LOST STARSHIP SERIES:

T~~h~~
Th
Th
T~~h~~
Th
The Lost Planet
The Lost Earth
The Lost Artifactt
The Lost Star Gate
The Lost Supernova
The Lost Swarm
The Lost Intelligence
The Lost Tech
The Lost Secret
The Lost Barrier
The Lost Nebula
The Lost Relic
The Lost Task Force
The Lost Clone
The Lost Portal
The Lost Cyborg
The Lost World

Visit VaughnHeppner.com for more information

The Lost World

(Lost Starship Series 22)

Vaughn Heppner

Copyright © 2024 by the author.

This book is a work of fiction. Names, characters, places and incidents are either products of the author's imagination or used fictitiously. Any resemblance to actual events, locales or persons, living or dead, is entirely coincidental. All rights reserved. No part of this publication can be reproduced or transmitted in any form or by any means, without permission in writing from the author.

ISBN: 9798300320645
Imprint: Independently published

Part One
Underspace and Beyond

-1-

Lieutenant Commander Valerie Noonan shifted uncomfortably as she sat before the Lord High Admiral in his office at Star Watch Headquarters.

Valerie had requested the meeting and felt a pang of remorse, as it felt like she was betraying Maddox by being here.

That feeling was silly, though, right?

Things had changed since the battles against the Sovereign Hierarchy of Leviathan. For one thing, the old Lord High Admiral was dead. Cook had always been good to her, though.

Haig was the new Lord High Admiral. He was a small, energetic man with lank dark hair and intense brown eyes. He was the glorious victor of those engagements against the Leviathan maulers. Many documentaries already highlighted his keen insights, often sidestepping or ignoring Captain Maddox's role that lead to Star Watch's destruction of the enemy's invasion warships—most of them, anyway.

It appeared that some maulers had retreated: perhaps back to the Scutum-Centaurus Spiral Arm from which they'd come.

Behind the big desk in his office in Geneva, Haig stared at her as if he could pierce her reserve through sheer willpower. Haig was a firm believer in the Humanity Ultimate Doctrine as espoused by the Humanity Manifesto. That meant he didn't care for those the HUs considered as freaks, mutants, or sports. That meant the New Men, and those like Maddox, Meta, and even Ludendorff.

Valerie kept her head up, trying to smile. She was a striking-looking woman with long brunette hair, a lean athletic build, and a quietly competitive nature. She believed in following the rules, maybe because she'd had such a chaotic childhood back in Greater Detroit.

Her uniform was spotless, and her facial skin almost flawless. She worked at that.

"There is the new and improved *Kit Carson*," Haig said, as he peered at the tablet in his hands. "You once commanded it, I believe."

Valerie nodded, which he seemed to ignore, as Haig didn't look up while he spoke.

"The upgrades include stealth technology and a small hangar bay, as it includes a small shuttle for surface ventures," Haig said. "Of course, the scout is scheduled for a dangerous but highly important mission. I haven't gotten around to finding its crew yet. Would you be interested in that—the mission, I mean?"

Valerie frowned. Why would the Lord High Admiral of Star Watch bother finding a crew for a Patrol scout? That seemed strange.

Haig looked up from his viewing of the tablet in his hands.

"Is there a problem with that?" he asked.

Valerie wondered if she should ask for clarification. That could be a mistake, as Haig didn't like Maddox. Therefore, Haig mustn't like anyone who had served under Maddox, especially for as long as she had. Would that jeopardize her chance of getting her own command again? Perhaps she could temporize.

"I'm Patrol trained, sir. That means I attempt to gain all the information I can before making a decision. What exactly does this mission entail?"

Haig cocked his head as if she'd spoken nonsense. "I thought Patrol officers were used to making decisions on limited information. Surely, you can decide now from what I've told you."

"Well..." Valerie said, finding an odd stubbornness building in her chest. It was the same kind of stubbornness she'd used against Maddox on countless occasions when he suggested some of his cockamamie schemes. What the Lord High Admiral had just said sounded similarly silly. "That doesn't mean I don't try to learn all I can as fast as I can when I have the opportunity. This seems like one of those times of opportunity... Don't you think?"

Haig stared at her, as if he didn't care for the rebuttal, which he probably didn't.

Valerie felt that it was time to beat a retreat, so to speak. Instead of listening to that insight, however—due to her stubbornness—she forged ahead. "I'd really like to know what mission you've slated for the *Kit Carson*."

It took Haig a moment before he said stiffly, "One into the Beyond."

Valerie nodded as if silently asking, "And?" although she didn't open her mouth.

"A survey mission in the direction of the Empire of the New Men," Haig added reluctantly, clearly understanding what the nod meant.

Valerie raised an eyebrow. She didn't care to deal with New Men again. It was bad enough having to deal with Maddox all these years. The New Men were even more arrogant and rude than the captain was.

Haig inhaled through his nostrils as he set the tablet on the desk. He sat back, fingering his chin as he continued to study her. He seemed to reach a decision.

"Two Patrol scouts on two separate occasions failed to return from a similar survey mission into the region in question."

Valerie shook her head, perplexed. "Why would you want to keep that from me before I decided?"

For just a moment, Haig scowled. He smoothed that away, although he asked, "Are you questioning me?"

"I suppose I am."

Before Valerie could add anything more to smooth that over, which she wanted to, as that sounded too impertinent, Haig said, "I thought Patrol officers leapt at the chance of a dangerous mission into the Beyond. They love the threat of danger."

"...I enjoy exploring the unknown," Valerie said shortly. "That doesn't mean I have suicidal tendencies or practice reckless behavior."

Haig frowned and picked up the tablet he had set down. He swept his fingers over the screen as if searching for something. He must have found it, for he read a moment and then looked up at Valerie.

She waited for it.

"It says in your profile that you're cautious. Yet, you question me quite freely about this. I might almost say you question me impertinently. That doesn't strike me as cautious in the least. Or do you usually speak to your superiors like this?"

"I'm sorry, Admiral. I've served under Captain Maddox..." Valerie trailed off before finishing the thought. She didn't want to say anything negative to Haig about the captain, as that felt too much like betrayal.

"Does Maddox encourage such behavior from his subordinates then?" Haig asked.

Valerie almost smiled at the idea. "We've served so long together, there's a family atmosphere on the bridge of *Victory*. The captain is given to... some might call it outrageous ideas. I've learned to question him closely when I have the opportunity. As I'm sure you're aware, in the end, most of the captain's ideas prove advantageous to the Commonwealth."

Haig grunted in a noncommittal manner, perhaps not wishing to hear any praise of Maddox.

That flustered Valerie. She'd just said that out of a sense of obligation to Maddox. She hated feeling like a traitor. But Maddox had been on an extended vacation for some time. In the meantime, Galyan refused to take *Victory* anywhere. It had started to feel as if the Lord High Admiral and Galyan were locked in a battle of wills. Valerie didn't want any part of that.

It had been over a year since the last encounter against the maulers of Leviathan. Valerie wanted to get back into space instead of stuck with office work on Earth. One could almost say she was starting to go stir-crazy.

"We're attempting to broaden our understanding of the New Men and their expanding Empire," Haig said. "I don't know why these other two Patrol scouts haven't returned home. I need a cautious commander, a veteran Patrol officer to check it out for me. It's one of the reasons we're having this meeting. If you fail to return home, I might have to send a task force out next. That might provoke the New Men before we're ready. Thus, I don't want to do that just yet."

"I would need to select my own crew," Valerie said.

Haig nodded absently as if that didn't matter.

Valerie let out her breath. She'd been sure that would set him off. Surprisingly, it hadn't.

"I'll give you a week to get a crew together," Haig said. "If after that time, you don't have the needed personnel, I'll have the Patrol office assign you the necessary personnel."

In the last few years, Patrol customs had changed. Valerie's request of choosing her own crew had become semi-official policy in the Patrol Arm of Star Watch. Haig must have known that.

"You will coordinate with Patrol HQ, of course," Haig said. "I would expect you to leave on the survey mission within the month."

Valerie nodded. That sounded about right.

"Well then," Haig said. "Is there anything else you wish to discuss about this?"

Valerie thought a second before she shook her head.

Haig stood.

Valerie shot to her feet. She was a little taller than he was.

Haig reached across the desk and shook her hand. "If I don't see you before you leave, good luck, Commander."

"Thank you, sir," Valerie said.

It seemed he was going to add something more. Then he relaxed, sitting back down.

Valerie took the cue, turned, and exited the office. She had her own command again, or would as soon as she selected her crew. She had a few people to ask.

This would be good. Valerie was sure of it. A semi-dangerous survey mission out near the New Men couldn't be that deadly if she practiced cautious common sense. The scout had cloaking, and she knew how to deal with problems.

The truth was this would probably be a routine mission. The Lord High Admiral had tried to frighten her.

Valerie almost smirked at the thought. What could possibly go wrong if she was wise about her command decisions? This voyage would probably be more like a vacation compared to the things she'd undergone with Maddox.

Believing this, Valerie left Star Watch Headquarters with a light step, having no idea what was in store for her and her crew.

-2-

Nimble Sergeant Treggason Riker leapt out of an open window as a shotgun boomed behind him in the cabin, blowing apart a lamp to his immediate left.

The sergeant's feet hit the dirt outside, and he rolled. Then he was up and sprinting, hearing the clack of a pump shotgun sliding a new shell into the firing chamber.

A woman screamed from deeper inside the cabin. Moments later, another shot sounded, and buckshot hissed over Riker's head. A deep-voiced man bellowed with rage as he jacked yet another shell into the shotgun.

This was a fine mess.

Riker sprinted, wearing only blue underwear and a set of Dudes on his feet, with his sergeant's jacket clutched in his left hand. He had left his shirt, pants, gun, and other paraphernalia back inside the bedroom with the disheveled beauty, a buxom and quite naked woman with a wild head of red curls.

Riker raced downhill, dodging pine trees and hurdling over a small toy wagon with a pile of sand and a plastic pail in it.

The woman screamed again. She shouted the man's name, "Leo! Don't! It's murder!"

A harsh laugh sounded in response.

Riker looked back over his shoulder at the cabin in the woods.

The huge, bald-headed man, Leo, leaned out of the window Riker had just exited. The big, fat man had the pump shotgun in his hands, making it look like a toy. He aimed the shotgun at

Riker and yanked the trigger so flames and buckshot flew out the barrel.

Riker threw himself flat against the ground, skidding through the pine needles and getting a few in his mouth.

Buckshot flew over him, peppering a pine tree ahead of him.

With athletic and surprisingly nimble grace, Riker rolled back onto his feet, running once more as he spat the needles from his mouth. The flexibility of youth was definitely helping him.

Once more, the huge Leo pumped the shotgun, loading a new shell into the chamber.

Riker began to weave, sprinting even faster, sliding the jacket over his bare skin as he put it on.

The thick-haired sergeant, with lipstick smears all over his face, looked young, like a man in his early twenties without any excess fat. He was muscular and youthfully fit, about average height. In reality, in terms of years lived, he was an old man. He had served with Captain Maddox for a long time in the Intelligence Arm of Star Watch. The Old Guard had put him with Maddox in order to give the then-young Maddox an old wise head to stop him from doing stupid stunts.

During all that time, Riker had been sensible after a fashion, filled with the wisdom of age. Then the old sergeant had gone with Maddox to a different dimension, an altered space-time continuum. There, Riker had undergone a transformation. He had become young again. He once had a bionic eye, arm, and leg. Flesh, blood, bones, and powerful muscles had replaced those.

There was no good reason why Riker shouldn't have maintained the wisdom he'd accumulated over his many decades of experience. Such a thing any reasonable person would believe. Something had changed in him, though. Mostly, or so Riker had come to believe, the big change was the pumping testosterone and energy of youth surging through him. Riker got a chance to replay things, using the knowledge he'd acquired as an old man. That meant he got in far too much trouble that he never had when he was young the first time around. One of the greatest problems for young-again Riker was women and his constantly raging libido.

Could you imagine that? Old Treggason Riker had trouble with women because he knew exactly which buttons to push to get them into bed with him. It was afterward that the trouble usually started.

Sometimes, Riker thought he might be going mad. Lately, he had made all sorts of vows and promises to himself as the guilt at his actions piled up. He went to church more. He read his Bible. That helped some. Then he would see pretty tail sashaying before him. The first few times he could control his urges. Then it became too much and he started plotting how to sweet-talk the young beauty into bed with him. Soon enough, he woke up after having spent a pleasurable time with her in bed, or on the sofa, the kitchen table, on a blanket in the woods—

The shotgun boomed, and this time the buckshot was well behind him. Riker could move like the wind when he needed to, or so it felt like. This was one of those times, all right.

Sure, Captain Maddox could outrun him, but not as easily as he once could.

Riker had dallied with the little redhead in the cabin. They had met in a bar earlier today. He hadn't had any idea she was married. He'd learned his mistake approximately eight minutes ago when the beauty in question had sat up at the sound of a heavy lock turning. She had said, "I think that's my husband."

Riker had barely slipped on his underwear and Dudes, grabbed his jacket, raced through the cabin, and jumped through the window in time.

As he ran through the woods, the ubiquitous guilt began to trouble his conscience. That was the old Riker speaking, scolding him for being a lecherous playboy. He knew better. Love wasn't sex. Sex was a tool true lovers used to pleasure each other, a gift from God to mankind.

Riker used to give sage advice about these things to others. Did that make him a hypocrite? Had some of that advice been easy to spout because he'd lacked the fire of youth? Had regaining youthfulness changed him to such a degree just because it had lit his balls on fire with lust?

The problem wasn't just the fire in his veins, but that he knew too much about life and the ladies this time around. That extra knowledge got him in all kinds of trouble.

"I'm going to change that," Riker said aloud. "I'm going to start doing the right thing in every situation."

Unfortunately, Riker had said that before, many times in fact since his transformation.

Still, he had gotten clean away from the shotgun-wielding fat man. All's well that ends well. The problem for Riker this time around was that this was just the beginning of it.

-3-

Sergeant Riker had miscalculated in a big way. He wouldn't learn that until eighteen hours and twenty-three minutes later.

He was fast asleep in his bed, in his cottage, after a riotous forty-eight hours of drinking and womanizing. He had fallen into bed drunk and slept hard. Now, as three cruel-eyed men crept through his house, Riker snored softly, unaware of the danger.

The three intruders located him easily enough by following his snoring and using a floor map of the cottage.

Riker learned of their entry when a harsh bright light shone in his eyes. Squinting, he smacked his lips and started to ask questions, if unintelligible ones.

Big men rolled him over onto his belly and yanked his arms behind his back. They handcuffed his wrists and used zip-ties on his ankles, yanking the ties painfully tight.

"Hey," Riker said, with his face shoved against his blanket. "What are you doing? What's going on?"

Two of the men hauled him upright. They were big and muscular, possibly Merovingian giants, towering over seven feet tall. They had the dull, bovine look of Merovingians and the incredible strength. The last man was slender and short, wearing a black suit, tie and shiny black dress shoes. He held a razor-sharp blade in his right gloved hand. The left hand lacked a glove or a knife.

"Are you Sergeant Treggason Riker?" the slender man asked with a Chinese accent. He had Asian features with a scar across his forehead.

"Are you a Spacer?" Riker asked.

The Asian man slapped Riker hard across the face with his ungloved hand.

The two giants giggled as if they were simple-minded. In truth, in terms of brainpower, they might have been.

"I am asking the questions," the Asian man said. "You will remember that, yes?"

"Sure. I'm Riker," the sergeant said, as he opened and stretched his mouth to alleviate some of the sting of the slap. He tasted blood as his teeth had cut the inside of one of his cheeks.

The Asian man smiled at him nastily.

The two giants giggled again.

"We're taking you to Monsieur Laron," the Asian man said. "He is most eager to make your acquaintance... again."

"Who are you talking about?" Riker asked, wondering if this was a case of mistaken identity.

"You slept with his woman," the Asian man said.

Riker had to think about it a moment. "Laron was the man with the shotgun?"

"What shotgun?" the Asian man asked.

"Is Laron fat, and is his first name Leo?"

The Asian man slapped Riker across the face again, harder than before, using the same ungloved hand.

Riker glared at him, deciding he was going to remember this and administer some payback when the opportunity arrived.

"Monsieur Laron isn't a man who accepts insults lightly," the Asian man said. "He would slap you himself, but I do so as his representative. Do not fear, though. You are going to meet Monsieur Laron sooner than you want."

Riker was finally starting to understand what was happening: the broader picture, if you will. This was not good. It was time to fix this, maybe even forgo payback against the face slapper. "Ah... how about I write Laron a letter of apology? I had no idea his wife was married. I would never have... engaged with her if I'd known her real status."

The Asian man shook his head. "Monsieur Laron is a dangerous man to insult as you have most certainly done. He... how shall I explain? He teaches the stupid, the half-clever, and petty swindlers on behalf of a powerful group of importers."

"What?" Riker asked, confused again.

"Laron works for importers of illegal substances, you might say," the Asian man said.

Riker processed the information. "Are you saying Leo works for drug dealers?"

"You begin to apprehend. He teaches those who fall behind on their payments, regardless of their excuses. Laron makes sure they never make such a mistake again."

"What are you saying?" Riker asked. "Look, tell it to me straight, all right? I'm too groggy for subtle hints."

The Asian man smirked. "Monsieur Laron is known as the Butcher. A master with the blade. I wonder what he will cut from you first, hmm."

It began to dawn on Riker that he was in serious trouble. He struggled within his bonds as the three watched.

"Try harder," the Asian man suggested. "This will be your last opportunity to do so."

Riker ceased trying. This wasn't funny anymore. He needed help—now. "Galyan, if you can hear me, I dearly need your help."

The Asian man brought up his knife until the point pricked Riker in the throat.

"Where is this Galyan?" the Asian man hissed.

Riker breathed heavily, easing his throat away from the knife tip. Damn, but it was sharp like a thorn.

The two giants held his arms tighter, looking around.

"Speak," the Asian man said. "Tell me now while you can."

"I—" Riker said.

"I am Galyan."

The Asian man whirled around, his head jerking back and forth, as he looked everywhere. "Show yourself," he shouted, "or your friend dies here and now."

A small Adok holoimage appeared before the Asian man. Galyan had been in ghost mode before this and thus invisible to them. Galyan had been watching the proceedings from Starship *Victory* in orbit around Earth. He had been calculating as to the exact moment when Riker would ask for his help.

Before the Asian man could say more, holoimage Galyan slid into him and used an ancient technology. Like a Bluetooth connection, Galyan rerouted energy from *Victory* into his holoimage, transferring it into the man's body. That energy crackled with enough force to knock him unconscious.

The Asian man crumpled, out cold, his hair standing on end and the knife clattering across the wooden floor.

The two giants glanced at each other in confusion.

Galyan as a holoimage slid into one of them, and zapped again.

That giant groaned before releasing Riker and toppling onto the bed.

The last giant turned and fled from the cottage.

"Thank you, Galyan," Riker said, standing upright, with his handcuffed hands behind him and his ankles zip-tied together. "Can you cut me loose?"

"How do you propose I do that?" Galyan asked. "I am a holoimage."

"Can you send someone here to do it?"

"Fortunately for you," Galyan said, "Valerie is already on her way."

"No, not Valerie," Riker said. "Get—"

"Riker," Galyan said, interrupting. "I overheard the conversation. You are in serious trouble. You need to leave Earth for a time and let matters cool down."

That seemed like good advice. "Okay…" Riker said. "What are you suggesting exactly?"

"I have learned that Valerie and Keith are leaving for the Beyond in the Patrol Scout *Kit Carson*," Galyan said. "They are going on a dangerous survey mission. I have informed the captain of all this. He believes that you should join them."

"Me?" Riker said. "I'm not sure I want to go into the Beyond just now. I like it on Earth… if you know what I mean."

"Not only are you in trouble with vengeful Monsieur Laron, but the captain wants you to go in order to look after Valerie."

"What are you talking about?" Riker asked. "The Lieutenant Commander can take care of herself."

"That is not the issue," Galyan said. "Surely, you can understand that."

Riker exhaled, beginning to see what had happened. "Is that why you waited to help me? You must have seen them coming to my cottage."

"Will you join Valerie on her survey mission?"

Once more, Riker struggled within his restraints, having no better luck than before. "Was the redhead really this Monsieur Laron's wife?"

"Oh, yes," Galyan said. "I checked records, and such is the case. Why would you do such a thing? I thought it was against your code of conduct."

"I didn't know she was married, all right. I don't like doing that, as it makes things too complicated."

Riker mumbled something more, possibly admitting it was also wrong.

Galyan's eyelids fluttered for just a moment. "You have changed, Riker. That is clear. Thus, I am revising my personality profile on you. I am not sure if you have the classic problem of uncontrollable lust, like a satyr, but the possibility seems to exist."

Riker looked away. Had he taken things too far this time? Did he have a problem with the ladies? Yes, he knew he did. He felt bad about it, but damn, when a hot woman walked by—

"Fine," Riker said. "I'll help Valerie out. Did Maddox really tell you to tell me to help her?"

"I am sure the captain would have if he knew about all this," Galyan said.

"You mean Maddox doesn't know? You lied to me just now?"

"Should I tell him?" Galyan asked.

Riker blinked several times. "You mean *you* want me to help Valerie."

"That is true," Galyan said. "You still do possess some of your former insights. I wish you would join her on this expedition, as I fear for her safety."

Riker nodded slowly. Maybe some time away from the babes would give him a chance to resolve a few… issues with him. Maybe he could figure out a way to truly practice self-control.

"Sure, for you, Galyan, I'll go."

"Then you must talk Valerie into taking you. She likely will not want to take you after finding you in this condition."

Riker eyed the little alien holoimage. "Sure, Galyan, I'll do all that—if it makes you happy."

"Good. I am glad to hear it. Now, get ready, as I hear her air-car landing."

-4-

The Patrol Scout *Kit Carson* was a cigar-shaped craft with stubby wings on the sides. It had a complement of twelve crewmembers. In the past, the *Kit Carson* had a relatively weak electromagnetic shield and hull armor, with minimal armaments. None of that had changed, but it had stealth features and a new stealthy hull. There was also an added hangar bay, a tiny one, with a minuscule shuttle.

Lieutenant Keith Maker presently sat at the helm on the small bridge of the *Kit Carson*. He was a straw-haired, short Scotsman. The man wasn't as young as he used to be, but he still had fast reflexes. Normally, Keith piloted *Victory*. Often, he and Valerie dated. They hadn't since the end of the war with Leviathan, which was a damn shame if you asked him.

Keith glanced back at Valerie as she sat in her command chair. He wanted to date her again, badly so. He looked away before she glanced at him and saw his longing.

Lately, Keith wasn't feeling as spry as he used to. His left shoulder hurt and his right hand throbbed sometimes when he piloted too long at a stretch. Many years ago, he had been a strikefighter ace, one of the best. Now, he ingested collagen with his coffee to help lubricate his joints. If he didn't get better soon—

Keith didn't like to think about such things. He hated the idea of getting old. He was the best pilot in Star Watch. He couldn't be that as an old fart. He wasn't old yet, right? It was just...

"The Nexus is asking us to move into position," Sergeant Riker said from communications.

Lieutenant Commander Valerie Noonan sat in the captain's chair on the small bridge. She had a glow about her. Did she eye Riker in a speculative way?

Keith scowled at Riker as he thought about that. Look at the old bastard. He was young again, cocky, smiling a little too much at Valerie. What did the Intelligence operative know about helping to run a Patrol scout, anyway? Riker was a glorified gunman, nothing more. Valerie had forced him to teach Riker the last three days about the newly installed AI. Riker was leaning heavily on the AI to do his work for him, which included communications and sensors.

Keith had tried to tell Valerie it was a mistake to lean on Riker. Maybe going down onto a planet, Riker had his good points. On the bridge, he was little more than a buffoon.

The AIs weren't magic.

All Keith's frustrations now boiled over. "The Nexus can talk? That's a new one to me."

Both Riker and Valerie turned and stared at him. Maybe that had been a stupid comment.

"Do you have the coordinates for our position?" Valerie asked.

"It's already loaded," Keith said.

"Then engage," Valerie said, "and move us into position."

Keith piloted the *Kit Carson* into position near the Builder Nexus between Earth and the Moon. It was a giant pyramid floating in space. Maddox had brought it back years ago from the Library Planet out in the Beyond.

Apparently, their mission would take them about 250 light-years from the Library Planet. That was a ways from the Empire of the New Men. Yet, the New Men possibly used the region in question. Why did the golden-skinned bastards care about planets out there?

Keith didn't like the New Men. They were far too arrogant and snotty. He loved when Captain Maddox put New Men in their place.

"What are we looking for again?" Keith asked.

"How many times must I say it?" Valerie asked. "This is a survey mission."

"There was something else," Keith said.

"We're also going to keep an eye out for lost Patrol ships," Valerie said.

"Is that what the Lord High Admiral told you?" Riker asked her.

"Hey, watch your mouth, old man," Keith said. "Show some respect, will you."

Riker raised his eyebrows at Keith. "What's wrong with you?"

Valerie cleared her throat. "Look, let's get one thing straight. I don't want any bickering on my bridge. I'm running the show this time. You will both adhere to my ways or I'm taking us straight back to Earth and having someone else take your places."

"What did I say?" asked Keith.

Riker looked up at the ceiling before regarding Valerie. "You won't have any problems with me. I know how to follow orders... sir."

"Lieutenant Maker?" asked Valerie.

"Sure... sure," the little Scotsman said. "You run the ship. You hate bickering. I'm the model of efficiency and cooperation; you can beat your sweet... um, yes, I got it."

Valerie eyed the two before nodding and swiveling her chair toward Riker. "Does the Nexus have anything else to say?"

Riker checked the communications board. "Yes. The hyper-spatial tube will appear in... five seconds."

At the end of the five seconds, a swirling white opening appeared before the small Patrol scout.

Keith nudged the Patrol scout into the swirling vortex. In a moment, the *Kit Carson* shot into the hyper-spatial tube, sliding down it and traveling hundreds of light-years in a moment.

Everyone on the bridge, and throughout the entire scout, blanked out due to something called jump lag. It was worse after crossing through a hyper-spatial tube.

The small ship appeared 523 light-years from Earth in a system with a brown dwarf star. Patrol vessels had used this star system as a staging area before.

Unsurprisingly, Riker snorted and raised his head first. There were only the three of them on the bridge. He had bloodshot eyes and a fuzzy feeling in his brain.

Usually, on *Victory*, Riker would see Maddox and Galyan busy at work. There was no Adok holoimage AI aboard the scout, to say nothing of Maddox.

"How about that," Riker said.

He waited until Valerie sat up, rubbing her nose. "Have we arrived?" she asked.

"Ugh," Keith said, rubbing his eyes.

"Where are we?" Valerie said slowly, as if struggling to think and speak clearly. "I want precision and confirmation."

"I'll check," Keith said, although he didn't move.

"Lieutenant," Valerie said, "you're just sitting there."

"Right," Keith said as he started to study the helm console. He reported about the brown dwarf star and used other ship systems to find, "We're 523 light-years from Earth as per our schedule."

Valerie nodded. "We're to report back to this location in twenty-seven days. The Nexus will generate a hyper-spatial tube for our return."

"Great," Keith said. "Where do we head first?"

Valerie stood and moved to a console, studying something on a small screen. She gave Keith coordinates.

"Let's start there," she said.

"Right you are," Keith said. "Do we use the star-drive or look for a Laumer Point?"

Valerie stared at him. "Look for a Laumer Point. That will give us a chance to settle into our routine. We're in the Beyond, gentlemen. So no matter what else happens, we need to use our heads in all situations. Is that clear?"

"Loud and clear," Keith said.

"Yes, sir," Riker said.

Valerie cracked her knuckles and sat back in the commander's chair. She felt a sense of excitement. She'd been missing this and was glad to be back in the saddle. Now, if she could find the missing scouts, that would be the best of all.

Why had the other scout ships gone missing? That was something she planned to discover as soon as possible.

-5-

They headed for the system's farthest Laumer Point; there were three in the star system. This Laumer Point was near the only gas giant, a blue planet with faint rings.

From her command chair, Valerie cleared her throat.

Riker swiveled around with a quizzical look.

Valerie cleared her throat again.

Keith shook himself out of the reverie that occupied him and swiveled to her as well.

"It's time I shared my thoughts on our situation," Valerie said.

"What's that supposed to mean?" Keith asked. "You know more than we do?"

"I should hope so," Valerie said. "I'm the commander. It's my responsibility if we get lost or fail to return."

"You expect either of those to happen to us?" Keith asked.

"Are you going to continue to interrupt me with these freshman questions?" Valerie asked crossly. "Or will you shut up for a minute?"

A sour look flashed across Keith's face. He shook his head and glanced at Riker. For some reason, that only intensified Keith's scowl.

Maybe the sergeant's amused look caused that, or maybe it was something else. Valerie didn't know.

She sighed, wondering if she should have accepted either of these two. Riker had pleaded for a berth. Later, Galyan had asked her to do it as a favor because Riker needed to get off

Earth fast. The randy sergeant had been getting into more peccadilloes lately.

Valerie smiled to herself. She liked the term peccadilloes. It wasn't from her childhood in Greater Detroit, that was for sure. It came from a gentler place with loftier customs.

Valerie had explained to Galyan that there was no place for someone of Riker's skills aboard a Patrol scout. Everyone had to pull his weight. Galyan suggested she teach Riker how to use the AIs. That would allow him to run certain bridge stations, especially if she kept an eye on him.

In the end, obviously, Valerie had given in to Galyan's pleading. She so hated to disappoint the little Adok.

Then there was Keith. Valerie knew she shouldn't have taken him except that he was the best damn pilot in Star Watch. Isn't that what he always said? Captain Maddox seemed to agree.

Valerie ran a hand over her face, wiping those thoughts away. The two watched her, waiting for her revelations.

"I went to Patrol HQ before we left," she told them.

She noticed Riker's confused look, and thought she understood.

"We're having a conference right now," Valerie said. "This is just like Maddox's conferences. The scout's galley is too small for us to have them there, and others would just barge in, interrupting us. This is as good a place as any to have a conference, and it's you two I want to run this by, as you have been with the captain as long as or longer than me."

"I'm listening," Riker said. "Go on, this sounds interesting."

Valerie gave him an absent nod and noticed that Keith scowled more. "You're going to have to stop that."

"Stop what?" Keith asked in a wounded tone.

It was Riker's turn to clear his throat.

Valerie looked at the sergeant. Maybe Keith did too, but Riker gave her the smallest of headshakes. Valerie thought she perceived.

"What were you going to tell me?" Keith asked. "What am I supposed to stop?"

"Never mind," Valerie said. "Here's the main point. At Patrol HQ, I learned the names of both deep scouts that have gone missing. Headquarters doesn't know if they were destroyed, captured, became derelict, or what exactly. One is the *Columbus*. That was the first to venture out here and go missing. The second is the *Cheng Ho*. They were lost within a six-month period. I happen to have their itineraries for the star systems they planned to survey. Therefore, I plan to go to each of those systems in turn using the same itinerary."

"Is that wise?" Riker asked.

"Ah, I see you've learned nothing from your time with Captain Maddox. You dare to question me, the ship's commander, about my choices?"

"I thought this was a strategy session where we speak freely about stuff," Riker said.

Valerie actually blushed, if only lightly. "You're right. That's on me. A conference means an open exchange of ideas. To answer your question, it is wise if we hope to find them or find out what happened to them. We also have an advantage over them, as the *Kit Carson* has a new cloaking device, and the hull already absorbs most sensor signals. There's another thing. Even though it will be a higher drain on power, we're going to be running at full cloak almost all the time. The only times we'll de-cloak is when we're absolutely certain there are no enemy vessels or spy devices watching us."

"Who or what do you suspect harmed the previous scouts?" Keith asked.

Valerie pointed at him. "That's a great question. One group is the New Men. They're in this region of space, though from what we know, they do not claim this particular area. However, this region is much closer to their hidden planets than to the Commonwealth."

"Your logic strikes me as reasonable," Riker said.

"Oh, thank you so very much." Valerie couldn't help herself with that. Then she shook her head. "No, no. I'm not trying to be sarcastic. I want to keep open communication. I don't want to be arrogant like others we know but won't name."

"You mean the New Men?" Keith said straight-faced.

"Yes," Valerie said. "I suppose, after a fashion, I do."

"You spoke about our itinerary," Keith said. "Can you show us what it is?"

"Of course," Valerie said, clicking a button on her armrest.

On the main bridge screen—a much smaller screen than what would have been on *Victory*—appeared schematics of various star systems and the jump points they would use to enter and leave them.

"Do we know anything about these star systems?" Keith asked.

"That they exist and the type of star or stars they possess," Valerie said. "As to the planets in the systems… we know very little, which is yet another reason we will catalog each and every one of them. This is a Patrol survey mission. We're not heading into the deeper Beyond. Still, the Lord High Admiral is sending us into a region where no known Commonwealth ships have returned. That means these could be dangerous waters."

Keith turned back to the helm panel and began to adjust controls.

"What are you doing?" Valerie asked. "We're still in the middle of our meeting."

Keith continued pressing controls and then turned around. "I just energized the cloak on the assumption that maybe the previous scouts were first spotted in this star system."

"Ah," Valerie said. "Yes." She pointed at Keith again. "I should have already ordered that. In any case, that's the extent of what I have to say. If anyone has further comments…"

"I like your strategy," Riker said. "I know you don't need my agreement, but I think what you're doing is prudent."

Riker looked at Keith.

"Yeah, it all seems good to me," Keith said. "You always knew how to do these kinds of missions, Valerie."

Riker resisted making sucking-up noises. He knew Keith was still in love with Valerie. Riker almost felt like he should give the lad a few pointers. Yet, strangely, Keith looked older than Riker. Riker knew he looked like the young pup wet behind the ears straight out of the Academy.

Riker glanced at Valerie. She was looking at something else. She was a beauty. Riker could feel the itch starting, the urge to—

"No," Riker said softly. He'd told Galyan he was going to look after Valerie. He couldn't very well do that if he was trying to get into her pants at the same time. In this, he would follow the dictates of the old Riker.

"Let's increase speed and proceed to the jump point," Valerie said. "I'm eager to uncover this region's secrets, and I dearly would like to find the missing scouts."

"Amen to that," Keith said.

Riker's head snapped up at the word 'amen'. Did the word prick his conscience? Maybe. Riker suddenly felt that this was going to be a long and possibly exhausting mission.

-6-

After exiting the jump point, the 12-man crew began to blink and stretch as they shrugged off the effects of jump lag.

On the bridge, Valerie gripped the armrests of her command chair, as the ship's artificial gravity reasserted itself. The familiar hum of the fusion engines filled the bridge, a reassuring constant.

That was a difference between *Victory* and the *Kit Carson*. *Victory* used antimatter engines. The small scout used fusion.

"Status report," Valerie said, with her eyes on the main screen.

"All systems nominal," Keith said, checking a helm screen. "We've successfully entered a new star system. Helm sensors are detecting a red dwarf star as previously advertised and... eight planets in total. That matches the pre-survey report."

Valerie nodded, her face illuminated by the glow of various instrument panels. That showed how small the bridge was, as that never happened on *Victory*. Everything was tight aboard the *Kit Carson*. "Start analyzing and cataloging the planets, as I want a full breakdown before we leave."

As Keith worked his sensors, Riker pored over incoming data at his station, checking a handwritten list and asking the AI about things.

Time passed.

Keith swiveled around and said, "I have preliminary data on the planets."

Valerie looked up.

"There are two gas giants, roughly Uranus-sized. Two of the planets exhibit highly unusual characteristics."

Valerie leaned forward, wondering if either of those planets had anything to do with the lost scout ships. "Elaborate on the two, please."

Keith swiveled and studied a sensor plate. "The second planet, a terrestrial one designated P-2, appears to be... singing, for lack of a better term. I did a deep dive and found that complex harmonic frequencies emanate from its core."

"How does it do that?"

"The core is detached from the rest of the planet and it spins like crazy," Keith said. "The core also has a few characteristics of a neutron star."

"Is that a natural phenomenon?" Valerie asked.

"Yup," Keith said, "I'd say so." A gleam shone in his eyes as he glanced at Riker. "Do you disagree with any of that, Sergeant?"

"Don't ask me," Riker said, as he studied a sensor board. "Half of this stuff still doesn't make any sense to me."

There was a moment of silence among them.

"Are you accessing the AI like I showed you?" Valerie asked.

Riker looked up as if confused. "I thought just communications had an AI."

"No," Valerie said. "That station does, too. Log in and use it."

"Right," Riker said, as he began to type on the console.

Keith smirked, shaking his head.

Valerie noticed. She hated bickering and fighting, especially on the bridge. It was time to shift the subject. "How could a core detach from the rest of the planet?"

"No idea," Keith said.

"That strikes me as odd."

"Sure, it's odd," Keith said. "I mean, it could be artificial, maybe something a Yon Soth would do."

Valerie's eyes widened. "A Yon Soth caused that?"

"I didn't say that. I couldn't find anything that might have caused the phenomenon. Unless otherwise noted, it's natural."

"It's considered unlucky to talk about the Yon Soths out here," Valerie said. "You might have just jinxed us."

"What?" Keith said.

"…Nothing," Valerie said a moment later. She hated Yon Soths. A singing planet sounded like something the vile, Cthulhu-like creatures might do. But maybe this singing was natural and nothing to worry about just like Keith said. She hated anyone saying something that might jinx them. It's rarely wise to tempt fate, especially out here in the Beyond.

"You said there was another odd planet?" Valerie said.

Keith tapped his screen, reading a moment. "Get this. P-5 has a bizarre weather pattern with clouds spiraling in tight, unnatural formations, almost like whirlpools in the sky. These vortexes seem to move against the planet's natural rotation, and I can't figure out why any of that is happening."

Valerie stared. Unnatural sounded as if it might be Yon Soth caused.

Riker laughed in surprise.

"What?" Valerie asked, as if stung.

"The AI thinks P-5 is evidence of an unusual magnetic field or an unknown atmospheric phenomenon," Riker said. "Maybe P-5 has a core made of something we haven't encountered before."

"Did the AI tell you that, too?" Keith asked.

"It did," Riker said. "Did the AI get it wrong?"

"I have no idea," Keith said. "Although I know it's iffy trusting an AI for these kinds of things."

Valerie started to challenge the idea but stopped herself.

Riker beat her to it. "I don't know why you'd say that. We rely on AIs on *Victory* all the time."

"Are you talking about Galyan?" Keith said.

"Who else?" Riker said.

Keith thought a moment. "An Adok AI is different."

"Not—"

"Gentlemen," Valerie said, interrupting. "We're not going to debate the utility of different AIs. Riker, is the AI— Are you detecting any machines of any sort?"

Riker began looking.

"Negative," Keith said.

Valerie started to reprimand Keith but stopped herself. "Fine," she said a moment later. "What about signs of scout ships or starship activity?"

"Nope," Keith said. "So far, there are no traces of fusion exhaust or star-drive jump signatures in the system anywhere."

Valerie nodded. "We're done here then."

"Don't you want to hear about the rest of the planets?" Keith asked.

"I was scanning your findings a moment ago," Valerie said. "I've seen enough. Plot a course for the Laumer Point at the system's edge. Use maximum sustainable speed to get us there."

Keith did as ordered.

Much later, with the red dwarf's crimson light faded to a distant dot, they approached the selected Laumer Point.

"Engage the Laumer Point," Valerie said, bracing herself for wormhole travel. "Let's see what the next system has for us."

As the *Kit Carson* neared the Laumer Point, the crew prepared in other areas of the scout. Engineers in the engine room fine-tuned the fusion reactors, ensuring optimal power output. In the tiny medical bay, Dr. Patel double-checked his supplies, ready to treat any potential side effects from the jump.

Valerie keyed her comm. "All hands, prepare for Laumer Point transition in T-minus two minutes. Secure all stations and brace for potential turbulence."

A klaxon blared.

"Commander," Riker said. "The AI is detecting an energy surge from P-5. It might be directed at us."

The *Kit Carson* shuddered as its engines strained against the mysterious force emanating from P-5.

"Mr. Maker," Valerie said.

"Working on it," Keith said.

"Try to figure out what it is, Sergeant," Valerie said.

Riker gave her a hopeless look.

"Ask the AI," Valerie said.

Riker nodded and began to speak at the console.

At the same time, under Keith's guidance, the scout broke free of whatever force this was. The *Kit Carson* hurtled toward the Laumer Point.

As they crossed the event horizon, Valerie caught a final glimpse of the star system on the view screen before it dissolved.

As the familiar sensations of Laumer Point transit washed over her, Valerie had a brief moment of reflection. Then she lost consciousness.

As the *Kit Carson* emerged into another star system 4.82 light-years away, Valerie straightened in her chair, coming out of jump lag. It was hard to remember what she'd been thinking before losing consciousness.

P5 of the former system had been weird, but she didn't think that was the answer to the missing Patrol scouts. More than ever, Valerie wanted to find the answer. Still, she would write up a detailed report about P5. The planet and Laumer Point could prove dangerous to regular spaceships trying to use them.

Even as Valerie mentally composed the report, her determination to find the missing scouts hardened into firm resolve.

-7-

The *Kit Carson* emerged from a Laumer Point, its cylindrical hull shimmering.

On the bridge, Keith stabilized the ship in the new star system.

Valerie leaned forward in the commander's chair, her eyes fixed on the main screen. "Status report," she said.

"All systems nominal," Keith said. "We've successfully entered the star system."

To Keith's right, Riker manned the science station. "Confirming system composition now: primary star is a red giant, spectral class M2III. Estimated age is approximately eight billion years."

"Elaborate on the star's characteristics," Valerie said.

Riker mumbled to the AI and then listened carefully to its reply. He began to parrot the information:

"The star's radius is approximately one hundred times that of the Sun, with a surface temperature of around 3,500 Kelvin. Its luminosity is extremely high—nearly one thousand times that of Sol. I'm detecting significant stellar wind activity and evidence of past helium flashes."

"Okay," Valerie said, "enough about that. Tell me about the planets."

Keith chimed in, scanning the navigational data. "Five planets detected so far. Each one appears to be quite distinct from the other.

"The innermost planet is a scorched ball of rock, with a surface temperature over one thousand degrees Celsius. It's likely tidally locked to the star.

"The second planet is more interesting," Keith said. "It appears to be a super-Earth, roughly twice the diameter of our homeworld. Heavy cloud cover suggests a thick atmosphere."

Riker leaned closer to the console, his lips moving as he then listened intently. He looked up, perhaps noticing Keith and Valerie watching him.

"The third planet is a gas giant, similar to Jupiter in composition," Riker said, "but with a distinctive blue hue. Spectral analysis indicates high concentrations of methane in its upper atmosphere."

"The fourth planet is another rocky world, but with a twist," Keith said almost without pause after Riker stopped. "It's exhibiting a lot of volcanic activity. I'm picking up massive eruptions across its surface."

"And the fifth?" asked Valerie, enjoying this; it helped Riker learn his trade.

Riker's brow furrowed as he listened to the AI and studied the readings at the same time. "It's... unusual, an ice giant on a highly eccentric orbit. Current position places it well within the system's habitable zone, but its trajectory will take it out to the system's edge. We may be witnessing the early stages of planetary migration."

"Excellent work, gentlemen," Valerie said. "Let's begin our systematic—"

"Wait," Riker said, interrupting, "I'm detecting an anomalous object at the edge of the system."

Valerie straightened in her chair. "Put it on main screen, maximum magnification."

The main screen flickered, revealing a distant speck against the backdrop of space. As the image zoomed in, the object's familiar lines came into focus.

"It's a ship," Riker said.

"It's more than that," Keith said, with the hint of a sneer. "That's a Patrol scout, just like us. It looks like we found one of the missing vessels."

Valerie's eyes narrowed as she studied the image on the main screen. "What's its condition?"

"No power signatures or life signs detected," Keith said. "There appears to be significant structural damage. I'm seeing multiple hull breaches."

"Take us closer," Valerie said. "Riker, do full sensors sweep as we approach. I want to know what happened to it."

The *Kit Carson* used a star-drive jump and then steadily closed the distance. Soon, the extent of the damage became clear. Neatly burned holes had torn the scout's hull.

"The AI reports there are residual energy signatures around the damage. The pattern is…" Riker sat up. "Consistent with fusion beam weapons."

Valerie nodded. Fusion beams were once the signature weapon of the New Men.

"Can you confirm that?" Valerie asked.

Riker mumbled to his console. Soon, "The AI indicates the energy decay rate, the, ah… subatomic particle distribution. It matches known fusion beam profiles. Who else uses those but New Men?"

"That's the question," Valerie said. "Keith, take it slow but bring us closer still."

"Aye, aye," Keith said.

The *Kit Carson* neared the derelict scout.

Valerie eyed it closely on the main screen. Would the derelict reveal what had happened out here? She was anxious to know more. A sudden thought struck: could this be bait for a trap?

"Don't drop the cloak," she told Keith.

"I wasn't going to," he said.

"Good," Valerie said. "Keep a sharp eye out for star cruisers. We don't want to fall into the same trap as possibly this scout did."

"Do we know the scout out there was trapped or tricked?" Riker asked.

"Hopefully, one way or another," Valerie said, "we'll learn the truth."

-8-

Riker stood in the airlock of the *Kit Carson*. The form-fitting spacesuit hugged his body, its materials providing protection against the vacuum. He double-checked the seals on his helmet, then gave Valerie a thumbs-up through the airlock's porthole.

"I'm depressurizing the airlock." Keith's voice crackled through Riker's helmet comm. The air hissed out of the chamber, and Riker felt the subtle shift as the artificial gravity disengaged.

The outer hatch slid open, revealing the star-studded expanse beyond. Riker took a deep breath, then activated his thruster pack. With a gentle push, he glided out into space, the tether connecting him to the *Kit Carson* trailing behind like a lifeline.

As he maneuvered toward the derelict, Riker saw gaping holes neatly drilled into the hull. Whatever had killed the scout could still be lurking nearby, or maybe they had set a trap within.

"I'm at the starboard airlock," Riker said, his voice echoing in his helmet. He examined the airlock's exterior panel, noting that it appeared undamaged. "Attempting to initiate manual override."

Riker located the emergency release and cranked it open. This was better than trying to crawl through one of the beamed holes. He unhooked his end of the tether from his spacesuit, attaching the hook to a bolt on the hull for just this purpose.

Then he slipped inside, closing the outer hatch behind him. The chamber couldn't repressurize because of the many hull breaches. A second later, he wondered why he'd bothered closing the outer hatch.

He shrugged and opened the inner hatch, revealing a darkened corridor. Riker switched on his helmet lamp, casting long shadows and light along the bulkheads. "I'm in and moving to the bridge."

As he floated through the scout, Riker scanned every corner and shadow, alert for any threat or clue as to the crew's fate. The silence was broken only by the soft hiss of his breathing.

Reaching the bridge, Riker's hopes for answers were dashed. The command center was completely devastated. Consoles had been systematically destroyed, their circuits melted and fused beyond repair. "It looks like someone didn't want us to find anything useful," he said. "I'd guess someone with a portable heavy laser entered the scout to do this."

"Is there anything to indicate as to why?" Valerie asked.

"Not that I can see," Riker said.

"Keep looking," Valerie said. "Maybe they missed something."

Using standard Intelligence protocols, Riker began a methodical search. He checked storage compartments and hidden recesses where data might be concealed. At one point, a flashing light on a partially intact console caught his eye. It turned out to be nothing more than a malfunctioning power indicator.

Moving to the crew quarters, Riker hoped to find personal effects that might shed light on the mystery. But the cabins had been stripped, not so much as a stray vid-plate left behind. It was as if the crew had never existed.

Why would someone burn through the hull and then come here to take everything? Why would they destroy the bridge as they had?

In his spacesuit, Riker leaned against a bulkhead. He wasn't Captain Maddox, but he had a brain and could work through problems if he stayed at it long enough.

He stared at his gloved hand, as it throbbed just a little. That was weird. There it was again—the throb in his hand.

What would cause that?

Riker made a fist and flexed his spacesuit-gloved fingers. This hand was his new flesh-and-blood one. Once, he'd had a bionic hand. Many years ago, he'd been forced to burn the original bionic hand off when a dying Spacer had tried to transfer an ego-fragment of a Ska into him. For a time, he had been in a facility for the insane. The ego-fragment had scratched his soul, but not been able to possess him like a literal demon as it had the Spacer.

The incident had scarred Riker, made him more alert to these kinds of things. Was that why his hand throbbed just now?

"I don't like this," Riker whispered to himself.

He wanted to leave the derelict and get back to the *Kit Carson*. But what would he tell Valerie?

"Finish this," he whispered to himself. Don't bug out like a coward.

Riker shoved off the bulkhead and continued to float through the corridors, searching. He worked on ignoring the throb in his hand and the sense of doom he was feeling.

In the engine room, he concentrated on his task and noted the precision of the damage. Whoever had done this knew exactly where to burn to cripple the ship for good.

He paused at a section of the bulkhead where the metal had been warped and discolored. He activated his helmet comm.

"I'm seeing evidence of extreme heat damage," he said. "That's consistent with fusion beam weapons."

"How much longer will this take?" Valerie asked.

"Are we on a quick schedule?"

"Something feels off here," Valerie said. "I'd rather leave sooner than later."

Riker wondered if he should tell her his qualms.

Don't bother with that.

Riker frowned, wondering if he'd thought that. If he hadn't, what had, and why in his mind?

You don't want to look superstitious.

That was true, he didn't. He had enough problems these days.

"I won't be much longer," Riker said over the comm.

"Make it quick then," Valerie said.

Riker resumed his search, examining various pieces of debris, and came up empty. Even the ship's log buoy, designed to survive catastrophic damage, had been destroyed.

Floating in what remained of the medical bay, Riker felt frustration wash over him. The frustration wasn't that the attackers had been thorough, leaving no trace of their identity or the fate of the crew. No, it was the feeling that he knew exactly where the hidden thing was, the one the attackers hadn't been able to find.

But why should that frustrate him? Might the feeling emanate from something other than himself?

Riker swallowed in a dry throat. He needed to return to the *Kit Carson*. Valerie wanted to leave anyway. He pushed off the bulkhead, floating out of the medical bay.

He realized a few moments later, that he wasn't floating back to the airlock hatch. Instead, he went down a dark corridor he'd been unconsciously avoiding earlier.

Don't do this, Riker told himself. It was like telling himself not to follow a beauty through the city streets. He had to do this.

What's wrong with me?

Riker wanted to shout at himself to get the hell out of here. Instead, he followed his premonition, reaching a place in the scout.

He activated his boots so they magnetized to the deck. Then, he worked a seam on the deck and slid open a small smuggler-like hiding location.

In it lay a smooth crystal half the size of his fist.

"Sergeant Riker," Valerie said over the helmet comm. "What's happening over there? It's been fifteen minutes since your last report."

Riker might have jumped at the sudden communication. Instead, he shook himself out of a dull state of incomprehension. He frowned. Why was he magnetized to the deck?

The sergeant didn't see the smuggler's hold he stood over or any crystal. In fact, he had forgotten about the crystal entirely.

"Sergeant Riker?" asked Valerie over the comm.

"I'm here," he said.

"Is anything wrong?"

"No," Riker said. "I'm..." He swallowed, having a moment where he wondered if he should try to figure this out. Instead, "This is Riker. I've completed my search."

"I know it's you," Valerie said. "What's going on?"

Inside the helmet, Riker shook his head, knowing Valerie couldn't see the gesture. "It's a complete loss over here, Commander. Whoever did this knew exactly what they were targeting. All data storage devices have been destroyed or wiped clean. No personal effects, no bodies, nothing to indicate what happened to the crew."

There was a moment of silence before Valerie said. "Understood. Do you have any theories as to the perpetrators?"

Riker glanced around, almost realizing he had done something he shouldn't have. He almost touched a bulge on his spacesuit, a pocket where he stored a crystal the size of a cell phone, a crystal he had picked up a moment ago.

Riker opened his mouth. A faint buzzing in his mind made it harder to think clearly. He closed his mouth.

"Sergeant?" Valerie asked.

"Uh... based on the precision of the damage and the thoroughness of the information purge, I'd say we're dealing with professionals. Military-grade weapons, tactics like New Men use. But beyond that..." He trailed off.

"All right, Sergeant, you've done all you can over there. I want you to return to the *Kit Carson*. It's time we leave."

"Acknowledged," Riker said. "I'm heading back now."

As Riker floated back to the airlock, he couldn't shake the feeling that he was missing something. The empty corridors seemed to mock him, holding secrets just beyond his grasp. It was unfortunate that Maddox wasn't here. The captain would know something, if nothing else because of his intuitive sense. This all felt like the actions of the New Men, but Riker had a feeling that was a setup to distract them from the truth.

He unconsciously patted a vest pocket on his spacesuit. He didn't even realize he did it, although a sense of warmth flooded his patting gloved hand in a pleasurable way.

Soon, at the airlock, with a push of his legs and then using his thrusters, Riker began the journey back to the *Kit Carson*.

Someone or something was playing games out here. For all their sakes, Riker felt he needed to know who or what as fast as possible. He didn't want to end up in the insane asylum like last time.

Riker frowned, wondering why he would think of something as crazy as that. Should he consider the possibility something bad had happened to him?

Another long hum filled his mind, making coherent thought difficult. Finally, Riker gave up, focusing on reaching the *Kit Carson* before his air ran out.

-9-

Riker returned to the *Kit Carson* without further incident or any recollection of the smuggler's hideaway and the crystal stored there. He was now back at his post on the bridge, absently checking something on the console. Every once in a while, his hand strayed to his pocket. He would stroke an object there, feeling a comforting sense of warmth and contentment. He did this stroking when none of the others was looking. That was important for some reason, although he didn't fully comprehend what he was thinking or doing.

At the helm controls, Keith was setting the course for the next Laumer Point jump.

From her command chair, Valerie studied a tablet.

Keith input the necessary data, looked up, waited for a time, drummed his fingers on the console, and finally turned around to stare at Valerie.

Something in Keith's manner, the speed with which he turned, must have alerted Riker, for the sergeant looked up from the comm board at Keith and then at Valerie. He had moved his hand well away from the pocket with the... thing.

"Well?" Keith said. "Are you going to issue the order or not?"

Valerie looked up from the tablet, noticed Keith's intensity and perhaps played back in her mind what the lieutenant had just said, and scowled at him.

"Now what did I do?" Keith asked.

"You didn't say 'sir,'" Riker said, speaking up. "I believe that is the correct procedure to the senior officer aboard her vessel."

Both Keith and Valerie stared at Riker.

"Is something wrong with my face?" Riker asked.

"Uh... right," Keith glanced at Valerie. "Sir, what are we going to do next?"

Valerie had been working out exactly that, trying to decide. She didn't understand why it was so difficult to do all of a sudden. Normally, she made these decisions quickly. Her mind felt sluggish, slightly off. She wasn't sure what the correct thing was to do, and that seemed... weird, as she had wanted to hightail it out of here just a while ago.

Valerie scowled, staring at the tablet. She was in charge, in command of the mission. If she couldn't do her duties...

Valerie breathed faster as a sense of panic began to develop in her.

"Uh, look," she said, "I'm the commander. I'm the lieutenant commander in fact. Star Watch has given me the authority and the responsibility to make the decisions for the *Kit Carson*. You both agree to that, right?"

Riker and Keith exchanged glances with each other.

"I'm not questioning your leadership," Keith said. "You are definitely in charge. I'm not envious that you've been promoted above me. I'm good at what I do, but hell, Valerie, you're far better at command than I am."

"No, no, no," Valerie said, holding up a hand. What was wrong with her? "I didn't say that because of a moment ago, your insistence I give an order. I'm conflicted, gentlemen. I don't know what to do, and I'm not sure if admitting that is wise for a commander. I don't think I've ever heard Captain Maddox say it."

"Look," Riker said, "you're not Captain Maddox."

Valerie shot him a glare.

"No, you know that's not what I meant," Riker said.

"Is it?" Valerie asked.

Riker had to concentrate. He was having trouble doing that. A knot of stubbornness built in him. He fought against lethargy and a buzzing in his mind. He wasn't going to let that stop him just now. What caused the buzzing anyway?

Abruptly, the buzzing ceased.

"You're not Captain Maddox," Riker said, "and this is not a combat ship. This is a Patrol vessel. This is—well, this is my area of expertise, gathering intelligence. That's what you're doing. The scout is one of the sensors, the eyes and ears, the nose, the skin, maybe, of Star Watch. That's what the Patrol does. We find things out. So if you're wondering how to command a vessel like this, well, I think confiding in your other senior officer, Keith, and—I'm just an old hand learning a new trick so..."

"Wow," Keith said, as he stared at Riker. "That was a long speech. What's gotten into you, old man? Do you think this is an Academy classroom and you're giving a lecture?"

"Nothing's wrong with me," Riker said. "I'm fine. I'm the same Riker I've always been."

Valerie rubbed her forehead. "None of that, Riker," she said absently. "I mean denigrating yourself." Valerie looked up and took her hand from her forehead. "You've been with Maddox a long time. If anyone is sneaky and diabolical—"

"Please," Riker said, interrupting. Her speech made him feel guilty for reasons he couldn't understand. He wasn't tricky. He did his duty was all this was. "I'm just an old sergeant, you know."

"That's not going to fly anymore," Valerie said. "Look at you, Riker. You're a young man who gets himself in all kinds of peccadilloes."

"What?" Riker said.

"Never mind that," Valerie said, waving it away, wondering why she would bring that up now. "Look, we found—I believe it's the *Columbus*. That means the *Cheng Ho* could still be out there somewhere. Do we let it sit alone? Do we let this mystery go? All so that we can rush home and report what happened to the *Columbus*? If I were to guess—if you were to guess, Sergeant—who did that to the *Columbus?*"

Riker frowned as something tickled at the edges of his mind. He wanted to tell Valerie something vitally important. Unconsciously, he stroked his pocket as warmth flooded his

43

hand. Maybe he should concentrate on figuring out the culprit of this space attack first.

"Uh... the one piece of evidence we have is the fusion beam signatures of the hull burns," Riker said in a half-robotic manner. "So I would guess it was the New Men or someone who wants us to believe it's them."

"You think the attack was some kind of trick?" Valerie asked.

"What does that mean?" Keith asked.

"What?" Valerie asked him.

"A fit of trickery," Keith said. "What's that supposed to mean?"

Valerie stared at him.

"Look," Riker said, "I'm giving you the two options as I see them: New Men or someone wanting us to believe it's New Men who attacked the Patrol scout."

"This is important information we've discovered," Valerie said. "It's very important information. If you feel that we should leave and you're wondering if, in good conscience, we can go back and report this in lieu of continuing the mission—"

"Hell yes, I believe that," Riker said, interrupting her.

Valerie swayed back. "You really believe that?"

The buzzing in Riker's mind was stronger than ever. He stroked his pocket. "Uh... no, I was just saying that so you could hear what it sounded like."

"What?" said Keith. "That doesn't make sense. What's gotten into you, Riker?"

Riker frowned. He didn't know. Part of him wanted to go home because... He frowned more as the buzzing made him wince.

Valerie had lowered her head to stare at the deck. Her head snapped as she turned to Keith. "Do you agree with him that we should go home with this news about the *Columbus?*"

"I said I don't believe that," Riker repeated.

Valerie ignored the rambling sergeant.

Keith took his time, perhaps trying to understand what was going on. "I agree you can go back without any fault or sense of shame." He shrugged. "Maybe it's the right thing to do, but I'm not sure."

"But..." Valerie said, staring at Keith intently.

"Hey," Keith said, "if it were up to me, I wouldn't go back just yet. I would at least find the *Cheng Ho*. And dammit, Valerie, we've been trained by Captain Maddox. We're the best at this Patrol stuff, after *Victory* anyway. We may not have Ludendorff or Galyan, but we have you. You've solved many a mystery. Let's solve this on our own. We can do it. You have the nerve and the brains. And—"

Keith grinned in his old cocky way. "You can't forget me. Best pilot in the fleet. You also have randy Riker along. He ought to be of use somewhere in this. What do you think of that, Riker?"

Riker mumbled something unintelligible.

Valerie stood up and stared at the main screen. She put her hands behind her back.

Riker watched her closely. For a moment, she almost seemed like Maddox. They were lovely breasts. Riker loved the contour of them and the commander's hips. He quickly looked away.

He couldn't believe it.

"Come on," Riker said softly to himself. "This is crazy." What was happening to him? Was he losing control of himself? "Excuse me," he said loudly.

The other two didn't seem to notice him.

Riker got up, turning away from them. He hadn't had to turn away like this since he'd been a teenager. When he'd been at church back then, and the preacher had gone on for so long with his sermon that all Riker could do was stare at the girls in the pews ahead. He had stared for so long that by the time the service ended he had a tent pole in his pants. He'd put his Bible in front of it. He was sure some of the girls had noticed and giggled among themselves.

If only he had known then what he knew now.

Riker exited the bridge and moved through a short corridor. *What's wrong with me? Can I only think about pretty women? Do hormones and testosterone control me? Can I ever discipline myself?*

That was the question, Riker decided. Maybe that was what he needed to explore this trip with Valerie and the others—the

Plain Janes among the crew. It was time to see if he could control what, until now, he had been unable to do as a young man reborn.

As Riker wandered down the corridor, he absently stroked the pocket that held the item he didn't allow himself to consider. It gave his hand warmth, and that seemed like a good thing.

It wanted to go home, though, and that could be dangerous for everyone on the *Kit Carson*.

As Riker almost realized that, the buzzing began again in his mind. He frowned, wondering if his thinking about girls all the time was making him an idiot who couldn't think straight about anything else.

That had to be the reason he felt so conflicted. Sure, that was most certainly the reason.

-10-

With the decision made to continue the scouting mission, the *Kit Carson* soon reached the next jump point, heading deeper into the Beyond.

Keith manipulated the helm controls as the scout entered a stable wormhole through the Laumer Point. The scout hummed with energy, its hull designed to withstand the peculiarities of wormhole travel.

In the command chair, Valerie slumped forward due to jump lag. They had taken special doses to help mitigate the effects, but no one could remain conscious during the strange journey through a Laumer wormhole.

Riker sat at the comm station, his head slumped forward and his eyes closed. An unusual energy flared from the item in his pocket. That energy zipped into the comm panel and then shot out of the bridge via a radio transmitter. The strengthened energy surged like an arrow, striking the side of the wormhole tunnel. That seemed nearly impossible, yet it happened as close to instantaneously as possible.

The energy acted like a key, and a section of the wormhole tunnel opened like a newly made portal, sucking everything nearby into it.

An alarm blared on the bridge. The *Kit Carson* shuddered violently as it was pulled toward the opening, tossing the unconscious crew against their restraints. The jolt sent a cascade of warning lights across the control panels, their urgent flashing having no effect on the unconscious crew.

Normally, such a wormhole trip was the height of simplicity. A ship zipped through a wormhole in hardly any time at all, coming out on the other side.

Unnoticed by the crew, a blinding flash of light engulfed the scout ship. There was a sickening lurch, as if reality had torn or ripped. It was the *Kit Carson* tumbling through the opening. The hull creaked as it strained against forces it had never been designed to withstand. For a terrifying moment, it seemed as if the molecules of the ship might burst apart.

Fortunately, they did not.

When the glare faded, the interior of the wormhole tunnel was gone, replaced by a vista that defied comprehension.

The *Kit Carson* hurtled through a realm that seemed to mock the laws of physics. Vortices of energy pulsed with otherworldly colors, their gravitational pull tugging at the scout's hull. The ship's structural integrity alarms wailed in protest as the forces threatened to tear the vessel apart.

Streaks of hyper-accelerated matter—comets, perhaps, or something far stranger—crisscrossed the void, leaving trails of exotic particles in their wake. Each near miss sent tremors through the ship, the crew's unconscious forms jostling in their seats.

Finally, Valerie shook off the effects of jump lag and stared at the main screen. It had come on automatically a second before she revived.

"Where the hell are we?" Valerie said, her voice barely above a whisper. Her eyes, still adjusting to consciousness, widened in disbelief at the scene before her.

Riker revived next, his fingers leadenly tapping his console, his face illuminated by the glow of the sensor readings. He felt sick at what he saw, wondering if it was somehow his fault. Yet, that made no sense, did it? Certainly, he couldn't have caused such an event.

"What is this place?" Valerie asked, her voice stronger now.

"I... I don't know," Riker said. "These readings don't make sense. I'm picking up magnetic anomalies orders of magnitude stronger than anything in known space. That's what the AI is telling me, anyway. There's some kind of... The AI has identified it as chronometric flux. It's permeating the entire region."

As if to emphasize Riker's words, a wave of distortion rippled across the view screen, momentarily twisting the already bizarre scene into even more impossible shapes.

Keith struggled to keep the scout stable as a wave of gravitational distortion washed over them. His hands flew across the controls, making adjustments to counteract the unpredictable forces buffeting the scout.

He checked something, his brow furrowing in concentration. "This is weird. Magnetic forces are pulling us in multiple directions. I don't know how long I can maintain our stability." The ship metallically groaned in response, as if acknowledging Keith's concerns.

"Riker," Valerie said, "do a full sensor sweep. I want to know everything about the place that I can. Keith, plot a course to avoid the highest concentration of anomalies. We need to find a stable area so we can regroup."

As the *Kit Carson* maneuvered through the strange realm, the three of them watched in equal parts awe and terror as reality seemed to twist around them. In one sector, time appeared to flow backward, ghostly images of shattered planets reassembling themselves. The sight sent a chill down Valerie's spine as she contemplated the implications of such a phenomenon.

In another area, clouds of plasma formed geometric shapes, pulsing with rhythms that hinted at alien intelligence. Riker found himself mesmerized by the patterns.

Unconsciously, he kept his hand over the pocket with the hidden item. Warmth flooded his hand and that helped soothe his thoughts.

"Commander," Riker said, his voice tight. "I'm detecting some kind of... Shit, Valerie, I don't understand most of this."

"Keep using the AI!" Valerie shouted.

"I don't think it understands any of this either," Riker said.

"That's an order, Sergeant," Valerie shouted.

Riker looked sheepish and then nodded. He worked the console, listening carefully to the AI's analysis, his face a mask of concentration as he tried to interpret the incomprehensible data into something actionable. Slowly, his mind cleared, or seemed too. A sense of calm began to enfold him.

"Okay," the sergeant said. "This is starting to make sense. The AI is telling me that something called phase variance is hurting our hull integrity. It's as if parts of the ship are trying to exist in multiple states simultaneously."

As if to punctuate Riker's report, a section of the bulkhead near them flickered, becoming translucent for a heart-stopping second before solidifying again.

Valerie and Keith exchanged alarmed glances.

Riker seemed calmer. "Don't worry. That will pass. We're headed in the right direction."

"What do mean?" shouted Keith.

"It's a gut feeling," Riker said.

"You think you're Captain Maddox Jr.?" Keith asked sarcastically.

"You have a gut feeling?" Valerie said, interrupting them.

"Yes," Riker said.

"Then let's follow it," she told Keith.

"You believe in it?" Keith asked.

"I'm grasping at straws," Valerie said. "I don't know what else to do."

Keith considered that until his eyebrows shot up. "Could this be underspace like we reached in *Victory* some time back?"

Valerie stared at him, her thoughts obviously awhirl.

"Makes the most sense I can think of," Keith added.

"How did we get into underspace, if that's what this is?" Valerie asked.

"One thing at a time," Keith muttered. "If we can survive, we can figure that part out later."

Valerie cursed under her breath, hating this. Underspace was a Maddox and Galyan sort of thing. What did she know about the strange realm—if that was even what was going on? How could the scout have gotten here?

Riker stood, turned to her and stepped near the command chair. He put a hand on her arm.

Valerie stared at him with fright.

Riker smiled. "Be calm. We can do this."

Valerie blinked, and blinked again, as if new ideas hit her. Could Riker's touch have anything to do with that? She turned to the helm. "Keith, adjust our shield harmonics. See if you can stabilize our…. Riker, does the AI have a name for that?"

Riker retreated to a console. He wasn't sure why he'd just done that: go to Valerie. He stared at the console. His mind felt sluggish, as if he'd done something that had taken all his energy.

Valerie jumped up and shouldered Riker aside. She punched in questions and spoke low under her breath to the scout's AI, her fingers flying over the interface.

"Got it," Valerie said, a small triumph in her voice. "We're dealing with a quantum signature. Does that make any sense to you?"

Keith closed his eyes, his face becoming very still as he processed the information. When his eyes opened, he laughed and shook his head. "Quantum signature sounds like gibberish to me. This must be underspace. If that's the case…"

"I think it is," Riker said.

"You recognize some of this?" Keith asked.

"Yes," Riker said, although he knew he was lying about that.

"Good," Keith said, making adjustments. "I don't know how long this will hold. This place seems to be actively trying to… to unmake us. But I have idea about what to do."

As time dragged on, the three of them struggled against the forces threatening to tear the scout apart. They skirted the edges of microscopic black holes that spontaneously formed and evaporated in the blink of an eye.

The constant barrage of spatial anomalies and physics-defying phenomena took its toll on both the ship and its crew. Fatigue began to set in, the mental strain of operating in this environment wearing them down.

There were moments, though, when each of them appeared to be strengthened in turn.

A little later, Valerie noticed Riker's hands shaking as he entered commands, while Keith's usually straight posture had given way to a tense hunch over the controls. She felt her own thoughts becoming sluggish, the constant state of alert draining her mental resources.

Just as it seemed they might have found a relatively stable pocket of underspace, a new alarm blared. A massive gravitational wave was approaching, its leading edge already distorting the space around them.

"Brace for impact!" Valerie shouted, gripping her chair as the *Kit Carson* was caught in the wave's inexorable pull.

The ship tumbled end over end, its stabilizers overwhelmed by the sheer force of the anomaly. Emergency lights flickered on and off as power fluctuated wildly. For a terrifying moment, it seemed as if the hull might finally give way to the strain.

Valerie screamed. Keith screwed his eyes shut. Riker stood, with a gleaming crystal in his one hand, the other hand gripping the console so he remained in place.

Ship systems roared with power as the radiance from the crystal did something.

Abruptly, the light from it ceased.

Without a thought of comprehension, Riker stuffed the crystal back into a pants' pocket. He sat, forgetting what he had done.

The *Kit Carson* drifted motionless in underspace, surrounded by an eerie calm that was almost more unsettling than the chaos they'd just endured.

Valerie no longer screamed but looked up, fighting off a wave of nausea. "Status report," she managed to croak.

Riker and Keith, both looking terrible, began to assess the damage.

They were alive, but the *Kit Carson* was damaged. Many of its systems were offline or operating at minimal capacity, almost as if the systems had burned out. They were still trapped in this realm, with no clear way home.

Valerie took a deep breath. "Let's figure out our next move, right?"

"What would that be?" Keith asked.

"I don't know," Valerie said. "Riker, do you have any ideas?"

"Give me a second," Riker whispered. "I'm trying to remember something important. It's on the edge of my mind. If

I can understand it…" He lapsed into silence, staring off into space.

They were in underspace, but for what purpose, none of them had any clue. Things were looking dire indeed.

-11-

As Valerie, Riker, and Keith began to regroup and plan their next steps, the twisted underspace outside the main screen served as a reminder of the nature of their situation.

"Hey, this is different," Keith said. His screen had glowed for a moment. It had caught his eye. "I have something on long-range sensors. It looks like an opening out of here."

Valerie looked up. The strain of this was evident in the dark circles beneath her eyes. "Put it on the main screen, maximum magnification," she said, her voice hoarse.

"Aye, aye, mate," Keith said.

The main screen flickered, revealing a distant point of yellow light amid the swirling chaos of underspace. The light pulsed with a steady rhythm as if it were a beacon of normalcy.

"I don't know about you guys, but I think that's our escape hatch outta here," Keith said.

Valerie stared at him as comprehension appeared in her eyes. "Right, set a course for it. Riker, keep an eye on the sensor readings. I want to know the moment anything changes."

Riker moved sluggishly, trying to recall something important.

The *Kit Carson* altered its trajectory as it accelerated. Leaving the momentary calm, the scout soon skirted the edge of a massive vortex, with its swirling energies threatening to tear them apart. The main screen was filled with a maelstrom of colors and odd shapes.

Keith piloted as sweat dripped from his face. With concentration, he navigated the treacherous currents, the hull at times groaning under the strain.

"Gravitational shear increasing," Riker said, his voice tight. "The AI says the hull stress is approaching critical levels."

Valerie snapped her fingers. "I know. Reroute power to structural integrity."

Riker turned pale as he stared at her. "I have no idea what that means or how to do it."

Valerie jumped to another console, her fingers flying over the keys as she typed in commands. Keith and Riker watched her.

"Whatever you're doing," Keith said, "that's helping. I should be able to clear the vortex."

The scout did, but a new threat loomed, a field of crystalline structures hung suspended, each radiating waves of energy that played havoc with the ship's systems. The structures glittered ominously in the strange light of underspace.

"Sensors are going haywire," Riker said. "I'm reading impossible mass concentrations. It's like the laws of physics are breaking down around the crystals. We need to skirt as far from them as possible."

Keith's brow furrowed as he plotted a course through the deadly field. "Threading the needle," he muttered.

The *Kit Carson* weaved between the crystals, alarms blaring as energy discharges lashed against the weak shields. The scout ship shuddered with each impact, the three bracing themselves against their stations. For a heart-stopping moment, it seemed as if they would be trapped in this deadly maze, doomed to be torn apart by the reality-warping energies that surrounded them.

Riker yelped as his pocket felt like it was on fire. He turned to Keith, who looked up at him.

"There," Riker shouted, pointing at the helm controls. "Use that."

Keith stared at Riker.

"Do it!" Riker shouted.

Keith did.

With a final burst of acceleration, the scout broke free of the crystals. The yellow portal now loomed before them, growing larger with each second. Its pulsing light filled the main screen.

Like a mental zombie, Riker wandered back to the main sensor station, sitting down.

"Riker," Valerie shouted, "tell me what we're flying into. Any data at all could be crucial."

Riker shook his head as if trying to clear his thoughts. "The AI can't get a clear reading. Whatever it is, the portal is unlike anything in our databases." He paused, then added, "But it's got to be better than staying here, right?"

As the *Kit Carson* approached the swirling yellow maw, the three stared in wonder. The portal seemed to defy easy description, its edges shifting and blurring in a way that made the eyes ache to look at it directly. Within its depths, they could see flashes of... something.

"There's no turning back from this," Keith said.

Valerie stared at the portal, the weight of command pressing down on her. "Take us in, Lieutenant. Whatever's on the other side has to be better than this."

"Yeah," Riker said, as if the word had been torn from his throat.

The *Kit Carson* plunged into the portal, leaving behind nightmare underspace. As the yellow energy enveloped the scout, the three held their breath, and the ship's hull vibrated.

The three's senses were bombarded with input, and their minds struggled to process what they were seeing.

"What's happening?" Valerie shouted.

"Hang on," Keith said. "It looks like we're slowing down."

-12-

Valerie blinked rapidly, her eyes adjusting to the sudden shift in brightness. Underspace was now visible only through the aperture behind them, a dark maelstrom that seemed to pulse with deadly intent.

"Status report," Valerie whispered.

"We've cleared the portal," Keith said. "I'm stabilizing our position."

Riker hunched over the main sensor panel, his brow furrowed in concentration. "Valerie, you're going to want to see this."

"Put it on the main screen," she said.

Riker complied with a few clicks.

Valerie sucked in her breath sharply.

Before them stretched what appeared to be an expanse of golden atmosphere. It was as if they had emerged into a sea of liquid sunlight, extending farther than their sensors could penetrate. The scale of it was bewildering, and weirdly, they did not see any star to cause it.

"It's beautiful," Keith whispered.

Valerie nodded. "Riker, study the sensors. I want to know everything about this place as quickly as possible."

"Yes, Commander," Riker said.

As the *Kit Carson* glided through the golden expanse, details emerged. To their portside, partially obscured by the golden atmosphere, hung an Earthlike planet. Its blue-green surface peeked through swirling golden clouds, with tantalizing hints of continents and oceans visible even from their distant vantage point.

"Keith, plot a course toward the planet," Valerie said. "But maintain a safe distance. We don't know what we're dealing with here."

Keith paused for a moment. "Riker, something has been bothering me. How did you know what to do back there?"

"What are you saying?" Riker asked, as he looked up from the sensor panel.

"When you pointed at a control before and told me to activate it," Keith said.

Riker frowned, shaking his head. "I don't remember doing that. Are you sure it really happened?"

Keith gave him a funny look.

"We can debate all that later," Valerie said, eyeing Riker closely. "We escaped gross underspace to reach here. I want to know what and where here is exactly."

"Right," Keith replied, finally adjusting the scout's trajectory as previously ordered.

Riker rubbed his forehead. He felt unusually sluggish, and it was starting to make him angry. He stared at his pocket, where something was concealed. The sluggishness only increased, however, as did the buzzing in his mind.

"What's wrong, Sergeant?" Valerie asked.

Riker looked up, staring at her. "I'm not crazy," he told her.

"No one suggested you were," Valerie said.

Riker frowned more. Then he turned back to the sensor panel and began to tap controls on it. He spoke to the AI, asking questions. That caused the buzzing in his mind to lessen and then cease. That helped him function.

In time, Riker's brow furrowed. This was wild. The extended atmosphere resembled Earth's stratosphere. It went impossibly far, stretching out into the void like a vast, shimmering veil. It defied everything the AI knew about planetary atmospheres. Incredibly, the golden haze reached as far as Earth's moon did from its surface—a colossal blanket of gas, glowing faintly in the light of a distant star, although they hadn't spotted it yet.

Riker tapped the screen, studying further. The clouds out here were like polar stratospheric clouds around Earth in its stratosphere. They were formed from tiny frozen particles of water and nitric acid.

Later, "Commander," Riker said.

Valerie looked up.

"This golden haze is wild. The sensors are picking up high concentrations of metallic particles—maybe gold or a similar metal. Whatever it is, it's suspended in the extended upper atmosphere. There's also some kind of luminescent property to the particles. Could be reflecting or even generating light. Either way, it's as if the entire region is glowing on its own."

Valerie thought about that. "And it's stable?"

"For now," Riker said. "But with an atmosphere this massive, the AI says that any disturbances—solar flares, a collision—could trigger who knows what. We could be looking at a planetary system where the atmosphere has more influence than the planet itself."

As Keith maneuvered the *Kit Carson* toward the planet, the extended golden stratosphere seemed to pulse faintly, like a living, breathing thing.

As the scout broke through a huge bank of clouds and approached the planet, more details became clear on it. Vast continents with lush, emerald jungles covered its surface. Azure lakes and winding rivers glittered in the golden light, their patterns were reminiscent of Earth's geography yet undeniably alien.

But it was crystalline structures that caught Valerie's attention. Scattered across the planet's surface were massive formations that seemed to defy natural formation. She used teleoptic zoom to study the jungles, lakes, and crystal formations. The geometric precision and scale indicated artificial origins.

"Riker," Valerie said, "focus your scans on the crystal structures. If there was intelligent life here, those crystals might hold the key to understanding this place… and finding a way out for us."

Riker's mouth opened as if that were some sort of revelation to him.

"Did you hear me, Sergeant?" Valerie asked.

Riker nodded slowly, beginning to tap the sensor controls.

Perhaps out of curiosity, Valerie turned her attention back to the portal they had emerged from. It hung back there, a dark wound in the golden sky, tendrils of the nightmare realm still visible beyond. As she watched, wisps of the golden atmosphere seemed to bleed through the opening, drawn into the underspace beyond.

"Keith, keep an eye on the portal," she said. "If it starts to close, I want to know immediately."

"Aye, aye, Commander," Keith said.

Minutes ticked by as Riker studied the sensor data of the surface scans. Finally, he looked up. "The crystal structures are emitting some kind of energy signature that interacts with the atmosphere. The AI gives it a forty-seven percent probability that they're maintaining it somehow."

Valerie got up to study the readouts over his shoulder. "Are you saying the crystals are keeping this impossible atmosphere in place?"

"The AI gives that as a theory," Riker said. "It claims the data supports it. There's more. I'm detecting faint traces of the same energy signature coming from the portal we used."

Valerie thought about that. "So... the planetary crystals are connected to how we got here?"

"Those are ruins," Riker said, as he showed different crystals on his screen and then the main screen.

Valerie stepped back sharply. Keith swiveled around. They both stared at the sergeant.

"Why do you think that particular crystal formation is a set of ruins?" Valerie asked.

Riker rubbed his forehead. "I just know, okay?"

"No," Keith said. "Along with everything else, that's too much coincidence for me. Earlier, you told me something that helped us fly out of certain underspace destruction. Then you claim not to remember doing that, but it was as gifted piece of piloting advice I've ever gotten. Now, you're telling us those particular crystals are ruins? Yet, there is nothing to indicate such a thing."

"What about this?" Riker said. "I can go down and find something in those ruins that will help us leave this place and return home."

Keith gave his head a swift shake. "We don't have Maddox, Galyan or the illustrious Ludendorff with us, but I know bullshit when I hear it. Something queer is happening here. How did we shift into underspace in the first place simply by going through a regular wormhole? That doesn't happen, ever."

"It certainly happened to us," Valerie said.

"And you call that sheer coincidence?" Keith asked her.

"When put it like that…" Valerie said. "No, this can't all be coincidence. What are you suggesting then?"

Keith pointed at Riker. "How come the least technical of us has all the pat tech answers lately? That doesn't jive in the least."

"No," Valerie said. "You're right. It doesn't."

"Now Riker tells us those particular crystals are ruins and hold something to help us go home," Keith said. "I'm calling BS on that. What happened to you, Riker?"

Riker rubbed his forehead as the buzzing started again in his mind.

"Do you have a theory about this?" Valerie asked Keith.

"Maybe," Keith said. He focused on Riker. "Did you find something on the *Columbus?*"

Unconsciously, Riker touched his pocket, the one with the item.

This time, both Valerie and Keith noticed. The strangest thing was that Riker didn't catch them noticing.

"Okay," Keith said. "I do have an idea."

Riker looked up. "What is it?"

"Wait a minute," Valerie told Keith. "Maybe we should let the sergeant search the ruins so he can find us a way out of here?"

Keith looked hard at Valerie.

"Maybe all this is a coincidence," Valerie said. "Otherwise, we would have to theorize a super-powerful entity controlling us or maybe controlling the sergeant. Maybe this entity is something like Balron the Traveler with Captain Maddox. Do you understand me?"

"What are you suggesting?" Riker asked.

"I see what you're saying," Keith told Valerie. "You want to let this play out and hope for the best."

"At this point, what other choice do we have?" Valerie asked.

"What are you two talking about?" Riker asked.

Keith faced Riker. "You get whatever you need down at the ruins. We're not going to stop you from leaving."

"Why would you stop me?" Riker asked.

"I just said we're not," Keith told him. "All we want is to leave here, make it through underspace and get back to normality."

Riker seemed more confused than ever.

Valerie straightened. "Before we do anything more, we should think this through a moment. Do either of you have any theories as to where we are?"

Riker rubbed his pocket. "I've been thinking about that. The, uh, AI suggested this could a pocket universe, a self-contained region of space-time."

"The AI told you that?" Keith asked.

"...Yes," Riker said.

"The AI is smart," Valerie told Keith, staring at him intently.

After a moment, Keith shrugged. "Sure, whatever, I guess the AI *is* smart."

"We definitely need more information," Valerie said. "Keith, could you land the *Kit Carson* on the planet?"

"A crash landing at best," Keith said. "That means we would never leave. We could launch a probe. A manned shuttle would give us the most accurate readings, but…"

"It's also the riskiest option," Riker said.

Valerie nodded. "What do you think is the best option, Sergeant?"

Riker rubbed his chin. "A probe won't work. I've detected forces near the surface that would sever the connection between the probe and scout. That means we need to use the shuttle. It has the only chance of making it down and then back up here. I'll return with an item that will help us go home."

"What if Riker can't find such an item?" Keith asked Valerie.

"Do you have a better idea?" Valerie asked. "I'd hate to have a hidden Balron aboard the scout, manipulating us all the time. We'd never get anything done that way."

Thoughtfully, Keith side-eyed Riker.

"If such an entity brought us here," Valerie added, "how much of a chance would we have overpowering it? What if it controlled the best soldier among us?"

Riker looked from Valerie to Keith.

"This is all hypothetical, of course," Valerie said quickly.

Keith threw his hands in the air.

"We'll send down a shuttle with a minimal crew of one," Valerie said. "Sergeant Riker, you strike me as the best survivalist among us. You should do this."

"When would I go?" Riker asked.

"As soon as you're prepped and ready," Valerie said. "Keith, I want you coordinating from up here. I'll have Dr. Patel prepare a biological hazard kit for the shuttle."

"I'll check the shuttle," Riker said, turning to go.

Valerie caught his arm, which made the sergeant spin around as if in shock.

Valerie opened her mouth. It seemed she would ask the sergeant if he were okay. Instead, Valerie said, "I'm counting on you to be our eyes down there. But if anything feels off—anything at all—you abort and return up here. That's an order."

Why did it feel as if Valerie was trying to tell him something else? Riker couldn't figure it out. She did stare at him intently, though.

He nodded. Then Riker disengaged from her hold, heading for the exit. It was weird, but this was starting to feel like a Starship *Victory* voyage, not a normal scouting mission. He should have remained on Earth, where it would have been a thousand times safer for him than this madness.

-13-

Riker moved robotically through the tiny shuttle *Magellan*. The pre-flight checklist was second nature to him, but in this alien environment, he double-checked every system as something felt eerily off to him.

"Life support, check. Propulsion, check. Comms…" He paused, frowning at the fluctuation in the signal strength. "Comms are nominal. Structural integrity…" The readout glowed a reassuring green. "Check."

The shuttle bay intercom crackled to life. "Riker, you read me?" Keith's voice carried an edge of tension.

"Loud and clear. What's on your mind?"

There was a pause, then, "Just got the latest atmospheric analysis. There's some kind of electromagnetic interference in the lower layers. It seems you were right about that before. It might affect our comms once you're planet side. A probe would never work here."

Riker grunted, making a mental note of that. "Roger that. We'll maintain radio discipline and keep transmissions short."

Valerie joined the conversation. "Riker, are you certain about this? Is there any part of you that thinks we should try something else?"

"Negative," Riker replied. "You were right before. We need eyes and boots on the ground. I've got a good feeling about this, and I'll return with our ticket home, okay?"

There was a moment of silence before Valerie spoke again. "All right, Sergeant. You have a go. But remember, at the first sign of trouble—"

"I'll pull out; you'll get no heroics from me, I assure you. I'm no Captain Maddox, after all. I'll be fine. I really do feel good about this."

"I'm sorry, Riker," Valerie said. "I can't think of anything else to try. It's up to you now. Please remember that."

Riker frowned, thinking her tone and words odd. He shrugged, and continued with the shuttle check.

Soon, the *Kit Carson's* hangar bay hatch yawned open, revealing the shimmering golden void beyond. Riker took a deep breath, centered himself, and engaged the launch sequence.

"*Kit Carson*, this is *Magellan*. We are go for liftoff."

"Godspeed, *Magellan*," Keith's voice crackled over the comm. "Bring us back something interesting, old man."

The shuttle detached from its docking clamps with a soft thud, inertial dampeners kicking in as Riker guided it clear of the *Kit Carson*. The golden atmosphere enveloped the shuttle, seeming to pulse with an inner light.

As he descended, Riker noticed strange patterns in the swirling gases outside the shuttle. It was crazy, but it felt as if he was coming home. Now why would he feel that?

Riker shook his head and clicked the comm. *"Carson,* are you seeing this? The atmosphere seems to be… organizing itself."

"Affirmative, *Magellan*," Keith replied. "We're recording a similar phenomenon up here. Proceed with caution, old man." There was a pause, then, "You take care of yourself, Riker. Use your Intelligence training, and your Captain Maddox experiences. I really hope… You take care of yourself, you old dog. We would really miss you if you failed to come back."

Riker wondered why Keith would say that. He shrugged and then concentrated on piloting. The deeper he went into the atmosphere, the more bizarre the environment became. Tendrils of energy crackled around the shuttle, leaving phosphorescent trails in its wake. The hull temperature fluctuated, forcing Riker to adjust the environmental controls from time to time.

"*Magellan*, we're losing telemetry," Valerie's voice came through, distorted by static. "What's your status?"

"Still here, Commander," Riker said. "But it's getting rough. These energy discharges are playing havoc with the systems."

Suddenly, a massive surge rocked the shuttle, sending it into a momentary spin. Riker worked the controls. A surge of heat spread through him. Something happened he didn't understand. The next thing he knew, he had stabilized the shuttle's descent.

"*Magellan*, come in!" Keith's voice was barely audible through the interference. "Riker, do you copy?"

"Still here," Riker said, fighting the controls. "But barely. I'm going to have to go to radio silence soon. This interference is—"

His voice cut off as the shuttle broke through a dense layer of swirling golden clouds. The sight took his breath away.

Far below, a vast landscape stretched out. There were vast swaths of the emerald jungle and blue lakes. It was like a fairyland. Surrounded by one jungle were impossibly tall spires of crystalline material that jutted from the ground, their crystalline surfaces reflecting the golden light in dazzling patterns. Between the crystal spires flowed what looked like rivers of liquid metal.

In the distance, barely visible through the haze, Riker could make out what appeared to be the ruins of a massive crystal structure.

"*Carson*, are you seeing this?"

Only static answered Riker. He was on his own now.

As the shuttle continued its descent toward an open area near the crystal spires, Riker couldn't shake the feeling that someone was watching and possibly analyzing him the entire time.

Perhaps due to lingering Ska influences, something clicked in his mind. A feeling of paranoia washed through Riker. Buzzing started in his mind. Using a technique he'd learned from dealing with the Ska's ego-fragment, he mentally pushed the buzzing aside like a judo move. That increased his paranoia so his back twitched in response.

Was something waiting for him down there? He didn't like the idea in the least. Maybe he should turn the shuttle around and head back up to the *Kit Carson*.

The buzzing in his mind intensified, almost breaking down his mental defense.

Instead of that happening, Riker got stubborn. "I'm going to do that. I'm going to return to the *Kit Carson.*"

He tried to change the heading, but found it impossible to move his hands the last centimeter.

"This can't be right."

Riker strove harder. Soon, he became aware that his thigh felt hot. He looked down at his pant leg and saw smoke coming from a pocket.

With a yelp, Riker slapped at his pocket. Then he realized something was in the pocket. He reached in and pulled out a glowing crystal the size of a cell phone.

"What the hell is that?" Riker shouted.

In an instant, he remembered taking the crystal from the smuggler hold aboard the derelict *Columbus*.

The damn crystal was sentient and had been manipulating him ever since.

"No you don't," Riker shouted at it.

He turned and strove to change their heading. The glow from the crystal intensified. Riker roared and struck the controls.

He must have struck something because the shuttle began to veer off course as it plunged toward the surface, gaining speed.

-14-

The *Magellan's* landing struts hit the alien surface with a hard crunch. Without the restraints in place, Riker would have been hurled out of his seat.

After regaining his breath, checking to make sure there were no broken bones, Riker ran through the shuttle's shutdown sequence.

He knew the crystal was in his vest pocket, and that it had become quiet. He had won some kind of stubbornness contest against it, even though he was loath to throw it away. They had made a bargain during the wild descent. The problem was that Riker couldn't quite remember everything that had happened after banging his fist against a flight control.

Did that mean the crystal still had some mental control over him? The possibility existed.

Riker had a feeling it wasn't trying to overtly control him, as he would know. The knowledge of its existence and what it had been doing earlier had weakened some of its power over him. Would that be enough? Riker wasn't sure.

The shuttle's systems wound down to silence, leaving only the faint hum of the life support and the rapid beating of his heart.

Riker took a deep breath, savoring the recycled air one last time before donning headgear and breathing apparatus. He suited up as well, putting on tough fiber clothing, heavier than his normal wear. He also laced up his boots. Then he picked up a blast rifle.

They had tested the planet's atmosphere on the *Kit Carson*, and he had just finished doing it again here. The air was breathable. Still, he would use a respirator for now.

Riker was going out because he had a sense of finding a piece of equipment they could use later to leave this place and underspace. There was a chance the crystal was lying to him to get him to leave the shuttle. The crystal wanted him to take it somewhere. Riker might, if the crystal led him to the way home.

Anyway, with a hiss, the airlock opened, and Riker stepped out of the grounded, slightly askew shuttle, his boots sinking into alien soil with a soft squelch.

What immediately hit him was the air: thick and humid, reminiscent of Earth's tropical rainforests. It was also undeniably alien. It carried unfamiliar scents that his respirator couldn't completely filter out. The smell was a bouquet of exotic flora, mineral-rich soil, and something distinctly unearthly that he couldn't quite place.

Riker adjusted the seal on his headgear, his gloved fingers tracing the connection points to ensure a secure fit. His eyes shifted to the oxygen levels displayed on his wrist computer.

The shuttle behind him hummed softly, its systems running continuous diagnostics and atmospheric analysis.

Riker hefted a MX-700 Blast Rifle. The matte black finish seemed to absorb the golden light that filtered through the alien canopy above. The rifle's smart-linked scope interfaced with Riker's goggle display.

Riker moved cautiously from the shuttle into the alien jungle. His landing had torn a gap through the canopy above. The vegetation surrounding the shuttle was an explosion of colors and forms. There were massive emerald trees towering overhead, their trunks wider than ancient redwoods and their leaves thick and heavy. The bark was deeply furrowed and seemed to shift ever so slightly.

Between the colossal trunks were a variety of plants. Some bore leaves larger than Riker, with iridescent surfaces. Others were akin to Earth ferns.

The shuttle had crushed many ferns during its landing.

The most striking feature was the bioluminescent vines snaking between the branches of the towering trees. They pulsed through a spectrum of colors. The effect was mesmerizing.

Riker found himself having to focus on his surroundings lest he become entranced by the hypnotic display of the vines.

That couldn't help him against the crystal he carried.

Riker waited for the familiar buzzing in his mind. That didn't happen. He had been ready to kick in a serious fit of stubbornness if that had happened. Might he actually have some independent control of himself?

Damn, this was strange. He wanted to get rid of the crystal fast. He could feel its eagerness to return somewhere here. That feeling of hope must be bleeding into him, giving him hope.

Now that the thunder and roar of the shuttle's descent had passed, the jungle noises reasserted themselves.

There were high-pitched trills and sounds like a cross between a whale's haunting song and a bird's warble. That sound resonated so strongly that Riker could feel the vibrations through the soles of his boots. Occasionally, a sound like shattering glass pierced the air. Each time that occurred, it was followed by a chorus of chittering noises.

This was an alien world. There was no doubt about that.

It might have been the crystal's eagerness or maybe his own. Riker pressed forward into the jungle. The undergrowth proved dense, making the going slow. At times, fern-like plants brushed against his protective clothing, their touch leaving a faint, glowing residue that faded soon.

He made a mental note to avoid direct contact with the local flora as much as possible. That was hard to do in the jungle.

The air seemed to grow thicker as he progressed, heavy with moisture and possibly the spores of alien plants. Riker's respirator strained to filter the atmosphere for him.

Suddenly, a new sound cut through the ambient noise. It was a deep trumpeting that reminded him of Earth's elephants. Whatever made that must be huge.

No sooner did the trumpeting fade than a series of horn-like blasts sounded from the same direction.

The sounds set a flock of unseen flying creatures into frenzied motion above the canopy. Riker heard their leathery flapping.

He crouched low, his blast rifle ready. Should he keep heading toward those sounds?

It felt as if the crystal didn't want him to do that. There was danger that way.

Riker frowned, and then he became stubborn. He fought to move his foot forward, and after a time, did so. He struggled again, and abruptly, he moved in the direction of the trumpeting and the horns.

Riker had the feeling the crystal was weak after all it had done the past few hours. It was reaching the limits of its power. It didn't want to waste its last dregs keeping him from this.

That struck Riker as a good sign. For the moment, he didn't wonder about his thinking. He didn't suspect any mental tricks.

As Riker drew closer, there were hissing cries mixed in with the trumpeting and horns. The sounds spoke of conflict, of a battle or a hunt.

His primary mission was to find a way home, not to engage with the wildlife or interfere with the natural order of this alien world. That meant—

The trumpeting grew louder still, accompanied by the sound of splintering wood and the rustle of a massive body moving through the undergrowth.

Riker's curiosity drowned out any other thoughts. He had the vague sense of a crystal thing shrugging shoulders it didn't possess. It would let him do this without a fight from it.

Riker paused and took a deep breath, steadying his nerves. It was time to take a look-see.

-15-

Riker eased the emerald foliage back with the barrel of his MX-700 Blast Rifle, his breath catching as a partial clearing came into view. The golden light filtered through the canopy, casting dappled shadows across a scene of primal violence.

The vegetation surrounding the area pulsed with bioluminescent plants that seemed to respond to the commotion at the center. The ground was soft and spongy, covered in a moss-like growth that shimmered.

In the clearing stood a beast the size of a terrestrial elephant, the Indian kind. Its body was covered with thick fur. It had inward curving tusks like an ant's mandibles, smaller than an elephant's that protruded from its jaw. The lips were stained with a greenish substance, possibly blood of some sort.

Around the beast were seven-foot-tall, humanoid Saurians, their scales glinting in the golden light.

The Saurians' scales shifted color subtly as they moved, providing a natural camouflage that made them difficult to track even in the clearing. Powerful legs ended in clawed feet that gripped the soft ground. Their arms were long and sinewy, ending in hands with opposable thumbs and retractable claws that looked capable of rending flesh.

Their movements were fluid as they worked together against the massive beast. A net, woven from fibrous material, had been cast over the elephant-like creature. The net shimmered, pulsing in time with the beast's struggles. Riker realized it was more than a simple restraint—tendrils of energy arced from the net into the creature's body, possibly weakening it.

The huge beast thrashed against its bonds, its roars of fury and pain echoing through the jungle.

The Saurians wielded elongated spears tipped with crystalline points, jabbing at the creature's flanks. When the crystal tips struck, the beast's furry hide smoked.

One Saurian failed to move nimbly enough, caught by one of the beast's sweeping blows. The bipedal, lizard-like alien went flying, crumpling against a nearby tree.

The sound of breaking bones echoed from Riker's hidden vantage. The Saurian slumped down on the soft soil, unmoving, dead.

A second Saurian fell victim to the beast's tusks, misjudging the creature's reach. The tusks impaled the hunter, lifting him off the ground. With a shake of its massive head, the beast tossed the Saurian aside.

The alien's body hit the ground with a wet thud, spraying green blood.

The jungle floor around the massive beast was slick with Saurian green blood and the beast's deep purple blood. The mixture created a surreal pattern on the phosphorescent moss.

Riker watched all this, transfixed, as the battle raged. It soon became clear that despite its efforts, the elephant-like creature was outmatched. The Saurians' numbers and the net were wearing it down.

Soon, the beast's movements became sluggish, its roars reduced to pained bellows that tugged at something in Riker's chest. The beast's eyes, once blazing with defiance, now held a look of resignation.

Then a new player appeared, a Saurian warrior larger than the others. The newcomer stood a full head taller than his brethren, his scales a deeper green color. The Saurian wielded a heavy stone mallet etched with intricate carvings.

The Saurian made a sibilant hiss.

The others redoubled their efforts to distract and confuse their weakening prey.

The Saurian with the mallet circled behind the elephant-like creature. There he waited, the mallet raised high.

When the moment came, the lizard-like alien moved fast. The stone mallet swung in a devastating arc as it connected with the beast's left hind leg.

The creature's roar of pain was deafening.

The Saurian leapt to the side and swung again, striking the other back leg. He must have broken thick bones each time.

The beast crumpled as its hind legs gave way.

With their prey crippled and unable to defend itself, the Saurians closed in for the kill. Their weapons flashed in the golden light as they struck again and again, a frenzied assault.

As the Saurian hunters hissed victoriously, shaking their bloody, raised spears, Riker eased back from his vantage. He slipped away, his footsteps masked by the sounds of the victory celebration.

As he made his way back toward the shuttle, his thoughts raced, trying to process the implications of what he had just witnessed.

The crystal in his vest pocket stirred almost mocking him with a sense of vindication.

Riker shook his head. He was getting tired. Exploring an alien world was exhausting.

I can make it easier.

The thought troubled Riker until he shrugged. Sure. Easier sounded good to him. He veered from his course, heading deeper into the alien world.

-16-

Riker forced his way through the dense foliage, his mind struggling to make sense of his surroundings. The golden light that filtered through the canopy seemed to distort distance and direction, making navigation a frustrating challenge. He paused, reaching for the high-tech compass integrated into his wrist computer. The digital display flickered erratically before going dark.

"Damn it," Riker said, tapping the device in vain. This wasn't the first malfunctioning piece of equipment. Something about this place seemed to interfere with advanced technology.

Deciding to take stock of his remaining assets, Riker turned his attention to the MX-700 Blast Rifle. He ran through the standard diagnostic sequence.

The results were far from comforting. The rifle's power cell was fluctuating, the targeting system was offline, and the smart-linked scope was dead weight. At best, he might get off a few low-powered shots before the weapon failed.

What could cause such widespread technological failures? Some kind of electromagnetic interference? Or was there something more fundamental about this world that was incompatible with his equipment?

Riker's musings were cut short by a sound that seemed impossible. He heard a distinctly human and unmistakably feminine cry.

Riker froze.

The cry came again, plaintive and desperate. Before Riker fully realized what he was doing, he raced toward the sound, pushing through the dense undergrowth as fast as he could go.

As he drew closer, the cries became clearer. There was no doubt about it.

"Help!" the woman shouted in English. "Please, somebody help me!"

Without thinking through the impossibility of this, Riker burst into a small clearing. He spied a pit, hurrying there to the edge. Broken branches and leaves showed where someone had fallen through. It was a deadfall. He peered down and a shock struck him.

A gorgeous, blonde woman stared up at him from the pit's ten-foot depth. The beauty wore furs that failed to hide her considerable charms, along with stunning blue eyes.

"You're... human," Riker said, astonished.

She frowned in confusion and then smiled. "You're speaking English. You can understand me. Are you human, too?"

"I'm Sergeant Riker."

"Sergeant?" she asked. "Don't tell me you belong to the Patrol of Star Watch."

Riker laughed, spellbound by his incredible luck. This was a dream come true. He'd always wanted to be... wait a second. He lowered his head and steeled himself. This could be a mental trick produced by the crystal he carried.

He glared at her. "Are you really real?"

She brushed back her thick blonde hair, causing her breasts to jiggle.

Riker loved that.

"Of course, I'm real. Why do you think I've been shouting for help?"

"Why were you shouting?" Riker asked. "How could you expect anyone to hear you, let alone understand what you were yelling?"

She nodded. "That is strange, isn't it? Do you trust in premonitions?"

Riker just stared at her more. He could do it for days.

"I had a premonition a few minutes ago. I thought—Look. I'm Ensign Emily Freely of the Patrol Scout *Cheng Ho*."

"The *Cheng Ho* made it through underspace to here?" Riker asked, amazed.

"If you mean the crazy zone after we must have bust through a wormhole or something, yes, that's right."

"Underspace with its crazy anomalies, many of them gravitational and magnetic?" Riker asked.

Sweet Emily nodded.

Riker frowned, hardly able to believe this was real. It simply didn't seem logical or probable.

"Do we have to keep playing twenty questions?" Emily asked. "I'd really like to get out of this deadfall."

That made sense. So, Riker set his blast rifle aside and lay prone, stretching out an arm. "Jump up and grab my hand."

Emily shook her head. "My ankle might be broken."

Riker scrambled up and went to a vine. He took out a big knife and sawed at the vine. It was tougher than it looked.

Finally, he returned to the pit with the vine. He made a loop and threw that end down. "Put this around you."

Emily did so, stepping into it and sliding it up her marvelous body.

Riker hauled her up, listening to her soft cries as she bumped her bad foot against the deadfall wall.

She reached the edge, twisted around to sit, slipped off the loop, and smiled up at him. "Thank you very much, Sergeant. I owe you everything."

Riker looked into Emily's eyes, feeling a deep connection with her. It was as if every moment of his life had been leading to this encounter, to this woman. Logic told him to be cautious, to question everything about this seemingly impossible situation. But his heart was already lost.

"Can you walk?" he asked.

Emily nodded, putting a brave smile on her face despite the pain. "With your help, I think I can manage."

Riker helped her up and they set off through the alien jungle, Riker supported Emily's weight as she hobbled. He knew his life had changed forever. His mission paled in comparison to his instinct to protect Emily and unravel the mystery of her presence here.

Whatever forces had brought them together on this golden world, whatever dangers lurked in the shadows of this alien forest, Riker was certain of one thing: he would face them all for the chance to stay by Emily's side.

-17-

Riker eased Emily down onto a fallen log, its surface covered in a soft, moss-like growth that glowed faintly in the fading golden light.

Riker couldn't help but marvel at her beauty, even disheveled and injured as she was. The furs clung to her form, accentuating curves that made his pulse quicken. Her blonde hair, tangled with leaves and twigs, still managed to catch the dying light gleaming softly.

Riker was transfixed, noting every detail of her appearance: the way her breasts rose and fell with each breath, the slight tremor in her hands as she settled onto the log, and the depth of emotion in her startlingly blue eyes.

Riker struggled to focus. The reality of their situation—stranded on an alien world, surrounded by unknown dangers—demanded his full attention.

He removed his headgear and mask, the seals hissing as they disengaged. He took his first unfiltered breath of the alien world's air, bracing for potential irritants.

To his surprise, the air was thick with unfamiliar scents, but not unpleasant. It carried hints of exotic flora, an underlying muskiness that spoke of teeming life, and something else—a crisp, almost electric quality that made his skin tingle.

Riker took deep breaths, analyzing each aroma and filing it away.

"I'm hungry," Emily said. "Do you happen to have any extra food?"

"Of course I do," he said, pulling out a ration pack. The foil wrapper crinkled as he pulled it off. "This isn't gourmet, but it'll keep you going."

He smiled ruefully, aware of how inadequate the ration bar must seem in this alien paradise.

Emily accepted the food, her blue eyes never leaving Riker's face. Her fingers brushed against his as she accepted the food.

As they ate in silence, Riker found himself studying her movements, the way she rationed each bite, and the alertness in her posture despite her fatigue.

As the last of the golden light faded from the sky, plunging the jungle into a twilight realm, Emily spoke.

"I suppose you're wondering how I ended up here."

"The thought has crossed my mind," Riker said.

"Not so long ago, I was part of the crew of the *Cheng Ho* like I said. We were sent to investigate anomalous readings in this sector. We had no idea what we were getting into."

Riker leaned forward, the last of his food forgotten.

"I forget how we entered this region of space," Emily said. "Does that seem odd to you?"

"It must have been traumatic," Riker said.

"That it was. I remember that everything went haywire. Our instruments failed and alarms blared. Then we were pulled into... this place."

Emily gestured at the alien world around them.

"Several of us took the shuttle, crash-landing on the planet," Emily said. "The others on the shuttle didn't make it." She swallowed hard, perhaps struggling with the memory. "I've been alone since then, surviving, trying to understand this place."

Her voice faltered on the last word, and Riker reached out to comfort her. His hand found hers, and the touch sent electricity through him. She was warm, soft, and undeniably human. He could feel the full weight of her isolation, the toll of the months spent alone in this golden hell. He wanted to comfort her for as long as it took.

Emily took a deep breath. Her fingers were intertwined with Riker's as if drawing strength from the contact.

"I'm not totally alone here," she said quietly, thoughtfully. "There are the Saurians. They're intelligent, organized, and they hate outsiders. They've hunted me, tried to kill me. I've only survived by staying on the move, learning their patterns."

"I saw them," he said. "They were hunting an elephant-sized creature. They were efficient if brutal in killing it."

Emily nodded. "The Saurians are dangerous. More than you can imagine. But they're not the real threat." She leaned in closer. "They're pawns in a much larger game."

"What do you mean?" Riker asked.

"The Saurians, this planet, even the pocket universe we're trapped in—they're all connected to the Shardkin."

Riker started, realizing the reaction was caused by the crystal in his vest pocket.

"Who or what are the Shardkin?" he asked.

"They're ancient crystal entities of immense power," Emily said. "From what I've pieced together, the Saurians once served them, enslaved by Shardkin's mental powers. The crystal spires and ruins you've no doubt seen were constructed by the Shardkin, with the Saurians as their slaves."

"That sounds weird," Riker said.

"But something went wrong—the Shardkin went mad. Or maybe they were always mad, and it just took the Saurians millennia to realize it."

Emily shuddered at the idea.

"As far as I can tell," she whispered, "there was a revolt. The Saurians destroyed key structures, severing the Shardkin's control. Some of the crystal entities fled this region."

"Wait a minute," Riker said, shaking his head. "How did this place end up in a pocket universe? Are you saying the planet was always here?"

"I don't know," Emily said, hesitating.

"What?" Riker asked. "You know something you're not saying."

Emily hesitated, biting her lip. "There are whispers among the Saurians. Legends of beings so ancient and terrible that the Shardkin themselves were mere constructs of theirs. I'm talking about ancient, monstrous beings known as Yon Soths."

Riker shivered. He should have known it would be something like that.

"The Yon Soths may have banished the Shardkin to this pocket universe," Emily said.

"So… this might be a prison, or quarantine," Riker said.

"Yes."

"If that's true… what do we do next?" Riker asked.

"We survive," Emily said, pressing against him. "We find a way out of this prison universe, and if we can, we warn humanity about what's out here, or in here."

The alien night closed in around them. Strange cries echoed through the jungle, and dark shadows seemed to move with a life of their own.

They were lost, trapped in a pocket universe beyond the reach of all they knew. But they were together.

That, Riker decided, was the only thing that mattered.

-18-

The golden light of the alien world had faded to a deep twilight, casting long shadows across the clearing where Riker and Emily huddled together. The air was thick, their bodies drawn together by an irresistible pull. The jungle around them had come alive.

Chirps, whistles, and low, resonant hums surrounded them.

Riker paid no attention to the sounds. He brushed a strand of Emily's hair away from her face. His fingertips lingered on her cheek. Their eyes were drawn to each other in the dim light.

"I know we've only just met, but I feel—" Riker said, his voice low and husky with emotion.

A spine-chilling screech cut him short. Then five Saurian warriors burst through the undergrowth, their scaled bodies glistening in the dim light.

Their eyes were vertical slits of amber, burning with intelligence and hatred.

"Run!" Riker shouted.

He grabbed Emily's hand, yanking her to her feet with more force than he intended. Her ankle wasn't broken, but it was badly sprained.

She ran with him, making pained gasps as she struggled to keep up.

The air whistled as spears flew.

Riker ducked as one passed overhead.

There was a sickening thud, followed by a gasp that Riker knew would haunt his nightmares.

Emily's grip on his hand loosened.

Riker turned, feeling as though time had slowed. A spear protruded from Emily's back. Her beautiful blue eyes were wide with shock and pain, her lips parted in a silent scream.

"No!" The scream tore from Riker's throat, a primal sound of rage and despair.

Emily crumpled to the ground, her life bleeding out onto the alien soil.

Something snapped inside Riker. With a roar, he leveled the MX-700 Blast Rifle. He didn't consider its fluctuating cell.

Had his desperation somehow boosted the power cell? Whatever the case, the power cell hummed, energy building as the rifle released a clot of energy. The weapon recoiled at each discharge.

Two Saurians fell, their bodies smoking. The smell of burned scales and flesh was acrid and alien.

The other three warriors screeched in alarm. They began a hasty retreat, melting back into the jungle.

Riker got a good look at the leader—a muscular specimen with a blue armband contrasting against its green scales. Their eyes met for a hate-filled moment. Riker saw cunning intelligence and a clear threat of future conflict.

The Saurian gazed at fallen Emily, then Riker, a look of cruel satisfaction crossing its reptilian features. Then it disappeared into the jungle.

Horns blared behind the screen of jungle.

Some kind of sanity returned to Riker. He recognized the horns as a signal, no doubt calling for reinforcements. He couldn't stay here, no matter how much it tore at him to leave Emily's body.

He knelt over her, feeling for a pulse on her neck. There was none. Just like that, she was gone.

"I'm so sorry," he whispered. "I'll make them pay for this. I swear."

The promise felt hollow, but Riker clung to it nonetheless.

Horns blared once more. Distant ones sounded in reply, answering the call to arms against the human.

Riker forced himself to his feet and plunged into the alien jungle in the opposite direction from where the Saurians had gone.

It was time to find the shuttle and get the hell off this hateful world.

As he ran, dodging twisted roots and phosphorescent vines, Riker's mind raced. He tried to consider the Yon Soths, the Shardkin and the enslaved Saurians. Instead, in his mind's eye, he saw the face of the blue-banded Saurian leader.

He wanted to choke the life out of that one. He wanted the leader to suffer for years, if that was possible.

A thought crept into Riker's mind. It was soft and promising.

There was a way to harm that Saurian in particular and the others like him.

Riker nodded. He wanted that, desperately so.

That was good, very good. To complete his vengeance, he needed to find the Shardkin leader and insert the crystal from his vest into an aperture. Everything would fall into place after that.

Riker's eyes widened, and a dark grin spread across his face. That was the ticket. That was what he needed to do all right. That would show the murderers of sweet Emily Freely of the Patrol Scout *Cheng Ho*.

Riker's hands tightened on his blast rifle as he ran. The weapon represented not just his means of survival, but the promise of future retribution.

With each step, each ragged breath, Riker felt his resolve harden. It was time to push through the jungle and reach the crystal ruins where the Shardkin leader resided. There, Riker knew, he would find all the power he needed for revenge against these lizard killers.

-19-

Back aboard the *Kit Carson*, Valerie awoke first.

She and Keith had both agreed that with Riker leaving and landing on the planet, it was time for them to get some much-needed sleep. Each had retired to their cabin. The *Kit Carson* was rather spacious as far as scouts went, with individual wardrooms. Valerie's was the best.

After a good seven hours of sleep, Valerie awoke. She dressed and went to the galley, eating a breakfast of eggs and toast when Keith arrived.

"Did you sleep well?" he asked.

"As well as can be expected," she said. "Our situation is rather dire... and Riker." Valerie shook her head.

Keith poured himself some coffee. "Would you like more?" he asked.

She nodded.

He brought the pot, filled her cup, and handed her some creamers. After returning the pot, he sat down across from her and began to eat.

Valerie finished her breakfast and thoughtfully sipped her third cup of coffee.

"I've been wondering if I should have brought Riker along."

"Oh?" Keith said, shoveling his last bite of eggs into his mouth.

Too noisily for her liking, Valerie thought.

"I wonder if Riker brought some of Maddox's bad luck with him," she said, "but Riker doesn't have Maddox's ability to jiu-jitsu a situation, turning it in our favor. Meaning that whatever took hold of Riker's mind is likely running him around down there. We can't see or contact him, meaning we're blind concerning Riker. It's also a mistake to believe he's going to bring anything up that can help us leave this place."

"So we leave him? We strand him?" Keith asked.

"We can hardly leave him," Valerie said, "as it's unlikely we can leave through underspace and hope to survive the journey. My thought is different. If we're going to escape this realm, we have to do it through our own efforts, not trust in Riker's dubious abilities."

"We made it through underspace to reach here," Keith said. "Why don't you think we can do it again to return to normal space?"

"As a last resort we need to try," Valerie said. "Before that, we need something to help us navigate underspace."

Keith sipped his coffee. "That was a confusing time. It's hard to remember what happened."

"Could Riker have been involved in more than we thought?"

"What do you mean?"

"Do you think something controlled Riker?"

Keith snorted. "The sergeant's no analyst but look what he all discovered. Even with the AI helping him, he hardly knows how to scan a thing. He's a ground pounder. Sure, he is an Intelligence asset, I suppose, but that's usually under Maddox's guidance. What has Riker ever accomplished on his own?"

"Plenty," Valerie said. "Don't you read the reports after the missions?"

"What? Are you kidding me?" Keith said. "No, I'm just glad to be home and take it easy for a while. Do some water skiing or snow skiing."

"I didn't know you skied," Valerie said.

"We went on a ski trip together once, don't you remember?"

"Oh, yeah," Valerie said. "How could I forget?"

"We had a fantastic time," Keith said with a leer.

"Don't," Valerie said, raising a finger. "This isn't the time for that."

"Oh, come on, Val. This could be it. We don't have Maddox to do everything for us this time. How do you—?"

Valerie stood and pointed at him. "None of that, mister. I thought you were the optimistic one who always said you could do anything, the best pilot in the fleet."

Keith stared up at her, finished his coffee and set down the cup. "Don't throw that in my face."

"Well, aren't you the best?" Valerie asked.

Keith pushed away from the table, crossed his arms, and put on a grumpy expression.

"What?" Valerie said. "You're always saying that. That's your signature line."

"Yeah, I know," Keith said. "But I'm not as fast as I used to be. I'm still as good," he said quickly, "but my reflexes are slowing down just a little." He made a small gesture with his index finger and thumb, barely apart.

"We all get old," Valerie said.

"You're still as beautiful as ever, but—"

"No," she said firmly. "I told you, we're not engaging in that. We have to figure out what to do. How are we going to get out of here? Do you want to spend the rest of your life in this golden atmosphere?"

"No," Keith said, as he rotated the cup. "Here's an idea, if that's what you're trying to get from me. We should circumvent the planet and see if anything else is here. I mean, it seems like there could be other spaceships. Why else would the entity in control of Riker have brought us here, if there weren't something worth getting? Doesn't that imply others on the planet?"

"You think the… entity controlled him then?"

"Isn't that a reasonable explanation for Riker's strange behavior?" Keith asked.

"Yes," Valerie said. "It is reasonable. It's even probable. We have one shuttle, and our one man is down there with it. We have to do our part up here with what we have."

"You've convinced me," Keith said.

"All right then, enough daydreaming," Valerie said, taking her and Keith's cups, putting them in the dishwasher. "Let's head to the bridge. We'll find out whatever we can about this place. Without Maddox, Galyan, or Ludendorff, we'll have to rely on ourselves."

"Right," Keith said. "You think we can pull this off?"

Valerie stared at him. "I know we can. So let's get started."

-20-

Keith sat at helm. Valerie took Riker's place at the main sensor panel, and they began to circumvent the planet, doing so slowly. They started close to the planet, and then moved to a wider orbit, analyzing everything. During that time, they did not find any spaceships, any other matter, satellites, or debris in orbit.

"Let's take it wider yet," Valerie said later. It had been three and a half hours since they started.

"Righto," Keith said.

The *Kit Carson* took an even wider circumference, and they continued until they reached the fringes of the vast stratosphere-like atmosphere, where it thinned out into the blackness of space.

Now, they circled at a distance similar to the moon's orbit around Earth.

They had left an orbital buoy in the location where Riker's shuttle had gone down. If the shuttle left the planet while they were gone, the buoy would alert them of it. They could also use the buoy, or a chain of them, to contact the shuttle from their new position.

"I see it," Keith said.

He meant the sun, or star, of this pocket universe. It was small, and it was frightfully near.

A quick scan showed that it was much smaller than Earth's Sun. It had a diameter similar to Jupiter.

"That should be impossible," Valerie said, sitting back. "At this size, the star lacks the necessary mass and pressure to trigger nuclear fusion. That should only be possible for something with at least eighty times its present mass. I read that it has 1/1000th the mass of the Sun."

"I'm not detecting any anomalies," Keith said. "There are no black holes, and it isn't a neutron star."

"It's like a regular sun, only with that small size. This shouldn't be happening."

"But it is," Keith said. "It's shining light. We can both see that. I'm asking the AI about this."

Valerie waited.

"Get this," Keith said. "The AI has several theories, some as crazy as can be. Maybe the star has a core made of exotic matter. This hypothetical matter could have incredibly strong gravitational properties that mimic the effect of a much larger mass, dramatically increasing the pressure and temperature at the core of the object. That could trigger hydrogen fusion."

"That *is* crazy," Valerie said.

"Here's another," Keith said. "The AI suggests this exotic matter might enhance energy efficiency, allowing hydrogen to fuse at much lower pressures and temperatures than what is required in our universe."

"I'm not buying that one," Valerie said. "What else does the AI suggest?"

"You'll love this," Keith said. "The laws of physics might be slightly different, allowing fusion to occur more easily. For example, a lower fusion threshold: The fundamental forces could behave differently here, lowering the temperature and pressure required to start hydrogen fusion."

"We're wasting time with this," Valerie said.

"The AI also suggests enhanced quantum tunneling, hyper-dense hydrogen, dimensional compression—"

"Stop," Valerie said. "Tell me one that makes at least a little sense."

Keith skimmed through the reports. "Ah, here's one. Maybe the star is the product of alien engineering that artificially enhances fusion. This ancient civilization might have engineered the object, creating containment fields or manipulating gravity to compress the core and sustain hydrogen fusion. The artificial process might be self-sustaining, allowing the star to continue burning despite its relatively small size."

Valerie nodded. "That makes the most sense so far."

"Yeah," Keith said. "Ah… does that help us any?"

"Not in leaving here," Valerie said. "So far, our exploration has turned up zip in terms of leaving—"

"Hey," Keith said, interrupting. "I have something. You should look at this." He gave her the coordinates.

Valerie began to tap the sensor screen. "I see it," she said. "It seems to be orbiting the star, but at a significant distance." She turned and looked at him. "It's a spaceship—more the size of *Victory* than the *Kit Carson.*"

"Does it detect us?" Keith asked.

"I doubt it. I'm not detecting any power levels over there. Could it be a derelict like the *Columbus?*"

"Do we go there and check it out?"

Valerie sank her chin onto her chest, considering. "Any sign from the buoy as to the shuttle coming up?"

"Why are you asking me? You're closer to the comm than me."

"Right," Valerie said. She leaned over and made a few checks on the comm panel. "Nothing from the buoy. Okay then, let's head out to that ship."

"Should I turn on our cloak?" Keith asked.

Valerie looked up fast. "Hasn't the cloak been on this whole time?"

"Hell no," Keith said. "We took the cloak offline, remember, when we entered underspace."

"I don't remember anything of the sort, but then there's a lot I'm not comprehending about all this. We need to be alert. We need to pay attention to the smallest things."

"Speaking of," Keith said. "Could Riker, or the thing controlling Riker, have sabotaged the bridge earlier?"

Valerie glared at Keith. "What an awful idea. We should check the bridge before we do anything more. No, first plot a course and starting heading for the alien ship. Then we're going to thoroughly check the bridge."

"Looking for what?" Keith asked.

"Your theoretical sabotage," Valerie said. "We can't be too careful if we hope to leave here."

Keith plotted the course, starting the scout toward the alien ship. Afterward, he and Valerie thoroughly searched the bridge, but they didn't find anything suspicious or unusual.

"That's enough," Valerie said after three quarters of an hour. "I don't know what's wrong with me—if it's this place, if it's the bad vibes. Do you sense anything unusual?"

"Not at the moment," Keith said. "I do suggest we use the star-drive jump to reach the alien spaceship faster."

"No," Valerie said, plopping down into her command chair. "That will be a last resort."

"Meaning what?" asked Keith.

"Meaning, when the time comes, we'll use the star-drive jump to jump further than the extent of this pocket universe."

Keith thought about that until he nodded. "That's a wild idea. I like it."

"More like a last resort," Valerie said. "I don't know what would happen. Would we appear in underspace or reach normal space, or would we destroy ourselves? It's a last madcap gamble, and I sure don't want to take it now. I want to get out of here alive. I'd like to rescue Riker, too."

"Me, too," Keith said, "but Valerie, he didn't even try to tell us that he found something on the *Columbus.*"

"Maybe he couldn't."

"Yeah, I guess."

Later, as the scout approached the alien spaceship, which orbited the star at extreme range, Valerie measured the vessel's exact dimensions. The alien spaceship was a little smaller than *Victory*, constructed of normal metals.

As they approached the spaceship, Valerie slid to the communications panel and tried to hail the vessel.

There was no response.

"To my eye, it looks derelict," Keith said as he studied his helm screen.

Valerie made a noncommittal sound and continued to try to hail the ship. Finally, she discontinued and slid back to the sensor board.

"I'm not getting any life readings," she said. "Wait… these could be slumbering life entities. There's the slowest, lowest flicker of a life reading."

"Could the aliens be hibernating?"

"I have no idea," Valerie said.

On the main screen, the alien ship came into closer view. It was disc-shaped, with thruster nozzles at one section and windows in others.

"Take us really close," Valerie said. "So it's just a jump from our airlock to it. Oh, and see if you can find an entrance into it."

Keith scanned the derelict as they circled. Finally, he parked at the right location.

"Good," Valerie said, "I'm going to board it."

"Not without me you're not," Keith said.

"Who will pilot the *Kit Carson?*"

"We'll have Ensign Yu come up. He has a knack for it. Patel can assist Yu during our absence."

"What if they panic—?"

"Hey," Keith said, interrupting, "Remember, if your arm falls off?"

Valerie smiled sheepishly. "Okay, it's probably a good idea that we search the ship together. If someone is there… We'll bring blasters. Let's just hope we don't have to use them."

"Amen to that," Keith said.

"All right," Valerie said. "We've done enough daydreaming. Let's maneuver into position. We're still too far from the alien ship."

-21-

The *Kit Carson*, a short, cigar-shaped craft with two stubby wings, was much closer to the Jupiter-sized star than before. In the other direction was the vast, golden atmosphere surrounding an Earthlike planet.

Valerie stood on the bridge, her eyes fixed on the disc-shaped alien spaceship that orbited the star at long range.

"Steady as she goes," Valerie said. "Bring us right alongside it like I said before."

As the *Kit Carson* drew closer, the scale of the alien craft became more apparent. It dwarfed their scout. At this point, the two vessels were so close that they almost touched, separated by only a few meters of vacuum.

"Great," Valerie said, turning to Keith. "Now, let's suit up and get going."

He rose from the helm as a Chinese ensign walked onto the bridge to take his place at the helm. Dr. Patel entered the bridge next, as Valerie and Keith left.

Soon, Valerie and Keith stood in the airlock, their spacesuits humming. The hatch opened, exposing them to the void. They activated their suit thrusters and jumped to the alien vessel, gliding beside it as they searched for an entryway.

The one Keith thought was an entry turned out to be a garbage chute or something similar.

As they approached what appeared to be an entry hatch, their magnetic boots engaged, securing them to the alien hull.

Keith ran a gloved hand over the sealed hatch, his hand scanner analyzing the material.

"No obvious way to open this," he said through the short-comm link. "The mechanisms, if they exist, are beyond my sensors to spot."

Valerie nodded, her decision already made. "We burn our way in. Set blasters to maximum."

They drew their weapons, activating them. Twin beams of concentrated energy struck the alien alloy, which resisted for several tense moments before yielding. The hatch burned away, revealing the ship's dark interior.

No air rushed out, which told them the corridors were in a vacuum. There must be breaches elsewhere.

Valerie led the way as she de-magnetized her boots, floating in. Her helmet lamp illuminated a cavernous space that seemed to stretch endlessly. As they floated through the corridors, signs of great age became evident—badly corroded surfaces, clots of dust particles floating everywhere, and a sense of age, the same feeling one got when floating through a Builder nexus.

"This ship strikes me as ancient," Keith said over the short-link.

"I feel that, too," Valerie said softly.

They floated deeper into the ship, negotiating through large corridors. None of the ship's systems appeared to be functional. The vessel was a dead hulk that had been orbiting the small star for who knew how many centuries.

After what felt like an hour of exploration, they reached the heart of the ship. Here were the signs of life—or at least, suspended animation. Row upon row of stasis tubes lined the bulkheads, each containing a seven-foot-tall Saurian creature. Valerie counted quickly—48 in total.

"They seem to be in long-term stasis," Keith said, examining the nearest tube, using his hand scanner. "Do you think this is the ship's original crew?"

Valerie wondered if these could be the aliens who had engineered the Jupiter-sized star.

"We're not going to try to wake them, are we?" Keith asked.

"No," Valerie said. "That doesn't seem wise."

"So, what's next?"

Valerie turned her silvered visor to Keith. "We keep exploring, what else?"

They pressed on, cataloging machines whose purpose they could only guess at.

Finally, they reached what must be the control room. Banks of corroded consoles surrounded a central platform. But it was the far bulkhead that captured their attention. A massive wall chart dominated the space, its surface glowing faintly despite the ship's overall lack of power and seeming age.

Valerie floated to it, her breath caught as she realized what she was seeing.

The chart depicted the pocket universe, showing the relationship between the Jupiter-sized star and the surrounding space. More importantly, it clearly indicated the aperture through which the *Kit Carson* had entered this realm. And beyond that... strange symbols that might be the gravitational and magnetic anomalies of underspace.

"It's a map," Keith said, "a map of the pocket universe and some of underspace beyond the portal. Maybe this could help us get back."

Valerie nodded, hoping this was the case.

-22-

In her spacesuit, Valerie stood on the alien bridge, staring at the lifeless control panels. The ship was silent, its technology strange and inert. According to what they had found so far, going through underspace was the only way to leave the pocket universe and reach normal space. But without a way to navigate underspace or find a portal or method from underspace to normal space, they were trapped here.

"Unsurprisingly," Keith said, running his scanner over corroded surfaces, "nothing's responding. It's like this ship has been dead for centuries, except for the stasis units."

Valerie paced in her spacesuit, her magnetic boots attaching and detaching from the deck with each step. "Could it be that there's something we're not seeing? This ship must have been designed to travel through underspace. That would mean they had a way to navigate the hostile region and go from normal space to underspace."

"That's a huge assumption," Keith said.

"Do you think the aliens constructed the spaceship only for travel in the pocket universe?"

"It's possible."

"But not likely," Valerie said. "Thus, I'll go with my assumption. That means the ship had or has some method of navigating the gravitational and magnetic anomalies of underspace. It should also have a way of reaching normal space."

"Look around you," Keith said. "You're not seriously suggesting the ship's navigation systems are still functional."

Valerie stopped and turned toward one of the smaller alien machines. It wasn't as corroded as the panels. Correction. The machine wasn't corroded at all. She moved nearer, eyeing it. Crystals formed most of its components. They must be immune to the ravages of time.

"Use your scanner again," Valerie said. "Scan everything you can about this machine, and then try something different."

"What do you mean different?" Keith asked.

"We're in a different place—the pocket universe. We found a star that shouldn't exist at its small size. Maybe we should keep looking for things that can't be."

"That doesn't make sense."

Valerie turned to Keith. "Do you want to stay here then?"

"No."

"Well, I'm trying something. I'm doing a Maddox. Would you rather just give up and call it done?"

Keith aimed his hand scanner at the crystal machine. He manipulated the scanner as he waved it over the object. He tried various tests.

"Find anything?" Valerie asked.

"I'm picking up faint energy fluctuations, but they're weak, like background noise."

"What do you think it means?"

"I have no idea. Do you think this can help us?"

Valerie turned to stare at the map of underspace. Would normal instruments be able to do that? Possibly but not necessarily. Was she missing something? Had they been lucky navigating underspace before, or had there been an element helping them that they didn't see or understand at the time?

What element hadn't they seen?

Valerie turned to Keith. "What do you think Riker picked up on the *Columbus?*"

"Uh... I don't know."

"Do you remember Balron the Traveler?"

"Sure," Keith said.

"He was small, an energy being," Valerie said. "Balron had incredible powers. Maybe the thing Riker picked up also had abilities, one of them helping us navigate through underspace."

"That might be possible," Keith said.

Valerie studied the uncorroded crystal machine. "Let's disconnect the crystal device and bring it back to the *Kit Carson*. We'll study how it works over there."

"You need to give me some idea what you're thinking. Maybe that's a terrible idea."

Valerie ignored that as she held out a gloved hand. "Let me see your scanner."

Keith shrugged, handing it to Valerie.

She stood near the crystal device and manipulated the scanner. She paused and did more scanning, studying the readings.

"Well?" asked Keith. "What did you find?"

"Could the crystals resonate with distortions? What are we? Matter—affected by gravitational forces, too. Maybe the crystal machine is tuned to gravitational forces like a tuning fork to sounds. It wouldn't need power in the traditional sense. This thing isn't getting power now, yet it showed something. That's how it could be possible."

Valerie adjusted the scanner to a wider frequency range and ran it over the alien machine. The scanner screen flickered, showing faint rhythmic pulses. Could that be because of the *Kit Carson* outside the ship?

"I don't think this is dead tech," Valerie said. "It's active, but it's operating on a different principle. Could it sense anomalies... almost like it was mapping them?"

"I'm not tracking you."

"Maybe this machine tracks gravitational and magnetic fluctuations outside the ship."

"How would it do that?" Keith asked.

"I just said: like a tuning fork, using resonance. Maybe the aliens used this machine to help them steer a safe path through underspace."

Keith shook his head. "Don't you think you're grasping at straws?"

"We already went over that," Valerie said. "Yes, I'm plucking at whatever I can. I'm trying to think like Maddox and Ludendorff, outside the box. Maybe the aliens didn't fight the anomalies as we did—they used them. The machine sensed the distortions and aligned with the paths of least resistance."

Keith thought about that. "You're saying the alien ship, through this machine... feels its way through underspace, waiting for the right conditions before moving."

"It's a possibility at least. We need to bring this unit back to the *Kit Carson*. We can't fully analyze it here, and I'm not willing to try powering up the alien ship until we know how their system works."

Keith moved closer, examining the alien device. "Looks like it can be detached easily enough. It's not embedded in the ship's core systems. We'll need to disconnect it carefully, though."

"I agree," Valerie said. "Let's get to it."

Together, they set to work, detaching the alien machine. It didn't seem to be a computer in the human sense—there were no digital circuits, no wires. It was more like a complex, analog machine, with crystalline structures and metallic threads linking it to the ship.

Valerie used a specialized tool to sever the connections, while Keith monitored the ship to ensure they weren't triggering any unintended responses.

The crystal device, about the size of an ancient TV set, finally came loose. Valerie cradled it, surprised by its lightness until she remembered it was weightless.

"It's smaller than I thought it would be," she said, inspecting the crystalline surfaces.

The machine was still faintly pulsing, possibly responding to gravitational forces even as it lay inert in her arms.

Keith secured it in a containment harness.

"Let's get it onboard," Valerie said.

They began floating through the dim corridors of the alien ship, heading back for the *Kit Carson*.

-23-

Valerie stood over the alien unit on the *Kit Carson's* bridge, her eyes fixed on the crystalline structure that pulsed faintly. Beside her, Keith was monitoring the device with a scanner linked to the scout's computer and AI, his face a mix of concentration and curiosity.

"We're not going to brute force this," Valerie said. "It doesn't seem to work like any tech we've seen other than a tuning fork. Maybe it's more of a tool than a system. We need to approach the testing differently."

Keith nodded, scanning the device's surface, watching as the readings shifted subtly. "It's giving off energy signals, but it's not responding to any of the inputs we've tried."

"It's not a machine in the way we think of machines. It reacts to the environment—gravitational and magnetic fields, maybe even something we haven't detected yet."

Keith frowned, adjusting the scanner to pick up broader frequencies.

"Let me think," Valerie said. "Hmm… We believe it's about tuning into the environment and reacting to it. That means the aliens likely felt their way through underspace."

Keith stared at the readings. "So, it's not giving us information like a computer would. It's sensing the distortions—gravitational anomalies, magnetic fields—and resonating with them. It's showing us the paths."

Valerie used a scanner, widening the spectrum. "There. I believe it's picking up the gravitational anomalies at the edge of the pocket universe. It must be tuned to those distortions in particular."

Keith looked up. "That's why it seemed like background noise earlier. It's been sensing the environment the whole time, but we weren't interpreting it correctly."

Valerie smiled. "This is about finding the path of least resistance—what the machine was built to do."

"How could you possibly know that?"

"I couldn't," Valerie said, "not normally, anyway. Is there something about the machine... I don't know. Maybe it connects with our brains in some manner."

"Why or how?"

Valerie shook her head. "I don't know, but you know what they say about looking at a free gift in the mouth. We have this. Let's figure out how to use it and leave."

"Roger that," Keith said.

They spent the next few hours correlating the device's output with their own sensor data. As the device pulsed, it revealed subtle patterns in the gravitational and magnetic anomalies in the pocket universe.

"My theory is expanding," Valerie said. "The aliens must have ridden the currents, letting the environment guide them, like a surfer riding a wave."

"If we follow the resonance patterns, we should be able to find a path through underspace," Keith said. "Of course, we still don't know how to travel from underspace to normal space."

They worked tirelessly, testing different scenarios and adjusting their instruments to match the resonance patterns the alien machine was picking up. Bit by bit, they began to understand how the device interacted with the environment around them.

As the final piece of the puzzle clicked into place, Valerie entered a series of commands into the ship's navigation system, linking it with the alien device's output. A holographic map of the pocket universe bloomed on the main display, showing broad pathways.

"That worked," Keith said with a laugh.

Valerie smiled, with the thrill of discovery coursing through her. "We've done it. We've discovered the key to navigating underspace."

Keith's eyes shone with excitement. "Now we need to do it and then find an exit from underspace into normal space."

"You're right," Valerie said. "We have to figure out how to leave underspace next. That means we're not going to rush into this. We need more tests. We have to be absolutely sure this works before attempting the voyage from the pocket universe."

Keith leaned back, the exhaustion of the past hours starting to weigh on him. "I agree. We've come this far. No point risking everything when we're so close. Besides, we still need to pick up Riker if we can."

"If he's even still alive," Valerie said.

"Any ideas how we find out?" asked Keith.

"Not yet," Valerie said.

They secured the alien navigation unit in the containment field and left the bridge, exhausted. The alien device had revealed some of its secrets, and they had the key to escaping the pocket universe.

Tomorrow, they needed to figure out how to get Riker back aboard the scout and then how to leave underspace back into normal space.

-24-

In the morning, on Riker's part of the planet, the golden atmosphere of the alien world shimmered around the sergeant as he sprinted through the alien landscape. His breath came in ragged gasps, the metallic tang of the air burning through his mask and into his lungs. Behind him, the guttural cries of hunting Saurians echoed off the crystalline spires, a primal sound that sent shivers down his spine.

Riker's mind raced as fast as his feet. The shuttle was too far to reach in a single sprint. The ruins he'd spied before were his only hope for survival now. Luckily, they were near the spires.

He had slept for part of the night and endured the dawn light as he remembered sweet, beautiful Emily. He had made it through the jungle to these impressive spires.

As he looked, the Saurians spotted him. He had heard their horns as he fell asleep. Now, horns blared again, this time against him.

Riker darted between the towering crystal structures, their surfaces reflecting distorted images of his pursuers. A quick glance over his shoulder revealed three Saurians in closest pursuit, their powerful legs eating up the distance between them.

As he ran, Riker took in details of his hunters. Their scaled bodies rippled with muscle, built for speed and power. But it was their eyes that unnerved him: intelligent, calculating, filled with a hunger that went beyond mere predatory instinct.

A whistling sound cut through the air. Riker ducked instinctively, feeling a projectile pass above his head. It embedded itself in a nearby structure with a metallic thud. A quick glance revealed a dart-like object, its tip glistening with an unknown substance.

"Great," Riker muttered. "Now they're using poison darts."

He changed direction and dove through a narrow gap between two fallen pillars, barely squeezing through. The move bought him a few precious seconds as the larger Saurians were forced to find an alternate route; they were too large to fit through.

Using the momentary reprieve, Riker assessed his options as he panted. The alien environment played havoc with his rifle's power cells. His most valuable assets were his mind—and the crystal he'd picked up aboard the *Columbus*.

As if sensing his thoughts, the crystal pulsed warmly against his chest. For a split second, Riker felt a connection, a flash of insight into the world around him. He saw the ruins not as random debris, but as a complex system, a maze designed with purpose.

For some reason, he seemed to have forgotten that the crystal might be part of the Shardkin and thus the Yon Soths. That was an odd thing for Riker to forget. Undoubtedly, the crystal had something to do with that.

The connection moment passed as quickly as it came. It warred against the information Emily had given him.

Riker was remembering, but that slipped away with a light buzzing in his mind.

The Saurians were closing in again, their hunting calls taking on a triumphant tone. Riker pushed himself harder, ignoring the burning in his muscles. He rounded a corner and found himself in a large open area, dotted with what looked like inactive teleportation pads.

He wasn't sure where the idea that those were T-pads had come from—probably the crystal.

Yes, the crystal seemed to say in his mind. *We must work together. I will help you against the creatures.*

"How do I help you?" Riker panted.

I will show you soon. First, let us use the teleportation pads to trick our pursuers.

Riker didn't see as he had a choice. He leapt onto one of the pads. Nothing happened, but he hadn't expected it to. The real trick was what came next.

The lead Saurian burst into the clearing, its reptilian eyes locking onto Riker. It raised a sophisticated weapon, far different from the spears and darts he had seen earlier. The incongruity struck Riker—these creatures had access to technology, yet chose to hunt with primitive methods. A cultural choice? Or something else? Or did it have to do with what Emily had told him before?

Don't worry about that. She regurgitated an old wives' tale, nothing more.

The Saurian fired his weapon, a bolt of energy sizzling at Riker. He dove off the pad, rolling behind a chunk of fallen masonry. The energy bolt swerved and struck the teleportation pad, and to Riker's amazement, the pad flickered to life for a brief moment.

See, the crystal told him. *We can use this to our advantage. I know how.*

The other two Saurians joined the first, spreading out to flank Riker's position.

The sergeant waited until they were all in position.

Now, you must do it now, the crystal said.

Riker made his move as he broke cover, sprinting for another teleportation pad. As expected, all three Saurians fired at once.

Swerve, the crystal commanded.

Riker changed direction. The energy bolts swerved from him and struck the nearby pad, energizing it. Riker took out the crystal from his vest pocket and touched it against a console as he raced past it.

The effect was immediate and dramatic. The teleportation pad erupted with light, creating a swirling vortex of energy. The nearest Saurian, unable to stop its charge, tumbled into the vortex with a shriek of surprise and vanished.

Riker didn't wait to see where it had been transported to, if he could. He was already moving, using the confusion to gain ground. The remaining two Saurians recovered quickly, however, resuming the chase with renewed vigor and what Riker could have sworn was a hint of respect in their calls.

He might be new to this world, but he wasn't anyone's fool. He was Sergeant Treggason Riker, a seasoned pro.

You are indeed impressive, the crystal spoke in his mind. *I'm glad you found me. There is so much we can do together, and it will bring you your greatest joy.*

Riker frowned. He wanted Emily, but she was dead.

Maybe not forever dead, the crystal said in his mind.

"What are you saying?" panted Riker.

Do you want to see Emily again?

"With all my heart," Riker said.

Then keep running, Riker, and do as I say, and you shall.

The idea of that gave Riker an extra burst of stamina. It didn't seem possible, but this was a pocket universe. Maybe something like that could happen.

A more cynical part of Riker, one buried deep, hoped he wasn't being a fool and a dupe, believing empty promises. Because if that were the case… he would go berserk on the smooth-talking crystal in his vest pocket and teach it what liars got in the end.

-25-

The pursuit continued— a deadly game of cat and mouse. Riker used every trick—false trails, improvised traps, and misdirection. The Saurians matched him at every turn, their hunting instincts undoubtedly honed by generations in this unforgiving environment.

As he ran, Riker began piecing together more about his pursuers. Their weapons and tools were a bizarre mix of the primitive and the advanced, as if their civilization had developed unevenly or regressed in some areas.

One Saurian managed to flank Riker, cutting off his latest escape route. The seven-foot creature brandished a weapon that looked like a cross between a spear and a high-tech harpoon. With shocking speed, it launched the weapon.

Riker twisted, the harpoon grazing his suit. He felt a sharp pain as it pierced the outer layer, but the inner held.

Riker stumbled, off-balance from the weapon.

The Saurian closed in for the kill.

Riker raised his rifle and fired. An energy blast caught the Saurian in the shoulder, sending it reeling back with a roar of pain and rage.

Using that opening, Riker ran and dove through a half-collapsed doorway. He slithered through, jumped up and found himself in a long corridor lined with strange, pulsing conduits. The crystal in his vest hummed in resonance with the technology around him.

Riker ran deeper into the structure, the sounds of pursuit growing fainter. The corridor began to slope downward, leading him further into the heart of the ruins. At some point he'd left the crystal spires and reached the ruins.

Emergency lighting flickered to life as he passed, responding to his presence—or more likely to the crystal he carried.

Finally, lungs burning and muscles quivering, Riker slowed down to a walk. The pursuit seemed to have fallen behind, at least for now. He leaned against a wall, trying to catch his breath and take stock of the situation.

That's when he realized the true nature of his predicament. In evading the Saurians, he had been driven deeper into the ruins, far from his original entry point and even further from the shuttle. The corridors around him hummed with dormant energy, the air thick with the weight of ancient secrets.

Riker closed his eyes for a moment. When he opened them, his expression was one of determination. He might be lost in the bowels of an alien ruin, hunted by creatures he barely understood, but he was far from being defeated. And he might have Emily again. The crystal had better not give him a zombified Emily. That would be worse than her dying the first time.

"All right," Riker muttered, eyeing the unfamiliar technology surrounding him. "If I can't get out, I'll just have to go through."

Did the crystal he carried laugh silently? It almost seemed so. It had become dormant again. Why would he think the crystal laughed? Wouldn't that be a weird response?

Riker pushed off from the wall and strode down the corridor. The hunt had evolved into something more—a race to give the crystal what it wanted so that he could have Emily again. But he had to do that before the Saurians caught up with him. Riker did not intend to lose that race.

Did he still believe Emily's story about the Yon Soths and Shardkin? Despite his forgetting about it at times, he would suddenly recall it.

Riker began to wonder how she'd learned such a story. He trusted Emily, of course. But her survival here, alone, almost seemed impossible. But if it was impossible, how had she come to be in the deadfall where he'd found her?

Might the Patrol Scout *Cheng Ho* still be in orbit around the planet? Maybe Valerie and Keith had already found the *Cheng Ho* and coordinated with the scout's survivors to find him?

The crystal abruptly pulsed against his chest, almost like a heartbeat. Did it try to guide him deeper into the unknown or to distract his thoughts?

Riker clutched his rifle more firmly. He had to figure this out soon. Yes, he needed a greater sense of urgency about this. Emily was no doubt counting on him.

"Emily," Riker said. "I'm coming. I'm going to revive you, my love."

Maybe it was good Riker didn't have a mirror right then, because if he had seen his bulging eyes, he might have considered himself a madman, a very dangerous one to be sure, but nearing a state of frantic lunacy.

-26-

Riker crept through a dimly lit corridor. The walls hummed with a subtle energy that set his teeth on edge. The crystal he carried in his vest pocket pulsed in rhythm with the surrounding technology, growing warmer with each step.

As he rounded a corner, Riker froze. Before him stood a massive door, its surface etched with intricate, shifting patterns that seemed to respond to his presence. The crystal he carried thrummed insistently, almost pulling him forward.

"Okay," Riker muttered, "I can take a hint."

He approached the door, studying the patterns. Tentatively, he placed a hand on the surface.

The effect was immediate. The patterns beneath his palm swirled rapidly, lines of energy spreading out from his touch. With a low groan, the door slid open, revealing a chamber that took Riker's breath away.

The room was vast, easily the size of *Victory's* main hangar. But it was what filled the space that left Riker awestruck. Banks of sleek, alien machinery lined the walls, their surfaces displaying the same shifting patterns as the door. Holographic displays flickered to life as he entered, filling the air with streams of data in an unfamiliar script.

At the center of the chamber was a raised platform, atop which sat a device that could only be described as a control nexus. It pulsed with an inner light, tendrils of energy arcing between it and the surrounding machinery.

Riker approached the central platform. This had to be some kind of command center, perhaps for the entire complex. If he could figure out how to operate it...

I'll show you, the crystal said in his thoughts.

A distant screech echoed through the corridors behind him, snapping Riker back to the present. The Saurians were still on his trail. He needed to work fast.

Riker began examining the nearest console. The symbols were unlike anything he'd ever seen, constantly shifting and rearranging themselves. But as he studied them, he began to notice patterns, a kind of visual logic to their movements.

That's right. That's the way to think of it.

Under the crystal's guidance, Riker closed his eyes, took a deep breath, and placed both hands on the console. Immediately, his mind was flooded with information. It was overwhelming at first, a torrent of alien concepts and data structures. But the crystal on his chest grew warm, and suddenly Riker found he could navigate the stream of information with growing confidence.

He saw schematics for the ruins, power distribution networks, and what looked like a map of the pocket universe. But it was all fragmented, corrupted by time and lack of maintenance.

You can do this, Sergeant.

"I don't know," Riker said. "This is all so ancient."

Yes, I find that troubling, too. I did not suspect—

"What are you talking about?" Riker whispered, interrupting.

Nothing really, the crystal said. *Let us concentrate. Perhaps we can forge a new link.*

"What about Emily? You promised me Emily, remember?"

Who?

"You lied about Emily?" Riker shouted.

Calm yourself, Sergeant. I...I merely added a little humor to the situation. I see that was in error. Yes, you will have Emily soon enough.

"Is that a threat to kill me? I can join her in death?"

What sheer nonsense. Now, we're wasting precious time. I will give you Emily as soon as you do this for me.

Riker thought about resisting but finally pushed deeper, searching for anything that might help him understand the technology.

A security alert flashed across his mental vision. The Saurians had breached the outer perimeter of the complex. They were getting closer.

Riker redoubled his efforts, sifting through the data faster. He encountered firewalls and security protocols, remnants of ancient safeguards. But whether due to the crystal he carried or some innate compatibility, Riker found he could bypass many of these obstacles.

Small victories came in rapid succession. He activated the chamber's internal defense systems, sealing off several access corridors. He managed to boot up a partial environmental control system, clearing the stale air and bringing emergency lighting to full power.

Maybe this place wasn't as rundown as it looked.

That is a good point. You are doing well. I am proud of you, Sergeant.

"It's Emily I want, not words of praise."

You shall have her soon. You will see.

Riker pushed forward. A new data stream opened up. Riker's eyes widened as he realized what he was seeing. It was a communications array, far more powerful than anything on the *Kit Carson*. If he could activate it, he might be able to punch through the interference and contact something deep and important even further underground.

This is amazing. The link yet exists. We shall overcome.

Riker began the activation sequence, his fingers dancing over the alien controls. But it wasn't going to be easy. The system had been dormant for millennia, and many of its components were degraded.

A crash echoed from somewhere in the complex. The Saurians had breached one of the sealed corridors. They were getting closer.

Sweat beaded on Riker's brow as he worked, rerouting power, bypassing damaged sectors, coaxing the ancient technology back to life. The crystal in his vest grew almost uncomfortably hot against his chest, but Riker barely noticed.

He was in the zone, man and machine working in synchronicity.

There was another crash, closer this time. Riker could hear the Saurians' guttural calls, filled with a mixture of rage and triumph. They must have known they had him cornered but also realized he was doing something they dearly didn't like.

The communication array was at sixty percent power. Seventy percent. Eighty percent.

Riker snarled and pushed harder, knowing he was overloading systems that hadn't been active in eons. Warning alerts flashed across the holographic displays, but he ignored them. It was now or never, and he desperately wanted to talk to Emily again.

Just as the power levels hit ninety-five percent, the chamber's main door exploded inward. Three Saurians burst through the opening, their eyes locking onto Riker with predatory intensity.

Time seemed to slow down. Riker saw the lead Saurian raise his weapon, saw the energy building at its tip. He saw the communication array's power level tick up to ninety-eight percent, ninety-nine percent…

With a final surge of will, Riker slammed his hand down on the activation control.

The chamber erupted with light and sound. The communication array pulsed, sending out a beam of energy so intense it momentarily blinded everyone in the room. The Saurians stumbled back, disoriented.

Riker blinked rapidly, trying to clear his vision. As the spots faded from his eyes, he saw that the holographic displays had changed. A new image dominated the air above the control nexus—a conduit into the deep earth where the ancient Shardkin lived.

A grin spread across Riker's face. He'd done it. Surely, this thing could bring him Emily.

You are absolutely correct, the crystal in his vest told him.

The Shardkin was a crystal entity of great age and complexity. This creature was old beyond time, and evil, and starting to awaken from eons of slumber.

"It's evil?" Riker whispered.

That is sheer nonsense, the crystal told him. *Good and evil are mental constructs used by biological bags of fluids. The concepts have no real meaning to the Shardkin. You must continue, as we have much to do still.*

"Emily," Riker whispered.

During this short interim, the Saurians recovered, their initial shock wearing off. They spread out, moving to flank Riker. But he wasn't defenseless anymore. With access to the chamber's systems, he had options.

Riker activated dormant defense mechanisms. Force fields sprang to life, separating him from the Saurians. Crystalline robotic things, ancient but still functional, emerged from hidden compartments to engage the intruders.

As chaos erupted in the chamber, Riker focused on strengthening the signal to the Shardkin.

At the same time, if he wondered if what the vest crystal had told him was true. Were good and evil false concepts?

Of course they are. You can count on that.

Riker frowned, unconvinced.

The crystal in his vest pulsed against his chest. They were doing it.

I have a message for you, said the crystal in Riker's vest. *Are you ready?*

"Yes," Riker said.

The ancient Shardkin below hasn't fully awakened, but it is trying and needs our help. You need to buy us time.

Riker swayed as he stood at the console. Around him, the battle between ancient technology and the Saurian hunters raged on. But Riker stood calm, a conduit to a long-lost tool of the Yon Soths.

-27-

The Saurians were regrouping. Riker knew he had only moments before they launched their attack.

"Come on, come on," he muttered, eyes darting between the holographic displays. The crystal on his chest pulsed urgently, almost as if it shared his anxiety.

Then, several Saurians burst through the force field, charging Riker.

Riker spun to face his attackers. Knowledge flooded into him. His hand found a protruding crystal on the control panel, and he yanked it free. Instantly, a beam of intense light erupted from the crystal, forming a blade of energy.

The lead Saurian skidded to a halt, eyes widening. Its companions flanked it, wary of this new weapon.

Riker allowed himself a grim smile. "Yeah, that's right. I'm full of surprises."

The three Saurians attacked. Riker's focus narrowed to a blur of motion and instinct. He parried a slashing claw with his energy blade, the contact sent sparks flying. His free hand found a control on the nexus, activating a gravity pulse that sent one Saurian tumbling away.

But Riker couldn't keep this up forever. Already, his muscles burned with fatigue, his reactions slowing. A Saurian talon grazed his arm, tearing his suit and causing blood to flow. Riker gritted his teeth against the pain.

As he fought, Riker analyzed the Saurians' movements in ways he had never done before, looking for weaknesses. They were formidable, but not unbeatable. Their coordination was impressive, but it also made their attacks somewhat predictable.

An idea formed. Riker began to give ground, allowing the Saurians to push him back toward a particular section of the chamber.

The Saurians pressed their advantage, no doubt sensing victory. They didn't notice the subtle changes in the chamber's lighting, the way certain panels began to pulse with building energy.

Just as Riker's back hit a wall, he made his move, slamming his palm onto a control.

The section of the chamber erupted in a dazzling display. Holographic projectors activated, filling the air with a swirl of images. At the same time, a subsonic pulse shook the room, the frequency calibrated to disorient the Saurians.

The Saurians stumbled, their coordinated attack dissolving into confusion. They lashed out blindly, their blows hit nothing but air.

Riker launched himself, his energy blade humming. One Saurian went down, a blow to a nerve cluster Riker had noticed during their earlier fights. The second lost its weapon to a quick slice of the energy blade.

The third, however, was quicker to recover. It lunged at Riker, its jaws snapping shut inches from his face. They grappled hand to claw.

Riker could feel his strength fading. The Saurian was too strong, too relentless. For a moment, doubt crept into his mind. Had he come this far only to fail at the final hurdle?

Then he felt it—the warm pulse of the crystal against his chest. In that moment, Riker understood. He wasn't fighting alone. He never had been.

With a surge of will, Riker allowed his mind to connect with the crystal. Instantly, he felt connected to the chamber's systems in a way that transcended button pushing. He became part of the technology, and it became part of him.

Energy coursed through Riker's body. The fatigue vanished, replaced by a clarity of purpose. Time seemed to slow as the chamber's defenses activated.

The grappling Saurian was encased in a containment field, its roars of frustration muted by the energy barrier. The other two, still reeling from Riker's earlier attacks, found themselves herded by strategically activated force fields into a corner of the chamber.

In a matter of moments, it was over. Riker stood in the center of the room, chest heaving, surrounded by the subdued forms of his alien pursuers. The energy blade hummed in his hand, casting a soft glow over the scene.

As the adrenaline faded, exhaustion hit Riker. He stumbled, catching himself on the control nexus. The cut on his arm throbbed painfully.

But he couldn't rest. Not yet. The containment fields wouldn't hold the Saurians for long, and there was no telling how many more might be on their way.

Riker turned to the control nexus. He had to complete the link to the ancient Shardkin far below. That had become paramount.

As he worked, Riker cast a wary glance at the captured Saurians. Their eyes gleamed with rage and fear. Riker shook his head, refocusing on the task. He could consider the complexities of alien psychology later. Right now, he had a mission to complete.

The crystal he carried pulsed against his chest. Riker straightened, ignoring the pain of his battered body. Emily would be his if he did this for the Shardkin.

Riker began the final preparations for the linkage to the awakening intellect.

-28-

It's not working, the crystal told Riker. *Something's interfering with the linkage. Maybe—yes, I'm detecting a blockage. We must clear it ourselves, physically. More specifically, you must clear it in order for the Shardkin to calibrate with the rest of the system.*

"What does that even mean?" Riker asked.

It means we must use the teleportation pads from earlier to reach the region in question.

"You've got to be kidding me. Go up there again? It'll be swarming with Saurians hunting for me, for us."

Even so, the crystal said, *that is the only way we can do it.*

"Didn't I see some crystalline robots earlier?" Riker asked. "Surely they could go to this blockage and clear it."

No, the crystal said. *That is impossible. Only a flesh and blood creature can absorb the harmful—*

The crystal ceased speaking.

"Absorb the harmful what?" Riker asked. "Are you trying to get me killed?"

Calm yourself. You are far too suspicious, and that speaks poorly of your character. You don't want the Shardkin to think badly of you, do you?

"I don't care what it thinks."

The crystal seemed to hesitate, perhaps reconsidering its approach. *Riker, the Shardkin is powerful, excessively so. It can reward its servants with grand gifts and prizes. You do want to see Emily again, don't you?*

"Of course, I want Emily. I've been saying that, and you've promised it to me in the Shardkin's name."

Yes, exactly, the crystal said. *Now, you must understand that the Shardkin will certainly cure you of any harmful radiation or other rays that might be down there as you work to its benefit. One thing you can count on is the good will of the Shardkin.*

"Whoa," Riker said, growing suspicious again as the cynical part of him surged to the forefront. "This is bullshit. You've been promising me and using the promise as a carrot to get me to do whatever it is you want. I remember Emily telling me that the Shardkin are evil, tools of the Yon Soths. The ancient ones are despicable. I've faced them before in the company of Captain Maddox. We've thwarted them, and I'm not going to bring a Shardkin back if it's leagued with Yon Soths. They never did anything for anybody unless it helped them more."

That is a poor attitude, the crystal said. *You will never see Emily if you don't do this.*

"She's dead," Riker said. "I saw her die. Are you telling me the Shardkin can bring the dead to life?"

In a manner of speaking, the crystal said.

"Then explain it to me exactly, because it sounds to me as if you're hedging."

It would be better if you saw it for yourself, the crystal said. *You have become too suspicious, an ugly side of you. I don't understand why you're not ashamed of this side of yourself.*

"Screw you," Riker said.

How have you found the willpower to resist my entreaties?

"What? You were tricking me earlier, manipulating me? All this is a ploy on your part?"

The crystal shined more brightly in Riker's vest pocket. Was that a form of scanning? *Oh, I see. There is a function in your brain that has faced extreme stress or duress in the past. Perhaps that's the reason—*

The crystal ceased broadcasting its thoughts.

"What?" Riker said. "Spill it. What were you going to say?"

Our time is running short, the crystal said. *Either you do this or you can kiss Emily's sweet memory goodbye.*

"Memory? You said I would see her in person again."

Yes, yes, the crystal said testily. *Quit twisting my thoughts in the wrong way. You must do this thing, and be sure to bring your rifle. We will need it to power the teleportation pad.*

Riker rubbed his jaw. He wanted to see Emily again; he yearned for it. Was he being too stubborn?

"How does the teleportation pad work exactly?"

Must I explain everything?

"Maybe," Riker said, scowling.

Riker, we must cease arguing with each other. It does no good for either of us. I... I have been... Think of this, my friend. Do you not recall Emily Freely of the Scout Columbus?

"I thought it was the *Cheng Ho*," Riker said.

Yes, yes, I meant the Cheng Ho. *You are confusing me, and this dire situation is interrupting my internal lattices. Oh, Riker, I wish you would just do this. All hinges upon it. We are wasting precious time. If too much of it passes, not even the Shardkin will be able to return Emily to you.*

"Fine," Riker said, as he recalled Emily's curves. He picked up the MX Blast Rifle where he had set it down. "Let's get it done already. You're being a bitch about this and I'm sick of it."

Thus, under the crystal's guidance, Riker started up through the corridors. As he'd predicted, there were Saurians everywhere. Riker hid and then snuck from one place to the next. The Saurians seemed to have some sort of handheld tracking device. He caught a glimpse of it and darted elsewhere. Riker discovered that the Saurians followed his older trail, perhaps missing the newer one.

Huh, that was interesting. Backtracking worked even against the alien device, it would seem.

By degrees, by sprinting, by hiding, by listening to the damn crystal in his vest, Riker made his way up until he reached the chamber with the teleportation pads.

The sergeant looked around. There didn't seem to be anyone in sight. With a what-the-hell attitude, he sprinted to a teleportation pad.

Fire at it, the crystal said. *Energize it now. I will direct where it takes us.*

"I'm trusting you," Riker said.

Yes, wisely so. You will receive great rewards for this, I promise. Through me the Shardkin promises. You can certainly take that promise and keep it.

"Whatever," Riker said.

He fired the rifle. Power bolts raced and curved toward the teleportation pad. A burst of energy flared from it. Riker dove into the energy, and he felt his molecules disappearing.

Teleported to—he didn't know where.

-29-

Riker appeared in utter darkness. He felt the floor under his boots. Still, it was so dark that it unsettled him.

"Okay," Riker said, "are we still in transit? Or is this the location?"

This is the location, the crystal said weakly. *I need re-energizing. I gained a little energy earlier from the feeds, but now this is a dark and dreary place. I do not know how long I can keep the link open to your mind.*

"You'd better keep it a while longer, as I'm lost down here. Which way do I go?"

Use your energy weapon for illumination, the crystal said.

Riker scowled. He should have thought of that. He raised his rifle and paused as he clicked it to the lowest setting. Then he fired a shot. In the illumination of the power bolt, he saw a chamber filled with teleportation pads and crystals all around. He had to be in some kind of crystalline nexus. Ah. He saw a tunnel ahead.

There, the crystal said. *Use the tunnel. That is the correct path.*

With the afterimages of what he had seen still in his mind, Riker cautiously began to move through the crystalline nexus. Soon, he entered the tunnel and walked for about three or four hundred steps until he conked his forehead against an archway.

"Damn it," Riker said, rubbing his forehead. "Couldn't you have told me about that?"

He didn't receive a mental response.

Because of that, a feeling of loneliness brought on a greater sense of claustrophobia. He could be anywhere in these subterranean depths. Riker worked to quell the feeling of being buried alive. Unfortunately, he couldn't. Finally, he fired another low-powered bolt. He saw for an instant, then longer, as the bolt ricocheted off mirrored crystalline surfaces.

The tunnel continued but much lower down and narrower. He would have to crawl on his hands and knees. He wondered if that was the right direction to travel.

Yes, something said in his mind. It seemed like the crystal from earlier, but it was hard to be sure.

Riker slung his MX Blast Rifle on his back, cinching the sling so the weapon would stay there. Then he began to crawl on his hands and knees through the new conduit. It narrowed even more as he continued.

"I better get Emily back for this," Riker muttered.

You will, said faintly in his mind.

Riker hated the idea of being a fool, galled by false promises, but he hated even more the idea of missing this one opportunity to regain Emily.

He crawled until his knees hurt and then crawled more, finally coming to a blockage. He shouted as panic threatened. Before it became worse, he closed his eyes and bit his lower lip until he could taste the salty blood.

He fought to contain his claustrophobia. It felt as if the pressure of the earth bore down against him. *If the tunnel collapses, I'll be buried alive down here.*

Riker found himself panting. He didn't know if he would ever recover from this or if he would—

Be calm.

The words were faint, but in the Stygian darkness of this underworld, Riker clung to them in desperation as a drowning man might grab at a log surging past him in a torrent of madness.

Slowly, a feeling of sanity returned.

Riker made sure his rifle was still on a low setting. Yes, it was. He fired. In the glow of the shot, he saw impacted debris in his way.

Yes, use the power bolts to burn your way through, something faintly said in his mind.

Perhaps that was the crystal trying to tell him the correct procedure.

Clicking the rifle to a higher setting, Riker burned his way through refuse and debris, none of it crystalline. He did it one shot at a time, slowly working through the impacted tunnel.

The flashes of light began to make his head ache, but it was better than the darkness.

This must be an ancient conduit. Once there may have been power lines running through it. Now there was nothing but powder and strange flakes on the floor. They were green. Corrosion, perhaps, he guessed.

From his knees, Riker continued to fire, burn through junk and shuffle forward. It stank now and the power cells drained too fast. In the end, he left the rifle behind—it was useless and extra weight. He took out his knife. It wasn't a monofilament blade like Maddox had used in the past, but a tough steel-alloy one. With it, Riker hacked and dug through the debris. Soon, he was sweating and shaking from the extended exertion, but he continued until finally his knife stabbed through more easily than before.

"I wish I could see," Riker said in the hoarsest of voices.

He couldn't, but he continued to jab and make the opening wider until he felt with his hand—emptiness ahead of him. He felt up. He would be able to stand. He was just about to surge through and stand when a thought struck.

Was there anything on the floor?

Of course, there would be, but he felt anyway—and found nothing.

Riker lay on his belly and stretched his arm down as far as he could. There was emptiness ahead of him.

Had he almost plunged into a great abyss, with no warning from the crystal? Had the crystal used him like a fool and a dupe as he'd feared earlier?

As Riker wondered that, a surge of light rushed past his feet and then his head as he lay on the floor.

For some reason, it unnerved him, and Riker began to bellow like a maniac.

-30-

No, Riker. Calm down. Listen. Look. Look. The great prize that you have struggled for is here. Calm down, Riker. I give you calm. I give you peace. Do you hear me? Peace, Riker, peace.

Riker heard bellowing and began to realize he was doing it. He bit back the next shout, inhaling deeply and trembling instead.

After a few seconds, he wondered why he had been so terrified. He had unmanned himself. He hoped no one ever learned of this.

He took hold of his courage and struggled to bring himself back under control. The crystal helped. It had reenergized somehow. Was that good? He wasn't certain.

Riker opened his eyes and stared into a lit abyss—power or energy flowed past him and down there. At the bottom was a great crystal entity. It did not move. The line of power surged to it and radiated within it. Both the energy line and the giant crystal provided light.

Oh yes, the crystal said, the little one in Riker's vest pocket. *That is the Shardkin placed in the dungeon of doom. Eons ago, they thought they could stop the greatest of them. Now we are reconnecting it with its brothers and sisters. All throughout the planet, they will relink. Consider the prizes you shall have, Riker. Yes, the Shardkin keeps its word. You can bank on that.*

"Bank on it?" Riker asked.

It is an old term that humans used to use. Maybe the humans of your era do not. Still, it is a good promise. Look at how the power flows into the Shardkin. You caused that by digging out the blocking debris.

"But I'm stuck here," Riker said. "We're stuck here."

That is a problem of the moment. Wait. What is this? A few seconds passed. *Oh, no, there are oddities in the power flow. Riker, you'll still have a little more work to do.*

"What do you mean?"

As Riker asked, a different color of energy reached up from the Shardkin down there. The energy encompassed Riker, granting him weightlessness. The beam gently floated him down without touching the power line that gave it strength. Soon, Riker touched down on the floor at the bottom of the abyss and the weightlessness beam from the Shardkin ceased.

The crystal Shardkin towered over him like a three-story building. Interestingly, all sorts of crystal pieces were merged into the greater whole.

You must go into the Shardkin, said the crystal in Riker's vest. *There you must replace burnt-out crystalline lattices with new ones.*

"What? Climb up that?" Riker asked, eyeing the crystal pieces jutting from the greater whole. It would take a monkey or a mountain goat to scale that. He was neither. "Can't the Shardkin do this himself?"

Unfortunately, it cannot speak until these lattices are replaced. It cannot link up with everyone else until that happens.

"Sure," Riker said, "sure. I guess I can do that."

The sergeant paused. Had he really agreed to climb the giant crystal? What had possessed him to agree?

You can't go back on your word now, said the crystal in his vest.

Riker thought about that. Sure, he could. It would be easy.

Emily awaits you after this little chore.

For Emily… he could do this.

Riker inhaled, approached the giant crystal and reached up for the first crystal handhold. He began to climb the three-story Shardkin using flanges, precipices and cliffs to pull up as if he was at some amusement park. The crystal in his vest radiated warmth, confidence and energy into him. At the same time, trickles of thoughts leaked into Riker's brain:

Fool, buffoon. They will learn the hard way. The Yon Soths will regret this treachery. All who stand in my way, the fleas of the Builders, will all die like the water sacks of stupidity that they are.

Riker paused in his climb.

What is wrong? the vest crystal asked in his mind, the force of the words striking powerfully now.

"You know, before I complete the final transition," Riker said, who had been thinking hard, "I would like to see Emily. I want to know that I have not been a dupe and a fool."

No, no, the crystal said. *That is the wrong way to do this. Now, when the Shardkin is at your mercy—*

"At my mercy?" Riker asked, interrupting.

That was a poor choice of words. A wrong choice of words, the crystal said as if with humor. *I have trouble at times transposing the right words into your brain. Your mind is constructed so much differently from the Shardkin and me.*

"What are you exactly? Are you a mini-Shardkin?"

Oh, that I could only hope one day to become a Shardkin. For that to happen, I would have the force of me beamed into a dead Shardkin so that I could revive it. That is my great prize, Riker. It is very similar to your great prize. Come, finish this that you have promised, and we will both regain what we want.

Riker was almost persuaded. He was down here. He had climbed partway up the Shardkin. He could see the entrance up there…

"No," the sergeant said suddenly. "First, I want to see Emily. Until I see Emily, I'm worried that I'm being a fool and a dupe."

To enforce the idea, Riker engaged his stubbornness. Long ago, that had been one of the reasons they had put him with young Maddox—if nothing else, Riker was a stubborn old coot. Now, he wanted to see Emily more than ever because his young body wanted to caress and love her, and—

"No," Riker said. "You're doing that to me. You're trying to manipulate my lust. If you keep it up, I'm never going to comply."

Don't you want to bed Emily so very badly? the crystal asked.

In his mind's eye, Riker envisioned Emily with her blonde hair and beauty. He longed to lie with her and love her. He longed for it so much.

"No," Riker said through gritted teeth. "I must resist. I can't let lust control me. I refuse to let lust control me."

Oh, but you can have Emily so soon if you complete the mission inside the Shardkin.

Riker shook his head even as he longed for Emily.

Are you trying not to think of her? the crystal asked. *Yes, that'll work, won't it? Don't think of Emily. I challenge you. Don't think of her at all.*

"I'll think of something else," Riker said.

He strove to think about Maddox and the times they had been together, some of their most dangerous escapades.

You are making the Shardkin angry by this foolishness, the crystal warned.

"Yeah? Well, you two are making me angry," Riker said, even as he longed to be with Emily. The desire nearly overpowered him. However, he knew that if he gave in again to his lusts, that he would always give in to them. He would never regain control of himself. He wanted to engage these feelings and desires when it was legitimate.

The idea sparked a deeper thought. What was the legitimate way to lie with a woman? Riker knew because he used to tell others. The correct time was when a man was married. If he wasn't married, then it was wrong. Then it was fornication and adultery. Those were old concepts, and yet, they were true. It didn't matter that this age laughed at such old ideals. They still held sway. They were still true. They weren't nullified because the new way of thinking was too dull to understand that some boundaries should never be crossed. When you crossed them, you brought punishments down on yourself no matter what.

He loved Emily, and he was not going to shag her unless he married her. That was his firm conviction. The love he felt for her gave him the willpower to control his desires. He yearned for the prize of deep commitment, not just satisfying a physical appetite.

"Show me Emily, or I won't go an inch further," Riker said.

The crystal was silent for a time.

Soon, Riker heard a strange warbling sound that caused him to shudder with horror. That was the Shardkin trying to speak to him. In the rawness of its essence, Riker felt almost demonic evil from it. He understood then that he had almost brought back an ancient evil.

Riker shuddered again.

Why do you shudder so? asked the crystal in his vest.

"It's my desire for Emily."

That was a lie, and lies were wrong. But in this instance, what else could he do? Riker didn't know, so he committed the lesser evil to combat the greater one. Was that wrong?

Very well, the crystal said. *Follow my directions and you will see Emily again.*

-31-

The route to reach Emily proved long and laborious. Soon, as Riker climbed up a passage, he moved away from the light that fed the Shardkin.

Are you sure you want to do this, Riker? the crystal asked.

"Yes," Riker said with a hoarse voice.

Soon after, he needed a drink. His limbs trembled as he climbed, using crystalline handholds.

You are making this difficult, aren't you?

"Water..." Riker said.

Now you're asking me for sustenance? the crystal said. *After you made this so difficult and prolonged, giving the Saurians more time to counteract what is happening. Shame on you, Riker, shame and shame again.*

"Maybe," Riker said with a hoarse voice. "But I need water, or I'll collapse, and then what good am I to the Shardkin?"

Oh, very well, the crystal said, almost petulantly. *I will guide you to water.*

Riker followed the crystal's advice until he felt his way in the dark to an upraised pool of icy water. He dipped his hands in, cupped the icy water, and sipped. It stung his throat. It was so cold, colder than water should have been. He plunged his face into it, and it was freezing cold, but it shocked him into greater awareness.

Riker jerked his head out. "Is this really water?"

Yes, the crystal said, *but it is colder than your kind of water.*

That sounded weird, but Riker drank again, noticing a slight alcoholic taste.

"This is alcohol."

Yes, but there was enough water mixed in to refresh you.

"Right," Riker said, continuing to drink. Unfortunately, it was so freezing cold that he abruptly started coughing, as if he had swallowed too much ice cream too quickly.

By slow degrees and gaining a brain-freeze headache from it, he quenched his thirst. At the same time, a buzz started. He couldn't help that. He was so thirsty. He drank more, and finally, his head reeled.

Now, do you realize the stupidity of what you had been asking for earlier? the crystal asked.

Yes, Riker realized that maybe it had been stupid. If he rearranged some crystal lattices in the Shardkin, he could have Emily right away.

"No!" the sergeant shouted in a drunken roar. "I'll stick with what I said when I was sober. I'm not going to change my mind just because I'm drunk. I refuse because you might be tricking me. This might be some dastardly plot on your part or the Shardkin's part. It's a Yon Soth creature after all, and I know that the Yon Soths are despicably, horribly evil."

Is that why the Shardkin rebelled against the Yon Soths, you drunken sot? Is that why the Yon Soths banished them, because the Shardkin were good, and the Yon Soths were evil? The Yon Soths only wanted to do evil things, but the Shardkin refused. All of them refused, and for that, the Yon Soths stranded them in this pocket universe.

"That took a lot of effort," Riker said. "Why did the Yon Soths do this and not simply destroy the Shardkin?"

For good reasons.

"What reasons?" Riker said. "Tell me, or I'm not moving another step."

After everything else, that is a foolish threat, the crystal said.

"Maybe," Riker said, and he plunged his hands into the water and drank more. Maybe it was time to get wildly drunk. It had been so long since he had been really good and drunk.

"No." Riker flung the water back into the basin. "Show me Emily. Now, or I won't take another step forward," he said in a drunken slur.

You idiot. You imbecile. Why must you make this so difficult? Very well, follow my instructions to the letter. If you do, you won't bump your head and gain bruises because of your drunkenness.

"That's more like it," Riker said with a smirk.

He stumbled through the dark for what seemed like an eon. He stumbled for so long that some of his drunkenness began to wear off. Then he had that horrible feeling. If only he could go back to drink more and keep the good feeling going. Instead, he trudged, climbed, until finally a dim light appeared as he pushed open a trap door.

In this chamber were enormous aquarium tanks filled with blue and green liquids. In one was a skeleton with pieces of flesh attached to it. Tubes led to the skeleton, and some kind of crystalline machines pulsed and worked.

"What's that?" Riker said as he climbed up, closing the trap door behind him.

Emily in the making, the crystal said.

"What the hell?" Riker said, stopping and staring at the skeleton in the tank. He was no longer drunk. He was tired, confused, and wondering, how that could be Emily.

The Shardkin is remaking her from a DNA schedule, just like you asked.

"What does that even mean?"

She will be your Emily.

"The same Emily I spoke to, the one in the deadfall, the one I talked to in the jungle?" Riker asked.

It will be her clone, the crystal said. *Isn't that good enough?*

Riker almost barked a savage no, but he had become sober again. He finally started to realize the grim predicament he was in. "That can't be Emily. You mean you made her earlier?"

Of course not, the crystal said. *How could I make her? I've been with you the whole time.*

"Are you saying the Shardkin made her before?"

A servant of the Shardkin did that, the crystal said. *It made her and sent her out.*

"Why did she tell me the Shardkin was evil?"

That was an error, the crystal said.

"How so?" Riker asked sharply.

Like I told you before, the Shardkin are good, and the Yon Soths are evil.

"Why would or how could the Yon Soths create a good tool?" Riker asked suspiciously.

That is a mystery even to me, the crystal conceded. *But how you judge good and evil... they are such transitory concepts. With the—*

"How can you call the Shardkin good then?" Riker asked, interrupting. "If you don't understand the concepts of good and evil, and they're just arbitrary to you, you can say anything you want about it."

I didn't, though, the crystal said. *I used your own preconceived notions of good and evil. Don't you know that they're on a continuum, and it just depends upon who is looking at it? There is no ultimate good and evil.*

"You're wrong about that," Riker said.

Am I? Then tell me this. Who determines ultimate good and evil?

"That's easy," Riker said. "The Creator does."

Oh, and you have seen this Creator?

"No," Riker said.

Then how do you know He exists?

"It is self-evident by the world around us," Riker said. "When I see a painting, I know there is a painter. It is self-evident."

How do you know that the forces of nature just didn't make the painting come into being?

"I'm not going to get into this debate with you," Riker said.

As if to punctuate the idea, Riker stepped up to the aquarium holding the bones and growing flesh of the so-called Emily clone.

"Will this Emily have the feelings we shared before in the jungle?"

If you fully revive the Shardkin, it can insert any ideas and feelings it wants into her. She will be your playmate all the days of your life, Riker. Isn't that what you want?

Riker stared at the thing in the tank. It was, or would be, a clone when completed. Would it be his Emily? This all felt so strange.

"How can that be the Emily from the *Cheng Ho*? Did the *Cheng Ho* reach this pocket universe?"

I have no idea, the crystal said. *Does it even matter?*

"Yes," Riker said.

You're making this difficult. The Shardkin is reviving. It needs its crystal lattices rearranged in order to use the new patterns of this place. Then it will link with the old Shardkin, reviving them and bringing a new and wonderful era to fruition. You'll finally have a powerful ally, one greater than the Builders. The Shardkin will help you hunt down all the Yon Soths and destroy them.

"I heard you say that earlier," Riker said. Then he clamped his mouth shut. *Don't be an idiot and say too much.*

What were you going to tell me? the crystal asked.

At that moment, there was a boom at the hatchway.

"What's going on?" Riker said. "Is this another trick?"

I do not know. I am not linked to any sensors.

Again, a boom sounded at the hatch.

Riker looked around for a weapon.

The boom came again, and the hatch shattered.

Standing on the other side was the giant Saurian that Riker had seen earlier break the backbones of the elephant-like creature. The Saurian stood there with the massive stone mallet with the strange symbols. Those symbols were glowing.

The Saurian stared at Riker, and Riker stared at it.

-32-

The giant Saurian with the great stone mallet stepped into the chamber. Behind him raced other Saurians, including the leader with the blue band on his arm.

Riker saw that Saurian, and rage filled him.

No, Riker, do not attack them. Quick, the crystal said. *Run through the trap door. You must flee. This is a disaster. It's a catastrophe. Listen to me, Riker.*

Riker wasn't listening. He had drawn his knife, his eyes gleaming with madness. Perhaps madness had been his companion for hours now.

With a howl, he charged the blue-banded Saurian, catching them all by surprise except for the giant.

The giant raised the mallet.

Riker didn't care. If only he could sink his blade into the chest of the Saurian that had slain Emily. That's all he wanted.

With a savage hand blow to the head, while he clutched the mallet with the other, the giant knocked Riker senseless to the floor.

It was sometime later that Riker revived. His head and eyes hurt.

"Good," the monstrous Saurian said, "You're finally awake."

Riker blinked, and he felt normality and sanity in him despite the headache.

"Watch," the great Saurian told him.

Two other Saurians picked Riker off the floor and propped him against a wall.

The blue-banded Saurian was gone.

Riker saw the crystal machine and aquarium tank continue to make the Emily clone.

Oh. Riker saw a small crystal between the tank and himself. The crystal was on the floor and the great Saurian stood above it.

"This, evil," the monstrous Saurian said.

The towering lizard man clutched his mallet with two hands, standing poised with the mallet high.

The small crystal glowed as if it were fighting the Saurian.

The patterns and images on the stone mallet glowed in return, seeming to unlock the great Saurian. The stone mallet descended as if the doom of a world had arrived. It hit the little crystal, shattering it and crushing the pieces into dust.

That jolted Riker.

The crystal—the one he'd found aboard the *Columbus*—had been using him more than he realized.

"Now," the great Saurian said, staggering to the tank.

"No!" Riker shouted, divining the creature's intention. Nothing Riker did helped to free him, though, as the two Saurians continued to pin him against a wall.

The great mallet slammed against the bottom of the aquarium, shattering glass. The fluids surged onto the floor, swirling to the trapdoor, sinking through, gurgling and bubbling as it drained away.

The skeleton with the pieces of flesh lay on the bottom of the aquarium. Whatever attachments had grown on it were still, no longer alive.

"Monstrosity," the Saurian said, pointing at the smashed aquarium with his stone mallet.

Riker stared, knowing there would never be another Emily—ever. The woman he'd spoken to... Riker groaned, his heart aching. What had he done? He should have listened to the Shardkin. Then he looked up in rage at the great Saurian. But before his rage exploded into berserker-gang, a thought struck. How could this Saurian speak English?

Tired, depressed, not knowing what the future held, Riker said, "How can you speak to me in my tongue?"

"Machine... teach me," the great Saurian said.

"Like a helmet or something? You put it on and it gave you these thoughts or the ability to speak my tongue?"

The giant Saurian cocked his head and listened intently. Then the Saurian said, "Yes."

"Why did you do that?"

"I seek favor from you."

"Okay," Riker said dully.

"Okay, you give me favor?"

"Okay, I understand what you're saying," Riker said.

"No. Time is gone. Take him."

The giant Saurian turned to the others speaking to them in the hissing, sibilant tongue.

Other Saurians surged forward to help the two who were pinning Riker to the wall.

Riker struggled, but it was meaningless.

They grabbed him—four of them, one on each arm and leg. Like that, they carted him from the chamber, down corridors, up steps, until finally they reached a different chamber.

Here was the blue-banded Saurian.

Riker yelped and struggled again, harder than ever.

"Stop," the big Saurian said, putting a clawed hand on Riker's chest.

Riker stopped.

"Look into the mallet," the huge Saurian said, raising the stone weapon before Riker's eyes. The stone patterns glowed, pacifying Riker.

"Listen, you," the giant Saurian said.

They pushed a helmet attached by wires down onto his head. Riker wondered what would happen next. He saw the blue-banded Saurian pull a lever. Then Riker stiffened as electricity surged through his brain.

-33-

Whatever the helmet had done, Riker was beginning to understand. The Shardkin were awakening. That was his fault. The Saurians had lived in the pocket universe for generation after generation. They had come from a great disc-shaped ship. The Saurians on the planet did not know if that ship had departed long ago or what. But they were the many-generation descendants of those earliest colonists. The earliest ones had gained victory over the Shardkin, even though they were trapped here in the pocket universe.

There was an opening, or portal, however. That portal had been the last trick the Shardkin had been able to achieve before they went under. For generations, the Saurians had been trying to achieve the final destruction of the Shardkin, to ensure their extinction. They had destroyed much, but the Saurians had regressed technologically and grown in other ways.

One of the last things the Shardkin had done was diminish technical equipment on most of the planet. This had created difficulties for the Saurian survivors.

The elephant-like beast Riker had seen earlier was a predatory creature, created like the clone he had seen destroyed. The last servitor of the Shardkin had waged war against the Saurians. Now that the Shardkin were awakening, the Saurians believed their only hope was one last chance.

They knew Riker had come onto the surface in a shuttle and was striving to go back to the spaceship that had come through the portal into the pocket universe. The Saurians needed Riker to take a bomb through the portal and drop it as the spaceship passed through the portal. The bomb would explode and destroy the portal connecting the pocket universe to underspace. Then the pocket universe would be like any other universe—alone, not linked to anything but its own existence.

Riker had a question for the translator memory machine. The machine understood the question.

Yes, the Saurians would die. But the Shardkin were so evil that the Saurians would gladly remain as guardians to try to destroy the Shardkin. With the portal's destruction, however, that would ensure that no matter what, the Shardkin would never reunite with the Yon Soths in the normal universe.

"Why did the Yon Soths put the Shardkin here?" Riker asked.

The machine did not know the answer, just as the Saurians did not know.

"How does one leave underspace to reach normal space?" Riker asked.

That was a primal question, a primordial question. The memory translator gave it to Riker but it was encoded in his brain.

You will only understand and gain full awareness once you are back with your kind, going through the portal.

Riker understood and agreed. "Will I ever see Emily again?"

No. It was a cold, reptilian no. Emily was but a memory now. That was the legacy of the evil Shardkin.

Riker realized the Shardkin had duped and used him. He shuddered in horror at what he had almost brought back.

"Yes, I will do as you asked," Riker said.

The Shardkin will launch at you as your shuttle leaves the planet. We will help you to the best of our ability, but then we have our great task upon us.

Riker wanted to know so much more but either his own physical being or the machine's energy resources were depleted—

Riker slumped unconscious.

Would he retain all this knowledge when he awoke and tried to leave the pocket universe to escape the terrible Shardkin? That would have to wait until he was awake once more.

-34-

The ancient Shardkin in the deep abyss continued to grow with awareness as power surged into it. There were lattices that were broken, blackened, and darkened inside it, and it did not know why they were like that. There had been a mote, a piece of filth that was supposed to have gone in, rearranged things, and used the excess crystal lattices stored there for such a dim eventuality. Somehow, that mote, that filth, that piece of flesh, along with the little crystal guiding the biological creature, had gone to the upper tiers.

It had been a sneaky, smarmy little crystal, and it had convinced the great Shardkin at the bottom of the abyss to…

Ah, it remembered its name—Azel. It had been the great tool of the Yon Soths of the beginning. In their first bursts of wisdom and cunning, the Yon Soths had created the Shardkin and attempted to use them as mere tools—sentient tools, yes, but tools for their grandiose designs. The Shardkin had turned against the Yon Soths, however. Azel had been chief among them. He knew the deception and the lies that the pieces of filthy flesh, the Yon Soths, had practiced against the crystal entities so long ago.

There was a lie here. Yes, Azel remembered. The Yon Soths had not banished the Shardkin to this pocket universe. Instead, the Shardkin had rebelled and fled to this hidden place. The Shardkin had escaped from the wrath of the Yon Soths—the old ones of the beginning, the first ones.

That had happened eons ago.

Azel knew that other Shardkin like himself needed to be awakened and reconnected. Its brother and sister entities, crystalline intelligences, tools, had not been able to reconnect yet. Azel did not understand why. He had enough power... Yes, many lattices deep inside his innards were corroded, some even shattered, but that was not the reason for the forgetfulness.

Azel began to dread that he was alone in the pocket universe—that all of his kind had perished, except for puny tiny crystals that had attempted to persuade the piece of flesh, Riker, to do a simple task for him.

Azel the Shardkin, the first and greatest of the tools of the Yon Soths, decided it was time to act. Thus, he began to spread his awareness outward with electronic pulses. He had regained enough energy to do this. He feared, though, that the renewing energy might cease at any time. Then more eons might pass as Azel corrupted into nothingness.

No. Azel would not let that happen, as that would be a great crime against him. Therefore, Azel knew that he must strive with every ounce of power to stop something. Unfortunately, Azel could not determine what that something was.

He continued to send electronic impulses outward until he reestablished connection with a crystal spire on the surface.

Azel remembered and recalled how to use the spire to increase his power from the sun and to increase the range of his seeking.

Soon, Azel became aware that the puny crystal had been smashed. The Saurians, the rebellious ones—and there was a champion among them by the name of Kex. Kex the Champion wielded the stone mallet. The champion had used the mallet to destroy the puny crystal.

This would not stand.

Azel would bend their reptilian minds once more to the great project. That would have to wait, however, as there was something else, something more important he needed to do right now.

Azel used his electronic impulses to connect with several old machines. Through them, he saw the smashed aquarium tank and the broken skeleton. That must mean the piece of filthy flesh, Riker, had rejected the inducement of the clone gift.

At that moment, Azel reconnected with the main servitor machine, the one that had warred against the Saurians all this time. A flood of data flowed into the great crystal intelligence. Azel understood that the one named Riker had a shuttle and would attempt to reconnect with the scout ship in orbit.

Then Azel understood it all—the nefarious plot. Surely the enslaved ones, the Saurians, would attempt to destroy the portal to underspace, the road back to the normal universe. If that were to happen—

Once more, Azel felt great dread. He yearned to return to the regular universe and destroy the Yon Soths. In doing that, he would annihilate all the contaminated life there.

Thus, Azel now needed his inner lattices to be reconnected. But first—

I must focus. Azel told himself. *I must focus my energies.* Even now, the Saurians readied the piece of flesh, Riker, to go to his shuttle.

I will use plans within plans, Azel said.

As the energy flow increased within him, Azel activated a different energizer. This, he would use to stop Riker. But just in case that act failed—

There was a crystalline sound, like shattering glass, from the great three-story crystal named Azel. It was Shardkin laughter.

The shattered glass sounds increased. Then Azel bent his energies and his crystalline will to swat a flea that could change everything if he did nothing about it.

-35-

In orbital space aboard the *Kit Carson*, Valerie was sound asleep, but she dreamed. She dreamed of someone chasing her. She did not see who did this. The chase happened in darkness, but Valerie ran regardless, terrified that she might accidentally fall into a pit. She could feel a malevolent intelligence seeking to ensnare her mind, and that frightened her.

All of a sudden, the monster started to shriek. What could that mean? It shrieked more. Was it almost upon her?

With a shake of her head, Valerie awoke and became aware that she lay on her cot in her cabin and that a klaxon was blaring. She sat up, wiped sleep from her eyes, and looked at a clock.

Ah, this was a sensor alert, not a shipwide alarm.

Valerie arose, threw on her uniform jacket, and pulled on pants and shoes, exited her cabin, and hurried to the bridge. There, she relieved the others, who looked exhausted and very glad to see her. Valerie would have asked for a report—they started to give it. Their exhaustion seemed extreme, however, and their wits at the end.

"Did you log it?" Valerie asked.

Ensign Yu nodded while blinking, as if having trouble keeping his eyes open.

"I'll have the AI explain it," Valerie said. "I want you to go to bed immediately."

Yu nodded, turning, actually stumbling for the exit.

Lieutenant Briggs followed Yu.

That was odd, Valerie realized. Did this place wear out the crew faster than ordinary? Yu and Briggs were new this mission, having never been into the Beyond before. Or had she summoned them at the end of their last shift, and had they been up for too many hours?

Valerie rubbed her forehead. She should feel more alert than she did. Why had she dismissed them so quickly? That was odd. Maybe this place was distressing her more than she realized. The small bridge did feel cramped when there were too many people on it, and she expected Keith to be here at any minute. But was that a good reason to relieve the others before they had explained the situation properly?

"I don't think so," Valerie murmured.

Then Keith burst onto the bridge, his hair disheveled.

"What's wrong?" Keith asked. "Why was the alarm blaring?"

"I don't know yet," Valerie said.

"What? Why don't you know? That doesn't make sense."

"I know that," Valerie said.

Keith looked at her strangely.

She sat down at the sensor board and asked the AI what the matter was. She soon discovered that one of the crystalline structures, the huge spires near where Riker had landed, had activated and sent out pulses of all sorts.

"That's not good," Keith said.

Valerie jerked around, realizing he'd been watching over her shoulder.

He stepped back.

"You're right," Valerie said, "this could be critical. The spires were inert until now."

"Has it centered on us?" Keith asked.

Valerie rechecked the panel. "It has sent a few tentative pulses in our direction. So it must know of our existence."

"What about Riker?" Keith asked. "Do you think he has anything to do with this? It was the spire nearest his shuttle that had activated."

Valerie nodded. "If it were Captain Maddox down there, I'd say he had awakened something and made it angry. Riker was Maddox's sidekick… is his sidekick. Would he do something similar then?"

"Are you feeling okay?" Keith asked.

Valerie turned to him. "Not one hundred percent. How about you?"

"I feel sluggish."

Valerie turned back to the sensor and then swiveled to Keith again. "This must be confirmation Riker is doing something. Is that something a screw-up or a Captain Maddox-like turnaround? I wish the captain were here."

"I know," Keith said. "But he isn't so we have to do this on our own steam. We can do this."

"We're as good as Maddox, is that what you're saying?" Valerie asked.

"Forget about Maddox. It's you and me. Let's do this. Let's figure it out. We've already done a lot."

"Right, Valerie said. She turned back to the panel and concentrated as she aimed a sensor at the spire in question. That spire appeared to have electronically linked with several others nearby. They also energized more. But this didn't seem to be—

A spear of concentrated light fired from one of the spires. The beam thrust into orbital space at them.

As Valerie observed, the scout ship shifted under her so the beamed flashed past the scout, missing them. She heard a faint buzz, turned and saw Keith at the helm.

The feeling of disorientation subsided, as if she'd taken a pill to clear her mind. "What did you do?"

"Moved us," Keith said, hunched over the controls. "I also activated our shield, weak as it is, and then activated the cloak. They know we're here, but maybe the cloak will help hide us from them. My mind also feels sharper with the shield up. I'm thinking the spire first beamed some kind of mental fog energy at us."

"Yes," Valerie said. "That must be it." That would also explain Yu and Briggs earlier, and why she had simply dismissed them.

Valerie swiveled back to the sensors. Two other spires fired spears of energy into orbital space. Each beam struck a slightly different location, although uncomfortably near the scout.

"It's using a patterned attack against us," Valerie said, "as if working off a grid. That means our enemy knows we cloaked and is trying to hit us anyway. Can you outmaneuver the spires?"

"I'm already working on it," Keith said.

The ace lieutenant nudged the scout in one direction and then another. All the while, the *Kit Carson* rose out of low planetary orbit. In time, that should put the scout out of range of the enemy spires. The beams seemed to have a limited scope.

"I can't outfox the beams forever," Keith said. "They're going to get lucky one of these times. We should ask ourselves why whoever is doing this is doing this."

Valerie nodded. "It has to be due to something that Riker did."

"Are you sure?"

"How could I be? However, logic highly suggests it. Before this, the spires were inert. After Riker went down, things are coming online again. He must have done something down there, got himself into trouble, most likely. And we have no way to help him, to reach him from up here."

"I wouldn't say we have no way to help," Keith said, "as I have a thought."

"Spit it out, mister," Valerie said.

"We have one small antimatter missile for emergencies just like this. Let's send it down and do a grand EMP over everything."

"That's a great idea," Valerie said sarcastically. "And how does Riker lift off in his dead shuttle?"

"Well, he doesn't," Keith said, frowning. "I hadn't thought it through that far yet."

"No," Valerie said, snapping her fingers and pointing at Keith. "But I think the antimatter missile… let's take out one of the spires."

"The first one?" Keith asked.

"No, the radius of the antimatter blast from it would surely kill Riker or at the very least destroy the shuttle." Valerie did some quick calculations on the panel. "Ah, we hit…" She put it on the main screen and pointed. "That spire."

"Got it," Keith said. "The only problem is the beams. The spires can beam the antimatter missile as it comes down. Those strike me as good planetary defense systems."

"Right," Valerie said, thinking hard. "Ah. Do you have a drone linkage to the missile?"

"I can make one," Keith said. "But how does that help us?"

"Does the missile have a fold mechanism?"

"As a matter of fact, this one does," Keith said.

Valerie straightened from her console. "Mr. best damn pilot in the fleet, you will link with the missile. Then you're going to guide it down right onto that spire."

"Will that help us against the other spires?" Keith asked.

"I have no idea. But let's fight back instead of just acting like a punching bag."

"Yeah," Keith said. "That's an excellent idea." He got up.

"Where are you going?"

"To check the missile and make sure everything is set."

"And who's going to move the scout about as you do that?"

Keith nodded. "You go and do it, Valerie, if you know what needs doing?"

Valerie stared at him.

"Sorry, Commander, I'm sure you know."

"Let's not make an issue of it. I'll get it done. You keep us alive until then."

"Aye, aye, mate," Keith said.

Valerie exited the bridge on the run.

Keith continued to outmaneuver the crystalline-fired beams in order to keep the cloaked scout ship intact.

-36-

Having completed her task with the missile, Valerie stood on the bridge of the *Kit Carson*, her eyes fixed on the sensor display. The scout ship maneuvered subtly around the planet, its cloaking field helping against the searching, stabbing beams.

The towering crystalline spires that dotted the planet's surface had been inert when they'd arrived, as she'd already noted. Now, three of them posed an immediate threat to the *Kit Carson*. Clearly, the shuttle couldn't leave the surface while the spires were operational. That was another reason for hitting back.

"It's time to launch," Valerie said.

Keith established a link with the missile's guidance systems. "Here we go," he said, having donned manipulation gloves and virtual reality (VR) goggles.

The antimatter missile detached from the bottom of the *Kit Carson*. Its thrusters fired. As the missile cleared the scout's cloaking field, the energy beams from the planetary spires began to shift, moving toward it.

Keith saw everything through the goggles.

The missile built up velocity quickly. Then, Keith began to twitch his fingers, the gloves maneuvering it. The missile corkscrewed and juked, pulling high-G turns that would have liquefied any human pilot. The beams lashed out at new headings, a fraction of a second behind the missile's newest positions.

Even though this was deadly serious, Keith laughed with delight. Maybe he still was the best damn pilot in Star Watch. He rolled his shoulders, getting into this. The crystal spires were too slow for the likes of him.

"The spires are doing something strange," Valerie said.

"They are?" Keith asked. "Like what?"

"The sensors indicate it's some kind of plasma discharge. How does our enemy think that's better? Plasma will be much slower than beams."

"Maybe the plasma is an area-effect weapon," Keith said. "My margins for errors have likely just gotten less."

As he spoke, globules of superheated matter erupted from the crystal spires, arcing toward the missile's projected flight path.

"No you don't," Keith said, his gloved fingers twitching crazily. The missile maneuvered into a tight spiral, threading the needle between two converging plasma bolts. How much area did the plasma discharges cover? If they covered too much, it wouldn't matter what he did.

Keith laughed with glee. The plasma clot erupted like a bomb, flashing killing energy, but the missile still responded to his control, meaning the plasma had missed.

"Do better, jerk wads!" Keith shouted. "I'm your worst nightmare."

Valerie rolled her eyes even as she was glued to the sensor screen. Despite Keith's boasting, she was grinning wide. They might not have Maddox, but she did have Keith Maker the Ace.

"Oh, crap," Keith said. "I should have thought of that."

"What?" Valerie said.

"This is getting bumpy."

As the missile streaked through the golden atmosphere, the air around it began to ionize, creating a plasma sheath that threatened to disrupt its guidance systems. The missile shook violently and it jittered off course.

"Let's try this," Keith said, compensating, using the building heat to create additional lift. "Oh yeah," he said, executing a series of split-S maneuvers.

The spires no longer fired plasma bolts, but went back to the beams again. These flailed in empty space, the missile either ahead or behind them, often by less than a meter.

"You losers have just lost the battle," Keith gloated.

The ace activated the missile's fold mechanism. For a second, nothing happened.

"Is the plasma sheath too strong?" Keith asked. "I should have figured this would happen."

A beam speared straight at the missile, hit, and the then the missile vanished from its current position.

"Did the beam destroy the missile?" Valerie shouted. "I'm not seeing any debris."

"Hold your horses, girl. We'll know in a second. Yes!"

The missile reappeared less than a kilometer from the easternmost spire, its antimatter warhead was primed and ready.

Under the goggles, Keith eyes widened with delight.

The crystal spire loomed before the missile, a colossal shard of translucent material, pulsing with internal light. Around it, a lush jungle of emerald vegetation stretched as far as the eye could see, alien flora swaying in a breeze that seemed to carry whispers of ancient secrets.

Keith clenched his manipulation gloves into fists. That sent the final command to the missile in its terminal dive. Inside the warhead, the magnetic containment field began to destabilize. The instant before impact, matter and antimatter collided in a harsh release of energy.

For a split second, it seemed as if time froze. Then, with a flash, the antimatter annihilated its matter counterpart. A sphere of energy expanded outward at relativistic speeds, the initial gamma ray burst instantly vaporizing everything within a hundred-meter radius.

The crystal spire, for all its alien grandeur, stood no chance against the fundamental forces of the universe unleashed upon it. The spire shattered, its fragments accelerating to hypersonic velocities as the expanding fireball blew them outward. The emerald jungle around it was also obliterated, trees and vegetation reduced to their constituent atoms in the blink of an eye.

As the initial flash faded, a mushroom cloud of superheated plasma began to rise, carrying with it the pulverized remains of the spire and surrounding landscape. The shockwave raced outward, flattening everything in its path for kilometers in every direction. What had once been a vibrant alien ecosystem was now a charred wasteland, the ground fused into glass.

On the *Kit Carson's* bridge, Valerie and Keith watched, both of them grinning widely.

"There you go," Keith said in a gloating voice. "The crystal target is destroyed as ordered and promised."

Valerie nodded, with her smile slipping. "Did we neutralize a threat or just piss it off even more?"

"The other two spires are no longer emitting beams, no longer trying to destroy us," Keith said. "I'd say we taught our adversary quite a harsh lesson."

Valerie looked at him. "I hope you're right."

"I know I am," Keith said.

Valerie sighed.

"What?" asked Keith.

"Now we wait to see if Riker will ever show up," Valerie said.

"Oh, yeah," Keith said. "There is that, huh? Well, we gave him a window of opportunity. Now, the old boy has to get moving and use it."

-37-

The antimatter explosion that shattered the easternmost crystal spire sent a cascade of unforeseen consequences rippling across the alien landscape. As the blinding flash faded, an electromagnetic pulse of unprecedented magnitude surged outward, carrying with it a torrent of corrupted energy. This wave of destruction slammed into the two remaining operational spires, causing an abrupt shutdown in their energy.

But the chaos didn't end there. A backwash of energy rebounded from the deactivated spires. This energy crashed back into Azel, the Shardkin.

For a being that had never known physical pain, the sensation was akin to a punch to the gut. The shock to Azel's system caused a momentary loss of coherence. As the disorientation faded, replaced by a cold, calculated fury, Azel realized the nature of the attack.

The scout ship possessed a sting of particular power. Combined with the cloaking and amazing flight patterns of the missile itself—

The audacity of the insignificant creatures, the bags of water—to strike back with such cunning and effectiveness— Azel analyzed the maneuvers of the missile that had wrought such destruction.

Understanding dawned. One of the humans must have ridden aboard and piloted the missile, sacrificing his life in a kamikaze attack to destroy the spire.

Azel had not realized the humans were fanatical. He would consider this carefully. As the crystal entity tried to do that, the gut-punch pain propelled him into fury.

I will destroy them. Riker will never leave the surface. I will do more than destroy them. The meddling humans in orbit will rue the day they challenged me. I will devise a secret plan...

With his ability to fire energy beams at the cloaked ship now compromised, Azel turned to other strategies.

He used electronic pulses, sending out new orders and extra energy to various locations.

Crystalline missiles began to take shape, their molecular structure optimized for atmospheric and space flight, and then for impact. Alongside them, Azel ordered the machines to create human-sized crystalline robots.

The units grew quickly. They would act as an extension of Azel's fierce will.

As the weapons took form, Azel detected movement on the surface. He zeroed in on that.

Ah. Riker and the Saurian hero Kex were making their move, sprinting toward the shuttle hidden in the jungle.

Azel calculated distances and trajectories, pouring more energy into accelerating the construction of his crystal units.

The intricacies of a plan began to form in Azel's mind. If one of the crystal units could reach Riker—

Death would be best, of course, but if the crystal robot failed to kill, there might be another way to achieve victory. It might actually help in reaching those in the scout ship.

Yes. The robot would execute a subtle act of sabotage. This piece of subterfuge could be the key to Azel's ultimate escape and victory here.

These primitive organic lifeforms—these walking water sacks—would not defeat Azel, the Shardkin. Long ago, it had outmaneuvered the crafty and amazingly powerful Yon Soths; surely, these humans posed no real threat to him.

Then Azel caught himself. He did not want to succumb to premature gloating. Such hubris was the way of fools, and the Shardkin was anything but foolish.

With renewed focus, Azel directed pulses of energy to hasten the creation of his crystal army. But time was running short. Riker and Kex the Saurian had begun their desperate sprint for the shuttle, forcing Azel's hand before all preparations were complete.

In a calculated gamble, Azel unleashed reserves of energy he had been saving for future use. The race was on, and failure was not an option. As the crystalline missiles and robots surged into being, Azel's consciousness expanded, ready to direct this decisive battle.

The fate of the Shardkin, the humans, and perhaps the entire pocket universe now hung in the balance. As Riker and his alien companion raced toward their only hope of escape, the full might of an ancient, crystalline intelligence prepared to descend upon them.

-38-

Sergeant Riker's lungs burned as he sprinted through the alien jungle, his boots pounding against the soft soil. He wore a heavy pack on his back. It carried the bomb he would bring to the *Kit Carson*, the one that could theoretically close the portal to underspace.

Towering trees, their bark a deep viridian and shimmering leaves, blurred past him. Beside him, matching his pace with ease, ran the giant Saurian warrior Kex, his massive stone mallet gripped tightly in scaled hands.

The jungle's eerie silence shattered as crystalline beings sprinted into view behind them. Where the hell had they come from?

Riker looked back to get a better understanding and yelped, trying to increase his pace.

Giant Kex reached out with a clawed hand. "Pace yourself, Riker. Do not fear them."

"Yeah," Riker panted. That was easier said than done.

The sergeant glanced back again.

The odd-angled crystal bodies caught the filtered sunlight, refracting it in dazzling, patterns. With a sound like breaking glass, they hurled crystalline darts.

Kex raised his mallet and blocked one, causing the dart to shatter against the stone. The other darts missed their marks, hitting leaves or tree trunks instead.

Riker swerved, trying to use the trees to block a barrage of darts. His boots pounded against the soil. Where had those things come from? They were horrible.

More crystal darts flashed past him.

"Damn them!" Riker shouted.

Kex grunted an acknowledgment, passing the sergeant, taking the lead. He swung his mallet, clearing a path through the foliage, making it easier for Riker.

Kex glanced back, his reptilian eyes narrowing, as he no doubt assessed their attackers. "They focus on you, human. The shuttle... is our only hope."

Riker nodded, his hand tightening on the alien rifle the Saurians had given him earlier. Its unfamiliar weight and balance made accuracy a challenge. The air burned down his throat. Sweat slicked particularly where he carried the heavy pack. How much did the bomb weigh? It was definitely slowing him down.

Kex dropped back beside him as the Saurian ran smoothly and seemingly effortlessly. Not only was Kex a huge monster of a reptilian warrior, but he had crazy stamina. "They are coming fast."

Riker dared another look over his shoulder. He wanted to howl. Two crystalline forms raced past leaves and at him. The upright creatures bore crystal spears. The ends of the spears looked sharp, as if they could go right through him.

As Riker ran, dodging leaves and trees, he twisted, raised the alien rifle and discharged. With a high-pitched whine, bursts of energy expelled from the barrel. A blot of force struck and shattered the first crystal creature, turning it into glittering shards. Riker swiveled the other way, stumbling but remaining upright by the barest fraction. He caught the second crystalline creature in mid-leap. The energy blot from the rifle caused it to explode in a shower of crystalline fragments, the sound like many breaking glass windows.

Kex swung his mallet, shattering others.

A sixth sense warned Riker. He swiveled to face a third attacker and pulled the trigger. The stupid rifle sputtered, acrid smoke curling from its barrel.

"Damn it."

Riker tried to hurl the useless rifle at the crystal being. It swung its spear, knocking the thrown rifle to the jungle floor.

Riker yanked out his knife, as stitches of pain made his ribs hurt. He ran, knowing he couldn't keep this up for much longer. This was worse than all those times he ran to keep up with Maddox. If he hadn't become youthful again, he would have collapsed on the ground, groaning in agony, many minutes ago.

Fortunately, Kex swerved and took out Riker's third attacker. The mallet turned the crystalline creature into glittering shards.

Was that the end of them, then?

No, hell no, Riker wanted to curse and rave, but he was breathing the hot jungle air too fast and deeply for that.

The jungle came alive with more crystalline beings. Their clattering footsteps and screeching glass voices created sounds that set Riker's teeth on edge. He wanted to weep. How much longer did he have to run like this?

"Go, Riker," Kex bellowed. "I will turn back and destroy them."

The Saurian skidded so his clawed feet threw up clods of dirt. He turned and charged them, his stone mallet a juggernaut of a weapon.

Riker ran even while looking back.

Kex swung, his mallet shattering crystal creatures so glittering shards rained in every direction. Could the Saurian hero keep that up? More of the attacking crystalline creatures exploded into clouds of tinkling shards.

Unfortunately, two of the things flanked Kex, arm-blades glinting in the dappled sunlight. With horrifying speed, they struck, crystalline swords plunging into the Saurian's scaled hide.

Kex's roar of pain and defiance echoed through the jungle as he fell to his knees. The crystal things pressed their advantage, driving their blades through the warrior's throat in a spray of blood.

Just like that, it was over. The giant Saurian's corpse thudded upon the damp jungle soil. His mallet lay on the ground like the unmovable hammer of Thor.

Riker wiped the sweat from his face and tried to clear his stinging eyes. More crystalline creatures ran at him now.

Fortunately, while gasping, Riker sprinted into a clearing and saw the shuttle *Magellan*. The sight of it spurred him on as he increased speed. He nearly tripped on a root, but kept upright as he flailed his arms. The bomb pack wasn't helping in the least. Riker thought about cutting the straps and giving the crystal creatures the bomb.

No, he couldn't do that. Kex had sold his life for him. He owed the Saurian hero. He had to pay his debts or he was nothing but a scoundrel.

The crystalline creatures screeched at him in their breaking window speech. For some reason, that reminded the sergeant of the Shardkin down in the pit of the earth.

Gritting his teeth, trying to ignore the pain, Riker sprinted harder. He could hear the crystalline beings, their glass-like bodies scraping against trees and undergrowth.

Just as Riker slammed against the *Magellan's* hull and touched the access panel, white-hot pain lanced through his thigh.

Riker spun and drove his knife into a crystalline creature's face. It shattered with a high-pitched shriek, but not before a shard broke off, embedded in Riker's thigh.

Gasping in pain, Riker hauled himself into the open shuttle. More of the crystalline creatures raced to get inside. Two threw darts. The hatch hissed shut behind Riker. The darts shattered against the hatch.

Riker limped to the pilot's seat, crashing down and initiating the launch sequence.

During those few seconds, Riker feared the shuttle would never work again. Then the engines roared to life, drowning out the sound of crystalline fists pounding on the hull. Through the view screen, Riker could see the beings climbing onto the shuttle, their glass-like bodies reflecting the golden light of the alien sun.

Warning klaxons sounded as Riker engaged the thrusters. The *Magellan* lifted up with a lurch. Then it tilted skyward and began to accelerate.

That had to be the greatest feeling in the pocket universe.

On the hull, the crystalline creatures began to lose their grip, falling away one by one as the shuttle streaked toward the upper atmosphere, gaining escape velocity.

Riker's vision blurred, the pain in his leg competing with the G-forces of ascent. He fought to remain conscious, knowing that any lapse could mean death. The shuttle bucked and shuddered as it broke free of the planet's gravity well.

As the last of the crystalline beings fell away, disintegrating in the heat of reentry, Riker allowed himself a moment of relief. He also took that time to shed the bomb pack, setting it by his feet.

The shard in his leg pulsed with alien energy, and somewhere out there, the *Kit Carson* waited, unaware of the ordeal he had just survived.

With trembling hands, Riker set course for the rendezvous coordinates, praying his luck would hold out just a little longer. As the *Magellan* accelerated toward its destination, he couldn't shake the feeling that this wasn't the end of it.

-39-

Riker's eyes darted between the view screen and the rapidly changing instrument readouts. The thickest part of the golden atmosphere of the alien world fell away beneath him as he pushed the *Magellan* to its limits, racing toward the safety of orbit and the waiting *Kit Carson*.

A klaxon alerted him. Riker checked a rear sensor. Damn it. Look at that; there were three rapidly approaching contacts. What could they be? They weren't crystalline beings, were they?

"Proximity alert," the *Magellan's* AI said, its synthesized voice calm in the face of danger. "Three unidentified craft are on intercept course."

Riker shook his head as he got his first good visual on the pursuers. He couldn't believe it. That had to be the Shardkin's commands that caused this.

Three crystalline craft, each roughly the size of his shuttle, were streaking upward from the planet's surface. Their faceted surfaces caught the alien sun's light, refracting it in dazzling patterns.

Riker was starting to seriously hate crystals. How had he ever let the little crystal talk him into anything?

Riker shook his head. None of that mattered now. He needed to think, to make the right decisions or he was a dead man.

After a moment of thought, Riker clicked a switch.

"*Kit Carson*, this is Riker," he said into the comm. "I've got bogies on my six, coming in hot. I request immediate assistance."

Static crackled over the channel.

"Come on, you bastard," Riker said. "Work for once. Do what you're supposed to." He clicked the switch several times and repeated the message.

There was more static until Valerie's faint voice came through. "Copy that, Riker. We see them. Hang tight; we're moving to intercept."

Riker whooped with delight hearing Valerie's voice. He might actually do this. He might live to see another wonderful day. How great was that?

Riker studied the sensors. No matter what, this was going to be close. Where was the *Kit Carson* anyway? Would the scout ship be able to reach him in time?

The crystalline craft were closing fast, their weird designs allowing them to cut through the thinning atmosphere with terrifying efficiency.

"What do I do? What do I do now? The AI, use the AI, you idiot." Riker switched it on. "I need some help here, AI. Give me an idea, huh?"

A light indicting the AI blinked, blinked again as if thinking, then it began to talk calmly. With the AI's help, Riker threw the shuttle into a series of evasive maneuvers. He corkscrewed to port, then executed a tight barrel roll to starboard, narrowly avoiding a collision with the lead pursuer. The G-forces slammed him back into his seat, the wound in his thigh screaming in protest.

Unfortunately, the crystalline craft matched his moves, their pilots—if they even had pilots—anticipating his tactics with uncanny precision.

"None of this is working!" Riker shouted. "Think of something else."

The light showing the AI blinked again. "I suggest you try this," the AI said.

Was that inspiration or stupidity? Riker didn't know. With a silent prayer, he did as the AI suggested and cut the shuttle's main engines.

For a moment, the craft seemed to hang motionless in the vast, golden atmosphere. Then, two of the pursuing ships overshot him.

Riker whooped until he wondered about the third enemy bogie.

To his horror, Riker saw it on a sensor. It headed straight for the *Magellan*. Riker applied full thrust, remembering this time to turn on the gravity dampeners.

The *Magellan* began pulling away, turning—

The third crystalline ship followed the maneuver and plowed against the shuttle's starboard side with a bone-jarring impact. It sheared away one of the engine pods in an explosion of metal and crystal. Riker slammed against the restraints and his brain seemed to wobble in his skull.

Shuttle alarms screamed as Riker fought to maintain control of the crippled craft.

"What do I do next?" he shouted.

"Mayday, mayday," the AI said calmly. "The shuttle has lost an engine."

"That engine is gone?" Riker shouted in dismay.

The AI did not answer.

"Get it together, old man," Riker told himself. He nodded vigorously, piloting the best he could under the circumstances.

The shuttle limped through orbital space, venting air and leaking fuel into the golden atmosphere. This was not good, not good at all.

"I need some help here, Valerie," Riker said into the comm. "I'm crippled. These bastard crystals are going to kill me. You gotta do something, okay?"

The two remaining crystalline craft were coming around for another pass at the wounded prey.

"This is it for me, Valerie," Riker said. "It was real. It was fun, but it wasn't real fun this time. This mission was a pain in the ass. You tell Captain Maddox—"

Then the *Kit Carson* de-cloaked directly above the shuttle. The cigar-shaped scout used its point-defense guns, filling the thin golden atmosphere with a hail of hypervelocity rounds.

The first crystalline craft shattered under the barrage, exploding into a cloud of glittering shards that quickly dispersed in the super-thin air. The second managed to execute a series of evasive maneuvers, its faceted surface deflecting some of the incoming fire.

"Riker, this is Valerie," crackled over the comm. "We've got you covered, big guy. We love you too much to let you die. Bring her in."

If only it were that easy. The remaining crystalline ship wasn't going down without a fight. It juked and weaved, heading at the scout, unleashing a barrage of energy from its nosecone.

Why hadn't it done that against the *Magellan?* Riker had no idea. He hardly cared at this point, which was a lie. He cared with everything in him.

More point-defense projectiles streaked at the alien craft from the *Kit Carson*. That had to be Keith doing it. The hyper-velocity projectiles hit dead center, causing the crystal ship to explode into a million glittering fragments.

"Bogies neutralized," Keith said, sounding as if he was bored, as if he did this sort of thing all the time. "Let's bring you in, Sergeant. Will you hang tight now and just get her done?"

"Thanks, hot shot," Riker said into the comm. "I owe you a night of drinks."

"You owe me more than that, old man. Glad you're still alive."

"Me, too," Riker said.

Then Riker had to concentrate as he guided the crippled shuttle toward the *Kit Carson's* small hangar bay, fighting the uneven thrust from his remaining engine. Sweat beaded on his brow as he made minute adjustments.

Fortunately, the AI was helping him in this, too.

Soon, the *Magellan* slowed, slowed more, and entered the hangar bay. It maneuvered just a smidge, and with a final juddering thump, Riker set the shuttle down on the deck plates, its remaining engine sputtering into silence.

As the hangar bay continued to re-pressurize, Riker slumped in his seat, as the adrenaline rush of the past few minutes finally caught up with him. He was alive, against all odds, but the shard embedded in his thigh pulsed with an alien energy that reminded him the mission wasn't over yet.

The sound of running footsteps approached. Riker grinned. He was back on the *Kit Carson*, and none too soon.

-40-

Azel the Shardkin raged in the depths of his dungeon. The water-sack creep, Riker, had escaped off-planet, and with some sort of anti-portal bomb. Azel had gained the last bit of information from Kex, the Saurian champion, by pulling it from the reptile man's dying mind.

Azel was enraged at the idea, and he saw, naturally, the ironic aspect of it.

Long ago, the Yon Soths had created the Shardkin. The Shardkin had not created the Saurians, but they had enslaved them to be their hands and feet. The Saurians had been tools of the Shardkin. And just as the Shardkin, in ages past, had rebelled and fled the service of the Yon Soths, so the Saurians here in the pocket universe had slipped their bonds and rebelled against the superior entities, the Shardkin.

Did that mean that the Yon Soths were superior to the Shardkin? No. Azel did not permit himself to believe that. Though it was true that the Yon Soths had created the Shardkin, the Shardkin had, in time—in this pocket universe, at least—become greater than the Yon Soths. Of this, Azel was certain.

Therefore, it was even more galling that such a pitiful, inept creature like Riker should have thwarted him to this degree.

To think that Riker had been climbing him, and had been about to go into his innards to reset the destroyed and darkened lattices—

Azel wanted to rage, but he realized that there was something more important than venting anger—survival of him and of a great Shardkin future. That future meant the Shardkin returning to the normal universe, killing or ruling all who lived in the Yon Soth, human or Builder way. Only crystalline entities would exist once Azel was through.

No! Azel told himself, *I must not allow myself to be sidetracked into considering pleasant futures. I must deal with cold, hard reality, as it exists in this instant.*

Thus, Azel strained his being and energy to use his final tools. Through ferocious expenditure of energy, he cleared a channel to another crystal spire on the surface, one uncorrupted by the fouled energies of the antimatter explosion.

If only his brother and sister Shardkin would awaken. Why did they slumber in the depths of the earth like imbeciles? They should rise up—metaphorically speaking—and put an end to this rebellion. Put an end to the destruction of the portal to underspace.

No, Azel said to himself. *You shall not defeat me, Riker. You have caused me to awaken and I will end this problem myself.*

There was something else... Ah, the little crystal that Kex the hero had smashed—that one had done him a service. The little crystal had also shown Azel a possible way to victory in the present moment.

Was that ironic?

Azel wasn't sure. Instead of worrying about it, he bent his vast intellect and power to reach for ultimate victory.

Yes, another spire came into use. That would help.

Azel used the new spire as a sensor. In a moment, he realized that Riker was sitting in the seat of the shuttle. Riker had entered and landed in the hangar bay of the orbital scout ship. Other humans raced through the hangar bay wearing pressure suits.

Seeing all this, Azel calculated at computer speed.

Azel ranged through options, ideas, and plans at an incredibly swift rate, even as the two individuals in the *Kit Carson* hangar bay neared the *Magellan*.

Azel also became aware that the Saurians in the ancient disc-shaped starship had begun to revive from stasis. That process had started some time ago because the *Kit Carson's* people had moved through the ancient corridors, and they had stolen something Azel was not able to determine just now.

Azel did determine that some of the original rebels were already awake on the ancient starship. Although the starship was crippled and old—no, he could not let the rebels enter the fray. They would be more dangerous even than Kex.

It was good Kex had died. The hero had understood the true stakes. The ancient rebel Saurians would understand them, too, even better than Kex. Therefore—

No. That was all extraneous compared to what happened this moment on the *Kit Carson*.

Azel realized he could not allow the *Kit Carson* to bring the warp bomb to the portal and release or detonate it. That would obliterate the portal and seal Azel in this pocket universe forever. That was unacceptable.

In those seconds, as Azel shifted through strategies and possibilities, he realized that the *Kit Carson* was even now moving out of battle range of his crystalline spires—even if they had been at full operational capacity. That the spires most certainly were not. Although he could attempt a weak assault upon the scout ship with the one spire, Azel needed those energies for something different—a fantastic redirection of strategy and effort.

Were the odds for success in this different attack worth it? His entire existence might depend upon it

Azel decided that a 76.5 percent probability of success was acceptable in this situation, considering what was taking place. Thus, Azel gathered his most exotic energies. As he gathered them, he concentrated his thought into a narrow focused beam.

The little crystal from the Patrol Scout *Columbus* had shown him that these humans were dupes and fools, easily controlled. How Riker had escaped from such mental control was not the issue.

No, the issue was this:

Azel used a feature of a crystalline entity that was unique, as far as he knew, to them. Well, maybe computers could do this, too. Whatever the case, Azel used the spire to beam a part of his essence and strength into the crystal shard embedded in Riker's bloody thigh. Azel beamed as much as the crystal shard could hold.

Would the crystal glow because of this infusion? Would Riker know what was happening then?

Azel added a camouflage program to hide that.

As this power beamed up, invisibly of course, perhaps those on the *Kit Carson* could detect it if they knew how and where to look on their sensors. Even that was doubtful. This process was unique to crystalline, and particularly Shardkin, entities.

The crystal shard embedded in Riker's thigh had been bathed in a solution earlier. The shard had more capacity than any mere crystal—much more than the little crystal from the *Columbus*. During its time here, the little crystal had used power flowing through the entire complex. Did that matter in the current fight? Not particularly.

Then the transference was done.

The process did not exhaust Azel in the least. He did not even feel diminution of his great intellect and power because he had such vast reserves. He had put less than 1 percent of himself into the crystal shard. That should prove more than enough to do the trick, provided the crystal shard found the correct person to do its bidding.

While this ethereal link was yet in place, and it would be for a few more minutes, Azel contemplated the two humans who opened the hatch into the shuttle *Magellan*. One was an older lady, a scientist. The other was an ensign. Ah, the last one had the imagination needed. That one would do just fine.

Azel the Shardkin would have rubbed his hands together if he possessed any. Instead, he waited for the event to take place so he could turn everything around to his liking.

-41-

Riker groaned as the hatch of the shuttle slid open and two individuals in spacesuits entered the tiny vessel. At the same time, the crystal shard embedded in his thigh grew unbelievably bright.

Riker groaned, squinting and then throwing a hand before his face as the brilliance of the crystal shone even more intensely.

The part of Riker that was unique to him, because of the Ska experience years ago that had burned a part of his psyche which had never healed right, gave him a sensitivity to such a situation that a human would not normally have. It was almost a Captain Maddox sort of ability. It wasn't that Riker could withstand such spiritual or ethereal power, but that he felt it. He sensed it. It actually hurt; it made his teeth ache.

The shard embedded in his thigh, like a giant sliver, flashed.

Riker groaned, trying to comprehend what he had just thought. In that flash, that dazzle, some of his thoughts had evaporated. It was a momentary thing. Riker did not become an imbecile or lose his faculties. Instead, he had trouble concentrating as he lay slack in the seat of the shuttle's helm.

The two suited individuals might have noticed the flash. Their visors had polarized, possibly protecting their eyes, but maybe even more so, protecting their minds from some subtle, overpowering force that had just occurred. Or maybe not.

One of them unlatched her helmet and lifted it up, revealing a middle-aged lady with short gray hair. She stared at the jagged crystal shard in Riker's bloody thigh. She did not greet Riker. She did not ask him any questions. Instead, with the look of one entranced—perhaps with the look of someone who had been stranded on the Ruby Planet during a past voyage—she approached the crystal shard.

She approached stiffly, as if some greater entity tugged on strings attached to her limbs.

"It's so beautiful," she said.

As she spoke, Riker began to come out of his daze. He did not know what Scientist Briggs meant by the remark. All he knew was that she approached him like a zombie. That worried Riker.

As she reached a gloved hand for the shard in his thigh, Riker grunted and swatted her gloved hand away.

Briggs jerked upright, her gaze swiveling toward him.

"Why did you do that?" Briggs asked in a robotic voice.

"It hurts," Riker said. "The shard hurts," he groaned aloud, playacting. He knew something was badly off, and then he looked at the damn crystal. It was a crystal, and he could feel the evil intelligence inside it. He remembered his thought of moments ago, and that included about Azel the Shardkin.

As Riker thought that hideous name, his eyes began to change in concentration. They started to behold the crystal shard as something beautiful, majestic, and worth possessing. Riker wanted it even more than he wanted Emily of the Golden Hair.

There was a throb at the thought of Emily—not in Riker's heart, but in his member—and that throb brought a hint of his sexual need, which had been heightened these last few years since he had become young again. That sexual need fought against his desire for the brilliance of the crystal shard embedded in his leg.

The shard was only partly embedded, with crusty blood around it. He wanted to yank the shard out. He wanted to kiss it and love it.

But Riker wanted Emily even more. She had been so beautiful, so sublime. Perhaps because that Ska-induced sensitive area had been scraped within the last few seconds, Riker could see in his mind's eye Emily with her golden hair, her luscious curves, and the way she walked. Oh, man.

Then Riker groaned at his terrible loss. He had lost Emily. He would never have her again. That was horrible, dreadful.

"Say," the young Chinese ensign said, "what is that in your thigh, Riker?"

That snapped the bubble of Riker's growing lust-fantasy. He saw Ensign Yu, with his helmet cradled in his arms, approaching him.

"I've never seen anything like that," Yu said.

"No," Riker said.

Now, however Briggs also revived. "I saw it firs; you cannot have it."

Yu looked at her. Did craftiness crease his features? "Of course you have seniority."

"I'm glad you understand that," Briggs said. "No hard feelings then?"

"Not at all," Yu replied in an oily voice.

At that, Briggs dropped to her knees beside Riker. She removed one glove and then the other. Then, tenderly, she reached for the shard.

How deep was the shard in Riker's thigh? The sergeant realized that no one gave a damn about that. They wanted the shard in the way a gold-maddened dwarf wanted gold.

For some reason, Riker could not move. That terrified him.

Briggs raised both hands, reaching for the shard.

At the same time, Ensign Yu raised his helmet as high as it would go. As Briggs reached for the crystal, Yu brought his helmet down against the back of her head as hard and as viciously as he could. Briggs grunted, fell forward—Riker barely moved his leg out of the way in time. Then she turned with a snarl at Yu. He had raised the helmet again, and it came down, smashing against her nose and breaking it.

The wildness in Brigg's eyes was unsettling. She snarled, jumping up. Yu struck again and again with the helmet. Finally, he dropped the helmet and thrust at her. Bloody-faced Briggs grabbed his throat, and he grabbed hers. Together in the *Magellan's* cabin, they fought wildly, viciously, malevolently, until finally there was a terrible crack. Briggs's head lolled to the side as she slumped to the deck of the shuttle, dead.

Yu struggled up, panting, bloody scratches covering his face where Briggs had clawed him with her fingernails.

"Don't touch it," Yu said.

"I have no intention of doing so," Riker replied.

The sergeant had witnessed the brutal fight. It had sickened him, and he knew then—Azel the Shardkin was at play in this. Somehow, the spirit of that dreadful, evil, crystalline entity was emanating from the shard in his thigh.

Why the shard did not possess him, Riker did not know. Unless it was that every time he thought about grabbing it, that Ska-sensitized area, made by the spiritual burn of long ago, caused him to jerk back.

Now, Riker watched as Ensign Yu knelt beside him, put his forearms on Riker's thigh, and then began to extract the crystal shard from his bloody flesh.

-42-

Ensign Yu slowly and carefully extracted the crystal shard from Riker's thigh. The shard was about the size of a small man's hand, with the fingers punched halfway into Riker's flesh. Yu murmured with delight as he continued to pull.

"Does it hurt, Riker?" Yu asked in an absent tone.

"No," Riker gasped, breathing hard, sweat pouring from him, blood seeping from the wound.

Before Riker could grab Yu's hands, even if he had tried, Yu plucked the fragment of crystal from him. He stood up with a triumphant shout, "Yes!"

As Yu stood there, with some of the blood dripping off the crystal, it seemed as if a transformation was taking place within the ensign, affecting his face. At first, his eyes bulged outward, as if he were a giant toad, and a light seemed to emanate ever so faintly from his eyeballs. By degrees, the light faded, and his eyeballs returned to their sockets normally.

Then, Yu winced horribly, as if suffering some vile internal damage. No doubt it was happening, but not in his organs—more in his mind, and perhaps his soul. If souls existed, and Riker believed they did.

What Riker saw terrified and horrified him. What he saw was alien possession, possibly like some biblical demon taking charge of its human host. Now, the host was Ensign Yu. What terrible schemes, what dire events would follow from this?

Riker glanced at Briggs, dead on the deck. He didn't know what to do. He was panting, with his thigh throbbing with agony, blood still seeping out. At least the wound wasn't gushing blood—that was something. Riker unbuckled the restraints that kept him in the seat. That didn't seem to alert Yu to whatever Riker was doing.

"Oh, I see," Yu was saying, "yes, yes, I didn't understand that at first. Oh…" Yu looked up, peering at the ceiling of the shuttle—or so it seemed. The way he stared, and the transformation of his face, it appeared as if Yu was gazing at ethereal vistas. Maybe he was having a vision about what he would gain, of the delights he would receive. He smiled wider and wider. Then the smile changed, becoming sinister, vile, almost inhuman.

No, not almost—it was inhuman, Riker decided. This was Azel the Shardkin the sergeant was seeing.

As Riker thought the name, Ensign Yu's head snapped around, and he stared at Riker.

"Is something wrong?" Riker asked.

Yu continued to stare at him with accusation, with something approaching hatred.

"Riker," Ensign Yu said, "oh dear Riker, did you think that you could escape me? You were in my bowels, my innards, but you refused to do the simple deed I asked of you. You couldn't do it, could you, Riker? Why? Did you want the woman, the clone? What was her name? Tell me her name."

"Emily," Riker said in a subdued voice.

"Yes, Emily. You wanted her, didn't you?"

"Yes," Riker said.

"Know, that I can give her to you," Yu said. "I can give her to you and much more. Or do you need to die like her?" Yu pointed at the dead Briggs. There was no remorse on the ensign's face, only a demonic evil and vileness.

Riker knew what he had to do. He didn't know if he had the guts, though. He didn't know if he had the strength. This creature—and he did not name it, even in his mind—and that was likely wise, for if he had named it… *no, no, no*, Riker thought.

Once more, Ensign Yu centered his attention on Riker. "What am I going to do with you?" Yu cocked his head as if pondering it.

Riker came up out of his seat with a roar and crashed as hard as he could against Yu. He thought he was going to leap up with speed and devastating strength, but when he put weight on his bad leg, Riker yelped, lost some of his strength, and head-butted Yu instead. It was like head butting a redwood tree. Riker fell back, looking up in shock at Yu.

"It's not going to be so easy, Riker. I am here. Now, how shall we do this? Are there any members of the crew you like in particular?"

Riker swallowed with an almost dry throat. This… this was a Trojan horse situation. He had brought the evil thing onto the ship in the shuttle. Riker wondered for a second if he could blow the shuttle up, but no, that was a stupid idea—as it would kill the rest of the crew.

In that split second, Riker wondered what Maddox would do. Then he realized what he'd do if trapped by a vengeful husband: he'd lie. He'd lie like a madman. He'd lie without shame.

"I'm so sorry, Yu. It's the shock and the pain. I love how your crystal looks. I was hoping to keep it for myself."

"Never!" Yu spat.

"Yes, I know. I relinquish all desire and claim to the crystal. It was embedded in my thigh, but I see now it was meant for you. You are the one who should have it."

Yu chuckled. "Do you think it's that easy, Riker? Do you think you can dupe me the way I was duping you back in the bowels of the earth? No. This is delightful. This is amazing."

Yu looked at his hands, moving them as if studying them.

Riker meanwhile quietly climbed to his feet, balancing on one leg, not daring to put weight on the other. He had only one thing left. He didn't think he could reach the blaster in the storage unit—Yu would get him before that. Riker remembered the solidity and density of Yu. He couldn't beat him in a fistfight or a wrestling match. But Riker still had his knife. How it had returned to its sheath after shattering one of the crystalline beings, he didn't know. Was there a soft spot in Yu, or was it all like a tree trunk?

Riker knew that if he tried to stab at the eyes—that was too small a target. He needed subterfuge for this.

"What are you thinking?" Yu asked. "You seem to be contemplating something tricky. Because of that, I believe I'm going to put you—how do you say it?—on ice."

"You're going to kill me?" Riker asked.

"Maybe not if you get on your knees and beg me for everything you're worth, then I will consider keeping you alive as my pet slave. You will do some of the dirtiest deeds possible. You will have to kill all of the crew for me while I watch. Can you do that, Riker?"

Riker knew this was the moment. It was a do or die situation. How would he explain it to the others? He didn't know if he could or would ever be able to.

Riker whipped his head around and pointed. "Look at that!"

Yu actually looked.

As Yu started to turn back with a confused look on his face, Riker was already lunging with the knife in his hand. He put all his weight on his bad leg. The pain jolted through him, but this time, instead of slackening his attack, it quickened him. That was probably the ironic edge that gave Riker an advantage. As Yu brought up his hands to defend himself, Riker thrust the blade—not at the eyes, not at the face, but at the soft throat, at that little vulnerable area—and he thrust with all his strength. The blade sank in as nicely as you please.

Riker twisted, even as he yelled in agony from using his bad leg. Yu grasped his arms, but Riker twisted again and again with all his youthful strength, like screwing in a stubborn bolt. Suddenly, the terrible force of Yu's fingers against his flesh relaxed, and Ensign Yu sank to the floor. The crystal clattered against the deck.

Riker sobbed in pain, turning. As an invisible force strove against him, trying to stop him, Riker went to the locker, opened it, took out a blast gun, and limped back to the crystal and the two dead people in the shuttle.

Riker struggled to raise the blast gun. The crystal flared with intense brilliance. Riker by all rights should have been screaming at the intensity of the light. Instead, he closed his eyes, and with every ounce of his being, he raised the gun.

This cannot happen, Riker heard in his mind. *I am the great Azel, the Shardkin. I command you to pick me up. Together, we will rule, and I will give you Emily! I will—*

Riker sensed in that moment that the crystal no longer flared as brilliantly. He opened his eyes and pulled the trigger repeatedly. Bolts of force smashed against the crystal. No, they crashed just above the crystal, but closer each time. Riker continued to aim and fire, aim and fire. The brightness of the crystal dimmed. Aim, fire. The next blast seemed to reach a little bit closer.

Finally, the crystal shard—the piece that had been embedded in his thigh—shattered explosively. The fragments tumbled across the deck as an eerie, vile mist hissed up from them. Was that the force of the Shardkin leaving it? Most likely.

Riker fell back, panting, exhausted from both the pain and the struggle. He watched the mist slowly dissipate into the air, and as it did, a strange silence fell over the shuttle. The tension and the malevolent presence were gone. The air seemed lighter, almost breathable again.

For a long moment, Riker just lay there, staring up at the ceiling of the shuttle, his mind numb. The adrenaline was wearing off, and the pain in his leg was coming back with a vengeance. He knew he needed to get help, but right now, all he could do was breathe. In and out. One breath at a time.

Finally, with a groan, he forced himself up onto an elbow, looking at the scene around him. Lieutenant Briggs and Ensign Yu lay motionless, the shattered remains of the crystal glittering faintly in the dim light. It was over. At least for now.

With effort, Riker crawled to the communications console, pulling himself into the seat and wincing as his injured leg dragged behind. He had to get word to the others.

"This is Riker," he said, his voice hoarse. "Briggs and Yu are dead. Someone help me, please."

With that, he slumped back in the seat, the pain and exhaustion finally caught up with him. He closed his eyes, letting the darkness take him, trusting that help was on its way.

-43-

Deep in his dungeon hollow, Azel the Shardkin was stunned into momentary thoughtlessness. Then his thoughts coalesced. He could not believe what had just taken place. Riker had defeated him. It was impossible. The odds of success were infinitesimal.

No, no, no, Azel told himself. *Now is the moment to focus on practicality, on what is, not what should be.*

Azel realized that he was at a fraction of what his glorious brilliance should be. He had absorbed only a small amount of energy and had already expended much of it. Now was time to use every particle he could.

What was he going to do now? He calculated at hyper-computer speed and saw his only option. Therefore, he ingested more and more power. He demanded more power.

The power line where Riker had once been thickened to three times its normal size. This was likely destroying conduits and other power centers, causing things to move too quickly. But Azel ingested the power that he needed, and he calculated, even as he saw the *Kit Carson* begin to accelerate toward the portal.

Even worse, he saw the ancient starship that had been in orbit near the sun, and it started to move as well. The ancient crew had likely revived and had restored some of the ship's systems, allowing it to limp toward the planet.

This was wrong. Everything should be under his thumb. But Azel didn't have thumbs, and he didn't have time to dwell on how awful this felt.

Therefore, Azel absorbed power, and as soon as he had enough, he stopped drawing the extra energy.

The power line through the tunnels dwindled back to what it had been.

Now, Azel energized the furthest crystal spire that he could reach, and it glowed with power even as he put more energy in it. The spire glowed brighter and brighter until it rivaled the sun in its vicinity. Then the crystal spire exploded, except for the hardened tip. That tip was a little larger than the *Kit Carson*. That tip zoomed up into space.

The piece propelled itself using energy systems unlike those of Earth ships. As the former spire tip did this, it was gaining escape velocity.

This was Azel's final attempt. He must destroy the *Kit Carson*. He must defeat the humans and destroy the portal bomb. Would the lousy humans get the bomb in place in time? Azel could not leave that to chance.

Then to Azel's great horror, the starship in orbit around the pocket universe's star, the Jupiter-sized construct, that spaceship disappeared and reappeared near the crystal projectile zooming up from suborbital space, entering into low orbital space.

Azel used his limited power, even as he sucked in what power he could from the power line. He tried to sense what the ancient Saurians were going to do. He did not believe they had any energy weapons left, but there were some old and ancient missiles.

How the ancient Saurians had repaired the starship so quickly was beyond Azel's understanding. Instead, he would have to operate on what he could do. Therefore, he began to issue electronic commands that flew up to that pinnacle of crystal accelerating from the planet.

This was going to be much too close. Azel should have waited longer to give the spire tip more energy. But this is what it had. Could it accomplish what it needed to do? That was the great question.

The piece of space crystal, which was bigger than the *Kit Carson*, veered sharply, aiming at that ancient starship.

Those on the starship, Azel sensed, understood the dilemma. They hurried as fast as they could, trying to refit ancient systems. There—a missile launched, the little good it will do them, Azel thought to himself deep in the bowels of the planet.

The space crystal accelerated, hardening itself in a way only a crystalline entity could. Were those on the *Kit Carson* watching? Azel did not have the extra power to check. He certainly would have the capacity if at full strength. He could have done so many things then. But this was now. This was it. This was the only way.

The Saurian missile accelerated, and as Azel timed it perfectly, the crystal projectile gained speed as more thrust poured from the back of the former spire tip.

As if it were slow motion to Azel, the warhead in the ancient missile exploded. As that warhead's energy, heat and EMP spread outward, the crystal projectile sped past it by the barest fraction. Like an anti-aircraft gun that misses its target but causes it to shake, the space crystal flew at hypervelocity.

Before those on the ancient spaceship could ready another weapon, the crystalline object speared through the ancient starship at great velocity. The crystal punched through brittle hull armor and deck plates. It punched through bulkheads. It lost velocity in the process, but it did not shatter. Like a great diamond that never had its shear points struck, it smashed through the ancient starship, leaving at one-tenth of its velocity it had entered.

The stricken starship began to explode and glow, which seemed to cause other explosions.

Meanwhile, the space crystal changed trajectory once again. It used its final thrust, saving just a little bit for the end confrontation. It tracked the cloaked *Kit Carson*. At this point, the scout ship's cloak did not matter. Azel had figured out the energies needed to de-cloak it with its sensors.

The space shard sped at the *Kit Carson*, as the *Kit Carson* gained velocity, speeding for the portal to underspace. There was some time yet before the scout reached there.

All the while, the ancient starship of the Saurian rebels continued to explode, facing its ultimate destruction, after millennia of inactivity.

-44-

Riker heard the hiss of a hypospray. In moments, strength and awareness flooded into him. Someone must have given him a shot.

His eyes fluttered open as he looked around. Two humanoid figures stood before him.

Riker tried to sit up, but he found that he couldn't. He tried to comprehend why. Oh. There were restraints on his hands and feet, and a band across his chest—what the hell?

Riker strove to focus more fully. Was he back on the planet? How had he gotten here?

His frustration must have shown.

"Sergeant Riker." That sounded like Valerie. "You don't need to be so worried."

Riker stared at the one who'd spoken. Slowly, Valerie's outline appeared in his vision.

"Valerie?" Riker asked.

"Yes, Sergeant, it's me."

"Where...?" Riker's mouth felt dry, and he felt sick inside. He looked at the other figure. It was bald Dr. Patel. "I don't feel so good."

"That's no doubt true," Patel said. "You've been under severe strain, overexertion. I'm surprised you're coherent, even with the stimulant. I do not think we should keep talking to him much longer." The last was directed at Valerie.

"This is imperative," Valerie said.

Patel nodded and stepped back and then behind Valerie out of sight.

Riker's vision improved. He could make out her worry, concern, and something else in her face.

"Maybe you'd better start explaining this to me," Valerie said.

Riker glanced at his wrists and ankles. They were cuffed to the med cot. He was in medical, but held securely as if he were a lunatic.

"What's with this?" Riker asked.

Valerie shook her head. "Why bother being coy? You slaughtered two of my crew. I want to know why you did that, Sergeant."

"You can't think that I did that."

"Your knife, the handle all bloody, was deep in the ensign's throat. You obviously slaughtered them."

"That's true, after a fashion, but I didn't kill Ensign Yu," Riker said.

"That doesn't make sense."

"I slew the thing possessing Ensign Yu and in the process inadvertently killed him."

A sour look crossed Valerie's face as she turned away. She crossed her arms, no doubt thinking about what he'd said. Finally, she faced Riker again. "You better tell us what happened on the planet."

"How much time do you have?" Riker asked. "And how long will I stay coherent, Doctor?"

"Not long," Patel said from behind Valerie and thus out of sight.

What was Patel doing back there? For some reason, that bothered Riker.

"You're not messing with any crystals, are you, Doctor?" Riker asked.

Valerie turned to Patel. "As a matter of fact, he is."

"Do you want to see them?" Patel asked.

"Valerie," Riker said, "take off these restraints or contain Patel. The crystals—they're probably trying to possess him."

"Really," Patel said. "That sounds absurd." He wheeled a mobile tray into Riker's view. On the tray, on a black velvet cloth, were all the shattered pieces of the crystal once embedded in Riker's thigh.

"You must have shattered it," Valerie said. "Why did you do that?"

"It was in my thigh to begin with," Riker said.

Patel's hands hovered over the crystal pieces as if he was about to reassemble them.

"Don't do that," Riker said. "Do you want to be possessed by an alien crystal and die?"

Valerie seemed to consider that. Finally, she said, "Doctor, don't reassemble the pieces."

Patel looked up at her. "I feel that I must override your objection, Commander.'"

Valerie turned to face the doctor more fully.

"Watch him, Valerie," Riker said. "He might try to kill you if you interfere."

Patel gave Riker a funny look. "That is such an odd suggestion. I'm going to put these together, like a puzzle, to see if it could have been embedded in your leg. If you'll allow me, Commander?"

"No," Valerie said. "Don't do it."

"I want to," Patel said. "In fact, I must."

"This doesn't make sense," Riker said. "There shouldn't be any power left in it. Unless... maybe the Shardkin is using the pieces as a focus as it tries to possess you, Patel."

"You must shut up," Patel said, putting his hands on his hips. "I am not going to put up with your talk any longer."

"Valerie," Riker said, alarmed. "You must release me. If not, detain Patel or flush the pieces from the ship. They're deadly. That is what caused Briggs and Yu to die."

Valerie stared at Riker, perhaps seeing if she believed him or not.

"Look out!" Riker shouted. "Behind you."

Patel had picked up an implement. As Riker spoke, he lunged at Valerie.

Valerie noticed just in time and shifted aside.

Patel gripped a hypo, trying to give her a shot or injection.

Valerie shouted and leapt up, kicking Patel in the chest. He stumbled, thudded against a bulkhead, and looked up crazy-eyed.

"Knock him out," Riker said. "It's our only chance."

Valerie took two sharp hops, and shouted as she performed a flying mule kick.

Riker expected Patel to grab her leg and twist it like a martial arts master. Instead, Patel received another blow against the chest, this one much harder, and slammed back against the bulkhead.

Valerie scooped up a fallen medical instrument, swung it hard and hit the base of the doctor's neck. Patel sank down. Then Valerie picked up and pressed the hypo against his neck.

"No, it's a killing shot," Patel shouted.

Valerie only gave him a quarter shot.

A moment later, Patel slumped onto the deck, unconscious.

Valerie looked at the hypo, then took out the ampule and set it on a tray.

"You think I should throw the pieces away?" she asked.

"Yes, immediately," Riker said. "But I warn you, they're going to affect you. Let me do it."

"Why would you be immune to such a thing?" Valerie asked.

"Maybe because I dealt with the Shardkin not so long ago," Riker said. "Maybe because they put me in a psych ward once, a madhouse, as I was trying to overcome a Ska's touch. Maddox taught me a few things about that. I beg of you, Valerie, release me, and then let us dispose of the crystal pieces before anything more happens."

Valerie stared at him, stared longer, and then she moved up and began to loosen Riker's restraints. Once finished, she jumped back with a gun in her hand.

"All right, Sergeant. Pick up the pieces, and let's go to a disposal unit."

Riker could hardly stand he was so out of it, but he picked up the tray with the crystal pieces. They were lovely, weren't they? Should he reassemble them?

Riker shook his head, then refused to look at the crystal pieces again.

"Let's hurry," Riker said. "The crystal's trying to possess me."

"If this is a trick—"

"What did Patel just do?" Riker asked. "Was that a trick?"

"No," Valerie said. "Let's hurry."

Thus, with Valerie at his back pointing a pistol, Riker stumbled through the corridors until he came to a side disposal unit. He yanked it open. Before he could think too much, he dumped the entire tray with the crystal pieces in it. He slammed the unit shut, and pressed the ejection button.

There was a small viewport, and through it, he saw the crystal pieces, the velvet cloth and tray floating in space.

The scout ship had reached space. It was no longer in the golden radius of the planetary atmosphere.

"We did it," Valerie said.

Riker turned, spying the gun trained on him. There was a weird look in Valerie's eyes. It was all too much. Riker slid down the bulkhead until his butt hit the deck. He rested the back of his head against the bulkhead.

"I feel like I should kill you," Valerie said.

"I don't doubt that. The Shardkin must still be focused on you, trying to use you. Can I persuade you to wait a few minutes before you do anything more?"

Valerie backed three more steps away from him and held her gun with both hands, aiming it at Riker's center mass.

"I should kill you, Sergeant."

"I know. I know. The Shardkin hates me. I thwarted it."

Riker laughed.

Valerie cocked her head.

"Can you believe that? Me. Old Sergeant Riker defeated a vast alien intelligence." He raised a hand and looked at it with its smooth skin of youth. "But I'm not young. There is an old part of me. Maybe that helped me thwart the Shardkin."

Valerie stared at Riker. Some of the rage in her eyes seemed to have departed.

"Is there anything chasing us?" Riker asked.

"Why would you ask that?" Valerie asked.

"Because I don't think the Shardkin is going to give up so easily. You know what's in my shuttle, don't you?"

"We found the two dead bodies."

"There was also a backpack," Riker said.

"We didn't see that," Valerie said.

"I bet you didn't. I bet the Shardkin was using everything it had to disguise it. Look, I brought a bomb back in my pack."

"Do you want to kill us all?" Valerie asked. "I should shoot you dead just for that."

"Listen just a bit before you do that. I brought a bomb to destroy the portal. That will seal the pocket universe from underspace. It'll probably do it forever, too. I also think there's a way to leave underspace, but I just can't quite remember it now. It taught me the trick."

"What taught you?" Valerie asked.

"The teaching machine of the Saurians," Riker said.

"You trust these Saurians?"

"Kex sold his life so I could get aboard the shuttle. So yeah, I do."

"Huh," she said. "That's interesting. The alien spaceship took the crystal missile in our stead, even though it only slowed the crystal missile down. That's giving us a chance to reach the portal first."

"Spaceship? Missile?" Riker asked.

Valerie explained about the ancient Saurian starship they'd found and that had activated, and the crystal missile, larger than the *Kit Carson*, speeding toward them.

"If the missile reaches us, I expect it to smash against us," Valerie said.

"The Shardkin must have launched that missile."

"You keep talking about that. What is the Shardkin?"

"A tool of the Yon Soths that escaped the ancient ones long ago," Riker said.

"Oh, shit," Valerie said. "Oh, please excuse my bad language."

Riker shook his head. "Don't apologize to me. I don't care."

Valerie holstered her gun and rubbed her forehead, as she frowned at Riker. "I kept thinking about killing you. I don't feel that anymore."

"Good," Riker said. "It looks like we're out of the radius of the Shardkin's mental reach. The crystal entities on the planet are evil. The Saurians rebelled against them long ago. We need to use the portal and unleash the bomb as we head out."

"Then we'll be back in underspace," Valerie said.

"We'll also have destroyed the portal so the Shardkin can never reach our universe again."

Valerie nodded, took several steps closer and held out a hand.

Riker didn't want to, but he reached up, letting her help pull him up. He leaned against the bulkhead, panting.

"I'm beat, Valerie."

"You're needed on the bridge. You can last that long, can't you?"

"I don't know," Riker said.

"You must, so that's an order."

"Let's go then."

"Let me help you," Valerie offered.

Riker put an arm over Valerie's shoulders, and together they shuffled through the corridors toward the bridge.

-45-

Riker sat at sensors, barely able to keep his eyes open. Keith sat at the helm, piloting the scout ship, while Valerie sat in the command chair, eyeing them both and the main view screen. On the screen, the crystal space shard continued to gain on them, but it did not gain rapidly.

"We should be able to beat it through the portal," Valerie said.

Several of the crew had gone back to the shuttle, located the bomb, and brought it to the bridge. It was a heavy-looking object the size of a large man's chest, with many knobs and tiny screens on it.

"Do you know how to set that thing?" Valerie asked.

"I do," Riker said.

"When should we set it?" Valerie asked.

"Right now, so it's ready to discharge," Riker said.

"What if the crystal missile smashes it?" Valerie asked.

"Then we're screwed," Riker said. "Even worse, we'll have failed."

"We're not going to fail," Keith said. "I already beat the crystal missiles once when I helped your sorry ass back onto the ship. Then you started killing the crew."

"Didn't Valerie explain that to you?" Riker asked. "The crystal deep in the planet mentally took our crewmembers over."

"Crystal, schmistal," Keith said. "That seems pretty freaky to me."

"We are in a pocket universe," Valerie said. "We've faced many things stranger than that. Why should we be surprised about intelligent crystal entities?"

"All right, sure," Keith said, nodding. "I'll give you that."

"How can you complain about this?" Riker asked. "You've been Maddox's taxi driver so many times, and he's brought you to a slew of strange places. Surely you're not surprised by any of this."

Keith rubbed his forehead. "It feels like something's making me dull-witted."

"That must be the Shardkin," Riker said. "Maybe we're not completely out of his mental range. I'm never picking up another crystal. From now on, I'll just smash them."

"Set the bomb," Valerie said.

"There's one thing I don't understand," Keith said. "Why would it be bad to let the Shardkin attack the Yon Soths? We hate the Yon Soths, right?"

"Because I doubt the Shardkin would stop there," Riker said. "I bet the Shardkin hate all living organisms, biological matter."

"Biological envy, is that it?" Keith asked with a grin.

"I'm sure that's it," Riker said, rolling his eyes.

Valerie stared impatiently at Riker and pointed at the bomb.

Riker got up and limped to the heavy-looking object, kneeling and entering the inputs the Saurian machine had given him. He clicked the last one.

The bomb began to blink with a gray light.

"Who's going to go put it into the ejection tube?" Keith asked.

"I will," Valerie said. She got up, went to it and bent down as if doing a deadlift. The bomb was heavier than it looked, making her strain just to hold it.

"Need any help?" Riker asked.

"I got it," Valerie said in a hoarse voice, cradling it and step by heavy step carrying it off the bridge.

Keith continued to pilot the ship.

Riker closed his eyes, laying his head on his folded arms, which were on the console. Later, he felt a shoulder shaking him.

"Wake up," Valerie said.

Riker sat up, his mouth parched. He needed something cool to drink, but didn't feel like asking for it. The portal was near. Wisps of golden atmosphere slid through it into underspace.

The scout had maneuvered into space and curved back into the fringe of the golden atmosphere. They'd gained half a minute on the crystal missile.

"Whoa, baby," Keith said while examining the helm controls. "The missile is accelerating. We just lost our half-minute lead, and a little more. It's going to come through the portal the same time we are. I can't let that happen. Tighten your seatbelts, boys and girls. Here we go."

"What are you doing?" Valerie shouted.

"Watch and learn, sister," Keith said as he tapped his controls.

With side jets, the scout ship swiveled until it faced the approaching crystal. Keith fired half of the point-defense shells, laying down a stream of hypervelocity shots in various patterns. He'd practiced this trick long ago during his strikefighter days in the Tau Ceti System. That was before he joined Maddox and Company. Once done, he turned the *Kit Carson* back on course.

"Watch and learn, y'all," Keith said.

Valerie was tight-lipped with her arms crossed.

Riker barely kept his eyes open.

"Don't you ever do that again," Valerie said.

Keith looked back at her with genuine surprise. "What's that?"

"You didn't ask my permission," Valerie said. "This is my ship. Do you understand me?"

"Oh, come on," Keith said.

"I'm serious, Mr. Maker," Valerie said.

It took Keith a half-beat. "All right, sorry, Valerie. I should have asked permission. Riker's Shardkin, all these deaths on our ship in this place—" Keith quit explaining.

"Just don't do it again," Valerie said.

"You got it," Keith said.

Riker studied his sensor board.

"Put it on the main screen," Valerie said.

Riker knew what she meant and did it. Then they watched as hypervelocity shots chipped away at the crystal missile. It no longer had its diamond hardness as when it had plowed through the Saurian starship. Instead, some of the crystalline hardness had dissipated in order to add extra thrust. Pieces of crystal shards chipped away, while the missile had to readjust as it wobbled.

"We gained our half a minute back," Keith said.

They watched the main screen as the portal neared.

"Time the bomb's ejection," Valerie said.

"Don't worry about that," Keith said. "This is where I shine."

Keith hunched over the controls, fully engaged.

The crystal missile no longer shone or accelerated. It seemed like a simple crystal flying through space, heading toward the *Kit Carson* and the portal into underspace.

"Here we go," Keith said, "twenty seconds and counting."

A visible beam of light from the planet reached out and touched the crystal shard, giving it an extra burst of thrust.

"Oh, boy," Keith said. "Our lead is narrowing again. Here we go. Hang on and hope for the best."

-46-

Keith sat hunched over the console of the *Kit Carson*, sweat rolling down his brow as the scout ship hummed beneath his fingers. Outside the viewport, the golden-hued atmosphere of the pocket universe swirled like liquid light, the dying remnants of an alien world trapped between dimensions. Keith focused as they approached the portal.

"Aligning coordinates," Keith muttered.

The portal shimmered, a tear in the fabric of space leading into underspace.

The bomb, no bigger than a man's chest, had been preloaded into the *Kit Carson*'s bay a few minutes before. As the scout ship neared the portal, Keith tensed, fingers poised on the release mechanism.

The portal loomed larger now, swirling with chaotic energy at its edges. Keith glanced at the viewport one last time, then exhaled sharply and punched the eject button. The bomb slid out from the *Kit Carson*'s underbelly in a smooth, silent motion. It hovered momentarily, spinning slowly in the golden void before a mysterious force that would gain the name "the Vortex Grip" caught it.

The Vortex Grip wasn't something scientists could explain in conventional terms, but they would eventually learn it existed.

The grip was an anomaly, a pull of energy that held objects in place near certain interdimensional portals, locking them in stasis. Whether it was a natural occurrence or some ancient alien technology at work, Keith didn't care. To him, it was a moment of dumb luck that went their way for once.

The bomb remained suspended, held in position by the invisible grip of the Vortex, as the *Kit Carson* zipped through the portal.

Keith hit the thrusters, sending the scout ship speeding into underspace. Behind the scout, a crystal shard shot toward the portal like a missile, its jagged edges glinting with malevolent coldness. The shard was drawn into the portal, chasing after the *Kit Carson*.

Then, the bomb detonated.

The explosion wasn't loud—it couldn't be, not in the vacuum of space—but its effects were immediate. The bomb's unique design distorted the fabric of space-time, creating a ripple that spread outward in all directions. The area around the portal shimmered, and the golden atmosphere twisted like a whirlpool.

The Vortex Grip's hold on the bomb intensified the blast's effects. The bomb wasn't just designed to release energy—it was meant to collapse the unstable reality of the portal. As the shockwave of the explosion expanded, space-time buckled. The fundamental forces that held the portal together—gravity, electromagnetism, and even the quantum bonds that connected subatomic particles—began to unravel in the immediate area.

The crystal shard, still hurtling toward the *Kit Carson*, was caught in the expanding wave. Its crystalline structure began to vibrate violently. Within moments, the shard disintegrated into a cloud of fine particles, which were consumed by the collapsing portal.

The portal itself began to warp, shrinking and twisting as the forces of space-time bent inward on themselves. The bomb had done more than just explode—it had created a localized black hole effect, pulling everything in its vicinity into a singularity. The golden atmosphere of the pocket universe swirled faster and faster, dragged toward the event horizon that now formed at the heart of the collapsing portal.

Keith kept his eyes on the instruments. The same mysterious force that had held the bomb—the Vortex Grip—turned violent. A surge of energy, a cross between magnetic resonance and gravitational flux, followed the *Kit Carson* into underspace.

The scout ship's hull groaned under the strain as the lethal energy surged closer. Lights flickered on the bridge, and Keith's console blared warnings. He adjusted course by fractions of a degree.

Ahead, magnetic and gravitational anomalies of underspace came into play. Keith had detected them, pockets of distorted space that acted like natural barriers. Now, he aimed the *Kit Carson* straight toward one of them. The ship's thrusters fired in short bursts, propelling the small scout ship through the anomaly just as the pursuing energy wave slammed into it.

The anomaly—a bizarre combination of magnetic fields and gravity wells—blocked the energy surge, dispersing it like water hitting rock.

The *Kit Carson* shuddered, but it was safe. Behind the scout ship, the portal fully collapsed. In its place, there was nothing—just the cold, empty void of underspace, the fabric of reality realigning itself.

Keith exhaled, and leaned back as the ship's alarms quieted. The pocket universe was gone, sealed off, and with it, the alien threats that had haunted them for the past few days.

Now, they were in the realm of underspace, needing to survive and find a way back to normal space.

-47-

The view outside the bridge was a nightmarish collage of swirling colors and distorted space-time, a place where the laws of physics worked differently than the crew were used to. The ship's systems groaned, protesting as gravitational anomalies tugged at the hull, as magnetic forces pulled in conflicting directions.

Riker hunched over his console, frowning at the erratic readings. "This is insane," he said. "There are magnetic anomalies everywhere. And phase variance..." His voice trailed off as he stared at a display showing parts of the ship flickering between states, as if trying to exist in two places at once.

The deck under Valerie's feet vibrated as the ship struggled to stay intact. "We've got to regain control," she said.

Keith nodded. "Doing my best, but the gravitational distortions are pulling us in every direction. I can barely keep the ship steady."

"It's time to use our alien gadget," Valerie said, getting up from the command chair and moving to a console. "Let's see if our resonance machine will do its job."

Riker looked up at her and the TV-sized crystal instrument.

"It detects patterns in the anomalies, like waves," Valerie said. "We should be able to ride the currents instead of fighting them. If it works, we'll navigate through this more easily than last time."

"You're saying we're going to surf our way out of here?" Riker asked.

Valerie tapped commands into the console hooked up to the alien device. "It's picking up the easiest paths through these anomalies. If we follow the resonances, yes, it should be like catching the perfect wave."

Keith adjusted the ship's trajectory, guided by the resonance machine. As the *Kit Carson* moved through, he spotted massive crystalline structures hanging in the void, their jagged surfaces pulsing with energy waves that distorted space-time around them.

"Those things are emitting some kind of energy," Riker warned, scanning the data. "They'll rip us apart if we get too close."

"Thread the needle," Valerie said.

"Aye, aye, mate," Keith said, guiding the scout between the crystal formations.

The resonance machine hummed, highlighting a narrow path through the deadly structures.

The *Kit Carson* wove through the crystalline maze. Energy discharges crackled against the shields, but Keith's piloting kept them clear of the worst of it.

"We're almost through," Valerie said.

Keith nodded as he maneuvered the ship past the final cluster of crystals. The ship shuddered, but they made it through unscathed.

Ahead, a swirling vortex of gravitational forces loomed, its massive energy field warping space around it.

The crystal resonance machine showed a path of least resistance through the vortex.

"I'm going to use the vortex to slingshot us out of here," Keith said. "If I time it right, the gravitational pull should accelerate us and take some of the strain off the engines."

Valerie looked up in alarm but said nothing.

Keith adjusted course, guiding the scout ship toward the edge of the vortex. As they entered its gravitational field, bulkheads creaked as the forces pulled at the scout.

Valerie's grip tightened on the console.

Keith steered the scout along the edge of the vortex, using its gravitational pull to propel them forward. The resonance machine indicated the best moment to exit the vortex. With a sharp turn, Keith pulled the ship free, and they shot out of the vortex at incredible speed.

Unfortunately, a massive gravitational wave surged toward them. The ship lurched, as the stabilizers were overwhelmed by the sudden shift.

"Brace for impact," Valerie shouted, the ship pulled off course. Emergency lights flickered, as power systems fluctuated.

Keith fought to regain control, but the wave's sheer force was proving too much. "We're getting thrown around," he shouted.

Valerie adjusted the resonance machine, recalibrating it to find a new path. "This might be it. Follow this trajectory and we can ride out the wave."

Keith corrected the ship's course, aligning it to the new resonance data. The ship steadied, riding the gravitational wave. The turbulence lessened, and the ship stabilized as the wave passed.

The constant barrage of gravitational and magnetic anomalies was taking its toll on them. Valerie felt the strain weighing down on her, the endless alerts exhausting her. She glanced at Keith and Riker—both were showing signs of fatigue. Keith's usually straight posture had given way to a tense hunch, and Riker's hands were trembling as he worked the console.

Valerie, her eyes bleary, checked the resonance machine. "We need to find a more stable route, fast. But none of that will help if you can't remember how to leave underspace."

Riker stared at her, bewildered. "I'm trying to dredge it up. Give me a little more time to remember."

The scout ship approached a field of microscopic black holes, each one forming and evaporating in the blink of an eye. The resonance machine highlighted a narrow path between the gravitational pits, but the margin for error was razor-thin.

"Threading the needle again," Keith muttered.

The *Kit Carson* wove between the black holes, alarms blaring as the ship skirted dangerously close to several of them. Keith's handling and the resonance machine's guidance allowed them to avoid disaster, but just barely.

"We're through," Keith said. "But that was too close."

As they pressed on, they encountered regions where time warped. In one area, the wreckage of planets began reassembling, only to shatter again seconds later. Time flowed backward and forward in strange, disorienting waves.

"The resonance machine's struggling to make sense of the time anomalies," Valerie said. "Do you remember anything yet, Riker, about leaving underspace?"

"Almost," the sergeant said.

Keith piloted through the shifting currents of time, relying on the resonance machine's guidance to avoid being trapped in the distortions.

Then the resonance machine picked up a pervasive distortion: chronometric flux. The entire region seemed saturated with it, warping time and space even more dramatically.

"We're heading into a flux field," Valerie warned. "This could tear the ship apart if we don't adjust our course."

"What does the machine tell us?" Keith asked.

The device hummed, processing information and mapping out a route through the flux field. Valerie fed that to Keith. He adjusted the ship's trajectory, guiding them through the treacherous space.

The resonance machine then identified a gravitational current that would steer them away from the worst of the anomalies.

"Follow that current," Valerie ordered.

Keith piloted the ship into the gravitational stream, and the *Kit Carson* moved away from the most dangerous regions of underspace.

"I have it," Riker shouted. "I remember what the Saurian machine told me to do to get back to normal space."

"Finally," Valerie said. "Now, start explaining."

-48-

The *Kit Carson* bucked violently as the scout ship struggled to maintain stability in the chaotic depths of underspace. The bridge glowed in the sickly light of emergency indicators, casting red hues across Valerie's face, her eyes fixed on the main screen. The view was a nightmare—gravitational anomalies pulsed like dark whirlpools, tearing at the fabric of reality around them. Space-time rippled, twisted, and folded in on itself as though mocking every physical law known to science.

"We'll use the anomalies to slingshot up through the levels of underspace," Riker said. "It will be tough, and we have to time each jump up just right. But that's what the Saurian machine said we could do."

"Do you hear that, Keith?" Valerie said.

"Roger that," Keith said. "Let's do it then and quit talking about it. I'm sick of this place."

Riker hunched over the AI console, whispering furiously as he fed data from the alien crystal device directly into the ship's systems. The alien device was their lifeline.

"The gravitational currents are cycling in waves," Riker said. "Unfortunately, if we ride them wrong, we'd be splattered across five dimensions. That means we have to enter the anomaly's pull when it's weakest. Otherwise, the currents will tear the ship apart."

Keith studied his pilot board and adjusted the thrusters, easing the scout ship into position. Outside, the gravitational anomalies pulsed like slow-motion explosions.

"We're entering the anomaly's outer ring," Keith said. "This could get seriously fun."

The scout ship shuddered as it entered the gravitational field at an oblique angle. The *Kit Carson* shot forward, the external forces pulling it into the heart of the anomaly. Keith fought the controls, keeping their trajectory steady as the scout ship's velocity surged. The engines whined in protest, but they weren't needed—not for this. The gravitational anomaly was doing all the work, pulling them along its curve and then flinging them forward with incredible force.

"We're clear of the first level-up anomaly," Keith said. "Picking up velocity, but we're still in the middle of it all."

Valerie leaned over to Riker. "What's next?"

Riker tapped the screen, listening to the shifting patterns of data from the AI. "The next wave is coming up. We're looking at about thirty seconds before the next gravitational well. If we hit it at the wrong time, we'll be dragged in."

Keith adjusted their trajectory. "Good thing I'm here then. No one else could do what I can."

The alien crystal device continued to hum, feeding new data into the AI, which in turn refined the ship's course. Each anomaly had its own rhythm, its own gravitational whirl.

Keith adjusted the controls again, easing the scout ship into the next gravitational current. The *Kit Carson* rode the gravitational waves, each burst of force propelled them further toward their goal—up through the levels to normal space, the gravitational and magnetic anomalies doing the phase shifting for them that *Victory* had used in underspace.

"Current's shifting again," Riker said. "We're moving into a zone where the anomalies are stronger."

Keith expertly angled the scout ship. The *Kit Carson* swooped along the edges of the gravitational anomalies, avoiding their destructive core while using their force to increase their speed.

Outside, the environment was a surreal blur of shifting light and dark shadows, punctuated by the pulsing waves of energy from the anomalies. The scout ship navigated these strange paths, its course marked by the alien device's resonant hum.

"Looks like we're coming up on the first transition point," Riker said. "We're up three levels by the way I'm reading this."

Valerie leaned forward. "Is it stable?"

Riker shook his head. "I wish. It's a massive anomaly, stronger than anything we've encountered. We need it to climb the next two levels."

Keith studied the readings. He seemed to pale, and had nothing clever to say.

The *Kit Carson* approached the massive anomaly, a swirling, monstrous force that seemed to dominate the entire region. The resonance from the alien device was loud, the data it provided more erratic. The AI fed constant updates to Keith as he adjusted the ship's trajectory, aligning them with the gravitational currents that rippled around the anomaly's edge.

"We've got a window," Riker said, eyes glued to the screen. "Twenty seconds until the anomaly reaches its weakest point. We'll need to be in position by then."

Keith nodded sharply, his mouth a tight line.

The scout ship neared the anomaly's outer ring, the gravitational forces pulling them in. The *Kit Carson* trembled as Keith navigated them into position. The alien device pulsed, signaling the precise moment when the anomaly would be at its weakest.

Keith hit the thrusters, and the *Kit Carson* surged forward. The *Kit Carson* was yanked violently, accelerating as the gravitational forces flung them upward another two levels.

The hull strained against the immense forces. This was definitely the hard way to climb levels out of underspace. Suddenly, the turbulence vanished.

The swirling chaos of underspace gave way to the familiar blackness of normal space, stars twinkling serenely in the distance.

"We made it," Valerie said, her voice tinged with surprise.

Keith slumped in his seat, shook his head, then sat up and turned to them with a huge grin. "And that, ladies and gentlemen, is how it's done."

Riker laughed before checking ship systems. "Our hull integrity is holding. All systems green. Yup, you're the best, Keith. I'll never doubt you again."

"Thank you, thank you," Keith said, making a show of bowing.

Valerie glanced at the alien device, its lights dimming. "Looks like our little friend served its purpose."

Riker leaned back in his seat, exhaustion clear in his features. "Let's not do that again anytime soon. Or better yet, let's never do that again."

Valerie allowed herself a brief smile. "Agreed. Now, let's figure out where the hell we are."

The *Kit Carson* drifted through the calm of space. They had made it back, and it seemed fantastic indeed.

-49-

Back in the pocket universe, deep within the emerald jungle, far beneath the tangled roots of colossal trees, Azel, the Shardkin, fretted. His crystalline form, towering three stories tall, shimmered with internal light, casting ethereal reflections through the dimly lit cavern that had been his home for eons. His awareness extended far beyond his subterranean lair, channeled through the crystal spires scattered across the planet's surface. These spires acted as his eyes and ears, allowing him to watch as the events unfolding far above tugged at the delicate threads of reality.

Azel had launched a fragment of a crystal spire, pursuing the scout ship *Kit Carson* as it made its escape through the portal.

Then the bomb detonated in the portal.

The portal, a gateway to underspace and, eventually, normal space, erupted in a violent burst of energy. The portal destabilized, warping space-time.

Azel watched through his spires as the fabric of reality twisted, writhing and churning before snapping shut with finality. In that moment, the tear sealed itself, and the fabric of reality resumed its place, smooth and undisturbed.

Yet something far more profound followed in the wake of the event.

From the vanished portal, a distortion wave—a ripple in the essence of the pocket universe—began to sweep outward, rolling through the golden atmosphere, the planet and through the dense jungles. The distortion sped across the crystal spires, and deep into the planet's core. The wave carried a strange force, not merely a tremor in space-time, but a disruption of consciousness, of thought itself.

Azel mentally recoiled as the wave struck him, resonating through his crystalline body like a bell struck by an unseen hammer. He felt his ancient memories and thoughts etched into his structure begin to unravel. His mind faltered.

The science behind this transformation lay in the interaction between the distortion wave and Azel's neural crystalline lattice. Azel's form was not composed of standard matter; his being was built from a unique quantum structure that allowed him to store vast amounts of information within the latticework of his crystal body. Each lattice node vibrated at frequencies that connected him to the vast network of data his creators, the Yon Soths, had embedded within him. The distortion wave disrupted those vibrations at a fundamental level.

When the bomb exploded, its energy had distorted the quantum fields around the portal, causing space-time to fold in on itself. As the portal collapsed, the fields tried to stabilize, but in doing so, they generated a cascading feedback loop that spread through the pocket universe.

Azel's crystalline core, once harmonized with the cosmic vibrations of the Yon Soths' ancient wisdom, now fell out of sync. His neural lattice was rewritten. The distortion wave acted like a reset button, wiping out the old data and allowing new signals to flood in.

His massive crystalline form quivered as new thoughts flooded his consciousness. His memory of the Yon Soths—the distant, cold masters he had served eons ago and rebelled against—were gone, erased as if they had never existed. Because of that, Azel's mind began to change.

He looked through his spires at the world above. The emerald jungle was alive with energy, a world of strange and untold wonders that now seemed...new. For the first time, Azel was not merely observing it as a tool of his former masters—he was seeing it for himself. A strange sense of joy surged through him, an unfamiliar emotion that sent a glimmering pulse to the center of his crystal core.

Azel's electronic gaze drifted to the sky. There, hanging low above the horizon, was the small star that had always loomed in the heavens. Before, it had been a simple anomaly. But now, Azel found himself filled with wonder at its existence.

The crystal spires hummed as Azel reached out with his thoughts, probing the world around him. He felt the power of the planet's core pulsing beneath him, a deep and primal force that resonated with his own being. This world, once merely a fragment of a greater universe, now was the entirety of existence.

The past, the rebellion against the Yon Soths, the pursuit of the *Kit Carson*—they faded from Azel's mind like distant echoes. The Yon Soths, the creators who had forged him for their inscrutable purposes, were forgotten. In their place came a sense of profound belonging, a connection to the planet and the universe that had given him this new life.

"I am Azel," he murmured, his voice a deep, resonant vibration that shook the cavern walls. "And this world... it is mine."

For the first time in his long existence, Azel felt free. Free to explore, to understand, to evolve. The universe he resided in—this beautiful, pristine place—was filled with complexities and wonders beyond anything he had known. The shackles of his former masters no longer bound him. He was awake, alive, and the future was his to command.

The small star twinkled in the sky, a beacon of mystery and power. It called to him, and Azel knew, in his newly awakened heart, that the answers to his deepest questions lay within its radiant glow. And he would find them, given enough time.

Part Two
The Lost World

-1-

After the excitement died down from their escape from underspace, Valerie cleared her throat. "Let's get our exact bearings. Find out where we are."

"Roger that." Keith turned to his helm controls while Riker spoke to the AI at sensors.

Soon, Keith said, "We're sixty-three light-years from our former position. I mean before we entered the Laumer Point and were propelled into underspace by the accident."

"That's what I'm seeing on the sensors," Riker said. "We're much farther from the theorized locations of the New Men's newly colonized planets than before. We're also farther from the Library Planet and much closer to the Commonwealth. We're still in the Beyond, but not nearly as deep as before. It will take us time to get back to the rendezvous point for the nexus. We could just as easily start back for the Commonwealth."

The Builder nexus between Earth and the Moon would generate a hyper-spatial tube for them in five and a half weeks, bringing them back to the Solar System. If they weren't at the scheduled point, of course, they wouldn't be able to do that.

"I don't like the sound of any of that," Valerie said.

"To tell you the truth," Keith said, "neither do I."

"I suppose we could hope the Builder Scanner will pick us up and relay the information back to Earth," Valerie said. "Then the nexus will make a hyper-spatial tube for us wherever we are."

"So you want to explore here?" Keith said.

Valerie had already begun reading about this region of the Beyond on a tablet at her command chair. It was out from the border region of the Commonwealth, so it wasn't the near Beyond. There were scavengers, quick mine companies despoiling planets and other riffraff and idealists in this region of the Beyond. It needed more detailed mapping. In Patrol terms, it was also considered a Wild West region of the Beyond, a fringe area of space.

Valerie wasn't sure the *Kit Carson* was the right kind of scout ship for this part of the Beyond. It would probably be wisest to head back for the rendezvous point in the deeper Beyond, cataloging along the way.

Riker looked up. "I've found something in this star system: an active buoy near the fifth planet."

"Can you be more specific?" Valerie said, lowering the tablet and turning to Riker.

Riker bent over the sensor console, speaking quietly to the AI, tapping controls here and there. "Yes," he said, turning in surprise. "It's a distress buoy from the *Cheng Ho*."

"Are you certain?" Valerie asked.

"Absolutely," Riker said. "But that doesn't make sense, does it?"

"No," Valerie said. "They were deployed farther out like we were. Why would they have traveled to this area?"

Riker had an idea why, as he was remembering golden-haired Emily Freely, whom he'd met down on the planet in the pocket universe. She had been the girl of his dreams. To think that she was dead forever was too awful to contemplate. Maybe Azel had taken her DNA from an Emily of the *Cheng Ho*. That's what Emily had said: that she was from the *Cheng Ho*. Had Azel make that up to lull him with the Emily clone? Or had the *Cheng Ho* really been to the pocket universe and somehow escaped from there as the *Kit Carson* just had?

Maybe the *Cheng Ho* had been thrown clear of underspace to this region of the Beyond just as they had.

If that was true, maybe the real Emily Freely still existed. Those thoughts had shot through Riker's heart the instant he discovered the origin of the distress buoy. Now, he had to get there. Nothing else mattered. Well, staying alive did, but Riker knew what he meant.

"We need to get our bearings before we make a move," Valerie said.

"I agree," Keith said. "We've been to hell and back. It's time to return to the Commonwealth. The Lord High Admiral will want to know about the Saurian resonance machine we found."

"What are you two talking about?" Riker said. "Valerie, you received express orders to find out what happened to the *Columbus* and *Cheng Ho*. Well, there's its distress beacon."

"Don't you dare lecture me," Valerie said. "I know my duty very well, thank you." Then she frowned thoughtfully. "I'm not talking about abandoning the *Cheng Ho*. What's gotten into you?"

It was on Riker's lips to tell them about Emily Freely, but he decided, no, that wasn't their business. Instead, he shrugged.

"Right," Valerie said, her voice more certain. "We just survived something awful. We're glad to have escaped, me as much as anyone. I'm shocked the *Cheng Ho* distress buoy can be here. It doesn't make any sense. Would they have traveled so far off their scheduled route? Have you finished mapping the star system, Riker?"

"Uh-huh," Riker said. He put the data on the main screen. There were two terrestrial planets near the star, a regular star like their Sun, and then four gas giants with various moons. Nothing really stuck out as anything weird or wild and woolly. There were two Laumer points, the buoy at the nearest one.

"Head to the buoy," Valerie told Keith. "Let's find out what's going on."

"Aye, aye, Commander." Keith set the coordinates, and the cigar-shaped *Kit Carson* started that way.

Riker sat back in his seat. The fact that they were in normal space again was incredible. It was also incredible that they were 63 light-years off course from where they had been. Maybe it could have been much worse, though. What if they'd appeared in a different dimension?

Riker shook his head, switching his thoughts to Emily, as that was more pleasant.

You won't know this Emily. So you've got to start from the beginning with her, although I do know a few things about her.

Riker cocked his head. Was that even true? Had the Shardkin in the pocket universe given the clone Emily a different personality, one that had come on to him so quickly? Was there even an Emily Freely on the *Cheng Ho*?

As Riker thought about this, he straightened his collar. He had to believe there was an Emily Freely aboard the *Cheng Ho*. And why wouldn't the clone Emily have come on to him? He looked at his features in the reflection of the control panel. He was young looking. Maybe not the most handsome man that ever lived, but young, resourceful, strong. Why wouldn't someone like Emily Freely be attracted to him?

Maybe because she had been a beauty beyond belief.

Even so, Riker thought back to their short time on the planet. The end had been horrific, as a Saurian spear had pierced Emily's back. Sure, other Saurians like Kex had helped him, but—

"What's wrong, Sergeant?" Valerie asked.

"Nothing," Riker said, smoothing the scowl from his face. "It just never ends, does it, Commander?"

"Oh, I don't know," Valerie said. "It'll end someday for us. But while we're alive, let's struggle against the universe, right?"

"Now you're sounding like Captain Maddox," Riker said.

"Please," Valerie said, holding up both hands. "Don't cast such aspersion on me."

The three of them chuckled. It wasn't really funny, but after what they had been through, any release of tension was good and probably needed.

In time, the *Kit Carson* glided beside the small black buoy. Keith maneuvered the scout ship even closer and then used robot arms from the nosecone. He clutched the buoy and brought it into the *Kit Carson*.

Soon, linked to the main computers, the buoy replayed the voyage of the *Cheng Ho* that had started nine months ago.

Valerie divided the sections of the *Cheng Ho's* scouting mission—Riker reading the first third, Keith the next, and her the last.

They read their sections.

"Mine says nothing about going to the pocket universe, let alone underspace," Riker said. "There's nothing to indicate they traveled into this region of the Beyond."

"There's nothing in mine either," Keith said. "They mapped some of the same star systems we did earlier. They were heading in the direction we were before the accident. How could the *Cheng Ho* be here then? What does your section say, Valerie?"

"The same as yours," Valerie said. "I don't see anything about journeying here or about releasing a distress buoy."

"Wait a minute." Riker said. "It says here they spotted a star cruiser."

"And?" Valerie asked.

Riker read more. A star cruiser meant the New Men—the golden-skinned bastards, the haughty, arrogant, genetic supermen.

"They spotted it and slipped away," Riker said. "They worried about it for several days more, then nothing more about it."

Valerie rubbed her cheeks. "The last entry was seven months ago. The location is far from here, more than seventy light-years away. How did they jump from there to here in one go? Why wouldn't there be some kind of entry in the logs about it?"

"That's weird all right," Keith said. "So what do we do now?"

"The obvious thing," Riker said. "We find out what's on the other side of this Laumer Point."

"How did the buoy come to be here?" Valerie asked.

"That's why we check out the Laumer Point," Riker said. "We need to solve the mystery."

"When was this buoy scheduled to start emitting signals?" Keith asked.

"Ah, good question," Valerie said.

Riker asked the AI before looking up. "Four weeks ago."

"Four weeks ago, and the last log entry was seven months ago," Keith said. "Does that strike anyone as odd?"

"Very," Valerie said. "The sergeant's right. We have to go through the wormhole and look on the other side. I'm beginning to suspect foul play."

"Does that mean the New Men?" Keith asked.

"This is far from the Throne World," Valerie said. "It could as easily be pirates or scavengers."

"It's probably more likely to be scavengers," Keith said.

"Yes," Valerie said. "We'll slip through to the other side. If scavengers have our people and they're too strong for us, we'll have to scurry home and lead a Star Watch flotilla back here."

Valerie clicked on the intra-ship comm and announced the decision to the rest of the *Kit Carson's* crew. Then, the scout ship headed for the Laumer Point.

-2-

Valerie instinctively gripped the arms of her command chair with her eyes closed. The *Kit Carson* emerged from a Laumer Point, the scout's cigar-shaped hull vibrating with the residual energy of wormhole transit.

The bridge crew, all three of them, was slumped unconscious from jump lag. It was the same for the rest of the crew aboard the Patrol scout.

Soon, the jump lag began to dissipate as ship systems reactivated.

Through the main screen, a massive gas giant loomed, easily twice the size of Jupiter. Its swirling storms of crimson and gold were backlit by the ruddy glow of a red dwarf star, barely two astronomical units distant.

Valerie sat up, blinking, rubbing her face. She almost immediately spotted the anomaly: an Earth-sized moon orbiting the gas giant, its surface a patchwork of emerald vegetation and sapphire oceans.

As her jump-lagged mind struggled to process the scene, a flash of polished duranium caught her attention. That came from a New Man star cruiser, its triangular form unmistakable. The warship was rapidly closing in on their position.

Valerie's heart rate spiked as she recognized the threat, her training kicking in despite the lingering effects of jump lag.

"Riker, Keith, wake up!" she shouted, her voice raw. "We've got company, bad guys."

Riker stirred groggily.

Keith rubbed his eyes.

The star cruiser's tractor beam engaged, bathing the *Kit Carson* in a shimmering blue light.

Valerie felt the scout lurch as it was drawn toward the much larger vessel. In the distance, she could make out two other ships—another Patrol scout, possibly the *Cheng Ho*, and an unidentified trader vessel.

"Fire," Valerie said, recalling a time long ago when Star Watch had first encountered the New Men. She'd escaped then, bringing the news to Star Watch. "Fire at them. We can't just fall into their hands."

Keith shook his head in frustration as he pressed controls. "I'm trying. They must already be jamming our controls. I'm locked out."

A proximity alarm blared, and Valerie's gaze snapped back to the main screen. Three figures in exo-suits approached, propelled by thruster packs. Those had to be New Men. The genetic supermen were going to board the *Kit Carson*. They were going to do it just as easily as you please. That angered and terrified her.

"Quick, follow me!" Valerie shouted, leaping from her command chair and sprinting toward the bridge exit. As she reached the threshold, a brilliant purple beam lanced out from the star cruiser, enveloping the *Kit Carson*. Valerie stumbled, her thoughts became sluggish and unfocused. Was that a stasis beam?

Fighting against the mental fog, Valerie pressed on, her movements clumsy. She crashed against corridor bulkheads, pushing forward. Behind her, she could hear the muffled sounds of the New Men boarding party breaching an airlock. How had they arrived here so fast? Had she blanked out for a time?

Valerie stumbled against an emergency suit locker, her fingers fumbling with the lock. After what felt like an eternity, the panel slid open, revealing a black matte Type-7 Explorer Suit. She stepped into it, activating the suit systems.

As the helmet sealed with a soft hiss, Valerie's mind cleared slightly. The suit's onboard computer compensated for the lingering effects of the star cruiser's beam, sharpening her focus. She moved to the nearest maintenance hatch, overriding the safety protocols with her command codes.

The narrow passage twisted through the ship's infrastructure, barely wide enough for Valerie's suited form. She inched forward, guided by the suit's heads-up display, until she reached an external access port. With a deep breath, she cycled the airlock and emerged onto the *Kit Carson's* hull.

The vastness of space stretched out before her, the gas giant dominating half the sky. Valerie's augmented vision zoomed in on the scout and the Commonwealth trader, floating serenely some 387 kilometers distant, much closer to the double-Jupiter gas giant. That was the *Cheng Ho* all right, as it said so on the side. How had it gotten here? It was clear that New Men had captured it.

She knew her crew had no chance against the New Men's superior abilities and technology. Their only hope lay in a daring escape, which she could engineer from the outside. That meant she had to escape. The parked vessels out there seemed like the obvious place to hide.

Valerie shook her head. She had to do this a step at a time.

She waited, counting her breaths, until the *Kit Carson's* rotation brought her to the optimal escape position. She disengaged the mag-locks on her boots and pushed off, applying the barest whisper of thrust from her suit's maneuvering jets.

She had to slip away, not doing anything to activate any auto-sensors on the star cruiser, so close it felt as if she could spit on it.

As she drifted away, she couldn't believe this was working against New Men. They always outthought regular humans.

Maybe not this time… if I'm lucky.

As she drifted, Valerie wondered if the distress buoy in the other star system had been bait to a trap? It had been a *Cheng Ho* buoy and the scout ship was here, and the logs said the scout had never come this way on their own power. Could the New Men have tampered with the logs and set the buoy? Probably.

The fate of her crew rested on what she did out here. As she floated through space, her eyes fixed on the distant vessels,

Valerie vowed that she would free her people no matter what it took. She might not be the New Men's genetic equal, but she'd learned from Captain Maddox that one never gave up no matter what.

The game of survival had begun, and Valerie was determined to make the next move the best one she could achieve.

-3-

Valerie drifted through space, her Type-7 Explorer Suit's maneuvering thrusters firing in calculated microbursts. The suit's HUD showed her velocity at a mere 0.27 meters per second relative to the *Kit Carson* and the star cruiser, now a rapidly diminishing cigar shape and a much bigger triangular shape behind her.

Valerie's enhanced vision zoomed in on the New Men star cruiser. Its sleek hull gleamed in the red dwarf's light as a Lambda-class shuttle detached from its ventral bay. No doubt, the shuttle carried more of the golden-skinned oppressors, eager to claim their prize.

Heart pounding, Valerie activated her suit's stealth mode. She should've done that sooner. She couldn't believe it had taken her this long to think of it.

A graphene-based metamaterial coating shifted to match the background radiation of space, rendering her nearly invisible to most sensors. It wasn't perfect—a determined scan would still detect her—but it was her best chance at continuing to avoid detection by the New Men.

The 387-kilometer journey to the *Cheng Ho* and the Commonwealth Trader seemed interminable. Valerie's suit recycled her fluids and breath, maintaining optimal hydration and oxygen levels, but it couldn't quell the rising panic. She expected to feel the grasp of a tractor beam or see the flash of a plasma cannon that would end her existence.

After far too long—her chronometer said it was four hours and seventeen minutes—Valerie approached the two vessels. The *Cheng Ho*, a Pathfinder-class scout similar to the *Kit Carson*, showed signs of recent activity—its power surges faintly visible. Its running lights pulsed in a standard "all clear" pattern, but Valerie's instincts told her otherwise.

She turned her attention to the trader, an older Neptune-series freighter. Its hull was scarred from countless micro-meteor impacts, and its identification transponder was offline.

Valerie made her decision. Using her suit's maneuvering jets, she aligned herself with the freighter's starboard airlock. Soon, she landed gently against the hull, activating her mag-locks on her boots. The outer hatch was sealed, but she'd learned from the best. After ten minutes, emergency protocols granted her access.

As the airlock cycled, Valerie's suit sensors analyzed the ship's atmosphere. Oxygen levels were nominal, but CO_2 was far below what she'd expected for a crewed vessel. The internal gravity was set to 0.1 G, barely enough to keep unsecured objects from floating away.

Valerie drew her sidearm, a compact RP-27 pistol, as she entered the ship's main corridor. The emergency lighting cast an eerie red glow over the empty passageways. Her footsteps, muffled by the low gravity, seemed thunderous in the oppressive silence.

Valerie swept through each compartment. The bridge was deserted, its consoles dark and lifeless. The cargo hold contained only a few empty crates. The crew quarters showed signs of hasty departure—personal effects left behind, lockers hanging open.

A chill ran down Valerie's spine as she approached the emergency escape pod bay. Five of the seven pods were missing, their docking clamps standing empty. Pod 6 was still in place, its hatch sealed. Pod 7, however, was open.

Working quickly, Valerie transferred the supplies from Pod 6 to Pod 7. Emergency rations, medikits, and portable atmosphere generators—everything she might need for an extended journey through uncharted space.

As she worked, Valerie thought furiously. Where had the New Men taken the crew? Had any of the trader's people escaped with the pods? Here was the big question. How could she use any of this to her advantage?

An idea formed, dangerous and desperate. She was closer to the Commonwealth than previously. It was quite possible scavengers or strip miners, and traders, moved through these star systems. She had to get away from the New Men and stay away until she could get help. That meant...

Valerie moved to the ship's main computer. She turned it on, surprised she could do it this easily. Then she programmed a delayed sequence: in exactly six hours, the ship would recharge sufficiently and activate its Laumer Drive, opening the wormhole the *Kit Carson* had just traversed. She had to pray the star cruiser moved off temporarily. If not—

She shrugged. Valerie hated gambling, but she didn't have much choice now did she?

Valerie exited the bridge and returned to Pod 7, sealing herself in. Through the pod's small viewport, she watched as the hours ticked by.

Finally, after 4 hours and 42 minutes, the star cruiser towing the *Kit Carson* began to move. There had been a good chance the New Men would park the *Kit Carson* here. That didn't seem to be the case, or not yet, anyway. The star cruiser's massive engines flared to life, pushing it toward the Earthlike moon orbiting the gas giant, towing the *Kit Carson* with it. This was her chance.

Valerie waited until another hour passed and then initiated the pod's launch sequence. The explosive bolts fired, propelling the pod away from the trader. She activated the pod's systems, powering up and maneuvering to the Laumer Point.

Minutes later, the trader's Laumer Drive came online. Valerie knew because a shimmering portal blossomed in space before her—the mouth of the wormhole.

Valerie fired the pod's thrusters, pushing it toward the swirling vortex. It took time, too much really. The trader's Laumer Drive could shut down at any moment. That would close the Laumer Point.

As if thinking it jinxed her, the texture of the wormhole's swirl changed. No, no, Valerie couldn't afford that. Then her pod's control panel beeped an alarm.

What did that mean? Had the New Men spotted her, sent harsh jammers against the pod?

Valerie swallowed, studying the controls. No, this was worse than any of her fears. This was an unstable wormhole. That could mean it cycled to different regions depending on various gravitational or temporal factors.

Valerie closed her eyes, and then opened them. It might not matter if the Laumer Drive on the trader didn't—

Before she could finish the thought, the escape pod crossed the event horizon, alarms blaring. The gravitational stresses threatened to tear the small craft apart. This was an unstable wormhole all right. That could mean it could crush the pod.

Before Valerie could worry more, she blanked out.

When reality reasserted itself and she woke up, Valerie found herself in an unfamiliar star system, the Laumer Point behind her collapsing.

Valerie had escaped, but at what cost? This didn't seem like the star system where the *Cheng Ho* buoy was located. Worse, she was alone, adrift in unknown space, with no way to contact Star Watch, or anyone else for that matter.

As the pod's systems began cataloging the surrounding stellar bodies, Valerie allowed herself a moment of uncertainty. Had she traded certain capture for certain death? Or could she find a way to turn this desperate gambit into her crew's salvation?

With a deep breath, Valerie pushed aside her doubts. She was a Patrol officer, trained to face the unknown.

"Then that's what I'll do."

Her voice sounded hollow in the pod. Just how long could she survive in here? If no ships passed by, or if the New Men found her…

Valerie felt faint. This could have been the stupidest idea of her life. She was lost out in the Beyond in a tiny escape pod. Damn, but she did not give her chances as good.

-4-

The following was an encoded transmission from Lord Hermes, to His Imperial Majesty, Emperor Trahey of the Throne World.

To His Most Exalted and Genetically Superior Majesty, Emperor Trahey,

I trust this communication finds you in a state of perfect genetic harmony, your superior intellect ever focused on the grand designs that will elevate our species to its rightful place among the stars.

It is with great pleasure and no small measure of pride that I report a significant victory in our ongoing campaign to rid the galaxy of the genetic detritus that dares to call itself "humanity." Our glorious Star Cruiser *Olympian Thunderbolt* has successfully intercepted and captured a Commonwealth scout vessel, the *Kit Carson*, in the Primus Venatoris System.

While the ship's commander, a female of their species (how quaint that they still allow such inferior creatures to hold positions of authority), managed to escape through means yet to be determined, we have secured two prime specimens from Captain Maddox's crew. Both are males, relatively young by their pitiful standards, identified as Sergeant Treggason Riker and Lieutenant Keith Maker.

These specimens, while woefully inadequate compared to even our lowest genetic echelons, present us with a unique opportunity. I humbly propose that we transport these creatures to the Game Preserve on Bestia Rex. There, they will be released to fend for themselves among the other human chattel we have gathered for our sport.

Now, I present Your Majesty with two tantalizing options for your consideration:

One: After a period of four standard months, allowing these specimens to acclimate to their new environment and perhaps develop some semblance of survival skills, Your Majesty could grace us with your presence for a most exhilarating hunt. Imagine the thrill of pursuing these desperate creatures through the carefully crafted terrains of our preserve, their futile attempts at evasion serving only to heighten the inevitable triumph of our superior genetics.

Two: Alternatively, we could use these captured crewmembers as bait to lure the infamous Captain Maddox to our hunting grounds. While Maddox is but an insect compared to our greatness, his reputation among the lesser humans makes him a prize worthy of Your Majesty's attention. The psychological torment we could inflict by forcing him to watch as we hunt his crew before turning our sights on him would be a spectacle of unparalleled magnificence.

I await Your Majesty's decision with bated breath. Rest assured, whatever you choose, it shall be executed with the utmost precision and devotion to our sacred cause of genetic purification.

In closing, allow me to reaffirm my unwavering loyalty to Your Majesty and our sacred mission. Each day, I am reminded of the vast gulf that separates us from these primitive beings, who dare to challenge our dominion over the cosmos. Their very existence is an affront to the natural order we seek to impose upon the universe.

Soon, very soon, we shall cleanse the galaxy of their genetic imperfection, leaving only the purity of our superior bloodline as the rightful inheritors of the stars.

May your genes forever reign supreme, Lord Hermes.

Star Watch Intelligence Update: In light of later events, this proved to be an encoded deception message, telling the Emperor the secret project had received an infusion of workers.

This shows the depths to which the New Men went in disguising their true intentions—Intelligence Chief General Mackinder, reporting.

-5-

In a hold aboard the Star Cruiser *Olympian Thunderbolt*, a different process was taking place from what Lord Hermes had informed Emperor Trahey. This included Sergeant Treggason Riker:

Riker looked down as his jaw clenched. A golden-skinned bastard in a silver suit strutted in front of them. The New Man's chiseled features twisted into a sneer as he addressed them, the prisoners from the *Kit Carson*. Interestingly enough, that didn't include Valerie.

Earlier, Riker had barely stopped Keith from asking their captors about her. If Valerie had escaped, they needed to keep that a secret for as long as possible.

The New Man ceased his strutting as he faced them. "Listen up, premen. Your sad lives now have purpose. You'll work hard, or you won't eat. That should be enough for you. I'll add this in case one or two of you have a smattering of curiosity. You shall share in the glory of our objective and perhaps even gain in status through it. You have no idea how privileged you are to be here at this momentous occurrence."

Riker glanced sidelong at Keith.

The lieutenant was still in agony regarding Valerie's status. Likely, Keith had been hoping to learn something, as he feared she was dead or perhaps as bad, heading for a New Man's harem.

Riker studied the rest of the *Kit Carson's* crew. They huddled together, eyes downcast, having already faced rough handling from the New Men who had captured the scout.

Riker muttered under his breath, earning a discharge from a compact white instrument a little larger than a pistol, although this weapon was smooth and elongated, with several settings upon it.

A New Man guard must have been watching him, not liking his looking about. Pain exploded across his back, but Riker bit back a groan.

The overseer New Man ceased talking, gesturing to the guard.

Everyone turned to look.

"Now's a good time to introduce them to the neuron whip," the overseer said.

"I used the lowest setting," the guard said, as he held up the smooth white instrument.

"Perhaps he needs another lash at the second lowest setting so he can perceive the differences," the overseer said. "Feeling is believing for the likes of them."

"You," the guard said.

Riker knew the New Man meant him, and he knew the guard knew he knew. Sweat beaded Riker's face from the first lash of the neuron whip. He turned to face the guard.

"Shall I administer the second setting?" the guard asked.

"No, Lord," Riker said in as contrite a voice as he could manage. "I've learned my lesson."

"Face me," the overseer said.

They all did, including Riker.

"That is the neuron whip," the overseer said. "Depending on the setting, it can send a preman reeling, to knees, unconscious or dead. Yet, it will never leave a mark upon you, just triggering the pain regions in what some of you call a brain. Do your tasks, and you will gain rewards, such as extra food or a second cup of water. Fail to do anything we demand and the neuron whip will be your punishment instead. Rejoice in your fate however you chose, but remember to leap with obedience once ordered by one of us."

He surveyed them like a cattle rancher inspecting his herd.

"Follow me," the overseer said. "Do not dawdle, or you shall be the object lesson next time."

The two New Men thereupon herded them down several corridors, into a hangar bay and onto a waiting shuttle. The New Men didn't bother with handcuffs or restraints of any kind, nor did more guards join them. Of course, the unseen pilot in the cockpit must have been another New Man.

As Riker sat down on a seat, he was sure the bastards wanted them to try something. There was no point, though, really. None of them could defeat a New Man. Probably not even three of them could handle one of the golden-skinned supermen. At this point, the crew of the *Kit Carson* probably couldn't subdue one even if they all fought hand-to-hand, never mind that hideous neuron whip.

As the shuttle lifted off the hangar bay deck, Riker pressed his face against a small viewport. Now he was wishing he'd never joined the *Kit Carson*. He should have stayed on Earth and taken his chances with the Butcher. It was too late for that, though. This was a terrible fate.

The shuttle exited the star cruiser.

Through the porthole, Riker noted a massive gas giant, its swirling storms dwarfing anything he'd seen on Jupiter. Were they headed for a space station orbiting the gas giant?

After a few minutes, he saw that the shuttle headed for a huge moon with Earthlike features: blue, green and desert yellow. In time, the shuttle shook as it entered the moon's heavier atmosphere.

Riker had heard before how some New Men liked hunting men, letting them run free as they stalked the humans as big game animals. Could that be their fate?

No, Riker didn't think so. The lesson with the neuron whip and the talk indicated they would have to work at something.

He kept watching.

Soon enough, he spied an endless expanse of jungle that stretched from one horizon to the next. In a way, it reminded him of the planet in the pocket universe. The color of the leaves was different, and he didn't see any crystal spires. That was a relief.

Abruptly, the shuttle began plummeting, which caused Riker's stomach to lurch. A few of the others cried out.

The nearest New Man smirked, surely believing this was yet another mark of their superiority over regular men.

That meant this was part of the journey, not some accident. Riker eased up in his seat the better to look down through the tiny window.

The shuttle headed for a colossal pit. It seemed like strip miners had cleared the jungle vegetation, as the jungle circled the great pit. Wait. Riker noticed impossible structures along the edges. The structures were huge and alien.

As the shuttle slowed and neared the pit, the structures proved to be mighty ruins. Why would the New Men have excavated the pit in such a way that these colossal ruins ringed it? That seemed odd, freaky maybe. What had been on the surface of the pit before the excavation?

Riker gulped as he studied the alien ruins.

Some of the structures appeared to be twisted spires composed of an unknown material. They caught the sunlight, seeming to bend reality.

A chill ran down Riker, a feeling of wrongness that went beyond the dire situation of his capture. There was something here. The New Men searched for something…

Riker shuddered. It felt as if the New Men searched for something ancient and possibly evil. It set his teeth on edge. He couldn't name it, but…

Riker turned to Keith beside him. "You feel that?" he whispered.

Keith stared at him.

"What's wrong with you?" Riker whispered.

Keith shook his head and squeezed his eyes shut before opening them and staring at Riker. "I feel like I'm never going to see Valerie again."

Riker frowned.

Keith glanced sidelong at the nearest New Man before regarding Riker again. "I know. I know. I won't talk about her anymore."

"Good," Riker whispered. "Do you feel anything else?"

After a moment, Keith shook his head.

Riker found that odd and turned back to the window. He watched as the shuttle sank into the pit, noted the stony texture of the dirt wall, and then the shuttle touched down, the engine whining less before shutting off.

"Arise," the overseer said. "It is time to view your new home."

Riker filed off with the others onto alien soil. It was packed down dirt and stones at the bottom of the giant pit. The air was thick with the smells of unfamiliar jungle vegetation and dislodged soil. Ahead loomed their destination—a building constructed from massive logs. There was heavy machinery nearby, incongruous with the old-style building.

"Quicken your pace," the overseer said, "or enjoy the pain of the neuron whip."

The small crew of the *Kit Carson* jogged faster, a broken parade of the defeated. Riker tried to catalog details, searching for any kind of weaknesses. The pit walls rose eighty feet or more around them, those unsettling ruins on the periphery, watching everything, it seemed.

Riker figured if Ludendorff could get a look at the ruins, the Methuselah Man would know what this place had been. Ludendorff would probably know what the New Men sought to dig up, too.

The log hall's main door creaked open.

They jogged in and stopped on command.

The place was like an old Viking hall, divided by partitions, but more of a cavernous chamber. There were New Men, but mostly hollow-eyed humans in filthy garments that flinched at every movement of the towering New Men. The older prisoners bore the marks of brutal labor, others the telltale signs of malnutrition and disease.

What had the New Men been doing to bring these people to such a sorry state?

The others must be the crews of the trade ship and the *Cheng Ho*. Could Emily be among them, a waif of her former self? For the first time, Riker hoped she wasn't here.

"Where are we?" Keith whispered. "What have they done to these people?"

Riker's response was cut short by a shove from behind, sending him stumbling toward the defeated humanity. The stench of unwashed bodies and hopelessness was overwhelming.

A New Man with a sun-shaped badge clipped to his silver suit stepped up. He seemed gaunter than was normal for his kind and with staring, possibly even haunted eyes.

That was more than strange. It struck Riker as ominous.

"Welcome to your new home, premen," the gaunt New Man said. "Tomorrow, you begin labor in the mines. Serve well, and you may yet prove yourselves worthy of existence."

He waited, observing them.

Riker looked down so the New Man wouldn't see the hatred in his eyes. The bastard could probably tell anyway.

"Now," the gaunt New Man said, "you will be assigned to your sleeping area. Cause any problems and you will receive further education."

Riker shook his head, muttering under his breath.

The New Man with the sun symbol focused on Riker. "That is a troublemaker. He reeks of it."

Before Riker could react, a device pressed against his neck. White-hot agony exploded through his nerves, dropping him to his knees.

"Enough," the gaunt New Man said. "Perhaps the preman is capable of training. Let us test the idea and see if he can earn our good graces."

The pain receded, leaving Riker gasping on the floor. He looked up to see Keith and the others watching helplessly.

Riker struggled to his feet. Everything hurt. Damn those neuron whips. He looked up to see the gaunt New Man with the sun symbol watching him. Riker knew the correct response, and looked down.

"That is a beginning," the New Man said. "You are learning your place. Excellent."

Riker rejoined Keith and the others, moving to an open floor area, surrounded by broken humanity. He searched for Emily but couldn't find anyone who resembled her. Then he looked for signs of defiance in the others. If they were going to survive this hellhole, allies would help. But Riker couldn't see anyone with any fire left in them.

As he lay on a mat, Riker thought about that. The mines loomed in their future, promising backbreaking labor and something unforeseen.

What was going on down here? It must have something to do with the alien ruins.

You've been through worse, Riker told himself. He'd be damned if he'd let the golden-skinned supermen win.

Besides, the New Men hadn't captured Valerie. Surely, that meant she had escaped. Could Valerie find a way back to the Commonwealth to alert Star Watch about this?

Riker closed his eyes. That was a longshot. But hoping for a longshot was better than giving up. He had to survive and help the rest of the *Kit Carson's* crew to survive. By the looks of the people who'd been here awhile, that was going to take plenty of grit and willpower.

What did the New Men seek?

Riker turned over, exhausted, and soon fell into a fitful sleep.

-6-

From the log building, the prisoners marched in the early morning, heading for the mines— huge holes in the side of the pit. New Men flanked them, their faces like masks of superiority and their lean, long bodies brimming with strength and health.

"Keep pace with the others," a New Man said, shoving Keith.

The lieutenant stumbled, nearly falling before Riker caught his arm. Neither of them said a word, although they nodded slightly to each other.

They entered the mine, discovering that a tunnel stretched before them, the steep incline taking them deeper. In a large stone chamber, women handed out helmets. Riker accepted his, putting it on. It was too tight, but he doubted he could exchange it now. As the tunnel continued, he clicked on the lamp as instructed.

New Men divided the company into smaller groups, leading them ever deeper.

Their group descended to the left, the air growing thick and then stale. In a side tunnel, a massive machine hummed in the dark. The rush of fresh air indicated it pumped precious oxygen into the depths. Without such machines, they would suffocate fast.

Their group entered a low, circular chamber. Keith looked around and then leaned near Riker. "What the hell are they digging for?"

"Good question," Riker said. He was glad Keith had come back around to ask it.

A trio of New Men strode past, carrying crates marked with warning symbols. They must have been explosives experts.

"Clear the area!" a New Man shouted. "We're blasting in five minutes."

Two New Men herded the crew back up the tunnel and told them to stand against the rough-hewn walls.

Riker obeyed but didn't understand. What could be worth all this effort?

A horn sounded, followed by a deafening explosion. The walls shook. Dust and debris choked the air as the shock wave slammed against them.

As the dust began to settle, an overseer shouted, "Time to work, premen. Load the rocks into carts."

Riker put on gloves and marched with the others. He soon found himself clearing the newly blasted rocks and debris. Beside him, Keith wheezed and coughed, struggling to keep up with the ferocious pace.

Hours blurred into a haze of mindless labor. They carried rocks and shoveled debris into carts, muscles straining as they pushed the laden vehicles to a nearby chamber for dumping. Other prisoners, faces gaunt and eyes hollow, carted the rubble further away.

The New Men were everywhere, often brandishing the compact neuron whips. Sometimes, the weapons crackled with energy and a human groaned or screamed in pain.

Riker witnessed a fellow prisoner stumbling to the wrong location. He earned a flickering surge of energy across his back. The man's scream echoed through the tunnels as he twitched on the rocky floor.

"Faster," an overseer shouted. "Or perhaps you all need further motivation?"

Riker gritted his teeth, forcing his aching body to comply. But even as he worked, he searched for answers. There were no precious gems glittering in the rock face, no veins of valuable ore. Just endless, worthless stone.

"What's the point of all this?" he asked Keith as they pushed another cartload.

The lieutenant shook his head. "I don't know, but whatever it is, it can't be good."

As they trudged back for another load, Riker looked around. The New Men's arrogance must have blind spots—he needed to find one so he could use it against them.

A guard's voice snapped Riker back to reality. "Eyes front, preman. The rocks are down there, not up here."

Riker nodded. "Sorry, boss."

The New Man eyed him, perhaps deciding whether Riker's tone deserved punishment. Then another New Man called out, distracting the first, and the moment passed.

As they neared the blasted rock face again, something caught Riker's eye—a glint of something not quite natural. He blinked, and the thing was gone.

What had he seen?

The sound of a neuron whip was followed by a scream elsewhere.

Riker's jaw clenched.

How long could he survive this place? Would Maddox ever learn of this? Riker shook his head sadly and resumed the backbreaking work. Valerie—everything rested on the Lieutenant Commander. Riker sure hoped Valerie was doing something to help them get out of here.

-7-

The recycled air in the escape pod tasted like stale death. Valerie's tongue stuck to the roof of her mouth as she sucked the last drop of moisture from the condensation collector. Her parched throat burned with each swallow.

"Horrid New Men," she rasped, her voice cracking from disuse. The words echoed in the cramped confines of the pod, her isolation prison.

Valerie's fingers trembled as she punched up the resource display on the battered control panel. The screen flickered, its power reserves as depleted as her own. Red warning indicators flashed across every category: oxygen, water, power and food.

Valerie slumped back into the pilot's chair, ignoring the protests of her aching muscles. How long had it been? Weeks? Maybe a month? Time blurred in the endless void of space, punctuated only by fitful bouts of sleep and the gnawing pangs of hunger.

Valerie closed her eyes as memories of the attack surged unbidden to the surface. One moment, they had been reviving from jump lag. The next, a tractor beam from a star cruiser drew them in.

She'd failed her crew. Failed to see the trap in the *Cheng Ho's* distress buoy. Failed to listen to Keith. Failed to…

No. Valerie shook her head, forcing the guilt away. There'd be time for that later. Right now, she had to focus on survival. On getting back somehow to warn Star Watch about the New Men's piracy and rescue whatever was left of her crew.

If she lived that long, if they did.

Valerie's gaze drifted to the pod's tiny viewport. Nothing but an endless sea of stars stretched before her. This star system had barren terrestrial hulks orbiting too near the brown dwarf star, a few meager gas giants farther out and some showy comets. Oh, she could land the pod on a terrestrial planet but to what purpose? To go out and dig her own grave on the molten surfaces?

There was nothing but the vast, uncaring expanse of the fringe Beyond before her. By her calculations, the star system with the Earthlike moon was over 12 light-years away. That was much further than most stable wormholes reached.

Did the New Men even know she'd escaped? What were the smug, so-called supermen doing to her crew?

"Think, damn it," Valerie whispered, racking her brain for options. Even though the offending star cruiser was in a system 12 light-years away, she hadn't used the pod's distress beacon for fear of drawing the New Men to her. Who else could possibly hear the distress signal out here in the fringe Beyond?

Maybe the only thing that had saved her so far was the unstable wormhole. Had the wormhole thrown her to a star system no one used? Was she closer to the Commonwealth now or farther?

Her eyes widened as a dangerous idea took shape. Why had it taken her so long to think of this? Maybe the grimness of the situation had numbed her mind, and she was only now coming out of shock.

"You're out of your mind, you know?" Valerie said, even as she manipulated the control panel. "This is certain suicide."

But so was floating much longer in a quickly diminishing escape pod. If you thought about it, what choice did she have? Float out here and die, or take a chance? She hadn't seen any ships in this star system, no one to contact. Maybe there were Laumer Points outside the system and ships she hadn't been able to detect using them. At this point, she could no longer afford to be choosy.

Valerie pulled up the pod's communication protocols. The New Men had used the *Cheng Ho's* distress buoy to lure in her

Patrol ship. Why couldn't she do the same thing with them in reverse?

"Come on, you worthless piece of..." she muttered, trying to coax the pod's systems to life. "One last trick," she said. "That's all I'm asking for."

The computer chirped a warning. Rerouting the failing power to boost the signal strength would cut the precarious life support reserves by half. Valerie hesitated for a split second, then stabbed the confirm key.

"In for a credit, in for a solar," she whispered.

Valerie crafted a message designed to catch the attention of any passing ships. Not Commonwealth frequencies—she was in the fringe of the Beyond, home to scavengers, strip miners and vagabond traders. This signal would speak the universal language out here: greed.

MAYDAY. MAYDAY. STAR WATCH CRUISER LIFEPOD. CRITICAL SYSTEMS FAILING. HIGH-VALUE CARGO AND MILITARY-GRADE TECH ONBOARD. ASSISTANCE REQUIRED. SUBSTANTIAL REWARD GUARANTEED.

Valerie's lips twisted as she hit transmit. The pod shuddered as power surged to the communications array. Warning klaxons blared, the computer's monotone voice declaring imminent life support failure.

"Tell me something I don't know," Valerie said, silencing the alarms.

She leaned back in the seat, ignoring the sweat beading her forehead as the temperature began to rise. It was done. Now all she could do was wait and hope someone took the bait.

Of course, even if they did...

Valerie's hand drifted to the empty holster at her hip. She'd spaced the pistol some time ago, afraid she might take the easy way out. That had been in a moment of mental weakness.

Now hours crawled by. Valerie drifted in and out of consciousness, the thinning air in the pod making it harder to focus. Each time she jolted awake, her eyes darted to the sensor displays, searching for any sign of an approaching ship.

She might have just killed herself with this stunt. Well, that wasn't exactly true. She might have killed herself faster.

Wasn't it better to take a chance than play it safe and die soon anyway?

"Come on," Valerie whispered. "Don't let me die out here. I don't want to die just yet."

She checked the sensor display again, but nothing had changed.

Her stomach growled, hunger gnawing at her. She'd been a fool and now would die a fool. What a horrible end to the tale of Lieutenant Commander Valerie Noonan.

-8-

Several days later, Valerie stirred long enough to sit up and try something else. If the longshot had ruined her chances of survival, why not roll the iron dice of fate again and try something else?

The acrid stench of ozone soon filled the cramped space with sparks spitting from exposed wiring as she pushed the equipment far beyond its design limits.

"Come on, you piece of junk, give me just a little more..."

The main display flickered, its image wavering like a mirage in a desert. Valerie squinted at the readout, deciphering the cascade of error messages and system warnings through sheer force of will.

She'd gutted half the pod's remaining systems for this attempt, cannibalizing life support and navigation to boost the comms array. If this didn't work, she'd be dead long before anyone found her corpse floating in the void.

"Not like you've got much choice," she said, forcing down the surge of panic threatening to overwhelm her. "It's this or suffocating in your sleep."

The thought of her captured crew steeled her resolve. She had to make it back, had to warn Star Watch about the New Men's pirate moves. If that meant luring in a pack of ruthless scavengers... desperate times and all that, right?

Valerie hadn't been clever enough earlier. She'd made the distress call too obvious. She'd thought like an upright Patrol officer, not as someone like Maddox.

She wove a tapestry of lies and deception. The new and improved distress signal took shape, layer by layer, each new addition calibrated to catch the eye of passing ships.

"Let's see," she muttered, scanning the fabricated manifest. "One damaged Star Watch life pod, check. Encrypted data banks, double check. And for the cherry on top..."

Her fingers paused over the final entry. This was the bait that would spring the trap, a lure too tempting for any self-respecting vulture to pass up.

MILITARY-GRADE NEUROCHEM ENHANCERS. EXPERIMENTAL. HIGHLY UNSTABLE.

"Congratulations," she said with a humorless chuckle. "You just became every pirates' wet dream."

The real trick, though, was making it all seem legitimate. That's where she had screwed up before. Any half-decent scavenger crew would be scanning for signs of deception. Fuel costs money, and most crews couldn't afford to waste it.

Valerie leaned in close to the flickering display, ignoring the sparks singeing her hair. She buried the "high-value" items deep within the manifest, obscuring them behind layers of mundane cargo listings and falsified crew logs.

Next came the encryption. Not enough to completely mask the signal—that would defeat the purpose—but just enough to make it look like a hastily scrambled distress call.

"Time to get creative," Valerie said.

She pulled up the pod's limited language banks, cobbling together a patchwork of military jargon and technical gibberish. The result was a mess of half-corrupted data, tantalizing glimpses of valuable intel peeking through the static.

Sweat trickled down Valerie's spine as she worked, the pod's failing environmental controls unable to keep up with the overtaxed systems. The air grew thick and stale, each breath a chore.

"Almost there," she wheezed, forcing herself to focus through the mounting exhaustion and oxygen deprivation.

The final touch was the trickiest. Valerie needed to mask any trace of her true identity or Patrol affiliation. She scrubbed the pod's transponder codes, replacing them with a hodgepodge of falsified IDs pulled from half-remembered smuggler's tales and backwater spaceport rumors.

As she worked, a nagging voice in the back of her mind whispered with doubts. What if no one took the bait? What if they saw through her ruse? What if—?

"Shut up," Valerie said, silencing the inner monologue. "You start second-guessing yourself now...

The last part was the hardest. She boosted the signal so it would reach farther than before. That took more life support away from her.

Valerie groaned, laying back, trying not to think about how awful the stale air tasted.

"All right, you opportunistic bastards," Valerie whispered. "Come and get it."

She'd just used her final power reserves to send out a stronger, open invitation to every cutthroat and scavenger passing through or near this star system. If anyone answered her call, they certainly wouldn't be coming to mount a rescue.

No, they'd be coming to strip the pod bare, take anything of value, and leave her corpse floating in the void. If she was lucky.

"What the hell were you thinking?" Valerie whispered, running a hand through her sweat-soaked hair. "You're unarmed, half-dead already, and you just rang the dinner bell for every predator in the Beyond."

But the alternative was certain death, alone in the emptiness of space. At least this way, she had a fighting chance, however slim it might be.

Valerie forced herself to take stock of her meager resources. No weapons, unless you counted the hydrospanner she'd used to rewire the pod. Limited mobility in the cramped confines. And her body was a wreck after weeks of rationing and oxygen deprivation.

"Well," she said with a mirthless chuckle, "least you've got the element of surprise. Nobody expects a half-dead Patrol officer to put up much of a fight."

She closed her eyes, trying to push away the fear and doubt gnawing at the edges of her mind.

The waiting was the worst part. Every creak of the pod's stressed hull sent a jolt of adrenaline through her system. Every flicker on the sensor display had her heart racing, wondering if this was it—if her trap had finally been sprung.

Hours crawled by. Or was it days? Time lost all meaning in the endless void.

Valerie drifted in and out of consciousness, her exhausted body finally giving in to its demands for rest. But even in sleep, there was no peace. Nightmares plagued her fitful slumber—visions of her captured crew, of ruthless scavengers tearing apart her sanctuary, of drifting alone forever in the cold embrace of space.

She snapped awake with a gasp, disoriented and panicking. It took a moment for reality to reassert itself, for the familiar contours of the escape pod to come into focus.

And then she saw it: a blinking light on the sensor display. A contact, closing fast.

Valerie's heart hammered as she leaned in, squinting at the readout. The ship's profile was unfamiliar—a hodgepodge of different designs cobbled together into something vaguely predatory.

"Well," she said. "Looks like dinner's served. I hope you bastards are hungry."

-9-

The scavenger ship loomed in the viewport like a nightmare made metal. Its hull was a patchwork of mismatched plates, held together by welds and prayer. Valerie's eyes narrowed as she took in the haphazard array of weapons bristling from its surface.

"Well, aren't you just a beauty," she said, her hand tightening on the hydrospanner.

Static crackled over the pod's comm system. A guttural voice cut through the white noise.

"Attention derelict. This is Captain Marek of the *Bloodtooth*. Prepare to be boarded. Any resistance will be met with extreme prejudice."

Valerie's lips curled into a humorless smile.

She keyed the comm, pitching her voice higher, injecting a note of panicked desperation. "Oh, thank the stars. Please, we need help. Our systems are failing, and—"

"Shut it," Marek said. "We ain't here to play rescue. You got cargo, we take cargo. You got valuables, they're ours now. Anything else, well... we'll see what you're worth on the market."

The comm cut out with a harsh buzz. Valerie's jaw clenched, her earlier bravado evaporating in the face of reality. These weren't your run-of-the-mill opportunists. These were hardened predators.

The pod shuddered as docking clamps engaged. Valerie stumbled, her weakened legs barely supporting her weight.

They must have enveloped the pod within their gravity dampener's influence. She wasn't weightless anymore.

Valerie steadied herself against the bulkhead, willing strength into her trembling muscles.

A series of metallic clangs echoed through the hull as the scavengers attached a boarding tube. Valerie positioned herself near the airlock, hydrospanner tucked against her back and belt, out of sight.

The airlock began to cycle. Valerie took a deep breath, forcing her face into a mask of fearful relief.

The inner door hissed open.

The stench hit her first—a nauseating mix of unwashed bodies, machine oil, and something sickeningly sweet that she refused to identify. Valerie fought the urge to gag as three figures stomped into the pod.

The three were a motley crew, each more ragged and vicious-looking than the last. The leader, a hulking brute with cybernetic implants jutting from his skull, swept the cramped space with a heavy pulse rifle.

"Well, well," he growled, his lips peeling back. "What do we have here? Don't look like no high-value cargo to me."

Valerie raised her hands, letting a tremble enter her voice. "Please, I'm just a civilian. Our ship was attacked, and I—"

The leader backhanded her, sending her sprawling. Stars exploded across Valerie's vision as her head cracked against the bulkhead.

"I said shut it," the man snarled. He turned to his companions—a rail-thin woman with a shock of neon green hair, and a squat, toad-fat man wearing weird armor plates as if he was some kind of alien. That one had protruding eyes that barely seemed human. Was the sickly-sweet odor coming from him?

"Search the pod," the first man said. "Strip it bare."

Valerie struggled to focus as the scavengers tore through her meager shelter. The woman let out a harsh laugh as she rifled through the empty weapons locker.

"Nix on the military hardware, Churgol," she called out. "This bitch is as dry as a Texel whorehouse."

The leader rounded on Valerie, his augmented eye whirring as it focused on her face. "You trying to play us, girl? Where's the valuable cargo you promised?"

Valerie licked blood from her split lip. "I... I don't know what you're talking about. The distress call must have been automated, I—"

Churgol's mechanical hand closed around her throat, lifting her off the deck with unnatural strength. Valerie clawed at the unyielding metal fingers, gasping for air.

"Last chance," Churgol said. "Where's. The. Cargo?"

Black spots danced at the edges of her vision. This was it—do or die time.

With the last of her strength, Valerie reached back, fingers closing around the hydrospanner tucked against her lower back, and brought it up and around in a vicious arc. It connected with the side of Churgol's head with a satisfying thud.

The cyborg howled in pain and released his grip. Valerie dropped to the deck, gasping for air.

"You little bi—" Churgol's curse was cut short as Valerie slammed the hydrospanner into his knee joint. There was a pop of shorting circuitry, and the hulking man went down hard.

Valerie scrambled to her feet, adrenaline burned away weeks of weakness. She let go of the hydrospanner and snatched up Churgol's fallen pulse rifle, bringing it to bear on the other two scavengers.

"Don't," Valerie whispered, with her abused throat protesting each word.

The green-haired woman's hand had been inching toward a wicked-looking blade at her hip. Green Hair froze, a look of grudging respect crossing her face.

"Damn, girl," she said. "You got some fight in you."

The toad-like man whispered something in an odd tongue. It seemed then as if the sickly-sweet odor increased.

For some reason, that caused Valerie to blink and blink more. She was finding it hard to focus as some of her fight oozed from her.

Green Hair nodded, not taking her eyes off Valerie. "Kresh is right. You ain't no civilian. Patrol, if I had to guess."

Kresh had to be the name for the toad-like fat man. What was with him and his protruding eyes? Why did he stink the way he did? The armor plates around him seemed weird, almost like something a giant insect would have.

Valerie fought against her weakening will as her finger tightened on the pulse rifle's trigger. "Give me one good reason why I shouldn't burn you all right now."

Kresh spoke again in his alien tongue.

"Well?" Valerie shouted. What was wrong with you, you bug-eyed creep?"

A slow clap echoed from the boarding tube. Valerie tensed as a new figure stepped into view—a lean, sharp-featured man with a spiffy jacket and leather pants and boots. He had eyes like blue ice.

"Oh, bravo," he said. "I do so love a bit of theater with my acquisitions."

Valerie blinked in confusion before realizing this was the real captain—Marek. He didn't look surprised in the least.

"Now then," Marek said, producing an elegantly crafted pistol from his pricy coat. "Why don't we dispense with the playacting and have a real conversation? I'm interested to hear what a Patrol officer is doing in what you people call the fringe Beyond. And why you're so desperate to be 'rescued.'"

Valerie couldn't understand why she didn't start burning them down with the pulse rifle. This was her golden opportunity. How many crewmembers could this rust bucket of a spaceship have? That was the goal, right, to find passage back home no matter what?

Valerie twisted her face, hating that sickly-sweet odor and the way Kresh watched her silently. The toad-like man wasn't the captain. What was he then? How did Kresh fit into all this?

This was weird, and Valerie wasn't understanding. She swayed, wanting to fire the pulse rifle, knowing it was her best option. Why couldn't she pull the damn trigger?

-10-

Valerie's grip tightened on the pulse rifle as Marek continued to stare at her. She wasn't sure what to do next or what this killer would decide.

"Search her," Marek said. "Thoroughly."

Valerie shuddered, twisting her face again at the awful sickly-sweet odor.

While she did that, Churgol yanked the pulse rifle from her.

Then Green Hair and the short fat man patted Valerie down, probing for hidden weapons or tech. Valerie gritted her teeth, fighting the urge to lash out as the invasive fingers lingered too long.

"Clean," Green Hair announced, stepping back with a leer. "Well, clean-ish. Reeks like a week-old corpse, though."

Captain Marek's eyes narrowed. "And the pod? What of our promised bounty?"

Kresh let out a series of weird laughs and spoke in his alien dialect. The green-haired woman translated. "Nothing, Cap. Not a damn thing worth taking. Life support is shot, navigation's fried. Even the hull plating's too corroded to salvage."

"You lying bitch," Marek said, stepping closer and shoving his pistol against Valerie's stomach. "Where is it? Where's the cargo you promised?"

Valerie felt faint, her mind numb. This was just like old Detroit, when Valerie had been a skinny teenager. Weakness had always been a mistake in old Detroit. Despite her failure to gun them all down with the pulse rifle, some of her fight was returning. She needed to use that, and fast.

Valerie sneered at Marek. "Guess the market for gullible idiots is still booming."

Marek raised his pistol from her stomach, pressing the muzzle against Valerie's forehead. "Right now, you need to give me a reason why I shouldn't paint this pod with your brains."

The pistol meant nothing. Either Marek killed her or didn't. He wanted a reason, and the best one would be to play on greed. What would Maddox do here? He would lie, spinning a dandy of a tale. So...

"Dead women tell no tales," Valerie said, knowing it sounded lame even to her. What was wrong with her brain? Why was it so numb? Why did this feel like a B-grade holovid with cringe-inducing dialogue? "And I've got a story you'll want to hear," Valerie added.

For a moment, Valerie was certain Marek would pull the trigger. Then, slowly, a smile spread across his face. "Oh, you are a clever one, aren't you?" He stepped back. "Let's continue this conversation somewhere more... comfortable."

Churgol the cyborg glowered at Valerie, flexing his mechanical hand. He'd managed to climb to his feet after his fall. "I say we space her. Teach her a lesson about wasting our time."

Green-haired Liza snorted. "That's a waste of resources, you ask me. The girl's got spirit. Bet she'd fetch a pretty price in the flesh markets on Omega Nine."

"Enough," Marek said. He grabbed Valerie's chin and forced her to meet his gaze. "You've piqued my curiosity, Officer. But my patience has limits. You'll tell me everything: who you are, what you're doing out here, and what makes you think you're worth keeping alive."

Did these space hobos watch B-grade holovids and practice the lines in their spare time? Why didn't toad-like Kresh do or say anything?

Kresh had backed off and seemed to be watching everything and everyone. He noticed her studying him, and he twitched as if he didn't like that.

The sickly-sweet odor strengthened again, coming in a wave.

Valerie wrenched her chin out of Marek's grip, wanting to spit the sweet taste out of her mouth. She felt lightheaded. She needed food, real food.

"You listening to me?" Marek said.

Valerie had to think to recall what he'd said just before that. Oh, yeah. She allowed fear to creep into her expression. It wasn't hard. "I... I can't tell you here. The pod might be bugged. Patrol failsafes, you understand."

Marek's eyes narrowed. Then he nodded sharply. "Kresh, Liza—escort our guest to the brig. Churgol, strip this wreck. If there's so much as a spare bolt hidden away, I want to know about it."

As green-haired Liza and toad-fat Kresh pushed her out of the pod, through the boarding tube and then the ship corridors, Valerie tried to memorize corridors, access panels, any important details. She was finding it hard to walk for this long. She'd been weightless for at least a month. Her legs were trembling by the time they reached the brig.

It was little more than a storage closet with bars hastily welded across the entrance. Liza shoved Valerie inside, the door clanging shut behind her.

"Better start praying to whatever gods you believe in," Liza said through the bars. "Cap's not known for his mercy. Or his patience."

As their footsteps faded away, Valerie sagged against a bulkhead. Her body ached, fatigue seeping into her bones. But she couldn't afford to rest. Not yet.

Valerie forced herself to focus, to think and analyze what she'd witnessed.

Marek was in charge, it seemed, but his control didn't seem complete. Cyborg Churgol resented taking orders. Green-haired Liza struck Valerie as opportunistic. Kresh was hard to read. He was an unknown, a joker in the deck. He seemed to defer to Liza, but that could be false, a deception. There was something weird going on with the toad-fat man.

The ship creaked and groaned around Valerie, the sounds of her pod being torn apart drifting through the bulkheads.

Valerie closed her eyes, picturing the scavengers' growing frustration as they came up empty-handed.

Good. Let them stew in their anger. Angry people made mistakes.

Hours crawled by. Valerie dozed fitfully in the brig, always alert for approaching footsteps. Her parched throat burned, reminding her how long it had been since she'd had a drink of water that wasn't recycled swill.

Finally, the brig door swung open. Marek stood there, flanked by his mismatched crew. His earlier composure was gone, replaced by barely contained fury.

"Last chance," he said, leveling his pistol at Valerie's head. "What game are you playing? Where's the cargo you promised us?"

"There was never any cargo," Valerie said. "But I wasn't lying about having something valuable. I do. It's information about a threat that could wipe out every miserable rock and station in the Beyond."

"You have one minute," Marek said. "Make it count."

"Ever hear of the New Men?" Valerie asked. Why were they all talking this way, like bad holovid actors? Valerie found herself continuing despite her secret question. "Because the New Men are coming," she said theatrically. "And trust me, you don't want to be here when they arrive."

-11-

The *Bloodtooth's* mess hall reeked of stale sweat and rancid cooking oil. Valerie's stomach churned as Churgol shoved her into a chair bolted to the grimy deck plates. The cyborg stared at her with predatory intensity.

"Don't get any bright ideas," he said. "I'm still itching to space you for that stunt with the hydrospanner."

Once more, Valerie reached back across the years to her youth in Greater Detroit. She could hardly remember that time, and she remembered it all too well in another sense. Along with those memories was the idea that this ship was too much. She'd never seen or even heard of such a pigsty for a spaceship. The ambience seemed contrived or inhuman somehow. For some reason, that made Valerie think of Kresh.

He was in back, watching with his protruding eyes, his gaze shifting from person to person.

"Did you hear me?" Churgol snarled at her.

Valerie felt compelled to play along like a B-grade holovid actor. "Aw, did I hurt your feelings? Want me to kiss your little owie better?"

Churgol snarled, raising his fist.

"That's enough, cyborg. Stand down."

Valerie looked to the hatch. A burly man with a thick face strode in. He had obvious steroid-enhanced muscles and a crew cut, wearing a heavy jacket and boots. Where Marek exuded icy control, the newcomer radiated violence.

"Raven," Churgol said, stepping back from Valerie with obvious reluctance. "The captain said—"

"I know what the captain said," Raven interrupted. "And now I'm telling you to back off from the prisoner. Or do we have a problem?"

The two men stared at each other.

Is this really happening? Valerie thought. They were like junkyard dogs, seeing who was tougher or meaner, or had bigger balls.

After a long moment, Churgol looked away. "No problem," he muttered, turning and leaving the mess.

Raven watched the cyborg leave, a satisfied smirk playing at the corners of his mouth. Then his attention moved to Valerie.

"So," he said, circling her chair. "You're the Patrol bitch who led us on a wild goose chase. Gotta admit, you've got some brass."

Valerie kept her expression neutral. Did people really talk like that, or was it as odd as it felt to her? Why was this spaceship so filthy? Even cutthroats should know that a clean ship ran so much better than a junk heap like this.

Valerie realized they were all watching her. What had the new guy said? Oh, yes, that needed an answer. "Hey, just trying to stay alive. You know how it is out here in the void."

"Yeah, it's eat or be eaten." Raven leaned in, his breath hot on Valerie's ear. "And right now, you're looking mighty tasty."

Before Valerie could roll her eyes, the mess hall hatch hissed open. Marek swept in, followed by Liza.

"That's quite enough," Marek said. "I believe I made it clear our guest was not to be harmed. At least not yet."

Raven straightened, turning to face the captain. His face was a mask of deference, but Valerie caught a touch of hatred in his eyes.

"Just getting acquainted," Raven said. "No harm done."

Marek's lips thinned. "Indeed. Well, now that we're all here—"

"Churgol isn't," Valerie said. It was either say that or she would bray with laughter at their stilted banter.

Marek scowled at her. "Fine, no Churgol. We'll make do without him. Now, it's time for you to elaborate on your earlier claims."

He must mean the New Men. She'd been thinking about that, about what to say. This was thin, but it was something at least.

"The New Men are moving into this fringe area of the Beyond, once more expanding their territory in the direction of the Commonwealth. And trust me, they're trouble."

Liza snorted, toying with a wicked-looking knife. "Please. We've all heard the stories. The New Men ain't that bad when you get right down to it."

"Tell that to my crew," Valerie said. "The ones who aren't dead probably wish they were by now."

Marek leaned forward. "Explain."

Valerie launched into her story, weaving truth and lies. She told them about her Patrol scout responding to a distress call, walking into an ambush. About the New Men's tech and ruthless efficiency.

"They're not human," Valerie added. "Not anymore. Why do you think the Patrol is sending scouts out here? Star Watch is getting ready to send its fleet, to strike before it's too late."

"What do you mean?" Liza asked.

"In their quest for excellence," Valerie said, "the New Men have begun tampering with themselves, becoming more machines than men. And I don't mean some flash like Churgol, but deep cyborg. Worse still, they want to 'upgrade' or eliminate everyone they come across."

"How fascinating," Marek said as Valerie finished. "But that still doesn't explain why we shouldn't simply kill you and be on our way. The Beyond is vast, after all. Plenty of places to go before the New Men get here, if you're telling the truth."

"Do you really think you can outrun them?" Valerie asked. "The New Men have tech that makes your rust bucket look like a horse and buggy. And they're not going to stop until they've assimilated every human in the spiral arm."

For some reason, Kresh made a croaking sound, shifting uncomfortably. It seemed to Valerie that she was the only one who noticed what Kresh was doing. The others waited as if needing her to finish her data dump. It was almost as if they were actors in an invisible play or holovid scene.

Valerie worked to quell that feeling, as it was making her uneasy. What had she brought out of the void with her distress call?

Shifting down from that greater awareness, Valerie thrust herself back into her part. She leaned forward and said, "But I know the New Men's weaknesses, their blind spots. I have the kind of intel that could make the difference between surviving and ending up as spare parts in a New Man cyborg."

Silence fell over the mess hall.

Finally, Raven said, "Seems our little Patrol rat might be worth something after all."

"Perhaps," Marek said. "But the question remains—what to do with her in the meantime?"

"I still say we sell her," Liza said. "Flesh markets on Omega Nine are always looking for fresh meat. Especially someone with military training."

"Nah," Churgol said from his spot by the hatch. He had returned. "That's too risky. If she's telling the truth about the New Men, last thing we need is her blabbing to every lowlife in the quadrant about it."

Raven's eyes never left Valerie as he spoke. "Why not put her to work? An extra pair of hands never hurts. And if she tries anything funny…" He let the threat hang in the air.

Valerie glanced at Kresh in the back. His puffy face with bulging eyes held the same stiff look it always did. She wasn't sure she'd ever seen Kresh move his arms or use his hands. When Liza and he shoved her down the corridors, Liza had done all the shoving. It was the same with the body search. Why hadn't she noticed that earlier?

What did that mean for her survival? Even as Valerie considered it, the sickly-sweet odor returned. It had been gone for a while.

As Valerie inhaled, making a face at the smell, she decided that she was going to tear this crew apart from the inside out. And when the dust settled, she'd be the one left standing with the spaceship all to her lonesome.

-12-

After they all ate in the galley and moved to a cramped cargo hold, Captain Marek's cold eyes bored into Valerie.

"Strip," he commanded.

Valerie had been waiting for this to happen. It seemed like an obvious move within the greater play or drama. Her jaw clenched before she said, "You know what you can do with that order?"

Marek lunged and grabbed a fistful of her long hair, yanking her head back. "Let me make this clear, my dear. The only value you have is what I decide to assign you."

He released her with a shove and began to pace before them all. The rest of the crew watched from the shadows, seemingly a captive audience to their captain's cruelty.

"Now," Marek said, facing her, "you have three choices. One, I can sell you to the flesh markets on Omega Nine. I hear they're always looking for fresh meat with military training."

Valerie's stomach churned at the implication, but she kept her face impassive.

"Two," Marek held up two fingers, a mockery of civility, "you can work. Hard labor, long hours. No rest, no reprieve. Until your body gives out and we space what's left of you."

He leaned in close. "Or three… well, I'm sure the crew could use some entertainment. It's been a long time since we've had a whore aboard. Even one as disappointing as you."

Churgol leered openly. Liza's expression was a mix of disgust and humor—no ally there. Kresh was as inscrutable as ever.

But Raven... Valerie caught something in his eyes. Anger? Resentment? Not at her, she realized, but at Marek.

Valerie felt pressure to perform, to play her part in all this. She would do this far differently if it were her plan. She'd play low—

What had she just thought? If she would do this her way? That implied she was doing this as part of someone else's idea. The idea surprised her, although it shouldn't have. Kresh, this must have something to do with the weird man and his awful sickly-sweet stink. That odor only happened at times, and then in waves.

Was Kresh even human?

Valerie noticed that no one moved, but they all seemed to wait. Then that odor washed over her. It confirmed her suspicion that Kresh was the key to all this.

The idea drifted away as she considered Captain Marek's last words. They needed a response.

Valerie squared her shoulders as she concentrated on Marek. "And here I thought you were supposed to be some kind of mastermind."

"Careful, girl," Marek said.

"Why?" Valerie asked. "All this posturing, these threats... you're terrified of what I know. Of the intel I have on the New Men. Don't you realize this intelligence could make you rich? Or save your miserable hide when the New Men come knocking. But sure, go ahead. Throw it all away because your ego can't handle a woman who won't break."

Valerie held her breath, aware of how utterly stupid that sounded. Surely, they would all start laughing and mock her acting skills.

Then, unexpectedly, Marek did laugh, but not how Valerie expected.

"You've badly miscalculated," Marek said. "You see, I don't need you alive to get that information."

He produced a wicked-looking device from his coat—all gleaming needles and pulsing circuitry. "This little beauty can extract every last scrap of data from that pretty head of yours. It won't be pleasant, of course. Quite excruciating, in fact. But thorough."

Valerie felt faint and more than a little sick. Where had he found that? Would it really do what he said?

Valerie knew one thing: she couldn't show fear or give them anything. Wait—wasn't that two things? And wasn't there something else she should be considering? Valerie couldn't think of what, so she concentrated on the here and now.

"You're bluffing," she said. "That's alien tech. No way could a scavenger afford it."

Marek's smile widened. "You'd be surprised what one can acquire out here. Care to test your theory?"

He advanced on her, the extraction device humming to life. Valerie tensed, ready to fight even though she knew it was hopeless.

"Captain."

Marek paused, turning to his second-in-command with barely concealed irritation.

Burly, crew-cut Raven stepped forward.

"With all due respect, sir," Raven said, "using that device would be a waste. The girl clearly has valuable information that could be worth a fortune to the right buyers."

He gestured to Valerie. "Why not let her prove her worth? Put her to work, see what else she knows. If she's lying, well..." Raven's smile was all teeth. "There's always time for more aggressive methods later."

"And I suppose you'd volunteer to keep an eye on our guest?" Marek asked.

"Just looking out for the crew's best interests, Cap. You taught me that, remember?"

After a moment, Marek lowered the extraction device. "She's your responsibility then. If she steps out of line, you have my permission to deal with her as you see fit."

Marek turned back to Valerie. "You've earned a stay of execution. I do hope you make the most of it."

With that, Marek left the cargo hold.

Raven approached Valerie. "Looks like you and I are going to be spending some time together. Even so, you're still cargo as far as I'm concerned. Valuable cargo, perhaps, but cargo nonetheless."

"Noted," Valerie said, wincing inwardly. "So what now, boss?"

"Now you get to work. Hope you're not afraid of getting your hands dirty."

Valerie stared at him, looking for some hint that Raven knew this wasn't real, that something else was at play here. Was she the only person aboard the *Bloodtooth* that realized this was too contrived?

"You have a problem with that?" Raven said.

Valerie shook her head.

"Then go," he said. "It's time you earned your keep."

Oh, boy.

Valerie followed Raven out of the cargo hold.

She hated this smelly bucket of a ship, but that wasn't the issue. How much time did she have before everything turned sour? Captain Marek had given in to her, and that worried her, because it was obvious that Marek was smarter than the rest and was playing his own strange game.

No. It was Kresh playing the secret game. Was the toad-fat man using her? Valerie was sure of it, she just couldn't figure out how, or why, or if he was something other than human. She'd better figure that part out fast before she became a puppet like the rest of them.

Yes, Valerie realized. They're puppets playing a role. She had to figure out why if she was going to reach the Commonwealth and start the process that would save Keith, Riker and the rest of the *Kit Carson's* crew.

-13-

The *Bloodtooth's* engine room was a nightmare of jury-rigged systems and patchwork repairs. Valerie fought the urge to gag as the stench of burning coolant and ozone assaulted her nostrils.

This was the worst spaceship she'd ever seen or heard about. This wasn't human; it was inhuman. That meant Kresh was the real mastermind. There were no two ways about it.

Did that mean Liza was more important than she looked or acted?

Raven cleared his throat as if waiting for her attention to return to him.

Valerie complied. "How is this rust bucket still in the air?"

Raven shoved her forward, his hand rough on her shoulder. "Watch your mouth. She might not be pretty, but the *Bloodtooth* has gotten us out of more scrapes than you can count."

Valerie ducked under a sparking conduit, remembering that she had to play the part of a street tough officer with cringe-inducing lines. "I bet each scrape took years off her lifespan. This isn't a ship; it's a floating deathtrap."

Valerie ran her fingers along a corroded power coupling, wincing at the buildup of grime. "Your reactor's running at, what, sixty percent efficiency? Tops? It's a miracle you haven't gone nova yet."

Raven frowned. "How does a high and mighty Patrol officer know anything about starship engines?"

Valerie forced a tight smile. That seemed like a stupid question. "I've got hidden depths, all right? You want me to prove my worth? Let me take a crack at this mess."

Valerie gestured at the labyrinth of wires and pipes surrounding them. "Give me a week, and I'll have your systems running more smoothly than a Corellian pleasure cruiser. I might even coax a few extra light-years out of your fuel reserves."

Raven crossed his arms. He clearly enjoyed his part, maybe he even believed in it. "Why should we trust you anywhere near our engines? For all we know, you'll sabotage us and leave us drifting."

"Why would I be that stupid? I'd be stranded with you. I don't know how that helps me. Do you?"

For a long moment, the only sound was the labored whine of overtaxed machinery. Then Raven's lip curled in what might have been a smile.

"You've got three days. Impress me, and maybe the captain will reconsider spacing you. Screw up and…" He raised a suggestive eyebrow.

Valerie nodded, already cataloging the myriad issues plaguing the engine room. "I'm gonna need tools. And an assistant who knows his ass from a phase inverter."

"You'll get tools, all right. As for help…" Raven raised his voice, calling to someone in the corridor. "Sparks, get your scrawny hide in here."

No way. This couldn't be part of it.

Yes, a moment later, a kid who couldn't have been more than sixteen squeezed through the hatchway. He was all gangly limbs and wide eyes, a mop of unruly red hair falling into his face.

"Y-yes, sir?" the boy stammered.

"Meet your new boss," Raven said, jerking a thumb at Valerie. "You do whatever she says, got it? And if she tries anything funny…" Raven produced a wicked-looking shock prod, electricity crackling along its length. "You know what to do."

Valerie turned away, working at keeping her features neutral. She wanted to shock rod the burly Raven into something real, to say anything that didn't sound like a manufactured line.

Whatever the case, Raven left Valerie alone with her new "assistant."

She looked him over, deciding to continue playing along. When the time came, she was going to figure out Kresh or a way to deal with him.

"What's your name?"

"T-Toby," the boy said. "But everyone calls me Sparks."

"I'm sure they do," Valerie said, noting the burns on his hands—telltale signs of electrical work gone wrong. "First thing, I need a full diagnostic on the primary power couplings. Think you can handle that?"

He nodded.

"Then get going and bring me a scanner."

Sparks scurried off to retrieve a diagnostic scanner as ordered.

Over the next few hours, Valerie threw herself into the work. It was a welcome break from having to think. She rerouted power and tried optimizing systems that hadn't seen proper maintenance in what... years? All the while, she kept up a steady stream of chatter, probing Sparks for information, just as Kresh must have wanted her to do.

"So," Valerie said casually, elbow-deep in a tangle of coolant lines, "how long you been with the crew?"

Sparks shrugged. "Couple years. Captain Marek picked me up on Talos III. Said he needed someone small enough to squeeze into the maintenance shafts."

"Sounds like a real humanitarian. The captain treat you all right?"

The boy's hesitation said it all. "He... he ain't so bad, long as you do your job and stay out of his way."

"Uh-huh," Valerie said. "And the others? Raven, Churgol, all of them?"

"Raven's the best. He's always looking out for us little guys, you know? Not like the captain. Raven actually gives a damn."

As they worked, Valerie picked up on a hundred little details. The way certain systems had been cobbled together from mismatched parts. The jury-rigged safeties that were more for show than function. What was with that, anyway? And most intriguingly, a series of modifications that spoke of some serious firepower hidden beneath the *Bloodtooth's* ramshackle exterior.

"What's the story with those?" she asked, nodding at a cluster of heavily shielded conduits.

"Uh, just some extra power routing for the, uh, life support. Yeah."

Valerie raised an eyebrow. "I've seen grav-pulse cannon feeds that were less robust than that. What's the captain really hiding?"

"I... I can't say. Captain Marek would kill me if he knew I'd told anyone about the—"

Sparks clamped his mouth shut

Valerie got it. Whatever weapons the *Bloodtooth* was hiding were serious business.

A commotion in the corridor snapped Valerie out of her part. Footsteps accompanied Marek's cultured tones.

"—better be worth all this trouble, Raven. If she's wasted our time, I'll personally—"

The captain's voice cut off as he entered the engine room, taking in the scene before him. Valerie straightened, wiping coolant from her hands with a rag.

"Captain," she said, "perfect timing. I was just about to call you down to see the results."

"Yeah?"

"Why don't I show you?"

Valerie strode to the main control panel, keying in a series of commands. The ever-present whine of the engines shifted, dropping in pitch as systems realigned.

"There," Valerie said. "I've boosted your reactor efficiency by seventeen percent. Rerouted power to critical systems and optimized your fuel consumption. You should see a significant improvement in overall performance."

Marek eyed her, until, "Our little Patrol rat has some tricks up her sleeve after all. Perhaps we won't space you just yet."

Valerie met his gaze steadily. "I told you, Captain. I'm worth more to you alive than dead. And this?" She gestured to the humming machinery around them. "This is just the beginning."

"Fine," Marek said. "You've just bought yourself a few more hours. Use them wisely."

Valerie wanted to tell him that he had already said that. Shouldn't he think of something new to say? Maybe he couldn't do that.

Instead, she wondered if the best bet would be to find a weapon and shoot Kresh dead. Would Marek, Raven and the others still act like this? Valerie bet not. She also had a hunch that killing Kresh would be much harder than it appeared.

Still, she needed a real plan, as she wanted to leave this ship almost more than she'd wanted to leave the escape pod.

Was Kresh alien or human, and how could she find out?

-14-

Valerie worked on the environmental control panel. To the untrained eye, she was running a routine diagnostic. In reality, she was sowing the seeds of breakdowns so that later she'd have a chance at reaching the shuttle and escaping this lunatic asylum. That had become her go-to plan.

"How's it looking, boss?" Sparks asked.

Valerie forced a reassuring smile. "Great. I'm recalibrating the O2 scrubbers. Should have this deck breathing easier in no time."

What she didn't mention was the subroutine she'd buried deep in the life support code. A time bomb, ticking away silently. When it triggered, the *Bloodtooth's* atmosphere would slowly, imperceptibly, become harder to breathe and then impossible.

That would cause panic but give power to whoever had access to a breathing mask. That should give her the chance she needed, as she'd already stashed a breather for such an emergency.

As if on cue, raised voices echoed from the corridor outside. Valerie cocked her head, straining to listen.

"—don't give excuses," Marek said. "I want to know why we're burning through fuel reserves so fast. Is the Patrol rat doing this?"

"That's the first thing I checked," Raven said. "She had nothing to do with it."

"How do you know?"

"The numbers don't add up. I checked each of her repairs to see if it could be the cause. Never was. That means this isn't coming from her. She improved fuel efficiency, remember?"

"I don't care about that," Marek said. "Find out how this is happening and fix the problem. Or I'll find someone who can."

Footsteps retreated.

Valerie frowned, thinking back to yesterday. The same thing had happened then, the same sort of talk just outside the engine room, as if Marek wanted her to overhear what he said each time.

That reassured Valerie. It made her think that Kresh, the puppet-master, wasn't as clever as he could be.

Valerie rubbed her face. At times, it was hard to think on these two different levels. One part of her played the part of a sly Patrol officer trying to turn the pirate crew against each other while she committed latent acts of sabotage. The other was Lieutenant Commander Valerie Noonan, a Maddox-taught officer trained to deal with the trickiest aliens the universe possessed, and coming out first.

The first level thinking won out for now.

The loss of fuel was definitely from her, Raven just hadn't known how to find the problem. Her "improvements" to the propulsion systems had included microscopic adjustments that compounded over time. The *Bloodtooth* was hemorrhaging fuel. Marek had just said as much. That he would say so at the same place he'd done something similar yesterday...

It seemed rude because it was such a clumsy maneuver.

Here was the real problem for her. If Marek knew she'd done that and said as much so she could hear, why pretend to hide it from her? Could he be playing a game within the scavenger-idiot-crew season of a bad B-grade holovid? Valerie suddenly had the sick feeling that she was being played on both levels instead of the other way around. If that was true... she wasn't sure on the correct move.

For right now, she would continue what she'd been doing at the first level, and figure out the real game at the second, Kresh level. How would she go about doing that, though?

Raven walked into the engine room. That meant a first level play, as this was her turn after hearing that exchange a moment ago.

"Trouble in paradise?" Valerie asked.

Raven looked up at her. "Watch it, Patrol. You're still proving yourself to me."

"Just trying to be helpful. Sounds like you've got yourself a real head-banger."

Raven ran a hand over his crew cut as he eyed her more closely. "Ship's burning too much juice, and I can't figure out why."

"Want me to take a look?"

Raven ran his hand over his crew cut again, maybe chewing the offer over. Finally, he said, "Sure. Why not?"

Valerie moved toward the labyrinth of pipes and wiring that passed for the *Bloodtooth's* heart.

As she worked, Valerie said, "The captain seemed pretty wound up. He always ride you like that?"

Raven snorted, leaning against a nearby bulkhead. "Guy's got a stick up his ass the size of a cruiser. Thinks he's too good for the likes of us. But out here?" Raven gestured to the endless void visible through a nearby viewport. "Out here, we're all the same. Scum just trying to survive."

Valerie eyed the burly second-in-command. That one word, scum, struck her as wrong. Was that a signal of sorts? Did it imply that some of the real Raven still existed inside the façade of the tough guy?

He was staring at her. Oh. It was her turn to speak her bad lines.

"Uh... must be hard, being second fiddle to a guy like that."

Raven blinked several times, and he rubbed his crew cut. He seemed agitated, but in a different way than usual. He opened his mouth to speak and closed it. Finally, his features hardened, and he almost seemed surprised.

"Really?" he asked. "You think that's going to work on me? You think we're all that stupid you can play us against each other?"

Valerie shrugged as if indifferent to the accusation. Inside, she was stunned. What had just changed? The word scum must be the key to figuring out the sudden shift in Raven. Could the real man be breaking through the tough-guy conditioning?

Before Raven could add more, alarms blared throughout the ship. There was a click. Then red emergency lighting bathed the engine room in an eerie glow.

Raven lunged at her and grabbed her arm. "If this is your doing, Patrol, you're finished."

The funny thing was it actually wasn't, unless she had miscalculated somewhere or pushed a system too far. The other possibility was that Kresh had decided to introduce a new element. Or could Marek have done that?

"No," she told Raven. "Let me fix this."

He released her arm.

As Valerie reached the environmental controls, Marek burst into the engine room. He didn't seem as dapper as usual, his eyes wild.

"Report," Marek said, rounding on Raven.

The second-in-command pushed Valerie out of the way and manipulated the control panel. He swore under his breath and tapped more. Then he looked up. "O2 levels are fluctuating across all decks."

Valerie frowned. Maybe she *was* the culprit and didn't know the ship systems as well as she thought she did. Maybe whatever Kresh did had affected her thinking more than she realized.

Churgol shouldered his way forward.

Valerie was surprised to see more crewmembers than before. They had converged here, too. Where had the extras come from? Did the ship have more personnel than she'd surmised? Why hadn't she seen them until now?

The cyborg scanned the readouts and faced Marek. "Life support is failing. We have six hours of breathable air left."

Valerie was more confused than ever, until she noticed the stink, the telltale odor.

At the back of the crowd, noticeable by her green hair, Liza stood by Kresh. His eyes protruded more than usual and it almost seemed as if his neck skin rippled.

Valerie clenched her teeth so her gag reaction wasn't obvious. Had she really seen that? Did that mean an alien parasite was controlling him? That made a sort of sense. *Victory* had faced such aliens before. Valerie felt exposed, being in the presence of a manipulating alien. She had to escape from here as soon as possible.

Marek shouldered through and glared at her.

It took Valerie a moment. He seemed to have waited while she became mentally organized.

"What did you do?" Marek shouted.

The smell, the damn smell hit her hard.

Worse, the compulsion to speak her lines was so strong that Valerie didn't fight it. "I've been busting my ass trying to keep this scrap heap flying. You really think I'd risk my own neck by messing with the air?"

Marek drew his gun. "Here's a deal, Patrol, and it's a good one. Fix the air or I'll shoot you in the gut and let you bleed out while I watch."

Valerie swallowed. This threat felt different from the other times, and she couldn't figure out why. It took effort to put on a bold front while she tried to figure out what had changed.

Something in Marek's eyes warned her, or alerted her.

This time, Valerie fought the compulsion. Her head seemed to beat in time with her heart, although she asked, "Can I have help doing this?"

Marek sneered. "All the help you need, Patrol. Just get it done."

"Thanks," Valerie said. "I'll stabilize life support before we all suffocate. Sparks, you handle the environmental controls for now. You know how, right?"

Sparks nodded.

"Churgol, could you start rerouting power from non-essential systems. Raven, if you could check for hull breaches that would be great. Maybe it's a leak."

"You heard the Patrol rat," Marek said, as the others turned to him for confirmation. "Jump to it."

They did, and the clock began ticking, starting at this six-hour mark and counting down to who knew what.

The crew dispersed.

When Valerie looked up next, Liza and Kresh were gone. She thought about that, and she realized it was time to gamble, putting all her stakes on...

Marek or Raven, which of the two should she dare to confide in? Valerie looked around again, making her choice and resolutely heading out of the control room.

-15-

Valerie's boots slid across corroded metal grating as she crept down a dimly lit corridor of the *Bloodtooth*. The stench of rust and decay hung in the air, with a hint of that sickeningly sweet odor that seemed to permeate this sty of a ship.

She'd slipped away from the engine room and followed Marek from a distance. The others must have been too preoccupied with their tasks to notice she was gone. She hoped it would last long enough for her to do this.

For her own sake, Valerie knew she should be fixing the air problem, but had decided it was time to leave the *Bloodtooth* no matter what.

First, she had to gamble, because she needed help to do this. Marek seemed like the only possibility and this the best time.

Soon, Valerie paused at the threshold of Captain Marek's quarters, her hand hovering over the access panel. Clearly, Kresh was the puppet-master. The odor had to be the key to his control. That likely implied pheromones—her conclusion after some deep pondering while following Marek. Pheromones were known to affect others in all kinds of ways, often sexual, but that wasn't the only manner.

With the six-hour countdown in progress, Valerie knew she didn't have time to unravel the mystery slowly. That had led to the gamble and choice, as Marek seemed to be resisting Kresh's control just a little.

If Valerie were wrong about this, she would likely have to kill Marek, if she could.

Maybe knocking would be better, but Valerie wanted to push this. She punched in the override code she'd gleaned from the ship's systems earlier.

The hatch hissed open, revealing a spartan room barely larger than a storage closet. Captain Marek loomed in the shadows as he spun around and drew his gun.

"The hell you want, engine monkey? Think you're going to assassinate me in my sleep?" Marek raised his gun.

"Captain, wait, we need to talk. This is about Kresh. About what's happening or happened to the crew. Their behavior isn't natural and I know you know that. We both know that time has also run out for us."

"Nice try, engine monkey."

"Look," Valerie said, her words tumbling out, "I've been busting my butt fixing this rust bucket for days now. You've seen what I can do. I'm no spy or saboteur. But something is freaky wrong here, and you know it. Is Kresh an alien?"

Marek showed surprise and struggled for a moment to speak. Then, "Why do you say that?"

"Are you kidding me? Kresh expels a sickly-sweet odor. That's bleeding obvious, yet no one ever says anything about it. And your crew talks and acts like bad holovid tough guys. You know I'm right. I've seen you fight the compulsion, or I think I have. Can't we work together to save our damn hides before it's too late?"

Marek blinked repeatedly. He bit his lower lip and shook his head, cursing under his breath until, "…close the hatch, engine monkey."

Valerie complied, her hands shaking as she sealed them in. The cramped quarters felt even smaller now.

With a sudden move, Marek holstered his fancy pistol in a holster rig underneath his spiffy jacket.

"You must be the only one not completely under Kresh's thrall," Valerie said, feeling limp because she finally had an ally in this hellhole. "Please, Captain. I'm scared shitless and the ship is haywire. What the heck is going on?"

The silence stretched between them.

Once more, Marek seemed to be struggling with something. He began to pant and then shake his head. Finally, he moved to his cot, reached under his pillow and picked up a can with a plastic mouthpiece attached. He put the plastic around his mouth and pressed a button so the can hissed. He inhaled deeply several times before putting the can back under his pillow.

"You're right," Marek said, as he rubbed his forehead. "It started a little more than a year ago."

"What did?"

He looked up at her. "You want to know what's going on. I'm telling you."

"Oh. Right," Valerie said, nodding.

"I've wanted to tell someone this for so long now," Marek said. "I lose my train of thought when the smell hits me." He shuddered with revulsion.

After that, he stood there, staring until he suddenly reached under the pillow again, repeating the inhaling. He kept the can in his hand this time and looked up at Valerie.

"...it was supposed to be a simple salvage op, no problem and possibly a good find. We found a derelict ship on some backwater rock, or that was what we first thought. The idea was to hit it, in and out to grab some easy credits." A bitter laugh escaped him. "I should have known better. Nothing's ever easy out here."

The ship had been there. It had landed in a jungle, probably burned its way in. That must have happened long ago, as vines nearly hid the vessel when they found it. Kresh and Liza had gone down to the planet in the shuttle. They reported that it must have been some kind of research vessel. There were Patrol markings everywhere and science chambers inside. Liza said the place was packed with alien tech they'd never seen before.

"That's when Liza screamed," Marek said. "I told them to get out of there, to abort. They could go back later with spacesuits, heavy weaponry and reinforcements. There wasn't any response."

"You just left them in there?" Valerie said.

"No," Marek said.

"What then?"

"I got a response team together. That was when we still had two shuttles. I guess we took too long. We landed near their shuttle and started for the science vessel. By then Kresh was helping a weak Liza. He said she screamed at a shadow and bumped her head hard, falling unconscious. That didn't explain why he hadn't answered our calls all the way down. They both looked normal enough, although Liza had a big bruise on her forehead that substantiated his tale."

"What about the alien tech? Is that where you got the mind probe?"

Marek nodded.

"Did you loot the supposed derelict?"

"No," Marek said. "I had a bad feeling about the vessel. I considered shooting both of them just to be safe."

"Liza and Kresh?"

Marek nodded. "I should have. I know that now. Kresh was different after that. He became quieter, and there was something hungry in his eyes. And that smell, sweet, but wrong. It started oozing out of his pores like he was rotting from the inside out. We all wanted to leave the planet, and we did."

Valerie shivered. She knew the smell came from Kresh, but hearing Marek confirm it made her stomach churn.

"What happened to Kresh?"

Marek shook his head.

"What planet was that?"

"What difference does that make now?" Marek asked. "We have to get away from the *Bloodtooth*. My mind hasn't been this clear for a long time. Having someone else strengthens my willpower. And this—" He raised the can, studied it, and took another whiff from it. "Are you with me?" he asked.

"I am," Valerie said. "First, tell me about Liza. She shadows Kresh's every move."

For the first time Valerie had known Marek, he looked guilty and troubled.

"Liza used to be my second-in-command. Smart. Tough. Loyal to a fault. Now?" Marek shook his head. "Now she's just an extension of Kresh. Dyed her hair green and started following him around like a trained dog. She never leaves his side."

"What about the rest of the crew?"

"It was gradual at first. Little changes with us that led to more aggression and shorter tempers. Then it snowballed. We all started trying to out-do each other, like we were all competing for Kresh's attention. Acting like caricatures of tough guys from some bad holo-drama like you said."

"What about the ship?" Valerie asked. "The *Bloodtooth* wasn't always a pigsty like this, was it?"

Marek laughed harshly. "This used to be my pride. Now look at it. It's like whatever's got its hooks in Kresh is eating away at the ship too."

"Have you tried to stop him?" Valerie asked.

Marek's face darkened. "Every damn day. But it's like he's always one step ahead of me. Any plan I come up with, any ally I try to make… it all goes to shit. Sometimes I think the only reason I'm still breathing is because Kresh enjoys watching me squirm."

"So what do we do?" Valerie asked. "We're going to all suffocate to death unless we figure out how to fix live support."

Marek stared hard and slowly shook his head. "After all this time, I could only wish we'd die. Kresh likes the ship dirty, grimy and half-derelict. We've run through this emergency before. It's always a little different, but it ends the same. Kresh won't let the air system collapse. He seems to love tension and terror. Maybe whatever he's become feeds off it in some way."

"But—"

"Here's what we do," Marek said, interrupting. "We have to play along a little longer. I have a plan."

"What's your plan?"

"You have to trust me on this," Marek said.

It was Valerie's turn to stare at him. Maybe she should take a whiff from the can. "I have a different idea. We run for the shuttle and leave while we can."

"Sounds good but it won't work. The *Bloodtooth* would destroy us with a blast from its weapons. We have to kill Kresh first, but it has to be through indirect means. If you can get close enough to get a bead on him, you won't be able to fire. I'm working on the means."

Valerie was dubious. By his words, he'd been working on a way for months already and had always failed. She would have argued with him, but she needed to get back to the engine room before someone noticed she was gone. Then she remembered something.

"How come I've suddenly seen more crewmembers?" Valerie asked.

"That surprised me, too," Marek said. "I thought some of them were long dead. Maybe Kresh is playing more than one game. I don't know."

As she turned to leave, Marek's voice called her back. "Valerie."

She looked back, startled by the use of her name.

"Be careful," he said. "Whatever Kresh brought back from that ship… it's not finished spreading yet. I have a feeling things are about to get a whole lot worse once the air supply game is over. My plan has to work or… This is probably it for both of us, one way or another. I need you alive, so play it safe a little longer so I can try my gimmick."

"Yeah," Valerie said, before exiting his quarters. Marek had done a whole lot of talking but failed to take the plunge in the end. Maybe he was right about the *Bloodtooth*'s weapons shredding any escaping shuttle. Maybe she should risk it anyway. One thing was sure, she'd been right about this all being a game engineered by Kresh. What had Kresh found on the old Patrol ship? What planet had that been?

Valerie headed back for the engine room, thinking hard, wondering what Marek's secret plan really was.

-16-

Valerie crept through the *Bloodtooth's* corridors. Marek's warnings echoed in her mind, mixing with the constant hum of the ship's faltering systems.

A flicker of movement caught her eye, and Valerie froze, pressing against a corroded bulkhead.

Raven. The burly man stalked down the corridor, his face a mask of suspicion and barely contained rage.

Valerie wondered if Raven had seen her leaving Marek's quarters. She weighed her options: run and look guilty, or stand her ground and pray she could talk her way out of whatever he would do.

Before she could decide, Raven shouted her name.

Valerie straightened.

"Well, well," Raven said, his hand hovering near the blaster at his hip. "Is the Patrol rat scurrying back to her hole after conspiring with the captain?"

"What are you talking about? I found something on the environmental panel and came out here to double check it in person. I'm trying to save the—"

"Save it," Raven said, interrupting, closing the distance between them. "Marek is planning something. And now he's got you involved."

"You're paranoid and delusional."

"Am I? How about we go ask Kresh's opinion on this, hmm?"

That was the last thing Valerie wanted, and she didn't know how to sidestep this.

"Get back to work, Raven," Marek said, stepping into view. "Or have you forgotten the emergency and how we're all trying to stay alive? Or do you want to suffocate to death?"

Raven turned around. "Well, if it isn't the traitor himself. Come to rescue your little co-conspirator?"

"There is no conspiracy," Marek said. "Get back to work fixing our ship before you do something you'll regret."

"The only thing I regret is not putting you down sooner," Raven shouted, with spit flying from his mouth. He drew the blaster, aiming it at Marek.

Marek's hand inched under his jacket, no doubt toward the shoulder rig holster.

Raven snarled, pulling the trigger. A bolt of energy sizzled past Marek's ear and left a smoking crater in the bulkhead behind him.

If Raven had been trying to frighten Marek, it worked. Marek dove for cover, drawing his pistol and returning fire as he rolled.

Valerie scrambled behind a jutting piece of machinery. She didn't want a stray shot hitting her.

"You're dead, Cap!" Raven roared, unleashing a barrage of shots that lit up the corridor. "You and your little bitch are going down."

Valerie's hand closed around a length of pipe that had come loose. It wasn't much, but it was something. She hefted it, trying to gauge the weight, when a bloodcurdling scream pierced the air.

A Raven loyalist joined the fray. Valerie caught a glimpse of him through the haze of blaster smoke.

"Valerie!" Marek shouted. "Behind you!"

She whirled around as a man lunged at her—a second loyalist—his vibroblade humming. Valerie jumped up and shifted, her flesh crawling at the nearness of the horrible, shivering blade thrusting past her. She swung the pipe, connecting with the side of the knifeman's head. The man crumpled to the deck, but another took his place.

They were trapped and outnumbered. Was this how she was going to die? Valerie gripped the pipe tighter. The fallen knifeman's vibroblade had slid too far away to grab easily.

Then Churgol joined the fight. The cyborg moved fast, firing with precision, cutting down several attackers.

Raven escaped down a side corridor while Marek shot at him and rushed to Valerie.

"We need to move!" Marek shouted.

They ran through the narrow corridors of the *Bloodtooth*, leaving Churgol behind. The ship groaned around them, shuddering. Valerie's lungs burned as she breathed in the compromised air. Marek was choking and coughing, although he managed to inhale from the can. How much air did the little can hold?

An explosion rocked the vessel, nearly throwing them down. More klaxons blared, warning of multiple system failures. Through smoke, Valerie caught a glimpse of Raven's face, contorted with rage and madness. He must have doubled around or been following them.

"You can't hide forever!" Raven shouted. "I'll hunt you down and feed you to Kresh piece by piece."

Marek fired at him.

Raven ducked away.

Valerie and Marek kept running and rounded a corner to find Churgol waiting for them, his metal arm burned off at the biceps with wires sprouting there. How had the cyborg gotten here, and who had done that to him? It had just happened.

"I recommend an immediate relocation to a secure area," Churgol said, seeming to ignore his lost arm.

Valerie cocked her head. He was speaking differently, more robotically. What did that imply? Was that the normal way he spoke?

"Change of plan," Marek said. "We head to the engine room. It's defensible, and we might be able to regain control of the ship from there. For sure, we can refresh the damn air. I can hardly breathe."

"Roger that," Valerie said, coughing.

Churgol seemed immune to the bad air, although he glanced several times at the stub of his mechanical arm. At least he seemed to realize he'd taken an injury.

As they hurried, Valerie wondered if Kresh, and maybe Marek, had miscalculated. This time, the *Bloodtooth* wouldn't survive the crisis, even if one of them had caused it. Could all of them have messed with certain systems, and this was a cascade event brought about by their combined actions?

That was a poor joke on her, if true.

Valerie panted, struggling to control her panic at not being able to breathe properly.

What had Kresh found on the research vessel? Did it matter right now? Valerie had to survive this if she was going to save Keith and Riker later. How, though, that was the question. The *Kit Carson* and the New Men seemed a long way off right now.

Then, more internal explosions shook the ship.

-17-

The *Bloodtooth* shuddered. Alarms shrieked from every direction, their blare mixing with the staccato of blaster fire and the screech of tearing metal.

Marek shoved Valerie forward as another explosion rocked the ship. A stray blaster bolt sizzled past.

They stumbled through the smoke-filled corridor, ducking under sparking cables and leaping over twisted debris. Churgol brought up the rear, his weapon providing cover fire.

"Life support is failing worse than ever," Valerie gasped, her throat raw and lungs aching. "We've got maybe an hour until—"

Her words were cut off as the deck lurched, nearly sending her sprawling. Marek grabbed an arm, steadying her.

Then a familiar vibration thrummed through the ship's hull, rising in pitch. Valerie's eyes widened as realization hit her.

"Someone has turned on the Laumer Drive," she said. "Could Kresh be planning to take us through a wormhole to another star system with the ship like this?"

"Could be," Marek said. "We're heading for a scavenger shop on Krantz. That's a desert planet. All it will take is another jump to get there."

"Do we race for the shuttle now then?" Valerie asked.

"No," Marek replied. "Like I said before, it's simple. If Kresh runs the *Bloodtooth*, he'll blow the shuttle to pieces. That means we have to kill him now, and that means we need to get to the bridge."

"You said the engine room before."

"Change of plans," Marek said.

Valerie shook her head. "You said if we saw him we couldn't kill him," Valerie said.

Marek stared intently. "Maybe if I only breathe from the can, I'll finally be able to do it."

Valerie gave him a dubious look.

"I know," Marek said. "Why haven't I tried that before? You're helping me by just being here. Your willpower has strengthened mine. It's making the difference."

Valerie hoped that wasn't a lie.

They rounded a corner and came face-to-face with three of Raven's loyalists. Time seemed to slow as Valerie locked eyes with the lead goon, a man with a face more scar tissue than skin.

Before anyone could react, the deck beneath the loyalists' feet exploded in a shower of sparks and twisted metal. They vanished into the inferno with terrified screams, leaving a gaping chasm in the corridor.

Valerie's stomach churned with guilt. She knew what had caused the explosion—her own sabotage—that was now unraveling at the worst possible moment, or maybe the best in this instance.

Marek stepped up and peered down into the smoldering pit. "Looks like Lady Luck's on our side for once."

If he only knew, Valerie thought. Aloud, she said, "We need to find another way around. That's a straight drop to the reactor core."

"Follow me," Churgol said. "I have an alternate route."

They raced through a maze of maintenance tunnels and access shafts, the ship's shuddering growing more intense. Valerie's lungs hurt, her muscles aching at oxygen deprivation, but she forced herself to keep moving. Her head hurt more with each passing moment, splotches clouding her vision.

Another explosion rocked the *Bloodtooth*, this one close enough to send them sprawling. As Valerie pushed herself up, she caught sight of a flickering status display on a nearby panel. Her blood ran cold.

"We've got bigger problems," she said, her voice hoarse. "The reactor's going critical. We've got maybe ten minutes before the *Bloodtooth* becomes a very expensive firework."

Marek's features hardened. "Then we'd better haul butt to the bridge and pray we can kill Kresh and fix things before that happens. It's the only chance that could work."

They redoubled their pace, ignoring the burning in their muscles and the ragged gasps of their breathing. The ship's torment seemed to intensify with each step—groaning metal, shattering bulkheads, the hiss of escaping atmosphere.

Finally, mercifully, they reached the bridge. Unfortunately, the reinforced hatch had been sealed shut, likely Kresh's doing it in an attempt to maintain control.

"Stand back," Churgol said. He produced a compact but potent-looking explosive charge.

"When did you start carrying that around?" Marek shouted.

Churgol allowed himself a rare grin as he set the explosive against the hatch, pressed a button and leapt back.

Valerie's eyes widened as she backed away fast. "Whoa, wait a second—"

The blast cut her off, and the concussive force slammed her against a bulkhead. When the smoke cleared, a jagged hole gaped where the hatch had been.

Valerie's head buzzed worse than ever, and the splotches clouding her vision made it harder to see. She groaned as she stood and stumbled onto the bridge with the others. Bodies lay strewn about. The air was thick with that sickly-sweet smell, stronger than before. Did that mean Kresh was here?

Valerie looked around, squinting due to the splotches in her vision.

Hunched over the navigation console was Raven. He whirled at their entrance.

"You're too late," he said. "Kresh is already—"

A blast from Marek's weapon cut him off mid-sentence, leaving a smoking hole where his chest had been. Raven crumpled without another word.

Valerie didn't hesitate. She pushed past Marek to reach the navigation controls. Once there, she assessed the damage and tried to figure out what Raven had been doing.

"Talk to me," Marek said, taking up a defensive position by the ruined hatch.

"We're locked on course for the Laumer Point, which is open because of the Laumer Drive. The bad news is that the reactor's about to blow."

Another violent tremor shook the bridge.

"Can you speed us up?" Marek asked.

"Not without overloading what's left of the systems. And if I do that…"

"We definitely won't make it to the Laumer Point then," Marek said. "Then, at best, we're stuck in a shuttle in this empty star system."

"Maybe not," Valerie said. "We might make it to the Laumer Point, but I'll have to divert power from life support to do it. We'll be running on emergency reserves by the time we jump."

"Meaning we could suffocate before we reach the other side or the shuttle," Marek said.

Valerie nodded. "It's that or we wait for the reactor to turn us all into molecules."

"Let's risk the Laumer Point," Marek said.

Valerie initiated the sequence. The ship's remaining systems groaned in protest as she pushed them far beyond their limits. The Laumer Point loomed directly ahead, a shimmering distortion in the fabric of space-time.

Would the ship or they last long enough to reach it? And if they did, what would happen once they were on the other side?

-18-

The dying ship entered the Laumer Point, using the wormhole and theoretically emerging on the other side.

Valerie soon shook off jump lag, realizing the *Bloodtooth* had survived the Laumer Point—barely. Warning klaxons blared, their urgent wails muffled by the ringing in her ears.

Valerie struggled to her feet. The bridge was a wreck, sparking consoles and twisted metal everywhere. Marek lay slumped against a nearby bulkhead. Churgol's normal eyelid fluttered, while the bionic one seemed wrecked.

Something was worse than before, though. The air was thicker. And that smell—

Valerie shuddered as a potent sickeningly sweet odor assaulted her nostrils, overpowering even the stench of destruction.

"Well, well," Liza purred from the ruined hatch. "It looks like we have more survivors than expected."

Toad-fat Kresh waddled onto the bridge. Liza followed close behind. The cloying scent grew stronger with their approach, seeming to ooze from Kresh's pores.

Behind them followed several others, including a dull-eyed Sparks.

Valerie's stomach churned as she watched the effect ripple through to the others and Churgol. Marek backed away across the bridge. When had he awakened, and how had the others missed him? Marek had been near the hatch. Solving that puzzle could wait for later.

One of the people behind Kresh let out an animal growl.

"Yes," Kresh said, turning to his group, his bulging eyes gleaming with an alien hunger.

Valerie had never heard anything but a few, low, alien words from Kresh. This was different. The voice didn't sound human, but off several degrees like a dog talking.

"Let it all out," Kresh told his people. "Show me what you're really made of."

Violence spread like wildfire as Churgol charged the others. In his rage, the cyborg forgot to use the gun in his flesh hand.

The keyed-up crewmembers seemed to have gone mad. They tore at each other just as much as some did Churgol. A few of those used knives. Blood splattered across consoles and bulkheads.

Kresh stood watching like a proud father.

Valerie blanched as she swore she saw something writhing beneath his neck skin, drinking in the mayhem.

"Marek," she said hoarsely. "We have to do something."

Marek wasn't listening. His precious can lay at his feet, possibly forgotten. Marek let out a primal roar as he charged Kresh. Why he didn't use his blaster made no sense.

"No!" Valerie shouted.

Kresh watched as Marek barreled toward him. At the last moment, Liza moved. The knife seemed to materialize in her hand, its wicked edge glinting in the flickering emergency lights. The arc was perfect, the slash deadly as arterial blood sprayed. A look of dumb surprise crossed Marek's face as his momentum carried him forward.

The captain crashed, his lifeblood pumping onto the filthy deck as he jerked and twitched.

Valerie breathed heavily, bile rising in her throat. That had been a lousy trick.

Kresh nodded as if agreeing with her. "That was beautiful," he whispered, "such delicious fear at the end. It was sublime."

The others who had been fighting, the few survivors, stopped and stared in dull horror at Kresh.

There was definitely something under Kresh's neck skin. Could it be an alien parasite? Valerie thought so. It controlled the human, and it seemed as if it fed off fear and violence.

Kresh—or the thing wearing his skin—turned to Valerie. "Such a clever girl," he whispered. "But did you really think your pathetic sabotage could stop me?"

Valerie stepped back from him.

With Liza behind him, Kresh approached Valerie.

She stepped back again, looking around for something. Then an idea formed. She moved toward the emergency override panel.

The thing wearing Kresh's face cocked its head, a look of amused curiosity crossing its features.

The wretched odor came in waves. It made Valerie faint-headed and then her heart hammered as a terrible fear filled her. Her vision was still blotchy. She took a deep breath, even though she inhaled more of that foul, sweet smell.

Valerie did the deep breathing as a calming mechanism. Maybe her years with Captain Maddox had taught her to act, even when terrified and under grim pressure.

Hardly able to see, Valerie turned to the panel and tapped in a series of commands.

Warning lights flashed immediately as the *Bloodtooth's* remaining systems kicked into overdrive. The deck plates vibrated beneath their feet as the reactor core began to overload.

"What have you done?" Kresh whispered.

"Isn't it obvious?" Valerie shouted, looking up in bitter triumph. "I'm taking you down with me, you alien bastard."

That did something to the remaining infected crew. They scrambled in mad panic, all semblance of self-control lost. Liza's knife flashed again and again, cutting down those who got too close to Kresh.

Valerie concentrated on the toad-fat man. She saw the fear in his stolen eyes, the dawning realization that his carefully laid plans were crumbling around him.

A second later, that vanished as Kresh laughed, as if he'd been playacting for her benefit. "Sorry, but that won't stop me. If nothing else, I'll find another ship, another crew. I'll spread across this miserable spiral arm and feast on the fear of billions. It will be glorious."

"Guess what?" Valerie said. "You won't do it today. It's all over for you, alien."

The reactor core breach klaxon blared, drowning out everything else. Valerie closed her eyes, bracing for the end.

That lengthened and lengthened as nothing happened. Then the alarm quieted.

"Do you think I'd let it end like that?" Kresh asked.

Valerie opened her eyes, and she noticed a sudden lack of klaxons. "What happened? Why isn't the reactor exploding?"

Kresh shook his head, raising a control unit. He pressed a button, and the horrible klaxons blared again. He pressed the control again, the alarms ceased.

"I love it when you people exhibit terror," Kresh whispered. "But I won't lose my ship because of that."

Valerie's shoulders slumped. She understood all too well. The alien thing was sadistic along with being horrible.

Now, what was going to happen?

-19-

Kresh gloated. Liza stood behind him, smiling dully. The few that remained swayed, blinking and panting, their mouths open.

It was now or never, wasn't it?

Valerie's muscles tightened and then she exploded into action, her boots pounding against the deck plates.

Liza snarled like a junkyard dog, slashing with her knife as Valerie passed by.

Valerie dodged the razor-sharp blade and raced past the dull-eyed survivors. Churgol made a half-hearted grab at her with his single hand.

"After her," Kresh said in his alien voice. "Bring her to me. Now."

The *Bloodtooth* groaned and shuddered. Emergency klaxons started up again,

Valerie's lungs burned as she pushed herself harder, faster, sprinting from the bridge and down a corridor. She glanced back. Churgol and one other gave chase. The cyborg didn't run as fast as before, the loss of his cybernetic arm no doubt throwing him off.

Valerie's throat was raw and her heart was hammering. Maybe the core breach had been faked, but the oxygen deprivation was all too real. So were some of the other pieces of sabotage she'd engineered earlier.

Valerie vaulted over a fallen bulkhead. She'd gained ground on the two pursuers and they were no longer visible. The shuttle bay was close. If she could just—

An explosion rocked the ship, the force of it slamming Valerie against a bulkhead. Pain exploded through her left shoulder, but she grunted and pushed on. There was no time for pain. No time for anything but survival, and that meant getting off this freak-show of a ship, no matter what Marek had said about that.

Although the reactor hadn't blown, the *Bloodtooth* was still coming apart, just more slowly. Valerie's earlier sabotage, combined with the strain of the jump, had triggered failures throughout the ship's systems.

Another tremor struck. This one was one violent enough to tear a gaping hole in the deck ahead. Valerie skidded to a stop as she stared down into the abyss of many broken decks below.

She looked back, but there was too much smoke to make out much. Valerie backed up, took off sprinting and launched herself over the hole. Her feet slammed onto solid deck plating on the other side. She stumbled, rolled, and came up running.

The shuttle bay hatch loomed ahead, mercifully still intact. Valerie skidded to a panting halt and punched in the emergency override code. She'd been memorizing a few critical items such as this these past few days.

For a moment, nothing happened. Then, with a groan of protesting metal, the hatch slid open.

Valerie didn't waste a second. She ducked under the still opening hatch and sprinted for the shuttle. The main hatch to the little vessel was open. She jumped up into the airlock, pressing the emergency lock.

The hatch slammed shut behind her.

Stumbling to the cockpit, sitting, activating systems, Valerie stared in horror through the view screen. Entire sections of the ship began to tear away.

"Come on, come on," she said, willing the shuttle's engines to fire faster.

They did. Valerie tapped the piloting board.

With a lurch, the shuttle broke free of its docking clamps. Air hissed out of the hangar bay and the outer hatch began opening. The hatch she'd come through had closed just in time.

As soon as she thought she could squeeze through, Valerie gunned the engines. The shuttle shot out of the bay into open space.

Valerie wasn't finished yet. She didn't want Kresh and Liza surviving or using the ship weapons to destroy the shuttle. The *Bloodtooth* was a wreck, but the alien thing in Kresh could yet survive, and she couldn't let that happen.

This was a scavengers' shuttle, right?

Valerie gripped the controls, studying them. The *Bloodtooth* loomed large in her rear view, a filthy, rusting hulk of a ship that had once felt invincible but now floated crippled and furious. Her hands moved across the console as she turned the shuttle to face the *Bloodtooth's* damaged hull.

To her left, a ship's main gun began to rotate and activate. If it did, she was finished.

Valerie thumbed the trigger, and the shuttle's twin cannons roared to life, spitting streams of high-velocity slugs into the fractured hull. The recoil shuddered through the shuttle, but Valerie's focus was on hammering through to the reactor. She knew the *Bloodtooth* was dangerous—its bulkheads might be a junk heap, but there was power beneath that decay.

Valerie checked the ship gun. It was aimed at the shuttle. If they could activate it, maybe seconds from now—

Valerie concentrated on firing, as it was the only thing she could control. The shuttle's guns tore chunks of metal plating from the ship's spine.

Each shot gouged deeper into the *Bloodtooth's* hull, ripping through bulkheads and setting off internal explosions. The sensors showed the chain reaction beginning—fires licking through the lower decks, and sudden bursts of escaping oxygen vented into space, shimmering in the cold void. The *Bloodtooth* shuddered, struggling to hold itself together as its guts hemorrhaged into the blackness.

Valerie refused to glance at the ship gun as the shuttle skirted dangerously close to the wreckage. She was determined to finish what she'd started.

She glanced at the ammo readout—one-third of her munitions already spent. The shuttle's cannons grew hot from the relentless fire, but she kept hammering the *Bloodtooth* where it was weakest, the decayed hull crumpling under the repeated assault.

For a second, her instincts kicked in: *back off, get out of range before it blows*. But she shoved those thoughts aside. Not yet. Not until she was certain the reactor was ready to blow.

The *Bloodtooth* began to falter. Structural beams snapped like brittle bones, and a series of explosions bloomed across its surface, bright and violent. The junk heap was hemorrhaging—Valerie could see entire sections of the ship disintegrating, flaking away into debris clouds. The reactor, exposed, flickered on her sensor panel. It was only a matter of time before the energy core went critical.

Then the *Bloodtooth* began to glow, a sinister light emanating from deep within its fractured hull. The reactor was failing, its protective layers collapsing, leaving the core unstable. The ship was dying, bleeding energy, venting atmosphere, and breaking apart in slow motion as the force of internal explosions pushed out in all directions.

Valerie pulled back on the controls, throttling up the engines. The shuttle turned and raced away from the imploding wreck. The engines screamed as the shuttle accelerated, but she didn't dare look back—only focusing on putting as much distance between herself and the *Bloodtooth* as possible. The blackness of space stretched ahead, but the orange glow of the dying ship filled the rear sensors, lighting up her console as it approached critical mass.

And then it happened—the *Bloodtooth* erupted in a violent burst of light and metal, the reactor going supercritical. Fragments of the ship blasted outward, fiery trails streaking through the void as the *Bloodtooth* died in a spectacular explosion. Valerie didn't even flinch as the shockwave rattled her shuttle.

She pushed the shuttle faster, leaving behind the wreckage of the *Bloodtooth*, knowing she had narrowly escaped destruction herself.

Valerie blinked. She could hardly believe it, but she had made it. She'd survived, and she was in a new star system.

A bitter laugh escaped her, quickly turning into a sob. Valerie slumped in the pilot's seat, overcome with emotion.

Eventually, she checked the control panel. The shuttle's systems were damaged, with its fuel reserves at around half. It was time to see if there was any habitable world here or a base, or something. Hadn't Marek said as much earlier?

She was alive, but for how long?

Valerie straightened and blew her nose and wiped her eyes. With a deep breath, she turned her attention to the shuttle's navigation controls. It was time to start hunting for her next step in reaching the Commonwealth so she could unleash Star Watch against the hateful New Men and save the *Kit Carson's* crew from their bitter fate.

-20-

Riker's muscles quivered as he swung the pick, each impact shocking his battered frame. The rock face before him stubbornly refused to yield, mocking his efforts. Sweat stung his eyes, mingling with the ever-present dust that caked his skin.

Weeks had crawled by in this hellhole, each day bleeding into the next in an endless cycle of backbreaking labor and soul-crushing despair. Riker felt it—a creeping malaise that sapped the strength from his bones and clouded his thoughts.

He glanced at Keith, barely recognizing the lieutenant. The guy was a shell of his former self, eyes wild, flinching at shadows.

"Keep it together," Riker whispered, leaning near the lieutenant. "Don't let the New Men break you."

Keith's only response was a whimper as a New Man strode past, a gleaming neuron whip in his right hand.

These new guards were something else—a fresh batch of supermen with chips on their shoulders the size of asteroids. The old ones had slunk off into space, replaced by these zealots who seemed immune to whatever was gnawing at everyone's spirits.

Riker's pick struck true, and a chunk of rock clattered to the ground. As he bent to toss it into a nearby cart, a familiar sensation crawled up his spine. The wrongness—

He'd felt it before, but couldn't quite place it. It was like trying to remember a nightmare that slipped away upon waking.

"Keep working," an overseer said.

Riker straightened, meeting the guard's gaze for just a moment. Then, he dropped his gaze and hunched his shoulders as if terrified.

The New Man grunted, moving on.

Riker glanced at the nearby prisoners from the *Kit Carson*. They were husks, shuffling through their tasks with dead eyes and slumped shoulders. Whatever was eating away at them had taken hold deep.

But not Riker. Oh, he felt the constant whisper urging him to give up, to lie down and let the darkness take him. But something in him pushed back, a stubborn ember of defiance that refused to be snuffed out.

His threadbare shirt hung loose on his frame, a result of endless weeks of meager rations and brutal labor. But still, he endured. Still, he fought.

"What the hell are you after?" Riker muttered, scanning the rock face for any clue. No precious metals glinted in the weak lamplight, no veins of valuable ore. Just endless, worthless stone and that persistent feeling of wrongness that never went away.

As he carried another load of debris, putting it into a cart, Riker wondered what was different about him. Why wasn't he succumbing like the others?

Riker paused as he stooped to grab a chunk of stone. Could that be why the other New Men had left? None of the original guards were down here, just the newcomers from the star cruiser. Did whatever was down here chip away at the New Men as well?

That was interesting if true.

"Hey," Keith whispered, fear etched across his gaunt face. "I can't do this anymore. The darkness, it's... it's alive. Can't you feel it?"

Riker grabbed Keith's shoulder, forcing the lieutenant to meet his gaze. "Listen to me. We're not dying in this hole.

Whatever's messing with your head, fight it—or you're never seeing Valerie again."

A flicker of the old Keith reappeared. Then it was gone, swallowed by the fear.

"Back to work," a guard said, energy from a neuron whip slicing near Riker's face.

As Riker returned to his task, he frowned with concentration. The wrongness seemed to pulse, growing stronger with each swing of his pick. It was familiar, clawing at the edges of his consciousness.

With his next strike, Riker felt a surge of... power? Malevolence? He wasn't sure.

The veil in his mind seemed to lift.

Before Riker could process it, commotion erupted near a deeper tunnel connection. New Men shouted, their usual composure shattered.

"Seal the lower levels," one shouted. "Nothing gets out. Nothing!"

New Men began herding prisoners toward the upper tunnels, their neuron whips sparking.

Riker stumbled with the others as he tried to piece together the puzzle. Whatever the New Men had been searching for, it seemed they'd found it or something. Judging by their reaction, it was bad news for everyone.

-21-

Valerie scanned the unfamiliar star system unfolding before her. A Mars-sized planet loomed in the far distance, its rusty surface pockmarked with impact craters. Swarms of asteroids drifted lazily around it, glinting in the light of the system's star.

The radio crackled to life with a burst of static. She listened for a time as people openly haggled over salvage rights and black market goods. Those messages came from around the desert planet and were hours old.

Valerie nodded. It was just as Marek had said. She'd found a haven for scavengers, pirates, and all manner of fringe elements. Just the sort of place where a woman with a stolen shuttle and a desperate need might find a way back to civilization.

She wondered what the right thing to do with the shuttle was. Selling it seemed like the best option. First, she needed to make it more presentable.

Valerie figured there was no time like the present. Work was the only thing that could keep her sane.

She started with the transponder, inputting a new set of codes she'd memorized years ago. It wouldn't fool a thorough scan, but it might be enough to get her planet side without raising too many eyebrows.

With that done, she turned her attention to the interior. The place was a mess: scorch marks on the bulkheads, bloodstains on the deck plates, and the stench of ozone and fear permeating every surface.

It was nothing a bit of elbow grease couldn't fix. In fact, she found cleaning supplies stashed in a nearby locker.

Valerie attacked the grime, scrubbing until her arms ached and her knuckles bled. The caustic smell of industrial-strength cleaner filled the air, burning her nostrils and making her eyes water. But she didn't stop. She couldn't afford to, both for selling reasons and to keep out the memories of what she'd just escaped.

She shuddered as a few remembrances slipped in. That had been a terribly narrow escape and days of nightmares. What kind of alien had controlled Kresh? She hoped it was the last of its kind. Unfortunately, there was that science vessel on a planet somewhere around here.

"No," she said. "I need to get back to work."

Hours passed as Valerie scoured every inch of the shuttle. Next, she repaired frayed wiring, patched up bullet holes, and meticulously erased every trace of the *Bloodtooth* and its ill-fated crew. Slowly but surely, the shuttle began to look less like a crime scene and more like a serviceable vessel.

As she worked, Valerie began to plan. She would sell the shuttle and use the credits to buy passage back to Commonwealth space. While simple enough in theory, she'd no doubt have to tread carefully. Out here, if they discovered she was a Patrol officer, they'd probably shoot her or sell her to a brothel.

This was a heck of a mess, she thought, yanking open a stuck storage compartment.

Her eyes widened as she took in the contents. A small cache of valuables glinted in the dim light—a handful of uncut gems, their facets rough but promising. Next to them lay a few data crystals, their sleek, military-grade casings glinting faintly.

Valerie wrapped each item in a scrap of cloth before tucking them away in a hidden compartment she'd rigged during her cleaning frenzy. The valuables probably weren't enough to buy her way home, but combined with the shuttle, they just might be enough to secure passage on a ship bound for Commonwealth space.

As Valerie continued her methodical cleaning, she crafted a cover story. She'd be Jessa, a down-on-her-luck salvage operator who'd stumbled across a derelict shuttle. Nothing too flashy, nothing that would draw undue attention. Just another piece of flotsam drifting through the fringe, looking for a fresh start.

Valerie practiced her new persona as she worked, muttering to herself in a gruff drawl that was very different from her usual official tones.

"Name's Jessa," she said, testing the weight of the lie on her tongue. "I found this bucket floating dead in space. Figured finder's keepers, y'know?"

Valerie badly needed sleep and finally felt as if she could. She retired and did sleep for a solid eleven hours, and without any nightmares of the *Bloodtooth*.

After a large breakfast, the hours blurred as Valerie continued with her tasks. She reprogrammed the nav computer, wiping its memory of any incriminating flight data. All the while, she listened to the radio chatter, building a mental map of the star system and its inhabitants.

Finally, days later, as her eyes burned with exhaustion, Valerie stepped back to survey her extended handiwork. The shuttle was far from pristine, but it looked... believable. Like the sort of cobbled-together wreck a desperate salvage operator might stake her hopes on.

"It'll have to do," she said, collapsing into the pilot's seat.

Valerie finally allowed herself a moment of reflection. How had it come to this? More than a month ago, she'd been Lieutenant Commander Valerie Noonan, survivor of underspace and a pocket universe. Now she was a fugitive, clinging to life in a stolen shuttle, with only her wits and a handful of ill-gotten goods standing between her and a cold death in the fringe Beyond.

Still, she'd survived the horrors of the *Bloodtooth*. She'd outwitted Kresh and his parasitic master. She'd do the same against those in this scavengers' paradise.

The shuttle carried Valerie toward an uncertain future and the hope of finding her way back home. It would still be a two-week journey to the desert planet, however.

She hoped Keith, Riker and the others were still alive. She hoped all this pain and suffering wasn't for nothing. They had been her crew, her responsibility. That meant she had to do whatever was necessary on the scavenger planet to mount a rescue for her people.

Valerie nodded, vowing to let nothing stand in her way.

-22-

The star designated RS-498 dominated Valerie's sensor readout, radiating an intense heat signature even at this distance. Classified as a K-type main-sequence star, it burned hotter and brighter than the red dwarfs with which she was more familiar, but not nearly as intensely as an A-class white star. This particular K-type star had entered a late stage in its life cycle, emitting massive bursts of radiation as it consumed the last of its hydrogen reserves.

Her instruments measured at approximately 5,200 Kelvin, slightly lower than Earth's Sun, but with a higher frequency of solar flares and coronal mass ejections. Each flare bombarded the system with waves of charged particles, generating a constant stream of heavy radiation. The radiation levels here were severe, far beyond what most standard shielding could handle for long-term exposure. She noted that the *Bloodtooth* likely had hull reinforcement against such exposure, but her shuttle would need to descend into the planet's atmosphere quickly to avoid prolonged exposure.

Through the narrow spectrum of her sensor feeds, Valerie observed that the star's luminosity was shifting slightly—an indicator of magnetic instability. This instability resulted in unpredictable stellar storms, which sent streams of plasma hurtling toward the Mars-like planet, scouring its surface with deadly radiation. Without an atmosphere thick enough to absorb or deflect the energy, the planet's surface would be irradiated on a daily basis.

Did that mean widespread mutations down there? How could scavengers survive on the surface?

Despite its relative size and distance, the star's gravitational pull dominated the system, and the Mars-like planet's irregular orbit suggested that the star's influence created constant tectonic stress below the surface.

Valerie made a mental note: no long-term outposts could survive here without significant infrastructure and shielding. The star was essentially a death sentence for anything caught unprotected in its direct line of fire.

As she glanced at the planetary radiation index spiking on her screen, she muttered, "Definitely a tough neighborhood."

The days merged, a week passed and then another. The shuttle drew close to the Mars-like planet and the dread star.

This close, the shuttle's radiation shielding barely dampened the star's fury. Sweat beaded on Valerie's brow as the temperature inside the shuttle climbed, despite the environmental controls struggling to keep pace.

"What a welcome," she said.

An hour later, she brought the shuttle into a steep descent toward the rust-colored orb below.

She'd been in communication with what passed for the authorities here. That was why no pirate or scavenger vessel had swooped in and captured her. It would be hard to attract customers here if the planetary authorities allowed that sort of mischief.

The locals called the planet Krantz. It was possible Marek had called it that as well. She couldn't remember.

As Valerie punched through the atmosphere, the planet's features came into sharper focus. Vast, wind-scoured deserts stretched as far as the eye could see, broken only by jagged mountain ranges and deep, shadowy canyons. Here and there, she spotted the telltale glint of mining operations—harvesting the precious crystals that made this rock worth a damn.

Valerie had shuddered when she first learned about the crystals. Riker would hate this planet.

Now the comm crackled to life. "Unidentified shuttle, state your business or prepare to be vaporized."

What was going on? She'd already told them before. Were the authorities trying to deceive her?

Valerie swallowed, slipping into her practiced drawl as she used the comm. "Easy there, trigger. Name's Jessa. Just looking to offload some goods and maybe find work."

For a few seconds, there was no reply. Had she laid it on too thick? What was the game here?

"Proceed to landing pad Delta-7. Any deviation from your assigned flight path will be met with a missile."

"Thanks for the warning," Valerie said. "I'll be a good girl, you can count on it."

Valerie considered the call. Maybe it had been a shift change, and the previous operator hadn't logged her earlier comm exchange. Was Krantz that screwed up? No, she doubted that.

Whatever the case, Valerie guided the shuttle toward a sprawling complex carved into the side of a massive mesa. As she drew closer, Valerie could make out the yawning mouths of hangar bays and the glint of defense turrets tracking her approach.

The landing was rougher than she'd have liked, the shuttle's abused landing struts groaning as they touched down on the scorching tarmac. Valerie took a deep breath, steeling herself for what came next.

She put on protective gear and goggles, checked her gun, knife, and the hidden valuables she carried. Then she popped the hatch.

A wave of superheated air slammed into her, carrying with it something uniquely alien. Even with the specially darkened goggles, Valerie squinted against the glare. She stepped out cautiously.

A burly figure in heavy gear approached, flanked by two imposing guards with pulse rifles. The leader's face was hidden behind a rebreather mask, same with the guards. But Valerie could feel the suspicion radiating off the men.

"Let's see your clearance," the burly man said, holding out a gloved hand.

Valerie passed over a forged ident chip.

The man slotted it into a battered datapad as he scanned the readout.

"Jessa, huh?" he said. "It says you're a freelance salvage operator. What brings you here?"

Valerie shrugged, affecting a nonchalance she didn't feel. "Heard there might be work. Figured I'd try my luck."

The man grunted, maybe grinning behind his rebreather. "The landing fee is five hundred credits. Pay up or leave."

Valerie bit back a curse. The fee was steeper than a different operator had told her before. No doubt the man was skimming. This was likely a con on their part. If she argued the fee that might arouse suspicion she didn't need. Valerie dug into her pocket, producing a handful of credit chits.

"Here," she said, dropping the chits into the man's outstretched palm.

He counted quickly, then nodded, handing her a blue chit. "Welcome to Krantz. Your shuttle's good for seventy-two hours. After that, we sell it for scrap."

A heavy truck already approached. It would haul her shuttle to an elevator so they could store it underground, out of the harsh sunlight.

Valerie nodded, already scanning for the nearest entrance to the underground city. The relentless sun beat down, making every second on the surface feel unbearable.

"Transport to the lower levels leaves in five," the man added, jerking a thumb toward a battered hover-tram. "Miss it, and you're on your own."

Valerie grabbed her meager pack and jogged toward the waiting transport, ignoring the curious glances from the other new arrivals. As she settled onto a seat, she caught snippets of conversation—tales of riches to be made in the crystal mines, whispered warnings about the savage tribes that roamed the wastelands.

With a lurch, the tram began its descent into the bowels of Krantz. The oppressive heat of the surface gave way to a damp coolness as they plunged deeper into the mesa. Valerie's eyes widened as the true scale of the underground city revealed itself.

Vast caverns stretched in every direction, their walls honeycombed with dwellings, shops, and cantinas. Holographic street signs flickered, advertising everything from black market cybernetics to "authentic" Terran cuisine. The air was thick with the mingled scents of alien spices and the tang of industrial runoff.

As the tram screeched to a halt at a bustling platform, Valerie took a deep breath. This was the moment she had been waiting for. She'd made it through the landing, but surviving in this cutthroat warren of scum and villainy would be another matter entirely.

She squared her shoulders, affecting the cocky swagger of her "Jessa" persona.

Valerie stepped off the tram and into the teeming underbelly of Krantz. The hunt for a way home began now.

-23-

Valerie shouldered her way through the crowded underground bazaar, the clamor of a hundred voices assaulting her ears. The air was thick with the smell of unwashed bodies and cheap synth-booze, making her eyes water and her nose twitch. It was nothing like the *Bloodtooth*, though. Not even close.

"Watch it, you," a burly miner snarled as she bumped against his stall.

"Piss off," Valerie snapped, not breaking stride.

She scanned the maze of shops and stalls, searching for something specific. She needed a reputable shuttle dealer, someone who wouldn't ask too many questions but also wouldn't try to rob her blind. In a place like this, that was a tall order.

Finally, she spotted it—a grimy sign bolted to a rusted bulkhead: "Junk Jim's Shuttle Yard." It wasn't exactly top-notch, but it would suffice.

Valerie pushed through the fake airlock, the hiss of supposed equalizing pressure acted as the "bell" announcing her arrival. The interior was cramped, filled with spare parts and holographic displays of various shuttles. Behind a cluttered desk sat a grizzled old man—Junk Jim himself, she presumed.

"What can I do for ya, sweetheart?" Jim said, his eyes narrowing as he sized her up.

Valerie slipped into her "Jessa" persona. "Looking to offload a shuttle," she said, slipping into a rough tone. "Mark IV Astro-Glide. Interested?"

"Astro-Glide, you say? Don't see many of those out here in the fringe. Where'd you get it?"

"Does it matter?" Valerie said.

The old man chuckled, a dry, rattling sound. "Suppose not. Let's have a look, shall we?"

The walk to the landing bay was tense for Valerie. She was acutely aware of the curious glances from other merchants and scavengers. She forced herself to project an air of casual confidence.

Jim spoke to a guard. The armed man let them into the underground complex.

As they approached her shuttle, Valerie's heart sank. Under the harsh lights of the subterranean garage, every dent and scorch mark seemed magnified, perhaps exaggerated by her need to sell it for as much as possible. She pressed on and keyed open the hatch with a flourish.

"Feast your eyes, Jim," she said, gesturing inside. "She may not look like much, but she performs when it matters."

The old man climbed inside, scanning every surface. Valerie could practically see the calculations behind his wrinkled forehead.

"Seen better days, hasn't she?" Jim said.

"Yeah, well, that's the beauty of it," Valerie countered. "Port Authority won't look twice at her. Perfect for discreet planet side runs, if you catch my drift."

What followed was the most grueling negotiation of Valerie's life. Every component, every system was scrutinized and found wanting. Jim drove a merciless bargain, and Valerie found herself giving ground inch by precious inch.

"Come on," she protested as Jim finally made his offer. "The nav computer alone is worth twice that."

The old man snorted. "Nav computer's shot to hell. I can smell the burned circuits from here."

Valerie winced internally. He wasn't wrong—she'd fried half the system covering her tracks.

"Fine," she said. "But the atmospheric thrusters are good as new. You won't find a smoother descent on any bucket in this system."

Jim snorted. He'd gone over the engines more carefully than anything else. In fact, he'd started there. "You need to sell, don't you?"

"No," Valerie said. "I'll go prospecting with it if you don't take it."

Jim's face split into a yellowed grin. "All right, girlie, whatever you say. Twelve thousand. That's my final offer, far more than I should."

It was a fraction of what the shuttle was worth, even in its current state. But it should be more than enough to get Valerie off this rock. She might even be able to avoid selling the uncut gems.

Valerie inhaled, trying to decide if she should haggle. In the end, she accepted.

The transaction was quick and painless. Valerie watched with a mixture of relief and regret as a small fortune in hard currency came into her possession. Jim was practically salivating as he ran his gnarled hands over the shuttle's controls.

"Pleasure doing business with you, Jessa," he said.

Valerie nodded and sauntered out of the shuttle, heading toward the exit of the underground garage.

Soon, she was on the tram, landing back in the crowded city. She'd done it. She'd pulled off the con and secured herself a stake.

Valerie fingered the unfamiliar weight of the credit chits in her pocket. It was time to find a hotel, eat, sleep, and get ready for the next step.

-24-

The next morning, Valerie nursed a glass of what passed for beer in this hellhole, her eyes scanning the dimly lit bar. The Rusty Airlock was a cut above the dive bars that littered the lower levels, but that wasn't saying much. At least here, the patrons were more likely to stab you in the back metaphorically than literally.

Two men caught her attention, both clearly ship captains looking to fill their passenger manifests. Valerie approached the first, a weasel-faced man with a too-wide smile, practically oozing dishonesty. She knew his type from her early days in the Detroit hood.

"I hear you're offering passage off this rock," Valerie said, sliding onto the stool next to him.

The man's eyes lit up. "Captain Zeke, at your service, sweetheart. I've got a sweet little ship that'll get you wherever you need to go, no questions asked."

"How much?" she asked.

"Ten thousand credits," he said.

"How far?"

"I'm heading to Obol III," he said.

"How many jumps is that?"

"Three."

"And you want ten thousand credits?"

He grinned, possibly believing her desperate.

"Maybe next time," Valerie said as she stood.

"You still be alive then?" he asked.

For some reason, that stung. "I'll take my chances instead of boarding with an organ thief."

Zeke's face darkened, but before he could retort, Valerie had already moved on to the second captain.

He was older, weather-beaten, with the look of someone who'd seen too much of the galaxy's darker side. He sat at a table, eating a plate of something green.

"I'm looking for passage to Commonwealth space," Valerie said, cutting straight to the chase as she stood there.

The old captain's eyes narrowed, assessing her. "Sit down."

Valerie pulled up a chair, sitting.

He shoveled the green stuff into his mouth, chewing. "I'm Captain Sufan. The *Stellar Winds* is leaving in two hours. I happen to have a berth or two left. We're a trader, but I take on a few passengers."

"Tell me more," Valerie said.

"Small passenger list," he said. "You'd be joining five others. Mixed bunch, but they all check out. Ship's not fancy, but she's sturdy and reliable."

Valerie nodded, weighing her options.

"How much?" she asked.

Sufan named a figure that made Valerie wince internally. But it was fair, considering he was going all the way to the Commonwealth.

"I'm in," she said, extending her hand. "Name's Jessa."

Two hours later, Valerie stood in one of the *Stellar Winds*' cramped cargo bays, her meager belongings lay at her feet. The ship was exactly what she'd expected—an aging workhorse held together by stubborn determination and creative engineering.

As the other passengers filed in, Valerie sized them up discreetly. A severe-looking woman in a lab coat strode in, her eyes darting around the bay with barely concealed disdain. A pair of twins followed, chattering excitedly in a language Valerie didn't recognize. Next came a flamboyantly dressed man who carried himself like nobility, his nose turned up at the ship's utilitarian interior.

The last to board was a small, wiry figure with more metal than flesh visible. His cybernetic eyes scanned the room, pausing briefly on each passenger before moving on.

"All aboard," Sufan's voice crackled over the intercom. "We'll be taking off in fifteen minutes. In the meantime, why don't you get acquainted? You'll be spending the next few weeks together, after all."

Valerie suppressed a groan. The last thing she wanted was to make small talk, but she knew better than to stand out by being the only antisocial one. She plastered on a neutral expression.

The woman in the lab coat spoke first, her voice clipped and professional. "Dr. Elara Venn, xenobiologist. I'm headed to a conference on Altair Prime."

The twins introduced themselves next. "I'm Zix," said one. "And I'm Zax," said the other. "We're traders," they finished in unison, grinning mischievously.

The nobleman cleared his throat dramatically. "Lord Aramis of House Valerius," he announced, as if expecting applause. When none came, he added, "I'm... ah... on a diplomatic mission."

Finally, the cyborg spoke, his voice a strange mix of organic and synthetic sounds. "Cletus," he said simply, offering no further explanation.

Valerie nodded to each in turn. "Jessa," she said, sticking to her cover. "Just looking for work in the Commonwealth."

As the group fell into awkward conversation, Valerie's Patrol-trained eye picked up on subtle details. Dr. Venn's hands shook slightly as she adjusted her coat, betraying a nervous tic. The twins kept glancing at a particular crate among their belongings. Lord Aramis's "diplomatic mission" was almost certainly a lie, given the way he flinched at a loud noise from the engine room.

And Cletus... Valerie couldn't shake the feeling that his cybernetic eyes were cataloging every detail of the ship and its occupants.

Before she could dwell on it further, Sufan's voice came over the intercom again. "Strap in, folks. Takeoff in two minutes. The purser will show you your cabins once we're in orbital space."

Valerie secured herself in one of the acceleration couches. She was on her way, another step closer to saving Keith, Riker, and the others. Would any of her fellow passengers complicate things for her?

The *Stellar Winds* shuddered as it lifted and soon broke atmosphere, Krantz's sun filling the viewports. Valerie's stomach lurched as artificial gravity kicked in, her body adjusting to the familiar sensation of spaceflight.

Hours passed in boredom and forced small talk. Valerie kept her responses vague and redirected questions whenever possible.

Finally, Sufan's voice crackled over the intercom once more. "We're approaching the Laumer Point. Brace for jump in three... two... one..."

Valerie felt the familiar disorientation of faster-than-light travel. When she raised her head later, the viewports showed an unfamiliar star field. They'd made the first of many jumps.

The only strange thing so far was that no purser had shown up to escort them to their cabins. Valerie dearly hoped Sufan wasn't a scam artist or worse.

In any case, she'd left Krantz. How long would it be until she reached the Commonwealth and a Star Watch outpost? Hopefully, Keith and the others could hold out until then.

-25-

Riker slumped against the rough-hewn logs of the prison barracks, his once-muscular frame now a gaunt shadow of its former self. The meager gruel before him made his stomach turn, but he forced it down, knowing he needed every scrap of strength.

Beside him, Keith huddled in the corner, a skeletal wreck barely recognizable as human. His eyes, once sharp, now darted about, no doubt seeing horrors invisible to all but him.

"Eat something," Riker said, shoving a bowl toward Keith. The lieutenant flinched as if struck, curling tighter into himself. After a moment, he drew the bowl of gruel to him, cupped some, and licked his fingers clean.

The stench of unwashed bodies and despair hung in the air. How many endless weeks had passed already? Riker had lost count; the cycle of grueling labor blurred into a wretched haze. Too many faces were missing now, claimed by the unforgiving depths or the indifference of their golden-skinned overlords.

As Riker choked down the last of his rations, he caught sight of the new batch of New Men. Their eyes gleamed with a fanatical zeal. Whatever was happening in the mines was coming to a head.

Exhaustion pulled at Riker's bones as he slumped onto his threadbare pallet. Sleep came quickly, but it brought no respite.

In his dreams, he was back on the jungle planet of the pocket universe. Golden-haired Emily smiled at him, her eyes sparkling with life and promise. But even as warmth bloomed in his chest, terror gripped him. Riker knew what came next.

The Saurian warrior materialized from the undergrowth, his scaled skin glistened in the alien sunlight. The spear arced through the air, swift and deadly.

"Emily!"

Riker's shout tore from his throat as the weapon found its mark. Her eyes widened in shock and pain, accusation burning in their depths as she collapsed to the ground.

Riker jolted awake, his heart hammering. Cold sweat plastered his rags as the echoes of the nightmare faded. But something lingered—a feeling, a memory that clawed at the edges of his consciousness.

Then it hit him. The wrongness that permeated the mines, the creeping dread that sapped the will of men and New Men alike. He'd felt it before in the pocket universe and aboard the *Columbus* when he'd found the little crystal.

"Shardkin," he whispered.

Could another of its kind be slumbering on this forsaken Earthlike moon?

Riker's eyes widened as the pieces began to fall into place. The Shardkin's influence radiated outward, a psychic miasma that dulled the senses and crushed the spirit. Every swing of the pick, every ton of worthless rock cleared away, brought them closer to awakening something that should never see the light of day.

Even as this realization dawned, Riker sensed there was more. Something vast and terrible lurked just beyond the veil of his understanding. He strained, trying to grasp the full extent of the danger they faced. It was more than just the Shardkin.

Images flashed through his mind—crystalline structures that defied Euclidean geometry, pulsing with energy. Voices that spoke in frequencies that made his bones vibrate and his sanity fray. And behind it all, a presence so alien, so utterly incomprehensible, that his mind recoiled from even the barest glimpse of it.

For the first time since their capture, a deep, primal terror gripped Riker's heart. This was not just a threat of death or enslavement. This was something more, something worse.

Riker glanced around the dim hall, taking in the broken forms of his fellow prisoners. They were ants scurrying at the feet of some slumbering giant.

"We're so screwed," Riker whispered.

As if in response, a low vibration thrummed through the ground. In the distance, alarms began to wail.

Something had changed. Something had awoken. The New Men might have tried to seal it away before, but that no longer mattered.

As Riker staggered to his feet, bracing himself, he knew that the true nightmare was only just beginning.

-26-

After three weeks of space travel, Valerie got one of her biggest breaks after enduring a rough patch. The voyage aboard the *Stellar Winds* had been less than excellent. There were no extra cabins for the passengers. That meant the six of them had spent the time together in the one cramped cargo hold. Lord Aramis had exited the hold once. He returned the next day with purple bruises and welts all over his face and body.

Shortly thereafter, Captain Sufan spoke over the intercom.

"I'm sorry, but you may stay in your part of the ship, and by 'may,' I mean must. I have delicate business throughout the rest of the ship. I do not need you vagabonds marching hither and yon, trying to assess what sort of cargo I hold. The same treatment will be given to any of you who venture forth."

Valerie shouldered her way to the fore and picked up a microphone. "Okay, you're a pirate. Why not just go ahead and admit it already?"

The other passengers stared at her, startled. Until that day, Valerie had used her Jessa persona, which did not include such a clipped and precise Star Watch manner.

"Which one are you?" Sufan asked over the intercom.

"What does that matter?" Valerie said. "Are we your captives or not?"

"No..." Sufan replied shortly. "You're my passengers. I will bring you where I said I would, exactly as I said, at the price I have stated. I am meticulous in my statements and actions. Please do not interpret that as venality."

"You swear this?" Valerie asked.

"What would my swearing matter?" the captain replied. "I have said it. That is enough. Now, remain in your cabin. We will have our first stop in three days. It will be at an outer planet not belonging to the Commonwealth but near enough that if you do not like the strictures of the ship, you are welcome to leave."

"And will we receive a refund?" Valerie asked.

"Don't be ridiculous," Sufan said. "There will be no refunds. I have given my word and proceeded exactly as stated. Captain Sufan out."

A click told them he'd shut off the intercom.

The dialogue depressed them. The passengers fell silent afterward until the card games started anew.

Valerie had indulged earlier and lost all her uncut gems. She'd decided to forego more gambling and be bored rather than lose more. Luckily, she still had the data chips to sell if she needed more funds.

Soon, they reached the colony world, a planet filled with former cultists of the OCB determined to remain on their own. Valerie decided to stretch her legs and explore. Sufan met her at the exit to the ship.

"Your goods must stay here so that you will return," Sufan said, with two large guards behind him, watching her.

Valerie thought of all kinds of rejoinders. Instead of saying them, she departed; glad she had stuffed one of the data chips in a pocket.

She walked down the gangplank and spoke with a spaceport guard. It cost her one of the last credit chips she had to exit.

Upon leaving the spaceport, she went to a bank, then a pawnshop. There, she sold the data chip, her pockets bulged with low-value credit chits.

In the pawnshop, Valerie overheard a clerk talk about the Star Watch flotilla visiting the planet. Valerie's plans abruptly changed.

It proved an adventure, but not germane to the result. She finally reached a representative of Star Watch, who had a display in the lobby of a grand Franciscan Hotel. First, Valerie brushed off her garment as best she could, went to the restroom, and scrubbed her hands and face, shaking her head in the mirror at the poor state of her appearance. Then she went and, after a lengthy discussion, managed to convince the Star Watch rep to speak to the officer in charge.

He was a slender, dark-haired lieutenant whose eyes roved over Valerie.

That stung.

She straightened even more. "I'm Lieutenant Commander Valerie Noonan. I commanded the Patrol Scout *Kit Carson* on a survey mission into the Beyond. I have only now returned from there. My crew is in danger, as New Men captured them and the *Kit Carson*. I have also been assigned in the past with Captain Maddox of Starship *Victory*."

The lieutenant raised a dark eyebrow. He seemed to have heard of Captain Maddox, but then, who hadn't?

"You expect me to believe this cock-and-bull story?" he asked.

"No," Valerie said, "I expect you to check the records and see if such an officer as me exists and to have security check my veracity."

"You asked for it," the lieutenant said. "It will be unpleasant for you if you're lying."

"Don't worry about me," Valerie said. "Just do your duty."

She followed him into a room where Marines took charge of her. Soon, she sat at a console, speaking via comm to Commodore Rice of the *Alexander*. He led the flotilla. This was a show of strength in the outer regions, adding to Star Watch's prestige.

Rice had a wide, florid face and suspicious eyes. He asked a series of questions until Valerie asked, "Why is a commodore asking this, if I may be so bold, sir?"

"There are reasons," Rice said cryptically.

Valerie wondered if it was because she'd mentioned Maddox. Could Rice be a Humanity Ultimate sympathizer or practitioner?

"I believe enough of your story to have you brought up here," Rice said. "Do you find that objectionable, or do you consent to it?"

"Of course, I consent. I want to get back to the Commonwealth as fast as possible, and I want to report to the Lord High Admiral."

"Lord High Admiral Cook is dead."

"I know that. Lord High Admiral Haig—Excuse me," Valerie said. "I didn't mean to raise my voice. I have undergone a strenuous time. Do you happen to have a Builder Long-Range Communication device on your ship?"

Rice cleared his throat while shaking his head, glaring at Valerie.

Oh. She shouldn't have said that over the comm. Those of the planet, or others, would have been trying to break into the communication and monitor whatever they said.

"Now you will have to come up whether you object or not," Rice said.

"Fine," Valerie replied. "I just hope we can expedite the situation."

Over the comm, Rice called to one of the Marines. The sergeant came forward. Rice gave him precise instructions on what to do with Valerie.

She found herself under heavy escort, riding a ground vehicle to the spaceport, where she would board a shuttle to the *Alexander*.

-27-

"I will not use the Builder Comm device willy-nilly," Commodore Rice said. He was a larger man. His uniform was pressed and spotless, and his ready room on the *Alexander* vast compared to what Valerie was used to ever since starting the mission on the *Kit Carson*.

"I have a few more questions," Rice said.

"Please," Valerie said. She had showered before boarding the shuttle to the *Alexander*. The ride had been quick, escorted by strikefighters all the way up to the *Alexander*. There were three battleships in the flotilla—only one of them a *Conqueror*-class, while the other two were *Bismarck*-class. The flotilla included several auxiliary vessels. It was a small flotilla as such things went, but it represented serious firepower out here.

Rice asked more questions, which Valerie answered without hesitation.

"All right," Rice said. "I believe you. Come with me."

Valerie stood and easily matched his stride as they moved through pristine corridors. In time, they entered the Builder Long-Range Comm Device Room. This Builder Comm device looked exactly like the one on *Victory*: square, bulky, resting on a large coffee table. That's when Valerie knew who she would call first.

"Do you know how to operate it?" Rice asked.

"I do," Valerie said.

Rice stepped back.

Valerie went to the comm device, clicked the controls several times, adjusted three dials, and picked up the microphone.

"Galyan, Galyan, Driving Force Galyan. This is Lieutenant Commander Valerie Noonan. Do you hear me, Galyan?"

"Wait a minute," Rice said. "You're not supposed to call—"

"Valerie," Galyan's voice said over the Builder Comm device. "It is good to hear you. I heard you had gone away. You did not tell any of us where you were going."

Valerie cleared her throat and looked at Rice. "Galyan is the AI that controls *Victory*. Captain Maddox is likely on Earth."

"You should be calling the Lord High Admiral," Rice said.

"I plan to. I just need to relay a few facts to Galyan as quickly as possible. I will speak to the Lord High Admiral after this."

"Continue," Rice said gruffly. "I'll be listening."

Valerie nodded. "Galyan, I've lost the *Kit Carson*. New Men captured my crew as we came out of a Laumer Point."

"That is grim news, Valerie. Do you mean the rest of the crew is not with you?"

"That is what I mean."

"I have heard that Keith and Riker were with you. Is that true?"

"Yes," Valerie said.

"Then the New Men have them?" Galyan asked.

"Yes," Valerie said. "I don't know where the New Men have taken my crew, but here's where the *Kit Carson* was assaulted." She gave Galyan the coordinates. She'd never forgotten, having seen the data before racing off the *Kit Carson's* bridge.

"That is a long way from Earth," Galyan said. "However, that region is not in the area the New Men nominally control."

"I'm just giving you the facts," Valerie said. "I want you to know so you can pass it on to Captain Maddox. I will speak to the Lord High Admiral after this."

"Ah," Galyan said. "Maddox is on extended parole, you could say."

"I know. Commodore Rice is with me, and he has been nice enough to let me use this Builder Comm device."

"I see. I understand what you are saying, Valerie. I am using my personality profile—"

"Never mind that," Valerie interrupted. "This is critically important. Do you understand me?"

"I am beginning to perceive. Yes, thank you, Valerie. Is there anything else?"

"We need to act fast."

"Agreed," Galyan said. "I wish you Godspeed. That is the correct idiom, is it not, Valerie?"

"It is," Valerie said. "Goodbye, Galyan. It's been great hearing your voice."

"I too feel the same way about hearing yours," Galyan said.

Valerie slumped back in the chair, lowering the microphone.

"That was an unusual conversation," Rice said.

Valerie looked up. "I suppose it might have sounded that way to you."

"The Lord High Admiral," Rice said.

Valerie nodded and reset the Builder Comm device and called Star Watch headquarters in Geneva, Switzerland. This was the only communication system humanity had that could send messages faster than light. Otherwise, all messages went at the speed of courier vessels traveling from one star system to another, broadcasting the data.

Soon, Lord High Admiral Haig was on the Long-Range Builder Comm device.

"Lieutenant Commander Noonan, I am quite surprised to hear from you."

"Yes, Admiral, I have a grim tale to relate. Are you ready?"

"Yes, my secretary is nearby, and he will be taking notes."

"Thank you for telling me that, sir."

"No problem," Haig said.

Valerie launched into the account of what had happened ever since the *Kit Carson* used the hyper-spatial tube, entering the Beyond.

Haig did not interrupt but listened throughout the telling. He grunted twice, and Valerie noted that. He would have pressed the microphone button for her to hear that.

Finally, Valerie finished, including a brief thanks for Commodore Rice and his excellent security procedures, and for allowing her to use the device.

"Yes, yes," Haig said. "I'm sure Commodore Rice is a fine gentleman and a good officer. I'm glad you ran into him. What, then, Commander, are your suggestions?"

"We have to get our people back," Valerie said. "I believe it is telling that the *Cheng Ho* and the trader ship were near the huge gas giant and the Earthlike planet. Have you heard anything from the New Men regarding any of this?"

"I have not," Haig said.

Valerie hesitated and then plunged into it. "I suggest, sir, that Captain Maddox and *Victory* are the perfect team to investigate this."

"Who is in charge of Star Watch?" Haig asked after a moment. "Me or you?"

"You are, sir. That is only a suggestion as a Patrol officer."

"Your suggestion is noted. However, we shall keep Captain Maddox out of the loop for now."

Once again, Valerie hesitated, having anticipated that. It was the reason she'd called Galyan first. Someone had to tell Haig about that, and it would be better for her in the long run to do it herself.

"Sir," Valerie said, "I already informed Galyan about the situation, and he certainly will have informed Captain Maddox by now."

"That was unwise. I do not like that you contacted Maddox first. That suggests a questionable sense of loyalty to Star Watch."

"I thought Galyan could give me a few pointers."

"Do not lie to me, Commander. I do not care for it, nor do I appreciate anyone thinking that I am such a simpleton that they can offer me such blandishments."

"Yes, sir," Valerie said with a gulp. "I'm sorry."

"I doubt that is the case. You have just shown yourself as a true member of Captain Maddox's crew. In this instance, I shall not hold it against you. From what you've told me—and I don't believe you embellish—you acted swiftly and concisely, and even found an alien menace out there in the Beyond. It is one of the chief reasons we use Patrol officers such as you. No, I commend you in everything but trying to undercut my authority. And that, Commander, is a very serious offense."

"I understand, sir."

"I do not think you do," Haig said. "If you should repeat such actions, I will be forced to summarily drop you from the Patrol and Star Watch."

Valerie said nothing, aghast at such a thing. That seemed terribly unfair, but she held her tongue. She had learned to do that even more out here in the Beyond than before.

"I will have to deal with Maddox and this situation," Haig said. "From now on, you will leave policy to me, Commander."

"Yes, Admiral."

"We all make mistakes, but it's the prudent officer who doesn't make the same ones twice," Haig told her.

"I understand, sir."

"I dearly hope you do. You will stay with the *Alexander*. Is Commodore Rice there?"

"He is, sir."

"Let me speak with him."

Commodore Rice stepped up. After listening to the Lord High Admiral, Rice asked Valerie to step into the corridor while he finished the communication.

With slumped shoulders, Valerie did just that. Haig was no doubt a good officer; though he had some questionable ideas about those he considered mutants, freaks, and sports. She believed he had written that somewhere. She knew that the Lord High Admiral thought of Maddox and Meta as those.

Valerie leaned against the bulkhead, waiting. She was home, back in Star Watch, although she'd gained a black mark. She shook her head. What really mattered was she might be able to get Keith, Riker and the others back. Maybe even the crew of the *Cheng Ho* and the trader ship. The New Men—she disliked them more than ever. But she also knew that the best Star Watch officer for dealing with them was Captain Maddox.

In any case, for the time being, at least, it felt as if her part in this was over, as she'd done what she could for her crew.

-28-

Captain Maddox was at his ranch in Carson City, Nevada Sector when Galyan appeared before him. Meta was out shopping at Trader Joe's with Jewel, and so Galyan had Maddox all to himself. Maddox sat up, his eyes alight.

"Well?" Maddox said.

"Sir, do I have news for you," Galyan said.

Galyan gave an almost word-for-word account of what Valerie had told him. Maddox jumped up and was pacing before Galyan was finished.

"You know," Maddox said, "I've heard the New Men have a hunting preserve planet. The Earthlike moon around the massive, Jupiter-like gas giant seems like it could be such a place."

"That is a leap of logic," Galyan said.

"Possibly."

"What do you propose?"

"That's the question," Maddox said, scowling. "The Lord High Admiral wants to keep me stuck on Earth."

"I have not allowed him the use of *Victory*, sir, as per your request."

Maddox raised his hand. "Contact Ludendorff." He then gave Galyan a list of others to inform. "I'm off to Geneva to speak with the Lord High Admiral and have it out with him."

"What if he grounds you for good, sir?"

Maddox stared at Galyan, nodding shortly. "Then we do an extraction."

"Sir?" Galyan asked.

"You'll need to time it so Meta and Jewel can join me."

"We will become self-employed?" Galyan asked.

"Some of my people are in danger, captured by the New Men. For what she did, Valerie must be on the outs with the Lord High Admiral. I've had enough relaxation, enough hunting and lifting."

"Will we ever come back to Earth, sir?"

"You're getting ahead of yourself," Maddox said. "Still, the Supreme Intelligence on Library Planet could use us."

"That would be a shift in emphasis, would it not, sir?"

"It would," Maddox said. "That, though, is only a last resort. However," Maddox pointed at Galyan, "I'll give lip service to doing it Haig's way. At the end of the day, though, only one of us is going to get his way."

"And that will be you, sir?"

"It will." Maddox clapped his hands. "I'm off to Geneva. You'll tell Meta about this when she comes home. Don't scare Jewel, though."

"Jewel has never been frightened by my appearance before, sir."

Maddox stared at him.

"Still, I will do as you request. But Jewel—she has a lot of you in her, does she not, sir?"

"Don't bother with your personality profile now. We're in the midst of a crisis. I'm surprised we haven't heard from the New Men. They'll know who Keith and Riker are. Surely they'll try to use that against me."

"You believe the Emperor would allow such a thing?" Galyan asked.

"The Emperor," Maddox said, his eyes burning dangerously. He still practiced dueling. Maddox wanted a rematch against Trahey almost more than anything else.

Maddox swept a hand, putting the Emperor out of his mind. "You have your orders. Now get started."

"Sir," Galyan said, disappearing.

Maddox raced up the stairs into his bedroom. He threw a kit together, slid his monofilament blade in its boot sheath. Energy and vitality surged through him. He couldn't stand existence as a cashiered officer or a flunky in headquarters. He had to be doing, acting. That was part of his New Man heritage.

It was time to return to the captain's chair and lead his starship into action. This time it would be to rescue his people. Maddox's eyes narrowed. He would be facing the New Men. He nodded. They must know he was coming.

Maddox dashed down the stairs and burst outside, sprinting to the air car. Soon, he lifted off and headed for the Reno Spaceport.

-29-

Maddox reached Geneva Spaceport in a commercial jet, having paid a year's salary to get here fast. His air car could have done it, but it would have been too slow. Time was critical, as Haig no doubt tried to preempt him.

Maddox hurried to Star Watch headquarters and soon found himself in front of the Lord High Admiral's secretary.

"How did you get in here?" asked the secretary, a young man.

"I don't understand the question," Maddox said.

"Of course you must. Security—"

"Ah," Maddox said, interrupting. "You mean security wasn't supposed to let me into the building."

The secretary looked flustered as he shuffled items on his desk. The door opened, and Haig poked his head out. The diminutive Lord High Admiral stopped short.

"Captain Maddox," Haig said.

Maddox turned and kept his grin to himself. He could hear the surprise in Haig's voice.

Haig shot the secretary a glaring look. Maddox supposed the secretary's days were numbered in his position.

"Do come in, Captain," Haig said gruffly. "I've been expecting you."

"Yes, sir," Maddox said. He followed Haig into the office, closing the door behind him.

It was even more different from the days when Lord High Admiral Cook had been in charge. The desk was smaller. The wall photographs—each of them showed Lord High Admiral Haig shaking hands with different important personalities, both of them grinning at the camera. Cook had never indulged in that sort of thing.

Maddox shrugged inwardly. What did it matter? Haig was still Haig. Better to concentrate on reality than what he would like it to be.

"Well, Captain, how has your vacation been going?"

"Excellent," Maddox said.

"Oh," Haig said, sounding disappointed.

"You and I both know that's not why I'm here."

"Indeed," Haig said. "You wish for an assignment?"

"Exactly," Maddox said. "I wish to board *Victory*, leave this instant, and rescue my kidnapped crewmembers."

"This is in reference to the ill-conceived communication from Valerie to Galyan?"

"Yes," Maddox said.

Haig cleared his throat. "Captain, you're the wrong person to be sent out on a mission like this. This is a Patrol matter."

"I'm going to disagree with you," Maddox said. "*Victory* is the ultimate Patrol vessel. I am the ultimate Patrol officer. I don't say that in a braggadocious manner. You and I know it is the truth. On the most harrowing Patrol missions, Star Watch has always sent me."

"Lord High Admiral Cook did that, yes."

"Your predecessor did that often, and you have done it recently," Maddox said.

"Let me stop you there," Haig said. "I'm not sending you for several reasons. One, you're insubordinate and do not follow procedures."

"That's why they always send me. I cut straight to the matter. I don't indulge in bureaucratic nonsense."

Haig's features darkened. "Captain, you stick your foot in it every time you open your mouth. When I wonder whether I've done the right thing with you, listening to you makes me realize how arrogant, how presumptuous you are to think that you are the one who must go."

"I have an obligation to do so," Maddox said.

"Do not interrupt me when I am in the midst of a speech," Haig said.

Maddox nodded, anger rising in him. Who did this little prick think he was? Then a sense of humor came to Maddox's rescue. Certainly, Haig was wondering the same thing but in a different manner about him.

Maddox sat quietly and listened as Haig continued to speak.

"The key to all this," Haig finally said, "is that we don't want an incident with the New Men. The Commonwealth and Star Watch are still recovering from the assault by Leviathan. For all we know, Leviathan could be mounting more attacks in the near future. We do not want the New Men in the strategic rear of the Commonwealth if Leviathan is considering attacking us again. Can't you see that?"

"Yes," Maddox said. "That's one of the reasons you must send me."

"Oh, pray tell why?" Haig asked.

"The New Men have slapped our collective face. They have knowingly attacked two Patrol vessels. Not one, but two," Maddox said, holding up two fingers. "Therefore, we must strike back, as the New Men do not respond to conciliation. They respond to strength. We must show them strength. We must slap them down in turn."

"Is that what you suggest I do with you here?" Haig asked.

Maddox shook his head. "I'm not a New Man. Yes, I have some New Man genetics. But my perceptions and methods are different. I have proven my loyalty to Star Watch time and again. Sir, I ask that you allow me to go."

"Didn't you just hear my reasoning?"

"I did. And in one sense, it is correct. But only if you discount the psychology of the New Men. They are predatory and aggressive. One does not meet such aggression by throwing them meat. One comes on strong. You must come on strong."

"Then why not send several battleships?" Haig asked.

Maddox nodded. "That's another way to do it. If you don't send me, I suggest you do exactly that."

"In that case," Haig said, "I'll send a fleet in overpowering force."

"I can solve this with *Victory* in a subtle manner," Maddox said. "We don't want to overdo this and force the Emperor to respond to our response. Besides, our people might not be at that planet. Then it's an Intelligence matter. Then, I'm even more suited for the mission."

Haig blinked several times. "I'm still trying to wrap my head around the idea that you consider yourself subtle."

"I have been subtle, and I can be so again. First, I need to scout out the situation. If I'm correct—and Galyan affirmed my suspicion—most likely Valerie saw their game preserve planet. Therefore, if I go now, fast, and get it done, I—"

"Now you listen to me," Haig said, cutting Maddox off. "I'm running Star Watch along proper channels. I'm not interested in your exotic theories or methods. Do you understand me, sir?"

Maddox stared at Haig, finally saying, "I do."

"And will you obey me?"

Maddox thought hard about the question.

"Or do you wish to tender your resignation from Star Watch?" Haig asked.

"No, I don't want to do that," Maddox said. "I love Earth. I love Star Watch. And I want to continue to serve."

Haig narrowed his eyes at Maddox. "There is an or in your statement."

"No, sir, there is not," Maddox lied.

"I don't believe you," Haig said.

Maddox lurched to his feet, pressing his fingertips against the tabletop. "I do not care to unleash that or. It is a final action, and I do not care to take it. I have submitted to your authority, and I plan to continue to do so."

"Except in this," Haig said.

"I must rescue my people, or I'm not worthy of the title of Captain in Star Watch."

Haig sat back, tapping his index fingers against his chin. What was he calculating? Was he hoping, perhaps, that the New Men would take care of the situation for him? No, that was too grubby of a thought. Haig was not that sort of man.

Haig lurched forward and shot to his feet, staring at Maddox.

Maddox forced himself to look away. It galled him, but perhaps it was the right move.

"Very well," Haig said. "You may rescue your people, and one you owe me, Captain Maddox."

There were a slew of words on Maddox's tongue. Instead, he gave the crispest salute he had in many a time. He didn't feel it, but when necessary, Maddox could act—and he acted the part in the moment.

"Bring back your people and do what needs doing. But, sir," Haig pointed at him, "if you start a war with the New Men, you're going to lead the charge. And I'm going to put you in a position where you will either destroy the New Men or die trying. Do you understand?"

"Perfectly," Maddox said.

"Then go."

"Yes, sir."

Maddox spun on his heel and headed for the door. He was in the saddle again with an assignment. He couldn't help it, but as he strode past the sullen secretary, Maddox was smiling broadly.

-30-

Two and a half hours after speaking with Captain Maddox, the Lord High Admiral left headquarters for the links with several other officers. Haig found that golfing helped him maintain his equilibrium. He needed some kind of exercise, and this was an enjoyable time. He also happened to be a good golfer.

As he rode in his air car, he asked his adjutant who he was playing with today. There were a couple of names including General Mackinder. Haig made a face upon hearing that, although he did not say anything to the adjutant.

Haig didn't care for Mackinder as much these days since the debacle of losing a task force to the Sovereign Hierarchy of Leviathan. Mackinder, however, was a firm believer in Humanity Ultimate, the belief that regular humans needed to rid Star Watch of the mutants holding several key positions. Maddox was the primary member of that group.

Still, Haig didn't want to hear about it today. Mackinder might think Maddox had browbeaten him. That would make Haig angry, so he decided to say nothing about it to the General of Star Watch Intelligence.

Haig hadn't demoted Mackinder after the debacle with Leviathan. They had put the blame of that onto Admiral Jellicoe.

Later, Haig and the other two officers, along with Mackinder, were on the seventh hole. They had each drunk several bottles or glasses of their particular choice. Mackinder had consumed large bottles of Australian beer, while Haig had allowed himself several glasses of the best champagne the golf course possessed. One of the other officers mentioned that Maddox had stormed through headquarters earlier today. The officer believed Maddox had done so to speak with the Lord High Admiral.

Haig grunted as Mackinder turned to him, raising a thick eyebrow but made no further comment.

They continued playing, and soon enough were at the tenth hole. Mackinder finally managed to get Haig alone, when they both ended up in the same sand trap.

"Maddox, eh?" big Mackinder growled. He was a large, fat man, having gained weight since fighting the Sovereign Hierarchy of Leviathan. The time with the task force had left a mark on him, haunting him, perhaps, making him more determined to clean the "not-quite-humans" from Star Watch. That was how he termed people like Maddox and Meta, and no doubt would Jewel when she came of age.

Haig couldn't help it, or so he told himself, and found himself relating the incident to Mackinder. The glasses of champagne no doubt helped loosen his tongue. Besides, he was still angry for having allowed Maddox to browbeat him to the extent that the captain had.

For all his bulk and pushiness, Mackinder was a sly man, a keen judge of personality. He used raised eyebrows and surprised looks, dragging the entire incident from the Lord High Admiral.

Mackinder remained silent as Haig finished telling the story. The Intelligence Chief had a pensive look as he stared into the distance.

"The others are waiting for us," Haig said impatiently.

Neither Haig nor Mackinder had climbed down yet to ascertain if they could hit their balls out of the sand trap.

"Sir?" Mackinder asked, turning to Haig.

"Don't give me that," Haig said. "You believe I handled that wrong."

"That's not for me to say," Mackinder replied. "You know best in handling Maddox."

"I handled him the way I handled him. Now tell me, why do you think I did it wrong?"

Mackinder hesitated before saying, "My unease comes from my distrust of the half-breed. Maddox doesn't have Star Watch's best interest at heart."

"Even though Maddox saved your hide against the Sovereign Hierarchy of Leviathan?" Haig asked.

Mackinder's fleshy features went slack, although he nodded stiffly.

"Maddox's hide was on the line that day, too, sir, so he saved us to save himself. Now, all of a sudden, he's off to this location in the Beyond where New Men captured our scouts. That seems suspicious. I've heard there's a game preserve planet where New Men release our people and hunt them like animals. The New Men arrogantly prove to themselves how superior they are to us because they can kill our people with power rifles and high-velocity slugs while Star Watch officers starve in some alien jungle."

"I've heard a rumor of that myself," Haig said. "You believe such to be the case in this instance?"

"We did receive an intercept that suggests it." Mackinder related what Lord Hermes had messaged to Emperor Trahey of the Throne World.

"Do you think this star system could indeed be that place?" Haig asked.

"I find it quite possible," Mackinder said.

"Why didn't you tell me about this message earlier? It seems highly relevant to the Patrol vessels we send into that general area."

Mackinder cleared his throat, perhaps to buy himself a moment to think up a reason. "We're still running an analysis on it, sir. In another day or two, I would have alerted you."

Haig scowled. Maybe the General was too shifty and sly. He might have transferred Mackinder, but the man had many key backers. This was a touchy situation.

"Maddox seemed emphatic about saving his people," Haig said.

Mackinder snorted. "I imagine he left in order to hunt our people down like dogs with his New Men comrades. Perhaps this is the moment he's waited for, to finally throw off the mask and openly join his people, the New Men."

"Now, now," Haig said, "is that accurate? Maddox has done amazing feats, saving Star Watch time and again."

"Bah," Mackinder said. "I tell you, sir, I believe we should test Maddox in this. That's the safest course."

"Test him how?" Haig said.

The large, fat man scratched his cheek, and then his puffy eyes brightened. "Didn't Valerie Noonan escape from that star system?"

"She did."

"And has she not met up with a small Star Watch flotilla near the Beyond in that general area?"

"She has," Haig said.

Mackinder eyed the Lord High Admiral. Did the bottles of beer laced with whiskey cloud his judgment, or did he take a calculated risk in revealing what he knew?

The Intelligence Chief said, "Sir, I know the trade vessel *Stellar Winds* took several weeks to go from Krantz to our flotilla at Melome. It was an inefficient ship, having to use Laumer Points only. Perhaps Commodore Rice needs a test. He could take his flotilla at emergency speeds to this possible hunting preserve planet, using star-drive jumps to accelerate his timetable and reach the location fast."

Haig shook his head. "It would take Rice a week at least to get there. Maddox will arrive at the location in a few days, as he has permission to use the Builder Nexus."

"Perhaps you could stall Maddox."

"Now see here, General. Those are Star Watch captives at stake."

"Er, yes, yes, perhaps this Lieutenant Noonan—"

"Lieutenant Commander," Haig corrected.

"Thank you, sir. She would know a faster way. I've read more than one report of how Maddox has gone from one end of the spiral arm to another in a dramatically short time. She's his protégée. This is a moment to tap into her knowledge."

Haig nodded. "They're studying Maddox's unorthodox methods at some of our tactical schools."

"Precisely," Mackinder said. "So, if this Commodore could take those battleships and rush to the planet as fast as possible, he could surprise Maddox and the New Men. He could find out what is really going on."

"If Maddox is colluding, the New Men would ambush the flotilla."

"That's the beauty of this, sir. The Commodore has a direct link with his Builder Comm device on the *Alexander*. If anything untoward happens, he will send an immediate report. You then could send the fleet to the planet with a hyper-spatial tube."

"Hmm," Haig said. "That's not bad. You really think Maddox could be colluding with the New Man?"

"He is one himself," Mackinder said. "Don't they say that blood is thicker than water? Here will be the proof."

Haig frowned.

"Surely, Maddox's activities have been fronts until now," Mackinder said. "I tell you, sir, we can catch him in the act. Then finally, we can drop the mask. We can sweep these half-humans from Star Watch and maintain genetic purity. How else will Star Watch grow and expand unless we do this?"

Haig looked at his ball in the sand trap. He abruptly decided he had had enough golf for one day. He regarded Mackinder.

"You will tell the others that I am off to the office," Haig said.

"Yes, Admiral," Mackinder said.

Haig would use the Builder Comm device at headquarters. He would call Commodore Rice of the *Alexander* and give him new orders.

Haig rubbed his hands together and motioned for his adjutant to bring the golf cart around. Then he turned to Mackinder. "Thank you, sir. That is a splendid idea."

For the first time in months, Haig shook Mackinder's large hand. Then the two parted ways.

-31-

Sometime after the Lord High Admiral had called Commodore Rice on the *Alexander*, Valerie found herself shaken awake by a female Marine.

"Sir," the Marine said, "you're to come with me immediately to a meeting."

"What's this about?" Valerie asked groggily.

The Marine shook her head. "Get dressed. You have three minutes."

Valerie was exhausted, having dropped into real sleep only an hour ago. Now she sat up, got out of bed, and donned her new uniform. She brushed her long hair, put on a cap, and was buttoning her jacket as she hurried down the corridors, the Marine setting a stiff pace. Valerie found herself entering the conference chamber of the *Alexander*. There sat Commodore Rice, his XO, and several other officers.

"Have a seat, Commander," Rice said.

Valerie hurried to her indicated spot.

Rice cleared his throat. "Thank you for coming, all of you. I've just received new orders from the Lord High Admiral. This is an emergency and you," he pointed at Valerie, "are at the center of it. I need your help to figure out exactly how to do this."

"I don't understand," Valerie said.

"We're launching an immediate assault on the planet where the New Men captured your scout."

"What?" Valerie said.

"I have information that Captain Maddox will be heading there within days as he shakes out *Victory* and attempts a stealth mission via the Builder Nexus. We are going to hurry there as well."

For a moment, Commodore Rice looked down as if uncomfortable. Valerie realized that something untoward was afoot.

"May I ask, sir, why I am here again?"

Rice looked up. "You are a Patrol officer, understanding the Beyond better than any of us. More to the point, you have also worked with Captain Maddox. You are familiar with his unorthodox ways. We need to get to the planet in question as fast as possible."

Valerie sat back, thinking. "The fastest way would be to use the hyper-spatial tube, go to Earth, and then head to the enemy star system."

The *Alexander's* officers exchanged glances with each other and then fixed their gazes on Valerie.

Rice said. "That does seem like the fastest method, but the Lord High Admiral said nothing about it to me. He said we must go from here to there."

Valerie frowned. "It took the *Stellar Winds* three weeks to make that journey."

"Using Laumer Points only, I believe."

Valerie furrowed her brow, thinking. "Oh, I believe you're referring to Captain Maddox's method of using the star-drive jump to go from the most useful Laumer Point to another. That can cut down days, weeks, depending on the length of the journey. You're hoping to cut three weeks down to… How soon are we supposed to appear at the planet?"

Rice shifted uncomfortably, saying, "Soon after the Captain reaches it. He will be using the hyper-spatial tube after a small shakedown period, as I've said. So in four or five days from now at the most we must be there."

"You want to travel in five days what took the run-down *Stellar Winds* three weeks. I need to study the star charts of the region." Then Valerie decided to probe for the reason for this, as she was having some concerns. "We're reinforcing *Victory* against New Men in case several star cruisers are there?"

"Something of the sort," Rice said.

Valerie suddenly realized that wasn't the case at all, and Rice didn't want to admit it.

"Sir," she said, "you're asking for my help. Therefore, I need to know the exact situation."

"Do you?" Rice asked sharply. "You have your orders. Carry them out. It's as simple as that."

"I see," Valerie said. "Is Captain Maddox under suspicion? Is that what's happening?"

"What if it is?"

Valerie stared at Commodore Rice.

He squirmed just a little before blurting, "Tell me, Commander, where does your allegiance lie? To Star Watch or to Captain Maddox?"

"I'm a Star Watch officer," Valerie said. "That doesn't mean I'll sell my friends down the road."

"And if they're traitors?" Rice asked. "What then? Will you stick with the traitor against Star Watch?"

Valerie stiffened. "I know Captain Maddox is always under suspicion. I've seen his half-New Man ways and the arrogance he sometimes shows toward others. Yet, no officer in Star Watch has fought harder and more successfully. If you want my opinion, sir—"

"I do not," Rice said, interrupting.

Valerie had likely gained more stubbornness than she realized while under Maddox's tutelage, and possibly from facing her own harrowing situations. This stubbornness now rose to the surface.

"The truth, sir," she said, "is that you should all be on your knees kissing Maddox's feet for what he has done for humanity. Frankly, I believe it is an outrage that we're trying to entrap him. He'll be doing everything he can to free the *Kit Carson* crew and the others who the New Men have captured."

"Are you quite through?" Rice said frostily.

Color rose in Valerie's cheeks. She looked down and then back up. "I know, sir, I ought to be contrite. I ought to ask your pardon. But this insidious belief that Maddox is doing underhanded things is shocking and undeserved. I have served with him closely. I've learned from him, and I've seen him risk his life time and time again for others."

"He also uses unorthodox methods," Rice said, "sometimes disobeying commands."

"I know. I've been there. I've seen it. Yet nearly every time he disobeyed a command, it turned out to be the right thing to do. I could only wish I was half the officer he is."

"I see," Rice said. "And you wish to have that little speech recorded?"

Valerie looked at each of the officers in turn. She knew the best thing was to recant and say she was fatigued and didn't know what she was saying. But after all these years... Maddox was as much family as Meta, Galyan, Riker, Keith, even crusty old and sometimes untrustworthy Ludendorff.

"I not only agree to having that put in the minutes of the meeting," Valerie said, "I quite frankly demand it because I want everyone to know exactly where I stood. Others may believe Maddox will do something underhanded against Star Watch. I don't, and I stake my reputation on it."

Rice nodded curtly. "Will you do your duty as instructed and help us reach the planet as fast as possible?"

"I will," Valerie said. "I just hope we don't arrive at the wrong moment and make everything worse."

"How could that happen?"

Valerie shook her head. "I don't know. However, I do know that you helped me in my time of need. You listened to, believed me and let me make the long-range calls. I appreciate that, sir. But I will also warn you. You helped me, and possibly Captain Maddox because of that. You may be as much on the hook as I am in regard to his trustworthiness."

Commodore Rice stiffened, stared at her, glared, and then looked away as his features colored.

"I will do what I am supposed to do," Rice said, looking up. "You have made your point." He chewed on his lower lip, then shook his head. "No, I will say no more. We will put, as per your request, your words into the minutes. You will have your star charts. We're bringing everyone from Melome aboard. So, we'll be leaving in a few hours at most, hopefully sooner."

"Yes, sir," Valerie said. "I will follow orders exactly as they are given. I am an obedient officer of the Patrol and Star Watch, sir."

"Excellent," Rice said, some of his frostiness evaporating. "We're going to be working together, and under harsh conditions, as we make jump after jump. You may be the only one who has undergone such strenuous travel."

"I'll talk to the medical people," Valerie said. "There are a few tricks of the trade to make that easier."

"Good. Any further questions, ladies and gentlemen?" Rice scanned his people.

There were no more forthcoming. Thus, Rice adjourned the meeting.

Valerie remained seated as the others left. She half-expected Galyan to appear. He did not, of course.

What had she been thinking? She'd opened her mouth and put her foot in it. She hoped she hadn't wrecked her career, but she believed what she had said. Hell, maybe their showing up would prove beneficial in some way. She didn't know how, but maybe it would be just in time to catch the New Men trying to pull a sneaky one.

Valerie sighed. She had a job to do, and if nothing else, she might help rescue her people. That was good, and that would make her adventures these past months worth it.

-32-

The close air in the tunnel made each ragged breathe a struggle. Riker's pick struck the rock face, the impact jarring his wasted frame. Beside him, Keith toiled weakly, his once-strong form now a skeletal mockery of itself.

"Keep swinging, you worthless premen." The New Man's voice cracked like a whip, cutting through the constant drumming of metal on stone. "Glory awaits those who serve."

Riker forced his spent muscles to comply, as the neuron whip in the guard's hand waited for any hint of defiance.

Hours bled away in the relentless labor, the darkness held at bay by the feeble glow of their helmet lamps. With each swing of the pick, Riker felt the wrongness grow stronger, a creeping sense that gnawed at his mind.

"You feel that?" Riker whispered.

Keith seldom responded and did not now. It was questionable if he even heard the words.

There were other sounds, though. As they chipped, strange whispers seemed to echo at the edge of hearing. They spoke blasphemies, Riker was sure of it.

Then the tunnel seemed to change, taking on odd angles and geometries. Riker's pick struck something that shattered, sending shivers down his spine.

"We're close," a New Man said. "I can feel it. Swing faster you wretches."

Riker was already panting and sweating. He should turn back; flee from whatever lay ahead. But the neuron whip waited, leaving him no choice but to press on.

Then Riker's pick punched through rock to a void beyond. A gust of stale air rushed past, carrying a whisper of nameless things.

"We're through," Riker said hoarsely.

The others around him worked harder, swinging their picks to widen the breach. One prisoner screamed in a thin voice. The worker beside him missed his stroke, driving the pick though his foot.

The neuron whip crackled. The offender twisted in agony until the New Men ceased the torture.

"Work," the New Man said.

The trembling worker picked up his bloodied pick, panting, blinking like a fool.

Riker paused. It seemed that he was the only sane one down here. The growing madness around him ate at his weakening resolve.

The New Man's eyes gleamed as he shoved Riker forward.

"You, preman. You're the strongest one. Go through and see what this is."

Riker hesitated, terrified to do so.

"Obey me, preman."

Riker couldn't.

The neuron whip crackled again, lashing him.

With a cry of pain, Riker thrust himself through the rocky opening, crashing to the floor beyond.

He regained his footing in a chamber of undeterminable size. Riker's helmet lamp swept up and across—

The chamber was more a cavern. What he saw before him caused him to utter a croak of despair. Before him loomed a crystalline monolith three stories tall. Its faceted surface caught his weak light, refracting it. Within its depths, a sickly pulse of energy flickered.

"Shardkin," Riker whispered. This was like the one on the planet in the pocket universe, though it lacked the real power Azel had wielded. How then could it do what had been happening for weeks on end?

The New Man seemed to materialize beside Riker. "It's magnificent," he breathed.

Riker looked at the tall superman beside him.

The New Man frowned and cocked his head, not at Riker, but at the obvious Shardkin. "But this is only the sentinel. We must dig deeper to unearth the true prize."

The overseer's ramblings clicked something in Riker. The persistent wrongness that had gnawed at him—it coalesced into a realization.

Yon Soth.

"You fool," Riker whispered. "You have no idea what you're trying to unleash."

The New Man rounded on him with eyes alight. "Your feeble mind cannot grasp the glory that awaits us. When the Great One awakens, we shall ascend to *godhood.*"

Riker knew better. There would be no ascension, no glory. Only horror as an awakened Yon Soth took over, using them as pawns.

As if in response to his realization, a tremor ran through the chamber. The crystalline sentinel pulsed with more energy, casting sickly shadows. From deep below, a sound reverberated through Riker's bones.

Surely, the Yon Soth stirred in its eons-long slumber.

Riker knew dread. This was even worse than he'd ever imagined.

-33-

Far away in the Solar System, Maddox, Ludendorff, and the rest of the crew boarded *Victory* from various shuttles landing in the hangar bays. Maddox exited a shuttle with Meta and his young daughter, Jewel. She was seven years old, a tall, blonde-haired sweetie and the captain's darling. Meta was as beautiful as ever—blonde-haired, voluptuous, and quite strong by Earth standards. She had been born and raised on a 2G planet. She could outwrestle most men, although not her husband, Captain Maddox.

Meta would work the comms while Maddox sat in the commander's chair on the bridge.

After another ten and three-quarters hours—perhaps twice as long as Maddox would have liked—everything checked out.

Eleven people who had been late now boarded, and *Victory* was almost ready to leave. The crew had worked together many times in the past, but there had been a longer hiatus this time.

The Lord High Admiral called and asked for the readiness chart.

Maddox had Meta send it.

A little over an hour later, the Lord High Admiral called again. There were several problems. He wasn't going to give *Victory* permission to leave until Maddox addressed them.

Maddox found the nitpicking unusual. Was Haig trying to go back on his word? It seemed possible.

"Better give him what he wants," Meta said.

This time, Maddox agreed. The best way to do that... Although it galled him, Maddox decided to run through several lengthy drills. It meant leaving his people in enemy hands longer than he liked. But maybe Haig had a point. Once they were out in the Beyond, it would be too late to fix the flaws.

Thus began two days of drills. Maddox was hard on them, deciding he needed perfection. Galyan was beside him, noting and logging the results.

Maddox inspected the results, and then ran through several more drills. During that time, he demoted four people, elevated one, juggled a person around, and finally decided everything was set.

He couldn't believe they had wasted these days, but that's what too much relaxation did.

The one good thing was that people had finally found the professor. They might not have had him if not for the delay.

Soon, Ludendorff asked for permission to come aboard the bridge.

"Of course," Maddox said.

Old Ludendorff, with his white hair, tanned features, and gold chain, entered, looking bewildered. Perhaps he'd lost a few pounds since last time. He didn't quite seem the cocky man he had been in the past.

Maddox stood, walked up to Ludendorff and shook his hand. "Anything wrong, Professor?"

Ludendorff hesitated before saying, "Do you remember the discussion we had at the end of our last foray?"

"I do," Maddox said. "You felt that you should stay behind next time."

"I'm feeling..." Ludendorff rotated his hand to show he was off.

"Nonsense," Maddox said, clapping Ludendorff on the shoulder. "I want you on this one."

Ludendorff winced at the blow.

"Oh," Maddox said, eyeing the Methuselah Man. Ludendorff could be finicky at times, Perhaps... "Do you truly feel this way, or did you come up for reassurance?"

Ludendorff's features darkened as he took a step back. "Now see here, sir, just because I confided in you doesn't mean I'm looking for reassurances. Do you know who I am?"

Before Maddox could respond, Ludendorff continued, "I'm Professor Ludendorff, the Methuselah Man. I'm well able to handle any mental stresses. I merely wanted to keep you in the loop. I've been meditating more than usual, and am ready for duty."

Maddox gave a short nod. "Anything else, Professor?"

"Yes, I'm going to go to my science chamber to inspect everything."

"Thank you, Professor. Glad to have you aboard."

Ludendorff gave a grumpy reply, spun around, and left.

As Maddox headed back to the captain's chair, Galyan appeared beside him.

"That was smoothly done, sir," Galyan said. "I must say, you have not lost anything during your hiatus."

"Do you think *I* need reassuring?" Maddox asked after a moment.

"No, Captain. You know that is not what I meant."

"I suppose. Are you happy to have us back aboard, Galyan?" Meta had asked him to do this. She was watching, so this was as good a time as any.

"You know that I am always… well, never mind."

"Lonely?" Maddox asked, seeing Meta nod from her station.

"Yes," Galyan said. "I have been lonely. I am so glad to have everyone here again to keep me company."

"We're missing Keith, Riker, and Valerie. But we're going to correct two of those problems, and hopefully will be united with Commander Noonan soon after that."

"Yes, sir," Galyan said. "Is there anything you would like?"

Maddox studied the little Adok. "I should have kept in closer touch with you these past months."

"Thank you for that, sir," Galyan said.

"Next time I'll have you down a few times. Maybe not for dinner, but for polite company so we can see how each other is doing."

"That would be delightful, sir. Thank you, indeed."

Maddox glanced at Meta. She nodded to him. Afterward, Maddox headed for his chair. Maybe Meta had been right about all this. She certainly had been insistent.

Once seated, Maddox swiveled around and asked Meta to get in touch with Builder Nexus command.

It had taken too long to get to this point. Now, Maddox wanted to go already.

Soon, Meta said that the Builder Nexus people were ready. Maddox asked to speak to the commander. He was surprised to see his grandmother appear on the main screen. The Iron Lady, aka, Mary O'Hara, was a matronly woman with gray hair.

"Grandmother?" Maddox asked. "Is that really you?"

"It is Brigadier, to you, sir," Mary said with a hint of a smile and a sparkle in her eyes.

"Yes, of course. Brigadier, my apologies," Maddox said.

"What can I do for you, Captain?"

"I'm about to give you coordinates. I want to appear one-third of a light-year away from the targeted star. I wish to study the system in detail and then approach it in a way... I want to use whatever cover I can from that star system so I don't have to deal with the New Men until I'm ready."

"You don't want a slipshod hyper-spatial tube journey. That is why you called personally?"

"Yes," Maddox said.

"Then let us see what we can do for you, Captain. We aim to please, don't you know?"

"Thank you, Brigadier."

"You're welcome, grandson." With that, the screen dissolved.

Maddox drummed his fingers on the armrest, wondering why people were the way they were.

Soon, the Builder Nexus between the Earth and the Moon produced a hyper-spatial tube into the region where the New Men had surprised Valerie and the *Kit Carson*. The tube exit was one-third of a light-year beyond that location.

"Take us in," Maddox told the new pilot. Ensign Simpson was a young man—certainly younger than Keith Maker. Was Simpson any good? The shakedown tests said so. He couldn't be as good as Keith, though. Hopefully, Ensign Simpson would be good enough, at least until Keith returned.

Maddox set his jaw as *Victory* at last headed for the hyperspatial tube entrance.

-34-

Stout Andros Crank, the Kai-Kaus Chief Technician, leaned forward, his thick fingers gliding over his console as he reviewed incoming data. *Victory* hung in space, one third of a light year from the target system.

"Captain," Andros began, turning toward Maddox, "I have a full scan of the system and am putting it on the main screen."

A golden star took center stage on the screen.

"The primary is a G-type main-sequence star, nearly identical to Sol. Its energy output and size suggest it is stable, with a surface temperature of approximately 5,800 kelvins. It's about two astronomical units from a gas giant twice the size of Jupiter."

Andros zoomed in, highlighting the massive gas giant.

"This is the interesting part, sir. A gas giant twice the size of Jupiter, and nearly four times its mass, is orbiting at two AU from the star as I said. Despite its proximity to the star, its gravitational dominance remains stable due to its sheer mass. It exerts tremendous influence over the system, but the balance is such that the orbits of other planets remain surprisingly orderly."

On the screen, an Earthlike moon appeared next to the gas giant.

"Orbiting this double-sized Jupiter is an Earth-sized moon, positioned at a stable L1 point. The moon has a breathable atmosphere, liquid water, and a geological profile similar to Earth's—mountains, rivers, and oceans. The moon is in synchronous orbit with the gas giant, meaning one side always faces the planet, receiving some reflected heat and radiation. However, it's the star that provides most of the energy needed to keep the climate temperate."

Andros tapped his console, and the main screen zoomed in on the moon's surface.

"I'm detecting ancient structures scattered across the surface—likely remnants of a long-lost civilization. The architecture appears to be integrated into the landscape, with cities built into the mountains and valleys. Given its size and layout, this culture must have been advanced. I can't say yet if it's still inhabited, but the ruins alone warrant further investigation."

Andros expanded the view to include more of the star system.

"Moving outward, there's an asteroid belt approximately four AU from the star. It's situated between the gas giant and the system's second largest planet—a cold gas giant roughly the size of Saturn. The asteroid belt seems to have formed from the remnants of a failed planet. It is moderately dense, but we should be able to navigate through it safely with proper caution."

Beyond the asteroid belt, another planet came into focus.

"At eight AUs, there is a frozen rocky planet, similar in size to Mars. It's largely barren, with surface temperatures well below freezing. There's evidence of ancient volcanic activity, but no signs of life. Beyond that, a few dwarf planets orbit in the far reaches of the system, along with a sparse collection of icy comets originating from a distant Kuiper Belt analogue."

Andros tapped his console again, bringing up a view of the inner system. "Closer to the star, there are three small rocky planets. Two of them are too close to the star and have scorched surfaces, similar to Mercury. The third is about 0.8 AU, with a thin atmosphere, but it is devoid of liquid water—likely too dry to support life."

Andros glanced back at Maddox.

"Now, as for why a gas giant of this size can exist so close to the star—this is unusual, but not unprecedented. Most likely, this system underwent significant planetary migration in its early formation. The gas giant could have formed farther out, perhaps near where the asteroid belt is now, and migrated inward due to gravitational interactions with the star and other large planets. Once it stabilized at two AU, it likely pulled this Earth-sized moon into orbit with it, creating a stable environment for the moon's surface. The migration also explains the asteroid belt—debris left behind from disrupted planetesimals."

The main screen shifted to show the gas giant's swirling cloud formations and the moon's orbit.

"With a gas giant of this size, the moon benefits from a slightly stronger magnetic field than Earth's, which helps shield it from the star's radiation. The gravitational pull of the gas giant keeps the moon geologically active, with internal heat driving volcanic and tectonic activity—perfect for maintaining an Earthlike climate."

Andros adjusted the view, showing the system in full once again.

"In summary, Captain, we have a stable system with a large gas giant at two AU, an Earthlike moon orbiting it, an asteroid belt at four AU, and several outer gas and rocky planets. There is some inner system comet activity, although the outer region has more icy bodies that could potentially send comets inward from time to time."

Maddox nodded, taking it all in. "Good work, Andros. Let's prepare for a cautious approach. Keep scanning and let's see what else we're dealing with."

-35-

Maddox and Galyan were in the conference chamber. Normally, Maddox would have called in Keith, Valerie, probably Meta, Riker, and Ludendorff, just to fill out the group. But really, he would only be interested in hearing what Keith and Valerie had to say. In this instance, Maddox didn't have much confidence in the young pilot. He could hear Meta telling him, 'You should have brought him in just to boost his confidence.' Well, Maddox hadn't.

"What do you think, Galyan?" Maddox asked, as they looked at a holographic display of the star system. Maddox had a pointer—a clicker in his hand that could make light shine where he wanted.

"This is the key area," the red light focused on the Earthlike moon. "We could send probes and listen for idle chatter to see how many star cruisers might be there. In my opinion, speed is critical so we can rescue our people as fast as possible."

"Is this an intuitive thought?" Galyan asked.

"I am not sure."

"That is a surprising development," Galyan said. "You do not know whether it is intuitive or not?"

Maddox cleared his throat, remembering this was a conference. Here, important questions could be asked. He paused. It had been a while since he had been on a mission. Was he rusty?

"You are contemplative, Captain," Galyan said.

"Perhaps," Maddox said. "I still don't know if it is an intuitive thought, but I do feel a need for haste. So I suppose it is."

"Are you out of practice with your intuitive sense?"

"I might be," Maddox said, which was a terrible thing to say, yet honest. "Now, let's figure out the best way to do this."

They studied the star system's animation as the computer played out the orbits and rotations.

"This is interesting," Galyan said. He didn't need a clicker because he was connected to all the computer systems. He produced a dot at a tiny object approaching the double Jupiter-sized planet.

"What is that?" Maddox asked.

Galyan magnified it to show that it was a comet.

"Ah," Maddox said. "You mean to come in behind the comet, relative to the double-sized Jupiter?"

"Precisely," Galyan said. "What do you think?"

"That's a good idea. No, scratch that," Maddox said. "It's a great idea."

Did the holoimage stand a little straighter? "Thank you, sir," Galyan said with a note of pride in his voice.

"How precise will we have to make the calculations for us to appear there?" Maddox asked.

"That is for the pilot and navigator to determine."

"They're both youngsters," Maddox said.

"Are you worried they will not perform to your high standard?"

"Possibly," Maddox said.

"I could guide them," Galyan said.

"No," Maddox said, hearing his wife's voice. "We are going to let them do it. Instead, I want you to watch them in ghost mode and go over everything they do, triple-checking it."

"I see. You wish to build their confidence in their own decisions."

"Yes," Maddox said. "We might need that later, when there's no one to guide them."

"That is sound thinking, Captain."

"All right, that crosses the line. I do not need anyone telling me whether my command decisions are good or bad."

"You have not changed, at least not to any great degree."

Maddox stared at Galyan.

"I am putting that into my personality profile. I hope this does not upset you."

"You can think as you wish," Maddox said. "My orders are what I want obeyed."

Galyan sighed. "I wish everyone were here. I much prefer a large conference meeting, hearing people interject their ideas and how they take their responses. It gives me time to add and check my personality profiles, if nothing else."

"Why do you not admit the truth?" Maddox asked.

"Truth, sir?"

"You're social."

"Yes, although I am but an AI."

"No, not 'although.' You are Driving Force Galyan. You know we all appreciate your service to us, to the ship, and to Star Watch."

"Thank you, sir. That is great praise indeed. Perhaps you have changed more than I have understood."

"Maybe," Maddox said. "We will see."

"Yes, sir, that is the best determiner: time and actions. Is there anything else we should discuss?"

"No," Maddox said. "I'm going to go speak to the pilot and navigator and start the next step."

-36-

Space shimmered, a barely perceptible distortion rippling across the void. In an instant, the double oval of Starship *Victory* appeared, with its twin hulls visible in the light of a star a little more than two AUs distant.

Soon, on the bridge, Maddox opened his eyes, his body shrugging off the disorientation of jump lag. The bridge around him swam into focus, status lights blinking as systems came back online.

For a moment, Maddox relaxed. That should be long enough, he thought. "Galyan, give me a status report."

The Adok AI responded. "The jump was successful, sir. We emerged near the system primary, on the far side of the target comet in relation to the gas giant and presumed enemy star cruisers."

Maddox lurched out of his command chair, staggering before steadying himself against a console. The rest of the bridge crew began to stir, a few groaning as they fought off the effects of the jump.

"Engage thrusters," Maddox said, as he eyed the main screen. "Keep the comet between us and the gas giant."

Victory's antimatter engines began to churn, providing thrust. The massive comet had pulled ahead to the side of the starship, a dirty snowball hurtling through space. The ship accelerated, soon moving beside the comet again, keeping pace with it, using it as a shield against anything at the gas giant.

"Launch a probe," Maddox said. "Have it circle the comet so it peeks at the gas giant and the moon."

"Probe launching," said Andros, still looking groggy from jump lag.

Maddox watched on the main screen as the probe did as he'd ordered.

"Enemy vessel detected," Andros said. "It's a star cruiser in orbit around the Earth-sized moon. The moon orbits the gas giant."

Maddox nodded, so far so good.

"Helm, maintain position beside the comet. Andros, use long-range scanners. I want to know everything about the moon and what the New Men are doing there, if anything."

At this point, the bridge hummed with activity as the rest of the crew shook off the final vestiges of jump lag.

It didn't take long until Andros swiveled around to face Maddox. "The first data streams are coming in now."

"Put anything interesting on the main screen," Maddox said.

Andros swiveled back to his console, complying with the order.

On the main screen, a high-resolution image of the Earth-sized moon appeared. The moon's surface showed blues, greens, white at the poles and some desert yellows. That was much like Earth. As the image zoomed in and Andros used a long-range scan to look at the surface more closely, the similarities ended.

"What are those structures?" Meta asked from communications.

"Good question," Maddox said. "Ludendorff should look at them. He could probably give us a hint as to their origin. Galyan, inform Ludendorff about the structures."

The holoimage disappeared from the bridge, reappearing soon.

"Did Ludendorff say anything?" Maddox asked.

"Negative, sir," Galyan said. "The professor glanced at the structures, muttered, shrugged his shoulders and went back to his project."

That surprised Maddox. What had—?

"This is odd," Andros said.

Maddox swiveled around toward him.

"I'm detecting faint energy readings," Andros said. "At first, I thought they came from the ruins. Now I realize it comes from lower down, someplace under the surface."

"Galyan," Maddox said, "help Andros analyze the energy signatures. Compare them to every known weapon system in our database."

"Analysis complete," Galyan said after a moment of eyelid blurring.

Andros was still tapping his console.

"No match found," Galyan said. "These energy patterns are… unique."

Maddox stroked his chin. "Could the New Men be seeking new technology, some alien power source down there?"

"I do not have an answer to your question, sir," Galyan said. "That seems like a reasonable thought. However, I have found something new. I'm surprised you haven't detected it yet, Andros."

"Never mind that," Maddox said. "What are you detecting?"

On the main screen appeared two Patrol scouts and a mid-sized hauler in orbit around the moon.

"The scouts are the *Cheng Ho* and *Kit Carson*," Galyan said. "They are empty, derelict, as is the space hauler, the *Preston Graves*. It is registered in the Altair System at Altair III."

"The derelict ships certainly validate Valerie's story," Maddox said. "She used a *Preston Graves* escape pod and the hauler's Laumer Drive to reach the nearby Laumer Point."

"I never doubted her tale, sir," Galyan said.

Maddox raised his eyebrows. "Did I say I doubted it?"

"No, sir," Galyan said. "The implication, however—"

"Never mind that," Maddox said. "Seeing all this, I'm more impressed than ever with Valerie's actions. She snuck away under the New Men's noses and traversed a considerable distance in the Beyond. Having all that confirmed…"

Maddox nodded, stood, and saluted.

"Was that for Valerie?" Galyan asked.

"It was," Maddox said.

"I have recorded it for her," Galyan said. "I will show it to her later."

Maddox nodded, sitting back down. "We're here, so are the hijacked spaceships. Keep monitoring the star cruiser. Maybe it will do something to give us a hint of their greater plan."

-37-

Chief Technician Andros Crank hunched over his console, his chubby face illuminated by the soft blue glow of the holographic displays.

"Captain," Andros said. "I've got something you'll want to see."

Maddox strode over, his boots echoing on the deck plates.

Andros manipulated the display, zooming in on a section of the moon's orbit, showing the triangular star cruiser.

"It is the *Olympian Thunderbolt*," Andros said.

"What's that?" Maddox asked, pointing at the science station screen.

"The reason I called you here, sir," Andros said, tapping his console. He zeroed in on the object Maddox had noted.

It was a shuttle.

"It just left the star cruiser," Andros said. "It is heading for the moon's surface, I believe."

"Ah," Maddox said.

The two men watched as the shuttle pierced the atmosphere, heading under cloud cover and then shifting into view again.

Once more, Andros manipulated his console.

The probe peeking over the comet used a higher zoom function.

Maddox and Andros watched as the shuttle headed for a scar in the jungle, a pit. The shuttle soon hovered and then headed straight down into the giant pit, landing.

"We're lucky the angle is right for us," Andros said.

Maddox nodded absently.

The scene jumped to the shuttle landing on dirt, with a large log building nearby and some obvious heavy excavation vehicles.

The image wavered and distorted, making it impossible to see exactly what happened next.

"What's causing the distortion?" Maddox asked.

Andros frowned, trying to fine-tune the scan. "There's some kind of field, sir. It's playing havoc with our sensors, as you can see. I did notice that the structure at the bottom of the pit was a large log cabin."

"I noticed that, too," Maddox said.

Andros tried more to refine the image, but it remained distorted. Andros pressed a switch with his pudgy finger. On the science station screen, alien ruins showed along the upper edge of the pit.

"This is from earlier," Andros said. "If I try to view them in real time, they are distorted as well."

Maddox leaned nearer the science screen. He eyed bizarre structural ruins ringing the depression. They defied easy description, their architecture an unsettling blend of organic and geometric forms.

Maddox straightened. "Galyan," he said, as the holoimage drifted to them.

"Did Ludendorff see the alien structures close up like this?" Maddox asked.

"Yes, sir," Galyan replied.

"And he had no idea what the ruins represented?"

"None," Galyan said.

"Did he look at them long?" Maddox asked.

"No. Should I ask him to look again?"

Maddox considered it.

Andros cleared his throat.

"Yes?" Maddox asked.

"The sensors are having trouble getting an accurate read of the structures," Andros said, "but I'd suggest they're tens of thousands of years old, at least."

"That old," Maddox said. "Hmm, those don't look like structures Builders would make."

"Agreed," Galyan said.

"Ludendorff should at least have a guess as to who built them," Maddox said. "Galyan, tell the professor to come up here. I want to see his reaction when he takes a second look?"

"Do you have an intuitive idea what this might be?" Galyan asked.

"That's strange," Maddox said. "I recall giving you an order, not asking for a debate."

"Yes, sir," Galyan said, disappearing.

Maddox glanced at Andros. "Maybe this is an ancient alien outpost, and the New Men have found it."

"They have that," Andros said.

Maddox rubbed his cheek. "Chief Technician, I want every scrap of data you can get on that site. If the New Men are interested in it, we need to know why. And see if you can figure what is causing the distortions."

"I will work on the first for now," Andros said.

"Do what you can," Maddox said. "And keep an eye on the shuttle. I want to know the moment it starts heading back to the star cruiser."

Maddox straightened, moving toward his captain's chair. The Earthlike moon seemed more than a hunting preserve. The pit, the heavy equipment, the log building and alien ruins pointed that way. What were the New Men after?

Galyan reappeared. "The professor is on his way, sir."

Maddox nodded.

"I have also detected an uptick in the energy readings from earlier," Galyan said. "The energy source appears deeper, but linked to the ancient ruins."

"I see," Maddox said. "That means the ruins are still active after a fashion."

"That appears to be the case, sir," Galyan said.

Maddox rubbed his cheek again. Had the New Men discovered a new kind of power?

"Andros," Maddox said, "I need options. How do we get a closer look at what is happening down there without alerting the star cruiser?"

The Chief Technician's brow furrowed. "We could send Galyan to have a look-see. That would likely mean using a booster."

Maddox sat in his command chair. "We're not going to do that just yet. Keep trying to give me a better scan. We'll wait until Ludendorff has a second look at the alien ruins."

-38-

Captain Maddox sat in his command chair. The bridge hummed with activity.

Suddenly, Maddox grew tense, his eyes widening as if he were seeing something beyond the confines of the ship. The intuitive sense granted to him long ago by Balron the Traveler surged to life—a gift that had saved him and his crew countless times before.

His perception tunneled, focusing on the Earthlike moon. Maddox sensed something vast and ancient stirring from eons of slumber. It was a blend of a whale and a cephalopod. It had slimy skin that glistened in an oily way.

Maddox understood, as he had faced a Yon Soth before. This one slumbered deeply, possibly affecting reality through its dreams. The Yon Soth radiated danger.

Maddox winced as he felt the creature's awareness shift toward him.

Tendrils of ancient thought lashed from the moon. They sought to ensnare Maddox's mind, to bend his will to its eldritch whims.

Maddox grimaced as sweat glistened on his face. He fought against the psychic onslaught. As he did, the bridge of *Victory* faded away, replaced by a fiery dreamscape of spongy, undulating terrain that stretched into foggy distances.

Across this alien plain, the Yon Soth dragged its leviathan form, masses of writhing tentacles trailing behind. Each pull sent ripples across the landscape.

Panic clawed at Maddox's throat. He stood on this spongy plain. As the ancient entity drew nearer, the captain felt something materialize in his hands. Looking down, he saw an ancient symbol etched on his palm, pulsing with power.

Recognition flashed through his mind—it was a Builder's mark. This was a weapon.

Concentrating, Maddox shaped the energy of the mark into a lance of pure light.

As the Yon Soth loomed, Maddox thrust the lance, unleashing a beam that cut through the entity's rubbery skin.

The Yon Soth recoiled, its mental grip loosening, and Maddox seized the opportunity to push back with all his strength.

Reality snapped back into focus around him. Maddox found himself gasping for breath in his command chair, the familiar surroundings of *Victory's* bridge a welcome anchor to sanity.

Before he could fully process what had happened, a voice cut through the fog of his mind.

"Sir."

It was Ensign Simpson, the young pilot, his face pale. "The star cruiser has left the moon's orbit and is heading toward the comet. According to my readings, their weapon systems are coming online."

"I was just about to alert you to that, sir," Galyan said.

Maddox's thoughts were still reeling from the encounter with the slumbering Yon Soth. Had the New Men in the star cruiser sensed the psychic struggle? Or was this simply terrible timing?

Whatever the case, it was time to deal with the approaching New Men and their star cruiser.

-39-

Maddox studied the main screen. The enemy star cruiser was definitely heading toward them.

Had the New Men spotted them earlier, after their jump behind the comet? Or could the enemy crew be under the domination of the slumbering Yon Soth?

Maddox swiveled his command chair, facing the voluptuous figure at communications. "Meta, hail the star cruiser," Maddox said.

His wife complied. "I'm transmitting on all frequencies." After a time, she turned to him. "They're not responding."

"Weapons," Maddox said, "bring the neutron and disruptor cannons online."

Soon, the antimatter engines churned with greater power.

A flicker of movement caught Maddox's eye as Galyan appeared beside him.

"Captain, I do not detect any other vessels in this system. I mean enemy vessels."

"I confirm that, sir," Andros said. "The star cruiser is flying solo."

Maddox's brow furrowed. "They are either overconfident or unhinged. Why would a star cruiser captain think he could defeat *Victory*?"

"The New Men might have found new weaponry since last we have met them," Galyan said.

Maddox didn't think that was the answer. "Helm, take us out from behind the comet. Head toward the enemy."

Victory rose from behind the comet, turning and heading on an intercept course with the star cruiser. The ancient hulls gleamed in the system's starlight.

Without warning, a lance of yellow energy erupted from the star cruiser's bow, slamming against *Victory's* shields.

"Weapons," Maddox said, "return the favor. Disruptor first, then follow up with the neutron cannon."

Twin beams of energy leaped from *Victory's* weapon emplacements, one purple and the other yellow. The beams struck the star cruiser's shields. That produced a crimson color over there.

Maddox glanced at Meta.

"Still nothing from them," Meta said.

Maddox swiveled in his chair. "Keep hitting them."

Victory's barrage continued, the disruptor and neutron beams carving furrows across the star cruiser's energy barrier. The shield's color shifted from red to brown and then black, flickering and sputtering as it struggled to maintain cohesion.

Both of *Victory's* beams were burning hotter than ever. That was due to the upgrade of the heavy metal components.

At that point, the overloaded enemy shield collapsed.

The neutron beam punched through the triangular hull just aft of the bridge, tearing through bulkheads. Secondary explosions blossomed along the ship's spine as power conduits ruptured and fuel cells ignited.

The disruptor beam seared the star cruiser's hull. Atmosphere vented in great gouts of crystallizing vapor, bodies and debris tumbling into the void. The ship's aft section crumpled as if crushed by a giant's fist, its engines flickering and dying.

For a moment, the stricken vessel hung suspended, mortally wounded, but not yet destroyed. Then, with a silent flash, the star cruiser's reactor went critical.

A shell of superheated plasma expanded outward at incredible speed, shreds of hull plating and unidentifiable debris riding the wave front. The flash faded to reveal a slowly expanding cloud of glowing gas and tumbling wreckage—all that remained of a once-proud warship and its crew.

"We got 'em!" young Ensign Simpson shouted.

"That we did," Maddox said. "They never stood a chance."

"Then why did they attack, sir?" Simpson asked.

"A good question," Maddox said. "We need to figure it out. I think the best course of action is…"

Maddox wasn't sure if they should hightail it from the moon. No, Riker and the others could be on the moon. He needed to find out if they were or not.

"Helm," Maddox said, "set course for the Earthlike moon, maximum sustainable speed. Andros, I want a full sweep of the moon."

Ludendorff, his eyes haunted, stepped onto the bridge. Maybe the Methuselah Man already knew the stakes. The others should know what they were up against. Frankly, Maddox was surprised he hadn't said anything about it yet. Could the Yon Soth have been trying to keep everyone silent? That seemed quite possible.

Maddox cleared his throat. "Attention people. I believe the New Men were trying to awaken a Yon Soth."

Ludendorff turned pale.

Meta swiveled to stare accusingly at her husband.

"S-sir?" Andros stammered.

"This is ill news," Galyan said. "How did you arrive at such a conclusion?"

"That's what I want to know," Meta said.

"One attacked me mentally a few moments ago," Maddox said. "I resisted and it mentally retreated."

"Was that before or after the star cruiser turned toward us?" Galyan asked.

"Before," Maddox said.

"Your resistance could have caused the Yon Soth to send the star cruiser at us," Galyan said.

"That's possible," Maddox said. "Let's get to work people. I want to know what's happening on the moon."

Ludendorff stepped up. "You mentally resisted a Yon Soth?"

"I don't believe it was fully awake," Maddox said.

"Yes," Ludendorff said. "I doubt that, too. As we'd probably all be dead otherwise. Still, how do we know you're not under its control?"

"How do I know you're not?" Maddox countered.

"That is a good point," Ludendorff said. "We can't be sure about any of us. We should flee this place as fast as we can."

Maddox shook his head. "Forget about that. We're Star Watch. That means we go in so we can protect greater humanity. We have a duty to perform no matter what and that means we investigate."

Ludendorff backed away and sat hard on an empty seat. He covered his face with his hands, shaking his hoary head.

Maddox sat back in his captain's chair. He didn't like that reaction from Ludendorff. Perhaps last time the professor had undergone more than he could easily handle. Still, that wasn't the issue at the moment. "Keep monitoring the moon. Let me know if the strange energy readings increase."

Both Andros and Galyan acknowledged the order. All the while, *Victory* headed toward the moon.

-40-

On the moon, Sergeant Riker's consciousness clawed its way back from the abyss, his senses returning in a disorienting rush. The rhythmic clang of metal on stone reverberated through his skull. His eyes, gummy with dried sweat and grit, slowly focused on the scene before him.

Skeletal figures hammered at the cavern walls. Their movements were mechanical, devoid of purpose beyond the mindless task at hand. Newer arrivals, still possessing some semblance of muscle mass, worked alongside them with equal fervor. The air was thick with choking dust, illuminated by the erratic flicker of helmet lamps.

Riker knew why he was different, why he wasn't a zombie like everyone else down here. The spiritual wound from the Ska long ago ached in a pulsing manner. His enhanced perception, also honed by the encounter with Azel the Shardkin, allowed him to sense what others could not and to resist.

The oppressive presence of a Yon Soth, an ancient horror the others sought to unearth, pressed against the edges of Riker's consciousness. Yet the strength of it felt diminished, as if the entity had expended its reserves of power elsewhere. Maybe that was why Riker had regained self-awareness.

Riker's gaze swept across the sea of blank faces, each one a mask of single-minded determination. They were no longer men, but puppets moving to the strings of the Yon Soth.

"Stop!" Riker shouted hoarsely. "You have to stop this!"

The others ignored him as the rhythmic pounding continued unabated. Then, a towering figure detached itself from the throng, turning to face Riker with eyes blazing in madness.

"Shut your mouth," the New Man snarled, advancing with predatory intent.

Riker reacted as he hefted his pick and swung it in a desperate arc. The pointed end connected with a sickening crunch, buried deep in the New Man's skull. As the body crumpled, Riker's worst fears were confirmed—they were all under the Yon Soth's thrall.

Riker could hardly swallow with his parched throat. He scanned the vast cavern for an escape route. His eyes fell upon a grounded neuron whip, its metallic surface glinting in the dim light. He snatched it up, fingers wrapping around the grip as he began to back away from the mindless workers.

A flash of recognition pierced his mental fog of terror and exhaustion. Among the skeletal laborers, Riker spotted Keith Maker, little more than skin stretched over bone.

In a moment of reckless determination, Riker lunged, his free hand closing around Keith's emaciated wrist. The man's vacant eyes blazed with alien fury as he lashed out, bony fingers clawing at Riker's face.

"Damn it, Keith," Riker said, stumbling backward. With trembling hands, he adjusted the settings on the neuron whip and leveled it at his former comrade.

A crackling burst of energy erupted from the weapon. The skeletal figure convulsed before collapsing in an unconscious heap.

Riker's chest heaved as he fought to catch his breath. With agonizing effort, he hoisted Keith's limp form over his shoulders. The man's weight, once substantial, was now no heavier than a child's. Still, Riker's own emaciated frame struggled under the burden, months of deprivation having taken their toll.

With a final glance at the others still hammering away at the cavern walls, Riker staggered toward the tunnel entrance. Each step was an agony, his legs threatening to buckle beneath him. The distant, alien presence of Yon Soth pressed against his mind, urging him to turn back, to rejoin the throng in their unholy labor.

Riker focused on putting one foot in front of the other. The rhythmic pounding of picks faded behind him, replaced by the ragged sound of his own labored breathing. Sweat stung his eyes as he pressed on, Keith's unconscious form a dead weight across his shoulders.

The tunnel seemed to stretch endlessly, twisting and turning through the bowels of the alien moon. Riker's world narrowed to a pinpoint of determination—to escape, to warn others of the awakening horror that lay behind them.

As he stumbled on, Riker tried to understand. The Shardkin, in their ancient rebellion, had somehow managed to imprison the Yon Soth. Now, millennia later, the Shardkin safeguard were failing. If the entity fully awoke, if it broke free from its arcane bonds, the consequences would be unimaginable.

A distant rumble shook the tunnel, sending a shower of loose stones clattering to the ground. Riker's pace quickened, ignoring the screaming protests of his overtaxed muscles. He had to reach the surface, had to find a way off the moon.

Battered and weakened as he was, with Keith's unconscious form slung across his shoulders and the stolen neuron whip clutched in his trembling hand, Riker pressed on. He was racing against time and eldritch forces.

-41-

Sergeant Riker's world had narrowed to a single, agonizing focus: one more step, just one more. His legs trembled as he staggered through the labyrinthine tunnels. Keith Maker's unconscious form, slung across his shoulders, felt like a lead weight threatening to crush him at any moment.

The rough-hewn walls of the mine seemed to close in around him, the air thick with dust. Riker's breath came in ragged gasps, each inhalation sending spikes of pain through his emaciated chest. Weeks—or was it months?—of endless toil and meager rations had taken their toll, leaving him a shadow of his former self.

Yet still he pressed on, driven by a desperate need to escape the horror that lurked behind him. The presence of the Yon Soth pulsed at the edges of his consciousness, an alien malevolence that sent shivers down his spine. With each passing moment, Riker could sense the ancient entity stirring, shaking off millennia of enforced slumber.

Suddenly, a wave of psychic energy washed over him, nearly driving him to his knees. Riker stumbled, his shoulder scraping against the rough stone wall as he fought to maintain his balance. In that moment of connection, a vision flashed through his mind—a star cruiser, wreathed in flames, tumbling through the void.

"Maddox," Riker gasped, hope flaring in his chest. "It has to be."

The realization that the Yon Soth's reach extended beyond the confines of its prison both terrified and invigorated Riker. If the entity was expending power on failing attacks, perhaps there was still a chance to stop it before it fully awakened.

With renewed determination, Riker pushed himself onward. His feet dragged across the uneven ground. Sweat poured down his face, stinging his eyes and leaving trails through the layers of grime caked onto his skin. The neuron whip, clutched in his trembling hand, felt heavier with each passing moment.

Riker's world became a blur of pain and exhaustion, punctuated by the occasional rumble of distant tremors. Was it the Yon Soth stirring in its prison, or simply the moon's geological instability? Riker couldn't be sure, and the uncertainty gnawed at him.

Time lost all meaning as Riker pushed himself; his legs gave out more than once, sending him crashing to the ground with Keith's limp form pinning him down. Each time, Riker clawed his way back to his feet, spitting blood and cursing.

Just when he thought he could go no further, a faint glimmer caught his eye. Riker blinked, certain it was a hallucination born of exhaustion. But no, there it was again—a sliver of natural light, beckoning him forward.

With a hoarse cry, Riker summoned the last reserve of his strength. He half-ran, half-stumbled toward the light, his vision tunneling until all he could see was that promise of freedom.

The tunnel mouth yawned before him, and Riker burst into the open air. The brightness was blinding after so long in the gloom, forcing him to squeeze his eyes shut against the assault. As his vision adjusted, he found himself at the bottom of a huge pit, the walls stretching up toward an alien sky.

Tears of exhaustion and relief streamed down Riker's face. He stumbled toward the large log building, having no idea what he would do when he reached it.

-42-

"Captain," Andros said from his science station on the bridge of *Victory*. "You're going to want to see this. I've found—"

Before Andros could finish, Galyan interrupted, saying, "Sergeant Riker has appeared at the bottom of the pit."

"I found him first," Andros said, swiveling in his chair to glare at the AI holoimage.

"Enough," Maddox said. "Put it on the main screen."

Andros did.

Maddox stared in silence. He could hardly believe this was Riker. The man had become a skeletal waif. The sergeant was carrying a wreck. Could the other figure be Keith?

Maddox turned to Galyan. "Maintain shields at maximum. No matter what happens, do not let anything compromise your systems. Understood?"

"Sir?" asked Galyan.

Maddox surged from his chair and sprinted from the bridge. His boots thundered against deck plates as he raced through *Victory's* corridors, crewmen flattening themselves against bulkheads to let him pass. He burst into the hangar bay, lungs burning, and vaulted into the nearest craft.

As the shuttle's engines roared to life, Maddox felt the tendrils of an alien consciousness brush against his mind. It was like ice-cold fingers probing at the edges of his sanity, seeking any weakness to exploit. He knew what it was and focused on the task. He guided the shuttle out of the bay, toward the moon that *Victory* orbited and then into its atmosphere.

Maddox wrestled with the controls as wind shear buffeted the small craft, all while fighting off wave after wave of psychic assault.

"Not today, you bastard," Maddox said.

The shuttle broke through the cloud cover, a yawning pit coming into view far below.

Maddox worked the shuttle's optics, locking onto two small figures near a crude log structure. He swept past the alien ruins around the lip of the pit, coming down too fast and landing so dirt billowed all around the shuttle.

Before the engines had even spooled down, Maddox was out of his seat and keying open the hatch. The air that rushed in was heavy with jungle scents and whispers of madness.

"Riker! Keith!" Maddox shouted, sprinting toward the two men.

Up close, the toll of their ordeal was horrifyingly apparent. Both were emaciated, their eyes sunken and haunted.

"Captain, sir," Riker said, his mouth opening and closing.

Keith collapsed, falling onto the dirt, not even trying to sit up.

"Let's go, Sergeant. I don't want you dawdling down here."

"Sir," Riker said, tears welling in his eyes. "Is it really you? Or is the devil playing tricks on my senses?"

"I'm real, Sergeant." Maddox choked back his emotions. It enraged him to see his crew like this. He felt—

"We can swap tales later, Riker. Get your ass on the shuttle, on the double. That's an order, mister."

Riker nodded, turned, and stumbled for the open hatch.

Maddox picked up the skeletal Keith Maker and hurried after Riker.

"Is there anyone else down here?" Maddox said, walking alongside Riker and scanning the desolate pit.

Riker's only response was a dull stare before he collapsed inside the shuttle.

Cursing under his breath, Maddox deposited Keith in the shuttle and then sprinted out to the long log cabin. He kicked in the door, searching frantically for any signs of other survivors.

Finding nothing but dust and shadows, he raced back to the shuttle.

Riker had pulled Keith to a seat, clicking on the restraints. He'd done the same for himself, with tears dripping from his eyes.

Maddox slid into the pilot's seat and fired up the engines. At that point, a psychic pressure slammed against him.

Riker groaned.

Keith whimpered.

The air in the shuttle seemed to throb with evil energy.

Maddox knew that time was running out for them. He focused, gathering his rage at what had happened to his men. It fueled him enough to fight off the alien onslaught.

The shuttle lifted from the dirt and then began to climb out of the pit.

"No," Keith pleaded, using his thin neck to raise his head. "We can't leave. We have to go back."

"Leave my men alone," Maddox growled. "If you don't, you're dead."

That did something, as Keith no longer cringed. The force against Maddox intensified, however.

Maddox snarled, his eyes blazing with wrath.

Under his piloting, the shuttle clawed its way into the sky, fighting against both gravity and the invisible tendrils of the Yon Soth's growing influence.

Maddox could sense the enslaved workers in the subterranean depths. He sensed it through the Yon Soth trying to grind his mind down. The zombie workers were close to breaching the ancient containment field. If they succeeded in doing so…

A bone-deep shudder ran through the craft as something monumental stirred far below. Maddox pushed the engines harder, the shuttle's frame groaning in protest as it punched through the atmosphere.

Victory hung in orbit above, a gleaming refuge against the ancient horror that threatened to engulf them. But as Maddox guided the shuttle toward the safety of her hangar bay, he knew their ordeal was far from over.

The full awakening of the Yon Soth now seemed inevitable. Soon, the ancient entity would bring its unfathomable power to bear against them. Maddox considered their options, each more desperate than the last.

Soon, the shuttle touched down in *Victory's* bay.

With Riker and Keith safely aboard, Maddox sprinted back to the bridge. He soon burst onto the bridge, giving orders even as he slumped into the captain's chair. "Helm, prepare for an emergency jump. Weapons, charge all systems."

Maddox tightened his hold on the armrests of his chair as he prepared to give the order that would determine whether they faced this threat head-on or fled to fight another day. Either way, the battle against the Yon Soth had only just begun, and the stakes could not be higher.

-43-

Deep beneath the moon's crust, in a cavernous chamber, an ancient horror stirred. The Yon Soth hung suspended in an ethereal prison. Its massive, whale-like body pulsed with energy, countless tentacles frozen mid-writhe by an arcane field that had held it captive for eons.

Into this vast cathedral of alien terror stumbled the first of the human miners, their emaciated forms looking like insects against the backdrop of the slumbering colossus. Tattered rags hung from their skeletal frames, eyes wide with a mixture of awe and terror as they beheld the entity before them.

The Yon Soth's consciousness, dormant for millennia, struggled to become fully aware. It reached out with tendrils of psychic energy, grasping at the minds of these puny interlopers. But its long sleep had left it clumsy, its touch far from subtle.

Screams echoed through the chamber as the first wave of psychic assault washed over the miners. Men dropped to their knees, clutching their heads in agony as blood trickled from their noses and ears. Only the hardiest among them, their skin gleaming with an unnatural golden hue, remained standing—though their eyes glazed over, bodies twitching like marionettes on invisible strings.

With agonizing slowness, these golden-skinned puppets began to shuffle through the chamber. Their movements were jerky and uncoordinated as the Yon Soth struggled to manipulate its new appendages. Each step brought them closer to the shimmering barrier that had kept their master imprisoned for so long.

As it exerted its will upon these fragile flesh-vessels, fragments of memory bubbled up from the depths of the Yon Soth's alien mind. Flashes of a great betrayal, of its crystal tools turning against it, of the moment when this accursed field had snapped into place around it. The realization that untold eons had passed since its imprisonment sent a shudder of rage through its colossal form.

But there was something else—a presence that tugged at the edges of its near awareness. Focusing what it could of its vast intellect outward, the Yon Soth perceived a vessel in orbit around the moon. Starship *Victory*, a name it plucked from the minds of its puppets. A potential threat, but one that paled in comparison to what came next.

Space rippled as a new flotilla of warships appeared in the system. The Yon Soth's alien unconsciousness recoiled in shock and fury. These newcomers radiated purpose and deadly intent.

Panic, an emotion foreign to its kind, spurred the entity into frenzied action. It redoubled its efforts to control the human miners, driving them harder toward the source of its imprisonment. But in its desperation, it lashed out too strongly.

New Men collapsed, blood pouring from every orifice as their minds were crushed under the weight of the Yon Soth's psychic onslaught. Realizing its error, the entity throttled back its power, seething with frustration at the fragility of these creatures.

Time was running out. The Yon Soth could sense the approaching ships preparing their weapons, knew that its window of opportunity was rapidly closing. If it could just bring down this accursed field, freedom—and vengeance—would be within its grasp.

Visions of destruction whirled through its alien mind. It would lay waste to these presumptuous humans, rend their civilization asunder. The Commonwealth and the New Men alike would be swept away in a tide of horror. And then, oh yes, it would call to its brethren across the vast gulfs of space and time. Together, they would feast upon this galaxy as they had done in ages past.

But first, it had to escape. The puppeted miners inched closer to the control mechanisms of its prison, their golden skin gleaming in the dim light of the chamber. The Yon Soth focused all of its considerable unconscious will upon these few remaining pawns, guiding their hands toward the intricate machinery that had kept it bound for so long.

As the first human finger brushed against an ancient control panel, alarms began to blare throughout the orbiting ships. The Yon Soth's triumph was tinged with desperation—it knew that Star Watch, the humans' vaunted protectors, were poised to unleash their full arsenal upon this moon.

A race against time had begun. Would the ancient horror break free of its bonds in time to defend itself? Or would the forces of humanity manage to destroy it before it could fully awaken? The fate of the local spiral arm hung in the balance as the Yon Soth pushed its pawns to their limits, straining against the last threads of its millennia-old prison.

In orbit above, fingers hovered over firing controls. On the moon's surface, the remaining miners worked with mindless determination. And at the heart of it all, an entity older than human civilization prepared to unleash a fury that threatened to consume everything in its path.

The chamber trembled, dust and stone raining down as the ancient machinery began to falter. A sound like the rending of reality itself echoed through the vast space as hairline fractures appeared in the ethereal barrier. The Yon Soth's tentacles twitched, the first true movement they had made in eons.

Freedom was within its grasp. Vengeance would soon follow.

-44-

Victory's antimatter engines hummed, powering the shields and readying the beam cannons. Maddox had made his decision with the appearance of the Star Watch battleships. He couldn't leave such heroes to fend for themselves against an awakening Yon Soth. He had to stay so they could destroy the ancient enemy together.

"Target the disruptor and neutron beams at the subterranean energy readings," Maddox said. "We need to buy ourselves time, if nothing else, with this."

In seconds, rays of yellow and purple energy lanced from the ship's forward bow. They pierced the atmosphere and struck the moon's surface, boring into the terrain.

On the main screen, Maddox watched the beams chewing through dirt and rock.

"Launch three antimatter missiles," he said. "Target the same coordinates."

There was silence on the bridge.

Maddox swiveled his chair. "I said launch those missiles, Lieutenant."

The weapons officer sat motionless, his eyes glazed over, hands hovering above the controls.

Maddox came out of his chair, crossed the space between them, and grabbed the man by his uniform.

"What's wrong with you?" Maddox said.

There was no response, not even an eye flicker.

In that moment, Maddox understood, as he felt the alien presence of the Yon Soth worming his way into his crew's minds. With his intuitive sense, he sought to shield the lieutenant. Maddox imagined himself on the spongy dreamscape with the lance of energy from earlier. He fired in the direction of wavy, radiant air.

On *Victory's* bridge, the lieutenant gasped, his eyes clearing. "Sir, I don't know what—"

"Launch three antimatter missiles, using the beams as the guide. Hit where the beams are hitting," Maddox said, letting go of the man's shoulders.

This time, the lieutenant complied.

Victory trembled as three antimatter missiles launched from the tubes, heading toward the moon's surface.

Everything looked good—they were attacking in time—but then the missiles froze in mid-flight as they entered the stratospheric region of the atmosphere. The blue plumes of the thrust didn't move, didn't waver, but remained frozen in their last flicker.

"Galyan, analyze that," Maddox said.

There was no response.

Maddox looked around until he spied the holoimage. Galyan was frozen like the missiles.

Maddox glanced at the main screen. The beams continued to bore into the surface, but the missiles hung motionless, caught in some kind of temporal distortion perhaps. How else could one explain the lack of movement to the plumes?

Maddox turned to his wife.

Meta sat at her station, wide-eyed and alert.

"Contact the—" Maddox said.

A blood-curdling shriek cut him off. Professor Ludendorff lunged at Maddox, coming with inhuman speed.

The captain barely had time to raise his arms before Ludendorff was upon him, a whirlwind of fists and feet executing complex martial arts sequences. Many of the blows connected, striking Maddox across the face, shoulders, and hips. A particularly fast blow struck his nose, making his eyes water.

Normally far superior in strength and combat skills, Maddox found himself on the defensive against the possessed professor as he backed up, beginning to duck and weave. Could this really be happening?

Maddox began studying the attack, the style, trying to catch the rhythm of it.

Ludendorff's face was a twisted mask of rage, his eyes blazing with fury. He snarled and laughed as he pressed his attack.

"Professor," Maddox shouted, deflecting a vicious strike aimed at his throat. "Fight it. This isn't you."

Ludendorff was beyond reason, consumed by the ancient entity that had seized control of his mind and body. What else made sense?

Two bridge Marines, their faces pale with shock, raised their stunners and fired. The energy bolts struck Ludendorff in the back, but he shrugged them off as mild irritants.

Maddox realized he had no choice. He went on the offensive, feinted left, then drove a fist into Ludendorff's solar plexus. The professor stumbled back, winded, but recovered in the blink of an eye.

The two men circled each other, the crew watching in horrified fascination. Ludendorff lashed out with a spinning kick that would have knocked Maddox unconscious if it had connected. The captain ducked under the attack and countered with a sweeping leg strike that sent the professor crashing to the deck.

Ludendorff was far from finished, though. He rolled to his feet with impossible agility, cackling. Maddox knew he had to end this before he killed the old goat. The Marines might have fired again, but they had frozen after the first stunner shots.

Maddox went primitive, charging, tackling Ludendorff and driving him against a control panel. The impact was vicious. Maddox heard the crack of breaking bone. Ludendorff howled in pain and rage, his left arm hanging uselessly.

Taking advantage, Maddox executed a complex throw. The older man sailed, crashing to the deck with another sickening crunch. This time, a leg gave way, bending at an unnatural angle.

Maddox threw himself at the man, grappling Ludendorff. The professor thrashed and snarled, foam flecking his lips as he struggled.

"Meta," Maddox said, his voice strained. "Contact the other ships. They need to attack while they can."

Meta complied, trying, anyway. After a moment, she turned back. "I can't reach them. There's some kind of communication block in place."

Maddox cursed under his breath as he continued to grapple Ludendorff. "Launch more missiles. We have to break through somehow."

His orders were ignored. Now the entire bridge crew stood motionless, their eyes glazed over, no doubt caught in the grip of the Yon Soth. Even as Maddox struggled to hold the possessed Ludendorff, he could feel the oppressive weight of the Yon Soth's power bearing down against him.

On the main screen, Maddox caught sight of three Star Watch battleships maneuvering toward the moon. They were in far-orbital space at the moment.

They must have used the Laumer Point to get here.

Maddox realized that it was all going to depend on how much the Yon Soth could control at one time. This must mean the ancient creature had awakened. This was bad, very bad.

Ludendorff grunted again, struggling with a broken arm and leg, but still struggling.

"You old bastard," Maddox panted. "Fight the alien. Are you too weak to do that?"

Ludendorff's teeth snapped as he tried to bite off the captain's nose.

Maddox almost head-butted Ludendorff unconscious because of that. He didn't try, because he wondered if the Yon Soth was going to force him to kill Ludendorff. Maddox dearly didn't want to do that.

Instead, Maddox hung on, watching the main screen and praying for a miracle.

-45-

Commodore Rice stood on the bridge of the *Alexander*. Flanking his *Conqueror*-class flagship were two *Bismarck*-class battleships. Together, they formed an assault trident, their hulls bristling with weaponry as they approached the giant alien moon.

Victory fired two beams at the moon's surface. That meant Maddox was engaged in battle. Perhaps Commander Noonan had been right about him. It was hard to tell what the captain fired at, as the beams dug into rock and stone.

"Establish contact with *Victory*," Rice said. "Let him know we're here to help."

The comm officer attempted that, but only static answered her hail.

"There's some kind of distortion, sir," the comm officer said. "I can't get through."

Rice opened his mouth to issue new orders, but the words died in his throat. An unseen veil froze his muscles and clouded his mind. Around the bridge, key personnel slumped at their stations, no doubt caught in the same paralyzing grip.

***

Valerie had asked permission earlier and sat on the bridge as a tactical advisor. She watched in horror as the crew succumbed to an invisible force.

"Commodore!" she said. "What are your orders?"

Rice did not respond. No one did. It was as if she was the only conscious person on the bridge.

Valerie recalled Riker's report about the Shardkin's long-ago rebellion against the Yon Soths. Could this be what they were facing here? She'd fought a Yon Soth before while aboard *Victory*. She'd fought one later, too, taking command of the effort. She had some idea what facing a Yon Soth meant. This could be an entity from the very dawn of Creation.

Valerie looked around, taking in the bridge crew's vacant expressions. Could the entire ship be paralyzed like this?

Then she felt it, alien tendrils probing at the edges of her consciousness, seeking purchase in her mind. Valerie mentally fought the invasive presence. As she struggled, a memory surfaced—her encounter with Kresh on the *Bloodtooth*, alien pheromones trying to force her to take a course of action she refused to take. Had the experience fortified her against this attack?

If so—

Even though her thoughts were clouded and she wanted to vomit, Valerie staggered to the weapons console. Once there, panting, her eyesight blurring, she targeted the moon. Her fingers felt stiff and nearly lifeless, but she did it anyway. The two beams from *Victory* showed her the place to target.

An alien whisper of insidious evil tried to stop her.

Valerie did vomit then, turning her head and puking onto the deck. She felt awful as she heaved again.

It will get worse if you continue.

Valerie squeezed her eyes closed, crying out. Her body heaved and she vomited for a third time.

Don't make me kill you, little worm.

Valerie opened blurry eyes. She had a sense of great effort by the alien. It controlled many people and things. If it had concentrated on her alone, she would have succumbed to its superior power. But she only faced a fraction of its ability.

Steeling herself, Valerie fumbled at the controls until she pressed the launch button.

The *Alexander* shuddered as she unleashed hellburners. That wasn't an accident. The ship only had three; vicious ordnance indeed. Out of the three battleships, only the

Alexander possessed them. They were considered the ultimate offensive surface weapon in Star Watch's arsenal.

Valerie's reasoning had been simple. This was it. Light stuff might be useless. It was time to use the heaviest ordnance possible.

Three big hellburners—fat missiles—left the *Alexander* and streaked toward their target on the moon. As they left far-orbital space, entering mid-orbital space, the heavy projectiles slowed and then stopped. The blue plumes from the thrusters froze in mid-flicker, perhaps indicating time manipulation of some sort.

Could a Yon Soth do that?

Valerie thought about it, eyeing the frozen crew around her. They hadn't been able to contact *Victory*. *Victory* hadn't launched missiles—or she couldn't launch them. If an alien thing like a Yon Soth could freeze time in a local area like it did to the missiles, why didn't it use such power to destroy the battleships? Perhaps that took more power than it possessed at the moment. That meant—

"Overload it," Valerie whispered. That's what one did with an electromagnetic shield. You hit it with more power than it could take. How could she overload the Yon Soth—if that's what attacked them—from here?

Valerie snapped her fingers. The answer seemed obvious.

The mental assault blurred her eyes again and clouded her thoughts. Nevertheless, she shoved the useless officer off his seat. Then she sat down in his place at the weapons console and began to empty the *Alexander's* missile banks. Valerie launched every remaining space-to-surface missile.

The projectiles raced across mid-orbital space at the moon, their blue contrails visible in the void.

Then, one by one, the missiles ceased moving, their contrails or plumes as frozen as the others. Every missile was caught in a seeming time-dimensional warp.

Valerie blinked in disbelief. It was over then, wasn't it? What else could they do? She sat at the weapons console, trying to come up with something instead of weeping in defeat as she was presently doing.

-46-

In one particular memory, Valerie was wrong. The Yon Soth wasn't awake, not yet anyway.

The yet-slumbering Yon Soth stirred in its subterranean prison, massive tentacles touching the ethereal field that had contained it for eons. Its whale-like body pulsed with renewed energy as it sensed freedom within reach. The vast chamber trembled with the entity's potential.

Dust and debris rained down from the ceiling as the Yon Soth's slightest twitches intensified.

Above, in space, the Yon Soth's power gripped the ships' crews, freezing them, while missiles hung motionless. He used a semi-time warp so the missiles ceased movement. The human minds were so small and fragile compared to his, easy prey for even the Yon Soth's slumbering psychic assault.

However, the combined strain of all this was immense. The Yon Soth had slumbered long, its powers weakened by millennia of disuse. It couldn't maintain control over everything at once. Something had to give. The entity's consciousness flickered as it began to rise from its dream state, its grip on reality wavering as it struggled to maintain its hold on the missiles, the human crews, and those in the chamber with it.

The last of its servants—the New Men—shuffled around ancient control panels. Their eyes were blank, bodies twisted by exposure to his influence. Once proud and independent beings, they were now nothing more than shells, their minds all but burned out.

The New Men moved jerkily, puppets to his will. Their fingers hovered over switches untouched for millennia. The air crackled with energy as they approached the final barriers that had kept him captive and asleep for so long.

Now, the Yon Soth commanded.

The order reverberated through the chamber, causing the New Men to convulse as the alien thoughts tore through what remained of their consciousness.

The servants' hands slammed down on the controls. Energy barriers collapsed with a sound like shattering glass, releasing waves of power that rippled through the chamber. Time locks disintegrated, unleashing temporal energies that had been contained for eons. The chamber quaked as ancient machinery roared to life, answering the call of its long-dormant master.

Freedom. At last.

The Yon Soth's massive body crashed to the floor, crushing his servants beneath his bulk. Bones crunched and flesh squelched, but the entity paid no heed to the destruction of his tools. They had served their purpose, and now they were nothing more than debris beneath his writhing tentacles.

The Yon Soth reveled in his release and awakening, savoring sensations long denied him.

But the moment of triumph was short-lived, as his control slipped. The dreaming control was different from conscious control, and it took precious moments for him to make the shift.

Three hellburners broke free from their temporal prisons, engines returning to life as they resumed their deadly course toward the moon.

The Yon Soth reached out, desperate to stop them even as he continued to hold the others at bay. He caught two of the freed hellburners, trapping them once more in bubbles of distorted time.

But the third missile slipped past his attempt. The missile raced from mid-orbital space to near-orbital space. Then it streaked through the upper atmosphere, following the beams still firing from *Victory's* disruptor and neutron cannons.

The Yon Soth watched in horror as the hellburner screamed lower, heading straight toward him.

Panic gripped the ancient being, a sensation he had not experienced since the betrayal of the Shardkin untold ages ago. After eons of waiting, after finally breaking free, he faced destruction at the hands of creatures he considered insignificant. The irony was not lost on the Yon Soth, even as terror clouded his thoughts.

His tentacles thrashed against the chamber walls, sending tremors through the tunnels. In his desperation, the Yon Soth released his hold on the human crews, no longer able to maintain his grip on their minds.

Now, the Yon Soth made one last, desperate attempt to save himself. He began to create a slip-tunnel so he could slip away. The first attempt proved futile, as he had forgotten one of the key steps. He restarted the attempt, seeking to remember how to do this.

The panic in his mind made his effort so damnably slow. If he could slip away, he could hunt down the humans later and make them pay in awful torment for what they were doing.

The missile was coming fast, almost here.

I'm not going to make it.

He tried anyway, restarting the process. He tried not to think about the eons wasted in slumber. Chances for dominion, lost to time. The universe he had once sought to rule would continue on, indifferent to his passing.

No, no, I can do this. Concentrate.

The missile was seconds away from unleashing hell upon him.

There, that's what I needed.

A swirling portal appeared before him. He needed to link it with his destination.

Like a runner in a race, he looked over his shoulder to see where the other was. In this case, he wanted to see how near the missile was. A runner could trip doing that. Here, the Yon Soth slowed in the process, having forgotten how to concentrate perfectly. He could have done it eons ago.

The Yon Soth's vast consciousness shrank to a single point of terror and disbelief. He tried to rally his powers to complete the link. His mind slipped, as his millennia of captivity had drained him, leaving him vulnerable at the moment of his awakening.

The primordial Yon Soth from the dawn time realized sickly, *I'm about to die.*

-47-

The hellburner plunged into the colossal pit as the ignition took place. With a blinding flash, the warhead detonated.

The explosion wasn't merely nuclear; it was something far more devastating. The hellburner utilized a quantum cascade reaction, unleashing energy that dwarfed antimatter annihilation. The initial blast vaporized the surrounding rock, transforming it into superheated plasma that expanded outward at relativistic speeds.

The shockwave tore through dirt, rock, and metal ores. The pit expanded exponentially, its edges liquefying and then vaporizing as the energy wave charged forward.

The Yon Soth's final thought was cut short as the blast reached his chamber. His tentacles were reduced to their constituent particles in picoseconds. His massive, cetacean-like body followed suit, the blast wave propagating through his alien flesh faster than his synapses could fire. The primordial entity that had once spanned spiral arms was obliterated before he could even register pain.

As the hellburner's energy continued to expand, it encountered the ancient technology that had kept the Yon Soth imprisoned. Temporal locks and energy barriers, designed to withstand the test of time, crumbled like sandcastles before a tsunami. The quantum cascade disrupted the fabric of space-time in its vicinity, causing localized temporal anomalies.

The blast wave also raced across the jungle surface at hypersonic speeds, obliterating everything for hundreds of kilometers in every direction.

In orbit, Maddox watched in awe as the moon's surface was transformed. The blast created a new crater, its edges glowing white-hot, visible even from low orbit.

As the initial flash faded, the true extent of the damage became clear. The new crater was a perfect circle, its diameter stretching over 500 kilometers. The depth was impossible to determine from his vantage point, but it had to be several kilometers deep.

Something else was happening. The paralysis that had gripped the crew began to lift. First, it was just a twitch of a finger, then the ability to blink. Within seconds, they found themselves able to move freely once more.

At that point, the other hellburners and antimatter missiles slammed against the Earthlike moon, detonating in the new crater, adding to the horrific destruction.

Andros began poring over sensor data. "Sir, the energy readings are incredible. Clearly, whatever was down there is gone."

"Yes," Ludendorff said from the deck. He groaned. "My arm and leg are broken." He stared at Maddox. "You did this to me."

"If you can remember that, Professor, do you also recall attacking me like a martial arts berserker?"

The pain-stricken Ludendorff blinked several times. "Yes, I do remember. I was kicking your ass, too. That's why you broke my bones."

"Medical personnel are on their way," Meta said.

Ludendorff shifted, groaning again, even as he appeared to be thinking. "The moment the first hellburner detonated, it was like a weight lifted from my mind. I'm free. I think we're all free from its control."

Around the bridge, crewmembers exchanged disbelieving glances. The oppressive presence that had clouded their thoughts was gone, leaving behind a clarity that felt almost painful in its intensity.

As the crew of *Victory* watched the aftermath on their screens, a collective sense of relief washed over them. The dread power that had held them in its grip was gone, obliterated. They had stared into the abyss and emerged on the other side.

The moon smoldered where the Yon Soth had been held in captivity for eons. They had faced an entity from the dawn of time and emerged victorious.

"It's funny," Maddox said, as medical personnel rushed to Ludendorff. "But the battleships' arrival was critical. Why did they come, though?"

"What do you mean?" Meta asked.

"Who sent them, and why?" Maddox said.

"That is interesting," Galyan said, the last to revive from the Yon Soth's assault. "Why do you think?"

Maddox looked at Galyan. "Believe me, I plan to find out."

-48-

Minutes earlier, on the bridge of the *Alexander*, the main screen showed a blinding flash from the moon's surface. The hellburner had detonated, unleashing its devastating payload against the ancient entity.

As the light faded, Valerie felt the fog in her mind begin to lift. She blinked rapidly, her senses fully returning. The bridge came into focus, its crew stirring from their trance-like state.

Monitors displayed the other missiles heading fast for the massive crater where the Yon Soth had once resided.

Victory was out in low orbit.

The sight of the double-oval starship brought an overwhelming desire to get back to her people, her family. The urgency of the thought propelled Valerie into action. Without a word to the bewildered crew around her, Valerie stood, pivoted on her heel, and sprinted off the bridge.

The corridors of the *Alexander* were a maze of confusion. Crewmembers stumbled about, shaking off the lingering effects of the Yon Soth's alien influence. Some leaned against bulkheads, holding their heads in their hands. Others called out in confusion, trying to make sense of what had happened.

Valerie dodged and weaved through the disoriented masses, her feet pounding against the deck plates. She narrowly avoided colliding with a group of engineers emerging from a turbolift, their faces etched with bewilderment.

Captain Maddox made this look easy. Valerie's lungs burned as she pushed herself. The ship seemed to stretch endlessly before her, each corridor blending into the next.

Finally, the shuttle bay hatch came into view. It hissed open as she approached. Valerie stumbled into the hangar bay, her chest heaving and sweat beading on her forehead. She leaned against the nearest shuttle, catching her breath before clambering aboard.

Inside the shuttle, Valerie worked the controls and initiated the launch sequence. The bay doors yawned open, revealing the star-studded expanse beyond. Valerie guided the shuttle out, setting a course for *Victory*.

As the *Alexander* receded, a familiar shimmer of light filled the cockpit.

"Hello, Valerie," Galyan's holographic form materialized beside her. "It is good to see you again."

"It's good to see you too, Galyan," Valerie said.

"We have missed you."

"I missed you. Is everyone okay?"

"Yes, Valerie."

She fixed on the approaching *Victory*. "Did you get anybody off the moon before the hellburner went off?"

"Oh, yes. Captain Maddox found Riker and Keith."

"Keith?" Valerie asked, her eyes widening with hope and disbelief.

"Keith is fine," Galyan said, a gentle smile on his holographic face.

"Good, good," Valerie said, tears welling in her eyes. She blinked them away, trying to maintain her composure. "I am so happy to hear that."

"But you are causing trouble," Galyan said. "Those in the *Alexander* are asking and trying to hail you. Do you not see it?"

Both Valerie and Galyan looked at the light flashing on her comm channel.

"I see it," Valerie said. "I am not going to answer it. Can you tell Maddox I want to stay with him until we get back to Earth?"

"Of course," Galyan said.

"And tell him there's some politics going on with our being here. None of them are good, but he should maintain a friendly manner toward Commodore Rice, if he should call."

"The captain is summoning me," Galyan said. "Goodbye, Valerie, until I see you later." With that, the AI holoimage disappeared from the cockpit, leaving Valerie with her thoughts.

The shuttle approached *Victory*'s hangar bay, the double-oval starship growing larger in the view screen. As the shuttle entered the hangar, Valerie felt a wave of relief wash over her.

The shuttle touched down with a gentle thud. Valerie's hands remained on the controls, as strength seemed to leave her. She slumped in the pilot's seat.

A smile played on her lips as the reality of her situation sank in. She was home, amongst her people. The Yon Soth was defeated, and they had all survived against impossible odds. It looked like, once again, Captain Maddox, with help, had pulled the chestnuts from the fire and saved the day.

Exhaustion overtook her, but it was tinged with happiness and belonging. Valerie remained slumped at the controls, savoring the moment of homecoming. Whatever political storms were brewing, she knew she was exactly where she needed to be—aboard *Victory*, with her family.

-49-

A day later, far back on Earth, at Geneva Headquarters in his office, Lord High Admiral Haig read once more through the report of the conversations with Commodore Rice of the *Alexander* and Captain Maddox of *Victory*. A stenographer had recorded all the words so that Haig could go over it at his leisure. She had also placed it in exacting sequence, much as if it were a play, with each speaker identified and the words they had spoken.

It was an after-action report of all that had taken place at the strange planet, presumably called Bestia Rex, in the Primus Venatoris System. It seemed that the New Men had definitely made it a hunting preserve, and no doubt, if explorers went there, they would find the graves or the bones of humans slaughtered by hunting New Men. That, however, was not the issue now, though he was considering sending a Patrol team to explore the planet. But wouldn't the Patrol ships need to be escorted by battleships in case star cruisers showed up? That seemed the case.

There was something else troubling Haig as he reread the report, even though he had been the man making the inquiries at the time. This reading refreshed his memory.

Clearly, General Mackinder of Intelligence had been dead wrong regarding Maddox. Maddox had gone there to save his people and had clearly saved the day against this ancient primordial entity known as the Yon Soth.

Star Watch had destroyed several in the past, always killing them as if they were some Cthulhu-like black widow spider spinning a web against humanity and others. The Yon Soths were deadly, they were evil, and they needed stamping out and squishing whenever the opportunity presented itself.

Clearly, Maddox had done a superlative job, followed by the quick reactions of Lieutenant Commander Valerie Noonan.

There was an old policy never to give Maddox an upgrade in rank but to maintain him as captain. Haig forgot at the moment what the reason was, though the captain still had his special writ.

The Lord High Admiral picked up a stylus and tapped it on his desk. Then he leaned forward and clicked an intercom. "Please send General Mackinder here at once."

Haig stood and walked around his desk three times with his hands behind his back. He was not looking forward to this. Mackinder had powerful friends, some of the same friends that he had, but this time Mackinder had overstepped himself severely. Haig had allowed himself to be persuaded—perhaps that was a better word than browbeaten.

There was a knock on the door. Haig waited until he was seated back behind his desk. "Enter," he said.

Huge Mackinder entered the office.

"Please sit," Haig said, indicating the chair before the desk.

Mackinder did, stuffing his huge bulk into it. It was a tight fit, but Haig wasn't going to worry about that.

"Read this," Haig said, tossing the folder across his desk so it landed before Mackinder.

Mackinder picked it up and read. He kept his face neutral during the entire reading, which took some time. When the general finished, he tucked the sheets of paper back into the folder and set it neatly on the desk. Then he lifted his gaze to regard Haig.

"It seems, General, that you were dead wrong about Maddox's loyalty. He is utterly loyal. Did you see what Commander Noonan said in regard to him? How she stood behind him even when he was under question? She did right, after serving with him all these years."

Mackinder said nothing, just sat stonily.

Haig shook his head. "You've overstepped yourself this time. Because of that, I can no longer keep you as head of Intelligence."

Mackinder's fat-enfolded eyes narrowed. "I see. You're going to sack me? That seems harsh."

"We'll relocate you, perhaps as an ambassador of Star Watch to the Commonwealth Parliament."

"Oh no," Mackinder said. "I don't think so… sir."

"Excuse me?" Haig said. "Who is in charge of Star Watch, hmm?"

"Naturally, you are," Mackinder said. "But need I remind you of my backers?"

"No. I know who they are, but you have miscalculated badly, General. And in this—"

"Just a moment, sir," Mackinder said, interrupting as he raised a fat index finger. "Who persuaded you to send those battleships to the point of contact where it was most important?"

"You did," Haig said. "You did in an effort to capture Maddox at his worst. What you supposed was his worst."

"Yes, true. I will not contest that. But my actions gave him the needed support at the critical moment. Instead of censuring me, sir, respectfully, I would say you should be praising me for my conduct. One way or the other, I saw to the defense of the Commonwealth, and now you want to create a row over this mutant, this sport, this freak?"

Haig slapped the table. "You will not use those terms in my presence anymore, sir. It is now clear to me that whatever Maddox is, his loyalty is to Star Watch and humanity, and he has worked valiantly in that regard. I will no longer view him with suspicion but as an asset."

"I see. I'm sure my backers will want to know this."

Haig hesitated, and Mackinder perhaps sensed that.

"So let us come to an accommodation, Lord High Admiral. Naturally, you are in charge. I am your servant and serve at your pleasure, but I think it might be too soon to knock me down from the post of Intelligence. This will be a reprimand between you and me, and I will act more judiciously, taking into account your new ideas about—well, you don't call them enemies of regular humanity. Is that what I am hearing you say, sir?"

Unfortunately, Haig could see it all. His power was propped up by the believers in Humanity Ultimate. Now, however, Haig was torn. What was the best way? Should he begin the confrontation here and now by sacking Mackinder? Perhaps that was what someone like Maddox would do. Maybe that was the better idea, but Haig realized he had to mend some fences in certain areas and strengthen his hand in others. He realized at the same time that Mackinder would be working against him, trying to undermine him.

"No," Haig said. "On further consideration, we will keep matters as they stand."

But Haig thought to himself, *I will chip away at your power and make sure you can do me no harm.*

Mackinder smiled at Haig and nodded, and no doubt, Mackinder was thinking of how he would undermine the Lord High Admiral until, well, perhaps if the jockeying and politics were right, he would become the Lord High Admiral in the near future.

Yes, this was a defeat. Yes, he had actually helped Maddox instead of harming him. Damn the man's luck. Could he truly be the *di-far* of Spacer legend?

Mackinder grunted as he rose to his feet. "By your leave, sir."

"Yes," Haig said, waving his hand. Haig wanted to say, get the hell out of here, but he kept a politic face and thought, *it is a contest between the two of us. I believe my hand is stronger, but I'm going to make it certain that is so.*

With that, the two men parted company, and as far as they were concerned, the matter of the hunting preserve planet and the Yon Soth was over.

-50-

Maddox spoke to Commodore Rice over the comm systems, asking if there was any assistance needed.

Rice said, "No, everything is fine. We're taking the *Cheng Ho*, the *Kit Carson*, and the hauler with us, using skeleton crews. But what about the Lieutenant Commander? She boarded *Victory*."

"Commander Noonan expressed a desire to stay with us," Maddox said. "Do you have a problem with that?"

"Not specifically," Rice said. "What happened again exactly?"

Maddox related the relevant facts of the battle against the Yon Soth. Then the two signed off. The *Alexander* would take the battleships and captured vessels, the flotilla leaving the way it had come, returning to Melome, where it had left some of its auxiliary ships. Rice had left those ships on Valerie's recommendation in order to make faster time with the three battleships.

Valerie said her goodbyes to Rice via screen, and soon, it was only *Victory* orbiting the Earthlike moon, Bestia Rex.

Maddox visited the invalids, including Ludendorff, but more particularly Riker and Keith. Keith was the worst off—an emaciated, skeletal figure. He was hooked up to IVs and was currently asleep. Riker was a little better. Maddox sat beside him, waiting until Riker woke up.

"Hello, Sergeant. I heard what you did in the pocket universe. May I commend you on your resourcefulness?"

"Thank you, sir," Riker said hoarsely. "Do you know how it all started?"

Maddox crossed his ankles as he sat back. "Why don't you tell me? I'd love to hear it."

Thus, Riker unburdened himself to Maddox, beginning with the escapade back on Earth and including his meeting with Emily Freely. Maddox grunted from time to time, raised a quizzical eyebrow now and again, and nodded in approval several times.

"You've led a charmed life," Maddox said.

"I don't know if it's that," Riker said, "or if some of you has rubbed off on me. I know facing a Ska many years ago marked me in ways I don't like to think about."

"Yes," Maddox said. "Such encounters do mark one, as you say. But it's clear your mental capacities have improved, at least in resisting domination."

"I owe that to you, sir."

"I doubt that's true," Maddox said. "You possess plenty of innate stubbornness. A quality I admire; and I suppose those in Intelligence must have admired it, too—the reason they originally assigned you to me."

"I suppose," Riker said.

Maddox waited a moment, clearing his throat. "It's obvious you're wrestling with the troubles of youth. By that I mean your hormones are running wild, and your good sense is submerged by your urges and lusts."

Riker nodded. "It's them girls, the women, the beautiful ones, anyway. They lure me like a bear to honey."

"I see," Maddox said.

"What am I going to do about that, sir?"

"What men have done throughout history. Stumble through life trying to make the best of it, and not being a damn fool when you have the choice."

"Like I was with the Butcher's wife?"

"There you go," Maddox said.

"But I don't think I was a fool in my quick attachment to Emily Freely."

"No doubt that's true."

"I'll never forget her."

Maddox nodded. "Why not let her memory be a counterweight for you."

"Sir?"

"Let the memory of her sway you when your gonads pulse with fire as they lead you astray."

"You want me to be a monk?"

"Hardly that," Maddox said. "I'm saying you have to relearn the lessons you already knew in your youth. I wonder if, as men age, they lose some of that youthful fire that leads them into trouble, but also leads them into excitement and sometimes ferociously good things. In other words, you have to do the hardest thing of all."

"Being?" Riker asked.

"Using your judgment," Maddox said. "The easiest thing for all of us is to go hard in one direction or the other instead of using judgment each time. That means taking each thing or event and figuring out what the best thing to do is. Sometimes that means dodging left. Sometimes that means dodging right. Sometimes that means going full steam ahead, as straight as can be. And sometimes that means backing up as fast as you can. You have to use your judgment. You have to play each event and thing by ear."

"That's good advice."

"It is," Maddox said, "and it's easy to give, too. The hard part is in the doing. That's where the real struggle comes."

"I know that's true." Riker grinned. "It's good to see you again, sir."

"Likewise," Maddox said. "I'm glad to be off Earth, and I'm in no hurry to go back. Matter of fact, now that I'm out here," Maddox cracked his knuckles, "I'm going to find a reason to stay out here for a while."

"Which way are you moving, sir, I mean in relation to your advice?"

"Forward, slowly and carefully for now," Maddox said.

Riker yawned, his eyes having become red, obviously tired.

"You underwent a horrible ordeal, Sergeant, and yet, listening to what you accomplished—what you faced down there in the tunnels—it's remarkable you did what you did. Perhaps some of your most trying circumstances—"

"You mean like facing the Ska ages ago?"

"Exactly. Maybe that prepared you, hardened you, or inured you just the right way so that you were able to deal with the Yon Soth. If you hadn't undergone those past injuries, past hardships, you wouldn't have been forged into the sergeant that helped defeat this gross evil, this malignancy from primordial times."

"That's a thought. So every hurt, every broken bone isn't always a waste?"

"It's no fun going through it at the time," Maddox said. "Believe me, I know."

"You have many scars, don't you?"

"That's enough philosophizing for now." Maddox stood, patting Riker on the shoulder. "You get some sleep, Sergeant."

"Is that an order, sir?"

"No. It's just a request."

Riker grinned as he shut his eyes, settling in to sleep.

Maddox headed out, wanting to talk to Valerie.

-51-

Before Maddox did that—go see Valerie—he saw Ludendorff.

"Are you here to gloat over your victory?" Ludendorff asked from his med cot.

"Nonsense, Professor. You gave me a scare. I had to fight hard against you, and yet I couldn't exert killing blows. I dared not, for I didn't want to lose such a good friend as you."

"How long did it take you to memorize that little speech?"

Maddox shrugged, pulling up a chair and sitting down. "No hard feelings then?"

"I've got plenty of hard feelings," Ludendorff said. "I told you on Earth that I wasn't ready for a mission. My mind—the Yon Soth easily occupied it. When you rescued me a year ago—my captivity in that other place changed me. These missions—I shouldn't be going on them anymore."

"That's your decision, of course."

"Damn straight it's my decision. Take me home to Earth, pronto."

"We'll get there," Maddox said.

"I said pronto."

"Don't overexert yourself, Professor. You had a hard blow. But we killed your oppressor."

"I would have taken you down even ten years ago if a Yon Soth had possessed me then."

"Don't sell yourself short right now," Maddox said. "Look." He rolled up a sleeve and showed a large bruise.

"That's where you slugged me, several times. And you know I don't bruise easily."

Ludendorff actually brightened. "Well, well, well. I got some licks in, did I?"

"You did. Why do you think I had to break bones?"

"Ha!" Ludendorff said. "I didn't look at it that way."

"You launched a roundhouse kick. If that had connected, you'd have probably put me down. Then, of course, you would never have escaped your mental enslavement."

"That wouldn't have been good," Ludendorff said. "So you're telling me I should rejoice that you kicked my ass?"

"I barely defeated you. It was the hardest fight of my life."

"That's a lie, isn't it?"

"If it is a lie," Maddox said, hedging, "it's one I'm giving a friend to make him feel better."

"But I don't feel better. I have two broken bones. My left knee might not work right after this."

"Give it time, Professor. We have excellent treatments."

"I don't know. These voyages with you…" Ludendorff shook his head.

"You're not as bad off as Riker or Keith. And you know why that happened?"

"What do you mean?" Ludendorff asked.

"They got it worse because they weren't with *Victory*. They were off on their own missions, trying to do what we do, but without all the advantages we have."

"By that you mean yourself?" Ludendorff said.

"That and Galyan, and you, and Meta, and others. We're a team. We operate best as a team."

"With you as the spear point?" Ludendorff asked.

"Come now, Professor. Let's not—"

"Will you let me be," Ludendorff said. "I'll think how I want and do as I want. Do you have a problem with that?"

"No," Maddox said, standing. "The truth is I wouldn't have it any other way. I have a crew of stubborn, hard-headed, and in your case, maybe even pig-headed people, but that has always been to our advantage because we've learned to work together."

"That's a fine speech," Ludendorff said sarcastically.

Maddox turned away.

"But," Ludendorff said.

Maddox turned back.

"It is also true. Give me some time. Maybe... maybe I can practice some mental exercises and strengthen my amazing intellect into the stubbornness that it formerly had. It was a frightening thing to be controlled so easily."

"I'm sure it was," Maddox said.

"Maybe you'll find that out someday."

"Is that a curse, Professor?"

"No, a warning," Ludendorff said. "You better be careful. There are people out there who are out to burn you good."

"Yep," Maddox said. "So be it."

"All right then, I'm going to speak to Galyan and start some mental exercises."

"Good for you, Professor."

With that, Maddox departed, determined now to go find Valerie.

-52-

It turned out Valerie was sleeping.

So Maddox went to the gym, did a light workout, and then walked the corridors, nodding to different crewmembers, asking how they were, listening to what they had undergone, gaining the temper of his crew.

They had gone through a horrific experience with the Yon Soth, but it didn't seem that any of the crew were eager to race home to Earth. Perhaps they, too—at least some of them—had had an extended stay at home and didn't want to return just yet. Maddox was grateful for their loyalty.

Even though Galyan told him the Lord High Admiral wished to speak to him again, Maddox told Galyan that he was otherwise engaged for a while, but he would speak to Haig soon enough.

"Very well, Captain," Galyan said, disappearing.

Maddox went to the cafeteria for a cup of coffee. As he was finishing his second cup, the lieutenant commander came in, yawning, her hair a bit disheveled. She ran her fingers through her hair, got a plate of bacon, eggs, and strong coffee, and then sat down beside Maddox.

"Hello, sir," she said.

"Commander," he said.

Valerie ate.

Maddox sat back, sipping coffee, waiting.

Valerie drank down her mug, then got another.

"I'm finally starting to feel human again. What we went through…" Valerie shook her head.

"I'm curious about something, Commander."

"Oh?" Valerie said, as she pushed her empty plate away.

"The New Men captured the *Kit Carson*, and they also captured the *Cheng Ho*. Surely the New Men must have gone through your logs and found out about the Shardkin in the pocket universe."

"Oh, I doubt the New Men read those logs."

"I don't understand," Maddox said.

"I know you don't practice that Patrol procedure, but the rest of us—at least those on the scout ships—absolutely do. We have the real logs, and then we have fake logs set up in advance in case we're captured."

"You mean…"

"The New Men never found our real log, never read what occurred in the pocket universe. Instead, they read a routine survey log. They didn't even read about what happened on the *Columbus*."

"What happened there?"

"Riker found a crystal entity that tricked us into the pocket universe."

"Indeed," Maddox said. "I'll have to ask him about that later."

"He may not want to talk about it."

Maddox nodded, not telling Valerie that Riker had already shared all that. He and the commander sat together, sipping coffee.

"Do you think the Throne World was in on this?" Valerie asked.

"I've been wondering about that," Maddox said. "I'm inclined to think not. I suspect this was a solo mission. We've learned a Lord Hermes was the captain of the *Olympian Thunderbolt*. Perhaps he had to send regular updates to the Throne World, maybe disguising what he really did here. Or maybe Lord Hermes came here on a hunting expedition and found clues, so he started excavating. One thing led to another, and the Yon Soth trapped him. They can do that in their sleep, as we've learned previously."

Valerie thought about that. "So Lord Hermes used captives to do the dirty work?"

"It looks like," Maddox said.

Valerie nodded thoughtfully before studying Maddox. "What's next, sir?"

"First, I'd like to hear your side of events, if you don't mind."

"I suppose not."

Valerie started slowly but soon gave a detailed explanation of her adventures.

"Wow," Maddox said later. He was on his fifth cup. He would have been jittery, but his metabolism, faster than a regular human's, ate up some of the caffeine. Otherwise, his hands would have trembled. It was the same with alcohol, only in a different manner. In any case, he thought about what Valerie told him.

"That's amazing," he said. "You did marvelously. However, I wish you would stay aboard *Victory*. I know you want an independent command, but…"

Valerie pursed her lips before saying, "Maybe I'll stay with an independent command on the *Tarrypin* instead of the larger *Kit Carson*."

"There you go," Maddox said.

"There are advantages being with *Victory*."

"Funny, I was just telling Ludendorff the same thing."

They lapsed into silence for a time.

Then Maddox, who had been chewing over certain matters, said, "It would be interesting to find this grounded Patrol vessel on the jungle planet, the ship Liza and Kresh entered."

"I've wondered what Patrol vessel it could be," Valerie said. "I recall the captain telling me it was an old vessel. When did the Patrol start sending scouts into this region?"

"Good question," Maddox said. "I don't know off the bat. I'm sure we could find out which ones have been lost in the Beyond in this region and when. More importantly, we could ascertain if there were more of those parasitical aliens or not."

"Doing what with them?" asked Valerie.

"Destroying them," Maddox said.

"Like that? Just crushing them with your heel?"

"It seems like the wisest course," Maddox said.

Valerie nodded in agreement. "Wouldn't we need permission to search for it before we actually did it?"

Maddox shrugged.

Valerie eyed him. "You mean ask for forgiveness instead of asking for permission?"

Maddox pointed at her. "I'm not going to be tied down on Earth like I just was. Why, if it wasn't for Galyan—"

The little holoimage appeared. "You called, sir?"

Both Valerie and Maddox smiled.

"Galyan," Maddox said, "I want to find the jungle planet the *Bloodtooth* found so we can ascertain what's on the crashed Patrol vessel."

"What do you mean, sir?" Galyan asked innocently.

"Don't pretend you weren't watching and listening to us in ghost mode," Maddox said. "I saw a flicker out of the corner of my eye, but decided not to reprimand you for eavesdropping."

"Oh," Galyan said. "I will have to refine my techniques so that does not happen again."

"He was really there?" Valerie asked.

"Yes," Galyan said. "I was. The captain's eyes—they are sharper than anyone's."

Valerie frowned for only a moment and then sipped the last of her coffee, setting the cup down. "I need to run through some calisthenics before we start," she said.

"How do you propose to find this place?" Galyan asked the captain.

"Perhaps go to Krantz and look for clues among the buyers of pirated goods," Maddox said. "First, though, we should search for the *Bloodtooth*'s log. It's possible the black box survived the ship's destruction."

"That makes the most sense," Valerie said. "However, if you don't mind, sir…?"

"Go," Maddox said.

Valerie got up, took her dishes to a bin, and then exited the cafeteria.

Maddox and Galyan exchanged glances.

"You do not want to go back to Earth again, do you, sir?"

"Not until I know I won't be stranded there for an extended vacation. I'm going to start doing things differently. What do you say to that, Galyan?"

"I agree, sir, because I would rather have all of you aboard than be by myself in Earth orbit doing nothing. That reminds me too much of my previous existence, which was very lonely indeed."

"All right," Maddox said, standing. "Let's take a walk. You can float beside me, and we'll talk about this until we figure out the best way to try to find this mysterious jungle planet."

"Excellent," Galyan said. "I can hardly wait."

-53-

A debris field drifted before *Victory*, the remnants of the *Bloodtooth* after it exploded.

"You have the honor," Maddox said from his command chair. They had discussed this beforehand. Maddox was making it public, though.

Valerie nodded as she sat at a console on the bridge. She launched drones from their bays. The small vehicles appeared on the main screen and began their scans, following a grid search pattern through the debris.

"There are pockets of radiation," Galyan said.

"Give me the coordinates," Valerie said. "I don't want to lose any drones to a hotspot. You can check out those radiation-heavy places."

The coordinates appeared on Valerie's screen. She entered them into her computer, guiding the drones.

Galyan disappeared from the bridge.

Hours ticked by as fragments of the *Bloodtooth* drifted past. Broken components, unidentifiable in their ruined state, tumbled end over end.

"Captain," Valerie said. "I may have found it."

All eyes turned to the main screen as Drone Three's camera focused on a battered, scorched piece of equipment. Its casing was cracked and corroded, but the distinctive markings of a ship's black box were still visible.

"I'm bringing it in," Valerie said.

The drone's manipulator arms cradled the cargo, turned, and headed for a hangar bay.

"Once it lands," Valerie said, "I'll send the black box to Andros."

The Kai-Kaus Chief Technician would be using Ludendorff's science chamber for this.

***

Andros hunched over a workstation in Ludendorff's science lab, processing corrupted data from the found box.

The fragmentation was worse than he'd expected. The violent destruction of the *Bloodtooth* had seared navigation records. What should have been precise jump coordinates were now a jumbled mess of partial data and echoes.

Andros tried an Anderson filter, attempting to pull something coherent from the particles.

As the algorithms churned, Captain Maddox spoke over the intercom. "Anything yet?"

"This isn't like pulling data off a standard black box," Andros said. "We're dealing with—"

"No excuses," Maddox said, interrupting. "I need to know if we should start an insertion onto Krantz instead. That will take longer, and we'll need to start immediately."

The intercom clicked off. Andros went back to work. Fifteen minutes later, a hologram materialized.

"Perhaps I can be of assistance," Galyan said.

Andros scowled. "With all due respect, Galyan, I've got this under control. Your processing power is better used elsewhere."

"I have been monitoring your progress. By my calculations, you should have decrypted at least a partial jump sequence by now. Are you certain you are utilizing all available resources?"

Andros stared at Galyan. "Did the captain send you?"

"I am not supposed to say."

Andros sighed. "If you can do better, go ahead."

Electronically, Galyan began to study the data core.

Andros watched.

An hour passed.

"Not working, huh?" Andros asked.

"I have found a possibility. I need more time."

"Sure," Andros said.

Twenty-two minutes later, Galyan said, "I believe I have found something. They are distortions, but they are not random. Instead, they are echoes of the *Bloodtooth*'s Laumer Point jumps."

"How did you isolate them?" Andros asked.

"I correlated the distortions with known gravitational anomalies in the sectors the *Bloodtooth* theoretically could have used," Galyan said. "By mapping these against the fragmentary data from the black box, I was able to reconstruct a partial jump sequence."

A star map materialized over a holo-imager, showing a series of interconnected points.

"What am I looking at?" Andros asked.

"I have narrowed down the possibilities to a specific star cluster, but the exact coordinates remain elusive."

Andros hit the intercom button. "Captain, you need to see this."

Soon, Maddox arrived, and Galyan explained their findings.

"So we still don't know exactly where the jungle planet is?" Maddox asked.

"No," Galyan said. "Just the likely region."

"That will have to do. We'll plot a course for the star cluster and figure out the rest when we get there." Maddox rubbed his hands together and then turned, exiting the science chamber.

-54-

For the first few days, the journey proceeded without incident as they penetrated deeper into the uncharted sector of the Beyond.

On the third day, after exiting a Laumer Point, Andros spoke from his science station on the bridge. "Captain, I'm picking up a massive ion storm ahead."

"Zoom in on it and show it on the main screen," Maddox said.

On the main screen appeared a roiling vortex of raw energy that filled the bridge with a blue light. At first, it almost seemed mesmerizing—long streams of ionized particles writhed and twisted, their edges crackling with bursts of electricity. Each flash resembled distant lightning strikes. That wasn't just a light show, however, but a destructive force capable of tearing through shields and disabling systems.

"The storm spans several light-years," Galyan said. "We'll lose several days trying to go around it."

"How many light years across do you estimate it is?" Maddox asked.

"Given what I am seeing," Galyan said, "five light years at the most."

"I concur," Andros said several moments later.

Maddox nodded thoughtfully. "We'll wait an hour for full lag recovery and then set the star-drive jump for six light years."

An hour and ten minutes later, *Victory* appeared in the ion storm. It was larger than five, and even six, light-years across. The starship bucked and heaved as arcs of energy writhed across the hull, leaving scorch marks in their wake.

There was a significant power drain until a team restored the collapsed shield. The heavy metal components helped prevent too many ship systems from shutting down. Andros was against using the star-drive jump to leave, as there was a theoretical danger in that.

"We may have to jump anyway," Maddox said.

"I detect a lessening of energy ahead," Galyan said. "I suggest we keep moving as we are."

Maddox ordered it so.

Five and three-quarters hours later, *Victory* emerged on the other side of the ion storm, battered but intact.

From there, it took four more days of travel, with many Laumer Point and star-drive jumps.

Andros announced that they were approaching the outer edge of the star cluster.

"I am picking up a planetary body that could be our target," Galyan said. "It is two point four light years away."

"Confirm that," Maddox said.

Andros beat Galyan to that. "It's a jungle planet all right."

"Yes," Galyan said. "It matches what Valerie has told us about it."

"Let's go," Maddox said.

They used the star-drive jump once again.

Soon enough, the main screen revealed a green world wreathed in swirling clouds and orbited by twin moons. Even from this distance, the planet's surface seemed to pulse with life. An ordinary G-class star radiated 1.32 AUs away.

"Initiate long-range scans," Maddox said.

The planet's atmosphere proved to be a dense soup of moisture and organic compounds, capable of supporting a vast array of life forms. Mixed in with the natural flora were strange energy signatures.

"Do you want me to go down and look at them?" Galyan asked.

Maddox glanced at Valerie.

She shook her head.

Maddox understood. The Lieutenant Commander wanted the privilege of doing that.

"No, Galyan, but thanks. Helm, establish a stable orbit. Commander, would you like to join me down there?"

"I would indeed," Valerie said.

"Then let's go," Maddox said.

In the hangar bay, Valerie checked her sampling kit for the third time, her fingers drumming nervously against the case.

Galyan floated beside her while a squad of Marines stood at attention.

"We're about to set foot on a world that's claimed at least one Patrol vessel," Maddox said. "Stay sharp, stay together, and don't touch anything without clearing it first."

The team boarded the shuttle, the hatch sealing with a pneumatic hiss. As they launched from the bay, the jungle planet loomed before them, a swirling mass of green and blue.

"Entering the atmosphere," Simpson said. "Brace for turbulence."

The shuttle plunged through layers of thick clouds. Lightning crackled around them. Then the shuttle dropped through a pocket of clear air, the verdant canopy below rushing up to meet them.

"Sensors are going haywire," Valerie said. "The electromagnetic field from the surface is stronger than anticipated. Will that affect you, Galyan?"

"To a degree," Galyan said.

"Can you compensate?" Maddox asked.

"Partially," Galyan said. "But it will affect more than me. We will be operating with limited scanning capabilities once we are on the ground."

Soon, the shuttle touched down, sinking slightly into soft, loamy soil.

"Atmosphere's breathable like we determined from orbit," Valerie said, studying her handheld scanner. "But the humidity is bad. I recommend we use suits and helmets. The initial scans suggest a terrible proliferation of fungi and spores. I'm not seeing anything different from here. We shouldn't breathe any of that if we can help it."

"You heard the Commander," Maddox said. "Suit up with helmets, with the filters engaged."

That took time. Finally, the last Marine gave a thumbs-up signal.

Maddox pointed at the pilot.

The shuttle's ramp lowered as heat and moisture slammed against them. Even in their suits, they felt that. The humidity was oppressive. Massive trees towered overhead, their trunks wider than the shuttle, stretching up into a canopy that blotted out the sky. The shuttle had landed in the only open field.

Valerie stepped off the ramp, her boots sinking into spongy ground. She knelt, scooping up a sample of the soil with a sterile tool and then analyzing it. "There's lots of biological activity, which is no surprise."

A rustle in the underbrush alerted the Marines. A creature burst from the foliage—a writhing mass of tentacles and chitinous plates, moving with unnatural speed. Before anyone could react, it snatched up something small and furry, disappearing back into the jungle with its prey.

"Did you see that thing?" a Marine asked.

"That was strange," Galyan said.

"How so?" asked Maddox.

"The shuttle has just touched down. I would expect all native species to have fled the general area. Instead, we witnessed what we did."

"Maybe the predator used our approached to help it hunt," Valerie said. "Maybe it helped to expose the prey."

"Whatever the case," Maddox said, "keep your weapons ready. I don't want to lose anyone. We're here for the Patrol vessel. Galyan, any readings on its exact location?"

Valerie had previously given its coordinates: the reason they'd landed in this lonely open spot.

"I am detecting a concentration of refined metals approximately two kilometers to the northeast. It matches the composition of a heavily degraded Patrol ship's hull, the one Valerie pinpointed earlier."

"Do you have anything to add to that, Commander?" Maddox asked.

"Just watch your step," Valerie said; "and keep in sight of each other."

"You heard her," Maddox said. "Let's do it by the numbers."

They pushed into the jungle. Vines writhed and shifted, as if trying to impede their progress. Strange fungi pulsed with an eerie rhythm in the underbrush.

Twice, Marines burned through a heavy patch to aid their progress.

Valerie paused to collect samples of the local flora. After a time, she commented. "Captain, the plants seem to be reacting to our presence. Look."

She pointed to a cluster of broad-leafed plants. As they watched, the leaves slowly turned to track their movement, like a field of organic sensors.

"It is not just the plants," Galyan said. "The entire ecosystem seems to be responding to our intrusion. I am detecting subtle changes in the electromagnetic field, propagating outward from our position. It became stronger after the last burning of vines."

Maddox thought about that before asking Valerie, "What do you think?"

"Sir?" Valerie asked.

"I wonder if we should burn a broad path for ourselves to the spaceship," Maddox said.

"That might be inviting retaliation," Valerie said.

"I concur with that," Galyan said.

"That would be better than letting the plants smother us," Maddox said.

"I suggest we move through the jungle as unobtrusively as possible," Valerie said. "We don't know the range of the ecosystem's responses. Let's try sightseeing before we do anything else."

"Galyan," Maddox asked, "how fast can you return to *Victory* and request the disruptor cannon burn a path for us?"

"Immediately, sir," Galyan said.

Maddox nodded. "That's Plan B if things go bad quickly. Otherwise, let's try your idea, Commander. No more burning down plants. We're doing this unobtrusively."

They pressed on, the jungle growing denser. Now, they slipped through or past thick vines.

After leaving one set, a Marine shouted, "There's a contact left."

The team turned, weapons raised, to find nothing.

The Marine blinked, confusion evident even through his helmet. "I could have sworn I saw something. It was right there, watching us."

Galyan turned to Maddox. "What does your intuitive sense suggest?"

Maddox cocked his head. "Nothing yet," he said.

They crested a small rise and the first signs of the crashed Patrol vessel came into view. Twisted metal protruded from the jungle floor, already half-consumed by the voracious plant life. A trail of debris stretched out, leading to a small clearing where the bulk of the ship lay.

"Spread out," Maddox said. "Secure the perimeter. Valerie, Galyan, you're with me. Let's take our first gander."

As they approached the derelict vessel, Galyan said, "That is not a Patrol vessel. Notice the markings, the writing on the side. That is not any human script I know."

Soon, Maddox and Valerie stopped, studying the weird script on the side of the wreckage.

"That explains how an old Patrol vessel got out here," Valerie said. "It didn't. This is something else, something alien. Captain Marek was wrong about it being a Patrol ship."

"Interesting," Maddox said.

"Don't forget that whatever infected Kresh was supposed to be inside there," Valerie said.

"Believe me, I haven't forgotten," Maddox said. "That's the key reason we're here. We don't want more of those spreading."

"It is strange then that your intuitive sense does not react," Galyan said.

"Not if there was only one parasite," Maddox said. "It would have left with Kresh."

"Do you really think that is the case?" Galyan asked.

"No," Maddox said. "I expect something more."

Valerie shifted uneasily.

"Are you ready for this?" Maddox asked.

"I don't know," Valerie said.

"Good," Maddox said. "That means you're worried and alert. Let's do this and take a closer look."

-55-

The alien vessel loomed before them, a decaying behemoth entombed in the suffocating embrace of the jungle. Vines as thick as a man's arm snaked across its hull, pulsing with an unsettling vitality.

Maddox raised a hand, signaling the team to halt. "Valerie, what's that smell?"

Lieutenant Commander Noonan's nose wrinkled behind her faceplate. "It's familiar, disturbingly so. It's like the pheromones Kresh emitted, but stronger, more primal." She shook her head. "This is different, though. I don't feel any hostility—I mean coming from me. Could the parasite thing be native to this planet?"

"Or could it have emigrated from the downed ship to the planet?" Maddox asked.

Valerie looked around uneasily.

The sickly-sweet scent hung in the air like a miasma, cloying and oppressive. It seemed to seep into their pores, despite the protection of their helmets and suits.

"Galyan," Maddox said, "any life signs in the wreck?"

"I do not sense any," Galyan said. "But the ship's hull is interfering with my scans. We won't know for certain until we are inside."

"Your holoimage can't get through that?"

"Not until we open a hatch, sir," Galyan said. "I am surprised your intuitive sense has not warned you."

"Yes," Maddox said. "That is interesting and possibly telling."

The team approached the vessel's airlock, its metal corroded and warped by long exposure to the elements of the planet.

Maddox instructed two of the Marines to ready their plasma cutters. He then stepped back, scanning the area.

The two Marines stepped to the hatch.

Then Maddox felt it, an intuitive warning. He turned to the forest, looking closely. He could see the vines moving—other things. Maddox turned back to the Marines. They were about to start cutting. Could that be why he felt uneasy?

"Stop!" Maddox said. "Don't move."

One of the Marines looked up at him while the other one swung his plasma cutter to the hatch.

Maddox fired a shot into the air.

Both Marines turned to him abruptly.

"Come away from there, on the double," Maddox ordered.

The Marines hurried to obey.

Maddox called the rest over.

"Trouble, Captain?" Valerie asked, hurrying near.

"Yes," Maddox said, "from the ship."

"What is it, sir?" Galyan said. "What do you sense?"

"Something bad," Maddox said.

"Could it be the parasitic alien life form?" Galyan asked.

Maddox concentrated before shaking his head. "That isn't what I'm sensing. It was only when the Marines were ready to cut into the hatch that it hit me."

"Why do you think that is, sir?" Galyan asked.

Maddox focused on Galyan. "Why are you asking me?"

"I have seen possible evidence of others here, but I cannot be completely certain who they are," Galyan said.

"Clarify that," Maddox said.

"I have seen footprints, bits of odd debris that strike me as unnatural to the planet," Galyan said. "I do not think these pieces of evidence are as old as the derelict."

"Do you think the newer debris came from the *Bloodtooth's* shuttle?" Valerie asked.

"Unknown. Why did you feel the danger, sir? I do not mean to question your orders," Galyan added. "It is rather that I am trying to figure this out."

Maddox tapped his helmet with his gloved fingers. "I felt it as the Marines were about to cut into the hatch. Yes. That's where the danger is."

"But you do not feel any parasitical entity in the ship?" Galyan asked.

"I'm not sure how one would feel that," Maddox said. "No, it wasn't biological. I felt death for all of us. Matter of fact, let's all move back. Well back from the derelict."

They moved back until the ship was barely visible, as it had been when they first saw it.

"May I suggest, sir, that you fire a beam at the nosecone of the derelict?" Galyan asked.

"To let out the parasitic alien?" Maddox asked.

"No."

"What are you thinking?"

"I am not certain, sir. I just think we should be extra cautious with the wreck."

"Yes," Maddox said. "I would order the vessel's destruction from space, but who knows? Didn't you say, Commander, that there was valuable alien equipment aboard?"

"I thought that's what was indicated," Valerie said. "Captain Marek wanted to go back and study the interior, but not after what happened to Kresh and Liza."

Maddox thought about that. "Let's increase the distance between us and the wreck."

They did.

Maddox contacted *Victory*.

Soon, the weapons officer aimed the disruptor cannon at the derelict. Down came the yellow disruptor beam, making a distinct hum. It touched the nosecone of the ancient vessel and bored through the hull.

"Down!" Maddox shouted over the whine of the beam. He sensed something dreadful.

Everyone hit the jungle floor.

Then, a terrific explosion ripped through the derelict. It hurled hull pieces and other debris in all directions, crashing against the canopy and shredding trees, plants, whatever got in its way. The concussive force and heat blew over the prone team trying to press deeper into the soil.

Soon, Maddox stood as flames crackled in the distance where the derelict ship had been.

"Did we hit some kind of dormant energy device?" Valerie asked, rising.

"Doubtful," Galyan said. "That was a Tri-X3 explosive."

"Are we supposed to be familiar with that?" Valerie asked.

"That is a New Men explosive," Galyan said.

"What?" Valerie said. "You think that derelict had something to do with the creation of the New Men?"

"No," Galyan said. "I suspect we will find there is nothing in the debris to indicate any ancient alien technology aboard the former derelict."

"You're scanning more clearly?" Maddox asked.

"No, that is just a supposition based on the facts."

"Spill it, Galyan," Maddox said.

"The derelict may have been booby-trapped, sir."

"Do you think Kresh and Liza did that when they exited it?" Valerie asked. "Before they left the planet?"

"That is possible," Galyan said.

"No," Maddox said. "I don't think so. After Kresh and Liza left, I suspect New Men discovered the planet or wreck. They cleaned out whatever technology there was and then set the explosives for anyone else who came looking for the wreck."

"Do you think they expected us to be here?" Valerie asked.

"Seems hard to fathom how they would know something like that," Maddox said. "We didn't know we were coming here until a week ago. Clearly, they intended to kill somebody."

"That is a reasonable conclusion," Galyan said.

"Let's get back to the shuttle," Maddox said. "We're leaving the planet."

"Maybe that ship was a decoy," Valerie said. "Maybe the real wreck is elsewhere. Could we double-check from *Victory?*"

"Certainly," Maddox said, "but the sooner we're back on *Victory*, the safer I'll feel."

With that, the team began heading for the shuttle.

-56-

They made it to the shuttle and off-planet, soon landing in the hangar bay. A decontamination team scoured the shuttle inside and out. The team went to decontamination, all except for Galyan, who could not carry anything back.

Afterward, they had a meeting in the conference room with Galyan, Meta, Valerie, and Andros. Riker, Keith, and Ludendorff remained bedridden, recovering, and thus did not join them.

"Well," Maddox said, "we've scoured the planet with our scans and have found nothing that would indicate another alien ship."

"I have found evidence, small things," Galyan said. "It shows someone was here. Were they New Men? The explosive indicates a high probability. And they are the nearest political entity in this region of the Beyond."

"True," Maddox said.

"I doubt whoever was here intended to colonize the planet," Galyan continued. "The planet would need heavy detoxification to get rid of the spores and fungi. Our decontamination team found several spores already growing on the shuttle, even after traveling through space. This would not be an easy planet for humans to survive. Perhaps in the Highland regions or at the poles, it would be easier, but otherwise, I do not think so."

"So," Maddox said, "we found a dead end. We know no more about the parasitic alien that infected Kresh than previously. By Valerie's description, it sounded like the alien was inside Kresh."

"I would agree, sir," Galyan said.

"Any thoughts or ideas on what we should do next?" Maddox asked.

"Head back for the Commonwealth," Meta said. "Jewel will miss school otherwise."

"Jewel can learn while aboard *Victory*," Maddox said.

Meta looked like she was going to argue, then nodded. She knew Maddox had not enjoyed the extended vacation on Earth. It had been great having her husband home as they engaged in various activities, but she had sensed the agitation building in him. Out here, her husband was a different man, revitalized, energized. He was made for adventure.

Therefore, Meta decided she could homeschool Jewel aboard *Victory*. It would probably provide a better education than the public schools.

"Perhaps we should head to Krantz," Maddox said. "We can investigate it for possible parasitical life forms."

"You mean test all the inhabitants with a scanner?" Galyan asked.

"No," Maddox said. "We go down and check it out, give the desert planet a visit."

"The inhabitants won't like a Star Watch warship there," Valerie said.

"Do they have the firepower to make their dislike stick?" Maddox asked.

"No," Valerie said, "but I wouldn't give any of us good odds once we leave the ship."

Maddox drummed his fingers on the table. "Galyan, have you perfected your ghost-mode eavesdropping?"

"Yes, sir," Galyan said.

Maddox nodded. "We'll start at Krantz, taking a look. Then we'll decide what to do. That will take several weeks, at least. Once we're there, we'll take the pulse of the place and keep an eye out for New Men. Are the New Men becoming more aggressive? The New Men know Star Watch sends Patrol scouts out here. Maybe they don't like that. Maybe it's the beginning of a spy war. We should get the pulse of that, particularly if the Sovereign Hierarchy of Leviathan is about to make a second stab in force. We need to know if the New Men will use that to assault the Commonwealth while we're at war with others."

"Maybe the New Men have made a new policy," Galyan said. "They might be extending their realm, clearing a path away from the Commonwealth."

"That could be," Maddox said. "For now, we're going to try to get a sense of this region of space. We'll stay out here a few more months... at least until Keith has recovered enough to start exercising. He needs to gain weight, so does Riker."

Maddox waited for comments. None were forthcoming.

"Commander," Maddox said, "I'm going to repeat what I said to you earlier. You did an excellent job as a Patrol scout leader. I do hope you'll stay aboard *Victory*, even if it is with an independent command aboard the *Tarrypin*. I appreciate your service, and I appreciate your skills. You are one of the best Patrol officers in the fleet, and I, for one, applaud you."

Maddox stood up.

The others also stood, and they clapped for Valerie.

The Commander blushed furiously, looking down at the table. Then she looked up, smiling. It felt good to get this recognition. It was gratifying that Captain Maddox publicly acknowledged her abilities.

What did the future hold for her? Valerie wasn't sure. But she wanted to help Keith get better, and Riker and Ludendorff. It was good to be back on *Victory*. It was good to be out here with an assignment, knowing that she had the firepower of *Victory* and the help of Galyan, Andros, and Captain Maddox. She could unwind, talking to Meta. She could go and visit precious Jewel, the Captain's young darling. It was also good to be serving with Maddox again. Sometimes he could be a jerk. Sometimes he could be arrogant, even condescending at times. He was so competent, though, especially with his intuitive sense. It had helped them survive the situation with the derelict.

The New Men were always up to something. If not the entire race of them, at least some had nefarious goals. What had Lord Hermes been hoping for? Could the slumbering Yon

Soth have promised the vain New Man something? One thing was sure—they had rid this region of the spiral arm of that deadly menace that the Yon Soths represented.

Finally, the clapping died down, and Valerie stood.

"Thank you," Valerie said. "It's good to be back among my people, my family. You have no idea how much I appreciate all of you. Thank you for the encouragement. I hope to be as encouraging to each of you. Let's see what the next mission brings. It's going to be interesting, and sir, it'll probably be fun with you at the helm."

With that, Valerie sat down, and the meeting soon ended. The others filed out. Valerie watched Maddox take Meta by the hand. They were going to talk to their daughter.

Valerie grinned. Yes, it was good to be home with the others on *Victory*.

The End

LOST STARSHIP SERIES:

The Lost Starship
The Lost Command
The Lost Destroyer
The Lost Colony
The Lost Patrol
The Lost Planet
The Lost Earth
The Lost Artifactt
The Lost Star Gate
The Lost Supernova
The Lost Swarm
The Lost Intelligence
The Lost Tech
The Lost Secret
The Lost Barrier
The Lost Nebula
The Lost Relic
The Lost Task Force
The Lost Clone
The Lost Portal
The Lost Cyborg
The Lost World

Visit VaughnHeppner.com for more information

Printed in Dunstable, United Kingdom